Praise fo

"Jam-packed with crosses, double-crosses, murders fair and foul, *Assassin's Lullaby* is anything but sleep inducing. An edge-of-your-seat thriller stretching from Israel to Russia to Brighton Beach, Brooklyn, it is a novel both grand in scale and incredibly intimate."

—Reed Farrel Coleman, *New York Times*
bestselling author of *Sleepless City*

"*Assassin's Lullaby* magically combines relentless action, psychological suspense, and emotional drama for a high-stakes thrill ride."

—Jayne Ann Krentz, *New York Times*
bestselling author of *All the Colors of Night*

"*Assassin's Lullaby* is a master class in crime fiction. It's a beautiful and moving noir creation, and if it is indeed a lullaby, then Mark Rubinstein is singing and writing in a new octave."

—Richard C. Simons, MD, former President,
American Psychoanalytic Association

"In *Assassin's Lullaby*, Mark Rubinstein is at the top of his game. As with all his suspense novels, he grabs you by the throat with his first sentence and then puts you on a roller-coaster ride of action and suspense. He is a master at misdirection, which adds dramatically to his storytelling. You will love Rubinstein's latest."

—Joseph Badal, award-winning
author of *The Carnevale Conspiracy*

"Mark Rubinstein is a member of the 'real pro' club when it comes to thrills, reversals, and creating gripping, real-time storylines, and *Assassin's Lullaby* will only advance his reputation."

—Andrew Gross, *New York Times* bestselling author of *The One Man*

"Eli Dagan is one hell of a very human assassin, and this is one hell of a story."

—Peter James, bestselling author of the Roy Grace series

Praise for Mark Rubinstein's Other Books

The Storytellers

"Psychiatrist and thriller writer Rubinstein (the Mad Dog Trilogy) collects more than 40 interviews with suspense and thriller writers in this fresh compendium of 'candid thoughts, opinions, inspirations, frustrations, backstories, and . . . sources of creativity.' . . . Thriller writers—and fans curious about the process—are in for a treat."

—*Publishers Weekly*

"Just look at this lineup: Lee Child, Patricia Cornwell, David Mamet, Meg Gardiner, Scott Turow, Kathy Reichs, James Rollins—and that's only a small fraction of them. This writer's guide to the genre takes the form of interviews with big name authors, experts in crime fiction, writers with proven track records and plenty of knowledge to share. A nice companion piece to the slew of more traditional how-to-be-a-writer books on the market."

—*Booklist*

Beyond Bedlam's Door

"Nobody knows the fascinating world of forensic psychiatry better than Mark Rubinstein, and he has given it to us in a brilliant book that is essential reading for everyone who likes crime fiction. *Beyond Bedlam's Door* is bone-chilling and thrilling, full of smart, strong stories. It belongs on your bookshelf!"

—Linda Fairstein, bestselling author of the Alex Cooper series

"*Beyond Bedlam's Door* is a real page turner. As an internist, I see many patients presenting with physical complaints who have undiagnosed emotional problems. These stories are important for all physicians to understand and use in practice to care for the whole patient. Dr. Rubinstein shows us firsthand his skills at listening and investigating beyond the obvious. He is a master storyteller."

—Kimberly Simons Patterson, MD, Exempla Good Samaritan Hospital, Lafayette, Colorado, Assistant Clinical Professor of Medicine, University of Colorado School of Medicine

"These fascinating true stories of discovery in psychiatric practice and court settings are compelling, dramatic, and often stranger than fiction. They are true page-turners—I couldn't stop reading! The worlds of the law and psychiatry often are an odd match, but Mark Rubinstein masterfully demonstrates his ability to bridge those worlds through his careful assessments, presented in clear fashion, unfazed by pressures to bend the truth."

—Roger Rahtz, Psychiatrist and Psychoanalyst, New York City

"*Beyond Bedlam's Door* offers an intriguing glimpse into a psychiatrist's world. Dr. Rubinstein is a skilled storyteller, and his recollections of provocative and challenging clinical and forensic cases make for a highly enjoyable and fascinating read for psychiatrist and patient alike."

—Donna Sutter, MD, MPH, Psychiatrist and former Clinical Assistant Professor, Baylor College of Medicine

"In *Beyond Bedlam's Door*, Dr. Rubinstein shows a working psychiatrist who is compassionate and curious, always making his patients' welfare his priority, even while negotiating the complex terrain of forensic psychiatry. Very few psychiatrists can communicate the best of what we do with such humble awe and respect for the complexities of the human mind."

—Howard Welsh, MD, former Director,
Psychoanalytic Institute, and Clinical Professor
of Psychiatry, NYU Langone Medical Center

"Mark Rubinstein's intriguing book, *Beyond Bedlam's Door*, explores the gritty truths about psychiatric practice. Rubinstein accomplishes an amazing feat—intertwining stories from practice and the courtroom that are simultaneously bursting with resiliency, sordidness, and hope!"

—Helen M. Farrell, MD, Psychiatrist and
Forensic Psychiatrist, Harvard Medical School,
and Instructor, Beth Israel Deaconess Medical Center

The Lovers' Tango

"Mark Rubinstein knows his stuff. A gripping legal drama powers this novel at a torrid pace. The tension in these pages never lets you go. But Rubinstein is a born storyteller. He knows that what goes on outside the courtroom is just as important as what happens inside."

—Michael Connelly,
bestselling author of the Harry Bosch series

"Legal thriller, medical mystery, and hauntingly suspenseful tale of a couple trapped in their final dance, Mark Rubinstein's *The Lovers' Tango* is a masterful story. The novel is powerful and poignant and kept me riveted through the last daring reveal."

—Linda Fairstein, *New York Times*
bestselling author of the Alex Cooper series

"In *The Lovers' Tango*, Mark Rubinstein proves that Nicholas Sparks is not the only author who can masterfully blend suspense, tragedy, and romance into a timeless story of love, loss, and the beguiling mystery of memory. Here is a story within a story, all entwined around a pair of lovers locked in a tragic dance. Once it starts, you'll be unable to tear yourself away as you're carried relentlessly forward to the novel's surprising and poignant ending."

—James Rollins, *New York Times* bestseller of *The Sixth Extinction* and *War Hawk*

"*The Lovers' Tango* is much more than a riveting courtroom drama. It is a powerful love story that kept me reading long after I should have been in bed."

—Phillip Margolin, *New York Times* bestselling author of *Woman with a Gun*

"Mark Rubinstein's *The Lovers' Tango* is a sultry, elegant piece of romantic noir. It has a terrific legal backdrop that merges the tale into a steamy courtroom thriller focusing on human frailty and the limitations of what we see before us."

—Jon Land, *USA Today* bestselling author of *Strong Darkness*

"Mark Rubinstein is a superb storyteller. His novels tap into the deepest of human emotions."

—Raymond Khoury, bestselling author of the Sean Reilly series

Mad Dog House

"I stayed up all night to read *Mad Dog House*. I didn't plan on it, but when I got into it, I couldn't put it down. It was fantastic, riveting, suspenseful, twisting, loving, horrific."

—Martin West, film and television actor and filmmaker

"The characters in *Mad Dog House* are compellingly real. It was a great read!"

—*Ann* Chernow, artist and writer

"In Mark Rubinstein's *Mad Dog House*, the characters—all well developed and dripping with authenticity—propel the novel along with style and edge-of-your-seat excitement."

—Judith Marks-White, author of *Seducing Harry* and *Bachelor Degree* and columnist, "The Light Touch," *Westport (CT) News*

"*Mad Dog House* is a gripping, harrowing, and provocative psychological thriller, featuring a plot packed with action and intrigue, staggering and brutal twists, and deeply disturbing possibilities. The author has a gift for delivering gut-punching surprises while raising unsettling questions about the basic nature of human beings and the inescapable hold of the past."

—Mysia Haight, www.pressreleasepundit.com

Love Gone Mad

"*Love Gone Mad* is a beautifully crafted suspense novel. The characters are people you care about; the story is fast paced and cleverly plotted."

—Scott Pratt, bestselling author of the Joe Dillard series

"I quickly found myself caught up in *Love Gone Mad*—part love story, part *Halloween*, and part legal thriller."

—Elissa Durwood Grodin, author of *Physics Can Be Fatal*

"Rubinstein's second foray into the fiction arena (after *Mad Dog House*) is an intense thriller that promises readers surprising twists, heart-pounding suspense, and a bird's-eye view into both the mind of a madman and a dizzyingly realistic account of how it feels to be stalked as prey."

—*Library Journal*

Mad Dog Justice

"What price must a man pay for doing a very bad thing for a very good reason? That is the question *Mad Dog Justice* poses, and the answer is written with great skill and creaks with tension and truth."

—Simon Toyne, author of the internationally bestselling Sanctus Trilogy and *The Searcher*

"*Mad Dog Justice* speeds along with more turns than a Vespa cruising through traffic. It's a smart, twisting thriller that grows into the weightier issues of friendship, vengeance, and betrayal."

—Andrew Gross, bestselling author of *Everything to Lose* and *The One Man*

"*Mad Dog Justice* thrums with relentless intensity and suspense. Rubinstein has created a palpable cast of characters who stay with you long after you finish the book."

—Jessica Speart, author of *A Killing Season* and *Restless Waters*

"Reading *Mad Dog Justice* is akin to being on a treadmill that's been programmed to perpetually increase speed until your heart threatens to burst from your chest. The tension in this novel accelerates to breakneck speed, and just when you think you might get a reprieve, Rubinstein shocks you again."

—Joseph Badal, author of *The Lone Wolf Agenda*

Mad Dog Vengeance

"Fans of *The Sopranos* will love this fast-paced thriller of Italian mafia versus Albanian gangsters versus an everyday guy who just wants to protect his family. Loved the explosive end!"

—Lisa Gardner, *New York Times* bestselling author of *Right behind You* and the D. D. Warren series

Assassin's Lullaby

Also by Mark Rubinstein

Fiction

The Lovers' Tango
Return to Sandara: A Novella of Love and Destruction
Mad Dog House (First in the Mad Dog Trilogy)
Mad Dog Justice (Second in the Mad Dog Trilogy)
Mad Dog Vengeance (Last in the Mad Dog Trilogy)
The Foot Soldier, A Novella of War
Love Gone Mad
Stone Soup

Nonfiction

The Storytellers: Straight Talk from the Planet's Most Acclaimed Suspense and Thriller Authors (Blackstone)
Beyond Bedlam's Door: True Tales from the Couch and Courtroom (Thunder Lake Press)
Bedlam's Door: True Tales of Madness & Hope (Thunder Lake Press)
The Growing Years: The New York Hospital-Cornell Medical Center Guide to Your Child's Emotional Development (Atheneum)
Heartplan: A Complete Program for Total Fitness of Heart & Mind (McGraw Hill) with Dr. David L. Copen
New Choices: The Latest Options in Treating Breast Cancer (Dodd Meade) with Dr. Dennis P. Cirillo
The Complete Book of Cosmetic Surgery (Simon & Schuster) with Dr. Dennis P. Cirillo
The First Encounter: The Beginnings in Psychotherapy (Jason Aronson) with Dr. William A. Console and Dr. Richard C. Simons

Assassin's Lullaby

MARK RUBINSTEIN

Thunder Lake Press

Thunder Lake Press
24338 El Toro Rd., #E227
Laguna Woods, CA 92637

Publisher's Note: This is a work of fiction. It is a product of the author's imagination. Any resemblance to people, living or dead is purely coincidental. Occasionally, real places or institutions are used novelistically for atmosphere and are employed in a fictional manner. There is no connection between the characters or events in this novel to any real-life people, places, organizations, or companies of any kind.

Ordering Information
Quantity sales. Special discounts are available on quantity purchases by corporations, associations, and others. For details, contact the "Special Sales Department" at the address above.

Orders by US trade bookstores and wholesalers. Please contact BCH: (800) 431-1579 or visit www.bookch.com for details.

Printed in the United States of America

Cataloging-in-Publication Data

Names: Rubinstein, Mark, 1942-, author.
Title: Assassin's lullaby / Mark Rubinstein.
Description: Laguna Woods, CA: Thunder Lake Press, 2022.
Identifiers: LCCN 2021925365 | ISBN 978-1-941016-31-2
Subjects: LCSH Assassins--Fiction. | Organized crime--Fiction. | Psychological fiction. | Thrillers (Fiction) | Suspense fiction. | BISAC FICTION / Thrillers / Crime
Classification: LCC PS3618.U3 A77 2022 | DDC 813.6--dc23

First Edition

27 26 25 24 23 22 10 9 8 7 6 5 4 3 2 1

For Linda

In every life, there lurks catastrophe.

—Eli Dagan

1

Knowing his life depends on stealth, Eli Dagan moves warily with the tide of pedestrians streaming along East Forty-Second Street.

Walking amid the late-morning crowds, he does a peripheral check of his surroundings, grabs glimpses of people in store-window reflections, and watches for danger that could come from any direction.

He's always been a hard target—tough to kill—because he's able to think exactly like those who would ambush him. That's one of the secrets of being a good assassin. And of staying alive.

It's reflexive to notice everything. He misses nothing—sights, sounds, smells, movement. It's all processed in milliseconds as his brain whirrs through the possibilities that could bring about the end of life.

Nothing distracts him: not the press of people or the clot of traffic, the blinking WALK–DON'T WALK signs, the blare of horns, the hiss of air brakes, the wail of sirens, or the clatter of jackhammers.

Because no matter where he may be, he's focused on one imperative: survival.

There's a chance he's being followed this morning—maybe by Chechens, or they could be Albanians. Or Russians—the most likely possibility given the jobs he's done for various Russian mob factions over the last few years.

The two guys he noticed on the subway are still near enough to make the back of his neck feel even colder than normal in the frigid February air. One wears a dark blue parka with the hood pulled over his head. The other is bareheaded and wears dark sunglasses. Each time Eli thinks he sees them, they somehow manage to disappear.

He picked them up easily on the subway platform while he was waiting for the uptown local. And he's kept track of them on the streets where he's been meandering in a seemingly aimless way for the last fifteen minutes. No matter how skilled these guys may be, it's tough to tail a moving target. Static shadowing is more effective when one man picks up where the other leaves off.

He's taken the usual precautions: he left the apartment through the garage exit, rerouted himself twice, ducked in and out of a few stores, and watched for anyone on the subway who appeared suspicious. Yet, there's a good chance they're still on his tail.

The life he's been living has primed him to be suspicious in even the most ordinary situations.

Is it paranoia, now at a full boil?

Is this any way to live? Maybe it's time to get out of the life.

He'll think about that later. Right now he's gotta focus on what's going to happen very soon. There's no room for distraction.

He's glad he decided to take the Beretta. Funny how when the piece is tucked into his waistband at the small of his back, it bites into the skin. But after a while, the pressure lessens and it's easy to forget the pistol is there. It just seems to disappear, as though it no longer exists.

If only guilt worked the same way.

At the intersection of Vanderbilt and Forty-Second, he turns abruptly and heads down the ramp into the southwest corner of Grand Central Terminal.

Veering right, he strides along a corridor that parallels Forty-Second Street and passes the Oyster Bar with its vaulted tile ceilings. At the entrance to the restaurant, he abruptly turns left, walks along a short corridor, and emerges into the terminal's echoing main concourse. Making his way across the expanse, he weaves through masses of people, then heads toward the Lexington passage and the subway.

Midway along the walkway, he darts into Grand Central Market's side entrance. The place brims with shoppers. He stops at a cheese stall, pretends he's examining the goods, then glances at the entrance to see if he's drawn anyone off course. He stays in place for a few more moments, waiting to see if any pair of eyes remains fixed on him for a beat too long.

It doesn't happen, so he decides to move on.

Threading through swarms of lunchtime customers, he passes a sushi stand, a butcher counter, a few more concessions, then slips out the door onto Lexington Avenue. Turning left, he reenters Grand Central through the Graybar passage.

Glancing back, he has a clear view for at least fifty meters. There's a good chance he's lost the guys tracking him.

Walking along the passageway, he passes a series of kiosks, then stops at the entrance to Track 13, near Zaro's bakery, at the periphery of the terminal's concourse. The aroma of freshly baked bread wafts through the air. Ordinarily, the yeasty smell would whet his appetite, but not today.

What's about to happen is serious enough to quell any desire for food.

There's no sign of the guys who'd been following him. He wonders how they managed to know his identity well enough to try tracking him. He goes by different names and for the last ten years has lived a sequestered existence. Escape, evasion, and deception have been a way of life ever since he left the Mossad, where he'd been a field agent.

But it's essential to focus on the here and now because he'll soon be meeting with Anton Gorlov, a major boss in the Odessa mafia. Eli has never before met with a client in person; discussions have always been over a satellite phone or through encrypted messages over the dark net. So Eli's breaking a long-established protocol by agreeing to meet with Gorlov. But the *pakhan* insisted the purpose of the meeting was so crucial it had to be face-to-face. Which makes Eli even more suspicious. Why take the chance? But here he is.

He scans the concourse. Streams of people crisscross the space in an array of intersecting lines. A choral roar fills the air as passengers stream in every direction. Armed, camo-clad National Guardsmen—some with bomb-sniffing dogs—stand at strategic points around the expanse.

Waiting for their scheduled train departures, conductors and terminal employees cluster near the tunnel gates. Over the intercom a robotic voice warns commuters to "Keep your belongings in sight at all times" and "If you see something, say something."

He's forty minutes early, plenty of time to reconnoiter the area. Was agreeing to this meeting a mistake? Has he unwittingly set himself up for assassination?

To ensure that doesn't happen, he'll soon alter the plan. Unpredictability is another requirement for staying alive.

Standing near Track 13, he eyes every passerby. That Russian gangster look is easy to recognize—there's the Slavic face, something reminiscent of Putin's, with high cheekbones, a more or less oval-shaped face, and almond-shaped eyes. Though there are exceptions, most of those guys are gorilla-like in size and often have shaved heads along with heavy facial stubble.

The Mossad taught Eli situational awareness. It's imprinted on his brain, as though his motherboard is hardwired to pick up the slightest hint of danger.

The sit-down was scheduled to take place at Cucina, a restaurant near the top of the escalators of the MetLife building. There's less chance of an ambush in a public place like that. A Russian boss like Gorlov—a pakhan in the Odessa mafia—might stay ensconced in Brighton Beach, Brooklyn, while two members of his crew could saunter into the restaurant, whip out shotguns from beneath their overcoats, and blow him away.

There are now fifteen minutes until the meeting. It's time to change things up.

Using his satellite phone, Eli dials Gorlov's cell phone.

"Da?" answers a deep, rumbling voice.

"Mr. Gorlov?"

"Yes."

"A change of plans," Eli says.

"I expected that," Gorlov replies with a heavy Russian accent.

Yes, Gorlov knows the terrain, is aware of the precautions Eli must take.

"We're still on for noon, but not at Cucina," Eli says, trying for a matter-of-fact voice. "There's a restaurant called Cipriani Dolci on the west balcony of the concourse at Grand Central. You know where it is?"

"I'll find it."

"Be alone."

Clicking the End Call button, Eli is certain Gorlov won't obey his instructions.

2

A few minutes later four men descend on the escalator leading from the MetLife building to the concourse of Grand Central Terminal.

At the foot of the escalator, they stop and talk among themselves.

It's them.

The Russians. They have that *look*.

Two older men and two younger ones.

The young ones look like muscle.

Gorlov's violating Eli's instruction to come alone. To be expected.

There's no way a crime boss of Gorlov's stature would come without foot soldiers. The top dog always has muscle nearby. Eli told him to come alone as a test to see if the guy was malleable.

As anticipated, the young ones are big and tough-looking, hard-core muscle, ready to do whatever it takes to protect the boss.

The four men walk to the center of the concourse and stop near the information booth. One older guy is a grizzly bear of a man. Really huge. Eli knows it's him. Even if he'd never seen photos of Anton Gorlov, he'd know he's the boss.

As Gorlov talks, there's a certain thrust and tilt of the chin, a posture Eli thinks of as the *Il Duce* look. It's the authoritarian Mussolini pose of a head honcho, a pakhan in Russian organized crime, the Bratva, or Brotherhood. This guy can't be taken lightly; you don't rise to his position in an organization like the Odessa mafia without being ruthless. And smart.

While the boss is speaking, the others nod in an über-respectful way.

Three of the men, including Gorlov, now proceed toward the marble stairway leading to the west balcony and Cipriani Dolci.

One bodyguard remains at the information booth. Leaning against the ledge, he takes out a cell phone and peers at it. It might be configured to pick up signals from Gorlov, who could be wired to transmit the conversation he'll have with Eli.

Squinting, Eli peers more closely at the guy. There's no earpiece in his right ear. But one could be inserted in his left ear, which faces away from Eli.

The three others continue walking toward the west balcony.

One bodyguard—a hulking fellow—stops at the bottom of the stairway leading to the restaurant and leans casually against the balustrade. Whipping out a *New York Post*, he begins reading, or feigns doing so. He's a study in pretense.

It's now ten minutes before noon as Gorlov and the other older man climb the stairway to Cipriani Dolci. The maître d' greets them and sees that their coats are taken, then seats them at separate tables adjacent to each other. Also predictable. The other one is positioned nearby to overhear whatever's said at Gorlov's table. The maître d' hands each man a menu and then makes his way back to the reception area's podium.

Gorlov picks up the menu and examines it.

A waiter approaches. As though he realizes he's serving a mobster, the waiter virtually bows and scrapes, scribbles on his pad while leaning close to Gorlov as the Russian speaks. If Eli can predict anything, Gorlov's ordering lunch without waiting for his arrival. Arrogant behavior, to be sure. This man waits for no one. The waiter nods, bows again, retrieves the menu, and disappears.

It's clear Eli will have to pass the soldier at the bottom of the stairway on his way to the restaurant. A reasonable precaution being taken by the pakhan.

Yesterday Eli did a methodical walk-through of the terminal. He's familiar with every part in the complex. If things get dicey, there are more than a few avenues of escape in the labyrinthine passageways of Grand Central.

Waiting another two minutes, he keeps his eyes on both bodyguards. Neither man seems to be wearing an earpiece. The one at the information booth turns his head to ogle a good-looking woman passing by him. Eli notices there's no earpiece in his left ear.

The guy loitering at the staircase flips through the newspaper. His lips don't move. No way is he speaking into a lapel microphone. It's unlikely there's any communication between or among the Russians.

It's time to move. Eli crosses the concourse and heads through the Vanderbilt passage. Exiting on Forty-Second Street, he walks around the corner.

At 15 Vanderbilt Avenue, between Forty-Second and Forty-Third Streets, he reenters the building, then takes the stairway to the Campbell Bar. He walks through the elaborately furnished room, waves off the maître d', and traverses a short corridor leading directly to a side entrance of Cipriani Dolci.

The Beretta tucked firmly into the waistband at his lower back feels reassuring.

He hopes he won't have to use it.

But in Eli Dagan's life, hope has always been in short supply.

3

At precisely one minute past noon, Eli enters the restaurant.

The decor is stark, modern. Every table is occupied.

From this height, the roar of the concourse is audible but muted.

Gorlov sits alone at a four-top.

Passing the other older Russian at the adjacent table, Eli approaches the pakhan.

"Mr. Gorlov, I presume," he says as he sits catty-corner to Gorlov. He can now eyeball the other man and view the concourse below. A simple and necessary precaution.

Gorlov's bushy eyebrows move upward. He tries to mask his surprise, but Eli notices the man's pupils dilate. A sure sign of fight-or-flight hormones pouring through his bloodstream.

"And you're Aiden?" Gorlov asks, using the alias Eli assumes with anyone from the Odessa mafia.

Eli nods. His eyes flit to the Russian at the next table. Pretending he's perusing the offerings, the man stares steadily at the menu.

"So, we finally meet." A smile breaks out on Gorlov's fleshy face. As was evident on the phone, the man's voice is a deep rumble. Though he speaks with a thick Russian accent, he sounds fluent in English.

"Yes, we do."

"Tell me, is Aiden your real name?"

"It is for you."

Gorlov looks to be about sixty and he's ponderous—has a thick chest, massive shoulders, and a protuberant belly. The man must tip the scales at well over a hundred kilos, maybe two and a half bills if you use the American weight standard. He has the thickest wrists Eli's ever seen. His huge hands sport gnarled knuckles, which were probably broken in street fights when he was a young man in Odessa. Though he's wearing a dark suit, he looks like a Russian or Ukrainian peasant, except this guy doesn't do farm work.

His weathered face has no doubt seen its share of tough times. A shock of iron-gray hair looks like a massive halo surrounding his head. His unkempt eyebrows are black, reminding Eli of hairy caterpillars.

Eli notices a dark blue tattoo of the Imperial Czar's crown etched on the outer surface of Gorlov's right thumb. In the Russian underworld it signifies a man of authority, a leader who commands respect, unquestioning obedience. To defy such a man guarantees death.

Eli senses something predatory about the man. But he's certain Gorlov doesn't need to threaten violence to get his way. He exudes a level of confidence shown by men accustomed to leading others, and it's clear he sees through artifice and deception. It's gotta be tough to bullshit this guy.

Eli thinks he detects something else: though they've said very little to each other, a deep sadness seems to lurk beneath Anton Gorlov's veneer of geniality.

Whatever this meeting concerns, it's important enough for the pakhan to have requested an in-person sit-down, an unusual situation—virtually unheard of—because ordinarily a man like Gorlov would insulate himself from even the most peripheral contact with an assassin. And it's critical enough for a guy who looks like an underboss to have accompanied him.

The Spytec bug detector in Eli's pocket isn't vibrating. He's now certain he's not being bugged. The slim, lightweight device can pick up analog or digital transmissions anywhere between 30 MHz and 6,000 MHz.

The instrument's stillness is comforting.

Anton Gorlov sizes up Aiden, or whatever his real name may be, because there's no doubt that's not the name he was born with. Equally telling, he has no surname, or at least, he's never used one in any contact with a member of the Odessa mafia.

He looks like he's closing in on forty; he's a bit under six feet tall, well built, with a thick neck and sloped shoulders. Athletic-looking, it's clear he'd be fearsome in a physical confrontation. He probably weighs about ninety-five kilos—about 200 pounds—and has a full head of black hair with a few threads of white at the temples.

He has a straight, prominent nose, high cheekbones, a strong jaw. His eyes are as black as coffee, but when he glances at Viktor, whom he clearly realizes has accompanied Anton, his eyes appear gray. Can eyes change color with an alteration in lighting?

And there's something else in those eyes: it could be tragedy or perhaps a world-weary sense of the world gone wrong. Terribly wrong. They're not the eyes of a stone-cold killer, though the man certainly kills. Something else is in those eyes, but it's impossible to make out what it may be.

He's dressed in black cargo pants and a dark blue turtleneck sweater beneath a waist-length black leather jacket. There's little doubt that tucked somewhere beneath that jacket is a small-caliber pistol ready to be whipped out and fired.

Gorlov can't quite make out Aiden's ethnicity. He could be Italian or French, Corsican, maybe Albanian, even Chechen. He doesn't look Eastern European, though it's always risky to try guessing ethnicity. You can never know a man's origins with even a hint of certainty.

This Aiden character's tough-looking and handsome in a rugged way. He's not a pretty-boy. He looks vigilant, ready for anything, the way Gorlov was as a young man.

Something disquieting seems to be at the core of this man: a hardness that's either inborn or the result of experience. Surely this Aiden has a military background. He's probably mastered many combat skills. And now uses them in the most deadly way.

Though the movement is subtle, Gorlov notices Aiden's eyes shift slightly. He's taking in his surroundings, including Gorlov's second-in-command, Viktor who's sitting at the next table. And there's something about those eyes. They're the eyes of a man who has seen the ugly underbelly of life, knows it for what it is: brutal, unfair, unforgiving.

He's not one to be fooled with. He hasn't blinked once since he sat down. It's the sign of a hardened man, a fearless man.

Before this moment, Aiden—or whatever his real name may be—was only a voice on an encrypted cell phone. Or a typed message on a secure server. No one in the Bratva—in any brigade—has ever seen him, though he's done many jobs for a number of the factions.

But now, seeing him in the flesh, Anton Gorlov feels an edge of discomfort, not just because this Aiden fellow radiates danger. Gorlov senses something else: though he's spoken only a few words, it seems clear this man possesses a fierce intelligence. He knows the world and has intellect to spare.

It would be difficult to outwit him.

Maybe it's the way he bypassed the bodyguards and appeared so suddenly, just popped up beside the table like an apparition.

Over the years, Gorlov has learned to read men the way a beast of prey picks out the vulnerable gazelle in a herd. But what he detects now is unsettling.

Something strange ripples through Anton Gorlov: it's not quite fear.

It's a sense of dread.

One thing is abundantly clear: Anton must use caution in dealing with this so-called Aiden.

Because this man exudes danger.

Of course he does; he's a paid assassin.

4

Eli feels Gorlov's eyes lasering in on him; the man is sizing him up, making moment-to-moment calculations.

Just the way Eli is formulating ideas about this Bratva boss.

"Up until now, Aiden, you've been a ghost. Why do you operate this way?"

"The less you know about me, the better it is for both of us."

"I don't disagree. In our lines of work, we need secrecy."

Eli shoots him a tight smile. There's no reason to be disagreeable, but Gorlov had better get to the point of this meeting, fast.

The waiter approaches with a plate of rigatoni alla Bolognese and sets the dish in front of Gorlov.

Of course, judging by his size, Gorlov is a man of great appetites, one who gives in to his urges. He finds it hard to delay gratification. He'll wait for no man, will put his own needs before all else.

"May I offer you a drink, Aiden? Or better yet, how about joining me for lunch?"

"No, thank you. I never mix business with pleasure."

Gorlov nods knowingly.

The truth is Eli rarely drinks. When he does, it's a bottle of beer, nothing more. On rare occasions, he may enjoy a glass or two of wine. But never during daylight hours. And never in the presence of a dangerous man about whom he knows so little, only what's been in the newspapers.

Gorlov cants his head, then says, "We can be sociable. Order something, anything. It's my pleasure. The chicken club sandwich looks excellent. I saw it at another table."

"Thank you, but no."

"Your choice." Gorlov shrugs as he spears two rigatoni, swirls them in the sauce, then slips them past wet lips. He chews vigorously, swallows, then downs another two pasta tubes with barely an interval between each mouthful.

Yes, the man has more than what can be called a robust appetite; he has an insatiable level of hunger. It says volumes about him.

Eli always notices the way someone eats, especially when the food is eaten as though it must be consumed before the dish is taken away. Gorlov probably grew up in poverty and food was precious. He's lived a hard life filled with uncertainty, with deprivation. He still feels life is unpredictable, that good things won't persist, so he must seize the moment.

"Tell me, Aiden, how did you get started in this business?"

Another mouthful of pasta passes his lips.

"Why do you want to know?"

"Because you *fascinate* me. I've always been drawn to mysteries."

"It's better that I remain a mystery."

"I see . . ."

"But there's no mystery about how you operate, Mr. Gorlov."

"Meaning what? And, please, call me Anton." Gorlov tosses him a quick smile and continues chewing.

"Sure, Anton. It's no mystery that three of your men are watching us."

"Oh?"

"There's one at the bottom of the stairway pretending to read a newspaper. There's another at the information booth, looking at his cell phone. And the third one's at the next table," Eli says with a nod toward the other Russian sitting nearby. The man is overweight, has a fleshy neck that hangs over his collar, and has dewlaps that remind him of the guy who played Clemenza in *The Godfather*. "He's staring at the menu as though it's the bible, yet every once in a while he glances our way. And, of course, the two men down below are carrying."

Though Eli's words are spoken softly, coiled energy seethes within him. But he reveals nothing that could give him away—no tightening of his muscles, no vocal tremor, no change in his pulse rate. Body control was part of his Mossad training—even the ability to control his blood pressure—and it's served him well over the years.

In this circumstance the movie reel of the next few seconds spools through Eli's mind.

He whips out the Beretta and puts a bullet into Gorlov's head, then pumps two rounds into the chest of the other man, rockets up from his chair and puts two slugs into the Russian climbing the stairway. The other patrons duck beneath tables. Shouts erupt, and the air smells of fear and gunpowder. He then melts into the crowd.

It's happened in a souk in Damascus, in a restaurant in Lebanon, a market in Tunisia, and a bazaar in Cyprus. It's happened throughout Europe and the Middle East. People never see what went down; at least that's what they tell the cops.

But he's way ahead of himself, and the movie ends abruptly with no rolling credits.

Gorlov nods. "Very observant, Aiden. I'm sure you know these are merely precautions. Let me assure you, these men are only here for my safety, and no threat is intended."

"I understand, Anton. And I'm sure *you* understand that I too have men positioned throughout this terminal," Eli lies. "They'll take matters into their own hands if anything happens to me."

Gorlov nods as though he appreciates Eli's safety measures.

Enough dancing around, Eli thinks. *Let's get down to specifics.*

He senses the Russian wants something unusual. Hence this unheard-of situation: an in-person meeting with a Bratva commander.

"So, Anton, why are we in a restaurant in Midtown Manhattan on a weekday afternoon?" Eli lets his tone of voice convey his impatience.

Gorlov sets his fork on his plate and leans toward Eli. "We're here because I want to discuss something important to me . . . *personally*."

"I'm listening."

5

Gorlov shoves his plate away.

"Let me put it this way. I am not getting younger, and things are changing," he says in a rumbling voice so deep, it sends vibrations through Eli's spine. "I cannot get into specifics, but I need certain things done to ensure my future."

"Yes?"

"I have two jobs for you. Actually, it's one assignment, but it has two parts. Both are unusual and of great importance to me. Rarely is there such pressure of time as there is now, but circumstances require that this be done quickly." Gorlov sighs, then leans close. "Let me tell you about the first part of the job," he says in a near whisper. "When it's been done, we can discuss the second part, which is just as important, maybe even more so."

"I'm listening."

"Have you ever heard of Ivan Agapov?" the Russian asks.

"Yes, of course."

"Tell me what you know."

"He commands a Bratva brigade in Brighton Beach, and he's been indicted by the Eastern District for racketeering. As far as I know, his trial's coming up soon."

"That's correct. And because of that, certain business dealings of Mr. Agapov's may come to light, and they could have consequences for other people."

Eli nods.

"One of those people is sitting at this table."

"I understand."

"I should clarify," Gorlov says, leaning back in his chair. "Agapov may cop a plea. His attorneys are trying to get him the best deal possible. If that happens, the feds will require him to talk about everything he knows—that's part of any deal arrangement—and there could be more indictments . . . of certain people."

Unless Gorlov's a better actor than Pacino, he's telling the truth. Eli knows this because part of his Mossad training involved interrogation techniques, ways to assess a man's truth telling or willingness to shade the truth, or even fabricate a story. Eli knows every tell, whether it's a change in vocal pitch, a shifting of the eyes, a barely detectable facial tic, even something so trivial as a quivering eyelid. He can sniff the slightest whiff of bullshit. And Gorlov doesn't display a hint of it.

"How do you know this?" Eli asks.

"I shouldn't even mention this, but to convince you I'm being truthful, I'll tell you there's a man in Brother Agapov's brigade who, we might say . . . belongs to me."

"So, you have an inside man."

"Yes."

Eli thinks about the enormity of what he's being asked to do. Ivan Agapov is notorious for his longevity as well as his brutality. Unlike most Russian mobsters, he's flamboyant, maintains a high profile. He's been in the local rags and is often covered on the six o'clock TV news, the way John Gotti was years earlier.

Agapov's notorious as one of the top dogs in all of organized crime. His brigade is involved in human trafficking, brothels, gambling dens, extortion, where, like vampires, they suck blood money from their victims, along with murder for hire, credit card and gasoline fraud, and other rackets. His operations are supported by an international coterie of criminals from the Balkans to the Far East. The man is smart enough not to bother with Medicaid or Medicare scams since most corrupt doctors will cave the moment a subpoena arrives at their door.

Gorlov says, "Have you ever done a job for Agapov?"

"No."

"Of course you're telling me the truth."

"Yes, I am."

"Good. So you have no loyalty to him."

"That's right."

Gorlov leans even closer to Eli. In a near whisper, he says, "With that in mind, the first part of this assignment involves Brother Ivan."

"I see."

"But there's an important condition."

Eli waits to hear more.

Gorlov's voice drops so severely, Eli can barely hear him through the ambient noise of the concourse. "Brother Ivan's demise must look natural. If an autopsy is done, it can't look like there was foul play."

Gorlov's voice takes on that low-pitched rumble, even deeper than before. "There can be no bombs or bullets," he continues. "If there is even the slightest hint he died by assassination, there will be a bloodbath. And if you know anything about war between Bratva brothers, bodies will drop everywhere."

"Understood."

"Now, Aiden, can you make a man die so it looks like natural causes were the reasons?"

"You want there to be no signature."

Gorlov nods. "Have you ever done a job where you've left no signature?"

"I can't talk about what I've done."

"But it's something you can do?"

"Yes."

Gorlov says, "Agapov takes precautions."

"The man is undoubtedly well protected," Eli says. "How do you propose I get close enough to do this?"

"I expected you to ask. Here is how it will happen. Believe it or not, Brother Agapov will call you."

"He will?"

"Yes. And he will ask to meet with you personally."

"And what will Mr. Agapov want me to do for him?"

"He'll offer to pay you a great deal of money to make good on a request."

"And that will be . . . ?"

"He will ask you to assassinate me."

6

Eli feels his heartbeat throbbing through his neck into his skull. Internecine warfare is ugly. Brother against brother can be unimaginably brutal. He recalls the infighting between Hamas and the PLO in the Gaza Strip. There were summary executions. The streets were littered with bodies.

"Why does he want you dead?"

"Because he and I once had common interests. We've had business dealings in the past, and given his situation with the feds right now, he's sure that I worry he'll reveal them to the authorities. That, of course, will be part of his plea deal. And he suspects that to protect my own interests, I want him dead."

Eli nods, thinking these mobsters will betray each other in a nanosecond. It must be chromosomal.

"So, it's a matter of who gets to the other man first."

"Exactly," Gorlov replies. "I expect you'll get a call from Brother Agapov's people very soon. But," Gorlov says, lowering his voice, "there's a fly in the ointment. He won't meet with you in a public place. He'll insist that you go to Brighton Beach for an in-person sit-down at his restaurant, Valentina's, located near the boardwalk. Are you willing to do that?"

"How will I know I'll be safe?"

"There's no reason for him to harm you since he'll ask you to do to me what I am asking you to do to him. He wants you to do the job. Besides, I'm sure you have a dead man's switch."

"I do," Aiden lies, knowing he's sending a message to Gorlov. "If I don't have access to the internet for more than a week, confidential computer files are programmed to be sent to certain people, along with all the user names and passwords. They describe what I've done for every organization that's ever hired me—names, dates, and details that'll help law enforcement build airtight cases against everyone named in the files."

"Very smart, Aiden." Gorlov nods as his lips spread into a thin line. "I can see that you're a smart man and know the latest technology."

"So, lemme get this straight," Eli says. "You want me to put this guy in the ground, and I can only meet with him at his restaurant, where his bodyguards will hover over me like hyenas on a carcass. On top of that, it has to look like he died of natural causes."

Gorlov nods.

"It's not an easy thing to do."

"I know you're a man of ingenuity, Aiden. Think about how you can accomplish this."

Eli glances about; his eyes sweep over the man at the nearby table. "Who's sitting there?" Eli asks with a slight nod toward the man.

"His name is Viktor Sorokin," Gorlov says in a soft voice. "He is my second-in-command, my brigadier. If we were Italian, he might be called my underboss. Of course, we're not Italian." Gorlov smiles. "We're the Odessa mafia. You may already know that our only real competitors now are the Albanians, but we have more peace with them than with Brother Ivan's brigade." There's a pause as Gorlov leans back in his chair. "So," he finally says, "are you willing to take on the job I've proposed?"

"I'll see what I can do. You said there's a second part of this job. What is it?"

"Now, that's a *very* sensitive situation, and I must tell you, it'll require even more finesse than the first part." Gorlov picks up the saltshaker and twirls it about between his thumb and index finger. "The second part is just as important as the first, maybe more so. But let's not discuss it now. We can talk about it after the first part has been done."

"Why keep it secret?"

"It is not a secret, Aiden. Brother Agapov is far too important for any distractions to interfere with what I'm asking you to do.

Discussing the second part now will only get in the way of your focusing on what must be done in Brighton Beach." Gorlov lowers his voice to a near whisper. "So, can I assume you're willing to take this job?"

"I'll do my best, if the terms are to my liking."

Gorlov taps the tabletop with his knuckles. "So now we turn from murder to money," he says.

Eli nods.

"The money will change how you live the rest of your life." Gorlov pauses, looks like he's waiting for a response.

Eli says nothing.

"How much do you want for the first part?" Gorlov says.

"It's high risk and tough to do."

"I'm aware of that. How much are we talking about?"

"Two hundred thousand up front. Another two hundred after it's done—*if* it can be done."

"Why such a modest amount, Aiden? As I said, this job is crucial for me. It determines how I spend the rest of my days. Why not three hundred thousand up front and another three hundred after Brother Agapov is gone? We can talk about the sum for the second half after the first part is done."

"I appreciate your generosity."

"I'm not being generous. I'm being practical. I want you to have an incentive to do this. I long ago learned there's no greater motivation than money." Gorlov's lips spread into a sardonic semismile. "Shall we pay in the usual way?"

"Yes, but with a slight change," Eli says, reaching into his jacket pocket. He produces a neatly folded piece of paper. "Here's the routing number for a bank I'm using now." He hands it to Gorlov.

"Another offshore account, yes?" Gorlov asks, picking up the paper and slipping it into his breast pocket.

Eli nods. "Have the first half wired today. If I decide it can't be done, I'll return the money."

"If it cannot be done, you may keep the money. If it gets done, the second half will be wired to this account."

"Much appreciated, Anton. To make it happen, I'll need a dossier on Ivan Agapov—where he lives, his habits and routines. I'll need to know his friends, his preferred means and routes of travel, if he has a medical condition. I want to know his tastes in food and booze, the entertainment he prefers—whether it's gambling or prostitutes, young boys or transvestites—anything. I need a complete picture."

"We'll get that to you. You usually deal with one of my people for communication."

"Your IT man knows how to reach me, but just in case, let me give you this."

Eli takes out a pen and small pad, writes the URL for the secure website he uses for Gorlov's brigade. After ripping the page from the pad, he hands it to Gorlov.

"Have your man upload the information."

Gorlov pockets the paper, nods, picks up his fork and begins tapping it on the plate of pasta.

"Do I have your commitment for this job? On both parts?"

"I don't know what the second half involves."

"You'll find out in due time. But I can tell you this: the money involved for that part will be even more than what we'll pay for the first part." Gorlov nods as if to emphasize the certainty of his words. "Will you commit to the entire job?"

"Yes, if the second part is to my liking."

"I suspect you'll be interested. This will be a great personal favor to me. And I won't forget it."

"It's a job, Anton. Not a favor."

Gorlov nods once again. "Understood."

There's a brief pause.

"I'm glad to have met you," Gorlov says. "You may go now. *Gei gazinta hait.*"

"That sounds like German. What does it mean?" Eli says.

"It's Yiddish, a form of old German."

"Meaning?"

"Go in good health."

7

Gorlov watches Aiden make his way down the stairway to the main concourse.

The man doesn't even glance at the bodyguard stationed at the bottom of the stairway, simply passes by him as though he doesn't exist. The assassin has nerves of steel.

This Aiden, or whatever his name is, has a walk that reminds Gorlov of a panther—catlike, stealthy, nimble. Above all, lethal. There's no doubt he served in some military force. Which one? There's no way to know.

But one thing's certain: he's a man best avoided. Unless there's killing that needs to be done.

He watches Aiden pass the information booth without so much as a glance at the other security guard. He cuts across the area and a moment later disappears into the crowd streaming across the concourse.

Viktor Sorokin gets up from the nearby table and sits in the chair that had been occupied by Aiden.

"A scary-looking man," Victor says as his eyes follow the assassin across the concourse.

"Yes. He has a certain look about him."

"A deadly one."

Gorlov nods.

"Do you think he can do it?" Viktor asks.

"We'll find out."

"There's not much time," Viktor says.

"I know, but there's something about this man that tells me he can do it."

"Even the second part?" Viktor says.

"Yes, probably. Though it will be tricky. But the money involved will be hard for him to resist."

"He's accepted the fee?"

Gorlov nods and hands the piece of paper to Viktor. "Make sure the money is wired to this account. Three hundred thousand. Have it done today."

"Anton, you've never paid this much before."

Gorlov leans toward Viktor and says, "Before this, we've never paid for a pakhan to be gone."

Viktor nods. "What if he takes the money, then says he can't do it?"

Gorlov shakes his head. "If that happens, it would just be the cost of doing business. But I have a feeling he'll figure out a way."

"He knew I was with you, didn't he?"

"Yes, and he picked out Stefan and Kolya too."

"He's highly trained."

"I suspect he has a military background, or maybe something in intelligence," Gorlov says.

"For which country?"

"Who knows? What kind of name is *Aiden*?"

"Sounds Irish."

"He's no more Irish than either of us," Gorlov says with a chortle. "I'm certain that's not his real name. He has some kind of mixed ancestry. Like I always say, we're all just a bunch of mutts."

Viktor says, "I think we're taking an unnecessary risk with him."

"When *haven't* we taken risks?"

Viktor shuts his eyes and nods.

"Could you hear what he said to me?"

"Only some of it," Viktor says. "This is a noisy place."

"That's why he chose this restaurant. I listened to him very carefully and for a moment thought I picked up a slight accent, but it was hard to tell. I doubt he was born here, but who can know where he's from?"

"Any idea?"

"When we parted, I said '*Gei gazinta hait.*' He pretended he didn't know what it meant, but I think he understood it."

"Really?"

"Yes. I could tell. And I think he knows a few languages. That would include German."

"You think he can be trusted?"

"I hope so." Gorlov's eyes narrow, and his lips spread into a thin line.

"You're not sure, are you?"

"Can we ever be certain of anything?"

"What if Agapov's willing to pay him even more?" Viktor says.

"You think he would double-cross us?"

"A man like that? Of course."

"I don't think so," Gorlov says.

"What makes you so confident?"

"He gave me his word he'll do this job."

"Both parts?"

"Yes. And he wants to know more about the second part, so it sounds like he's interested. And I hinted about the money we'll be willing to pay for the second half, that it'll be more than what he gets for the first part. It's an incentive he won't be able to resist. But even more important, Viktor, I have a feeling he's a man of his word."

"Did you give him any details about the second part?"

"No. Not yet. He was curious, as anyone would be."

"Did you say anything more about it?"

"No. We'll cross that bridge when we come to it."

8

Ignoring the bodyguard standing at the information booth, Eli moves quickly across the concourse toward the Lexington passage.

It's a cold February day, and he'll take the subway rather than walk downtown to the apartment. He'll forget about the two-hour trek he takes each day to stay flexible and keep up his endurance.

As he strides along the Lexington passage, Eli's thoughts wander to Gorlov's offer. Three hundred thousand and another $300,000 after Agapov is gone. Not a meager sum. The man must be desperate to get this job done. And there's the mysterious part two, with the hint of even more than the first $600,000.

The money will change how you live the rest of your life.

Not likely, but of course it's intriguing, even though Eli has more than enough stashed away to live comfortably for years.

Was he referring to something other than the money? Is he keeping the second part a secret to arouse Eli's curiosity, to keep him interested in what may be coming down the track? That's likely, but good judgment will decide whether or not to take on the second half of the job.

No matter what, if Gorlov wants to avoid extradition and a trial for a long string of felonies, there's plenty of housecleaning he needs to take care of before he leaves the country.

Eli scrambles down the steps of the Lexington line's Forty-Second Street station. The stairway ends at two wide platforms and four tracks—two for the express trains and two for the local in both the uptown and downtown directions.

Waiting for the downtown 6 local, he scans the platform. A dense crowd waits for the trains to arrive. Across the tracks, another throng waits for the uptown trains. Because of the cold weather, people are bundled in heavy winter outerwear, clothing that could easily hide a weapon. Or a bomb. Fortunately, there hasn't been a suicide bombing on a New York City subway train. Not yet. It's only a matter of time before it happens. When it does, life in the city will become nightmarish.

Eli's eyes scan everything and everyone, back and forth, barely miss a detail of his surroundings. By now it's his default way of being: to be exquisitely aware of everyone, a level of watchfulness bordering on paranoia.

Maybe he *should* set up a dead man's switch—configure his computer to unscramble his files and transmit them to law enforcement if he fails to log on to the internet for seven consecutive days. Threat of exposure is necessary in the killing business. Because with these mobsters, once your usefulness has ended, you're dispensable. A dead man's switch would be another layer of protection.

He's managed to stay safe because he constantly changes his routines. Most people are creatures of habit; their lives are patterned; there's a steady—and predictable—ebb and flow to their daily existences. They walk the same route every day, jog at the same time and place each morning, take the same train to work, dine at a favorite restaurant, go to the same post office, or visit their regular pharmacy. It can feel comforting to know what each day offers, whether it's stopping off at Starbucks for a latte each morning or going to the same ATM on Friday afternoon. It makes for a sense of reliability in an uncertain world.

But predictability is the prelude to death.

Eli's a hard target because he's renounced what most people cherish: family, friends, familiar routines, the luxury of knowing what each day will bring. He's an anonymous soul, unattached, ungrounded, floating amid the teeming masses of humanity. If he were to die tomorrow, there'd be no funeral service, no death notice, no mourners. No cemetery plot. Unclaimed, his corpse would be dumped into a hole in the potter's field on Hart Island.

No one even knows his real name. And he never provides a surname; if you give people your last name, they'll try to use Google or some other search engine to try to discover your identity.

Bottom line: give them nothing they can use to trace you.

His ability to hover at the edges of society was learned during his three-year training period with Mossad. He was taught computer technology and, among other skills, how to disappear—completely. His existence is ephemeral, as though his presence is merely virtual.

He has no fixed home or business address. His apartments—abandoned every six months—are rented under different names. He rarely food shops or cooks. Instead, he eats Chinese takeout from the white cardboard cartons or goes to any of a number of diners. Sometimes he grabs a quick bite to eat from a food cart vendor on the streets. Aside from an occasional Italian meal at Umberto's in the Village, he generally avoids restaurants. No matter where he may go, he always pays with cash he extracts from a small savings account held under a bogus name.

When he takes up residence in another apartment, he never calls a moving company. The furniture is left behind; he simply vacates the place without notice or leaving a forwarding address. Visiting a Goodwill store, he uses cash to buy used furniture, then sets up in a new place.

Rents are paid by wire transfers from an offshore account to third-party property management companies. He doesn't even keep a safe-deposit box in any bank registered under a name backed by a bogus birth certificate or a phony driver's license. There's nothing tangible to tie him to anything or anyone, anywhere on the planet.

Everything's digitized. Ephemeral. Untraceable.

The real Eli Dagan doesn't exist.

Floating through cyberspace, he's undetectable.

He might as well be a ghost.

The plastic seats on the 6 train are arranged in two rows along the length of the car.

He takes a seat on the platform side of the third car. The interior smells of fried food and tuna fish. The car is partly filled—fifteen or twenty people are seated, with another few standing and grasping the floor-to-ceiling poles or stainless-steel grab bars. It's not the jam-packed crowd of rush hour that begins as early as four in the afternoon.

The doors close, and the train heads downtown.

His eyes are suddenly riveted on a swarthy young guy sitting in the middle of the car on the track side. He's just a kid, no more than seventeen, maybe eighteen, years old. He wears a black parka with the hood raised over his head. Staring blankly ahead, he looks zoned out. Something about him is troubling: he rocks to and fro, and his lips move in silence. His left hand is buried in the coat's outer pocket.

Is he an Arab wearing a dynamite-packed suicide vest beneath that coat?

Has he downed an opioid-laced drink and now prays before he dies in a blast that vaporizes everyone in the car? Is he about to meet his seventy-two virgins?

A bristling sensation begins on Eli's neck. It's that familiar harbinger of danger.

But something mitigates against the guy being a suicide bomber. It's not rush hour, when the car would be crammed with wall-to-wall riders. He's not maximizing casualties.

But why overthink it? *Assume he's a suicide bomber.*

Eli subtly slips the Beretta 70 from his waistband. It's the Mossad weapon of choice for a close-range head shot. A .22-caliber semiautomatic handgun, it's small, lightweight, has low recoil, and in the right hands is highly accurate, especially at a distance of a few meters. After he slowly slides the piece into his cargo pants pocket, his thumb pushes the safety lever into the off position while his index finger rests on the trigger.

If the guy has to push a button to detonate the bomb, a brain shot could short-circuit his neural connections, and there'll be no explosive shock wave streaking through the car.

The kid's lips keep moving. He's lost in prayer.

Getting up, Eli moves toward him. He'll go for the kid's head.

The train slows as it nears the Thirty-Third Street station.

Only one meter separates him from the kid.

Suddenly the guy shoots to his feet. He slips an iPod bud from his left parka pocket and inserts it into his left ear. Heading for the door, he bobs his head up and down as he moves his lips.

Earbuds are buried in both ears. As the train rolls to a stop, the kid's lips keep moving and his head sways in time to the music streaming into his ears.

The doors open, and he steps onto the platform.

Eli sucks in air and his heart slows.

Sweat-soaked and feeling weak, he returns to his seat.

The doors slide together and the train continues downtown.

A woman is now seated across from him. She's in her thirties. A young girl, obviously her daughter, sits beside her. The child is ten or eleven years old, has pale skin, blond hair, and sapphire-blue eyes. It's a lovely face, sweet and innocent.

She reminds him of Hannah.

He first noticed Hannah standing in the apple orchard at Kibbutz Sharon. They were both twelve years old. He wondered if it was possible for a twelve-year-old boy to actually fall in love. Because that was how he felt the moment he saw her in the light-rinsed air that smelled of apples and pears and soil and cut grass. Sunlight washed through the tree canopies, and everything looked golden. When she smiled at him, his heart began drumming in his chest.

That smile—meant just for him—was so unexpected, it felt like a shock to his heart.

God, how he loved her. It was so intense the mere sound of her name—*Hannah*—made his heart beat erratically, and he knew he would love her all his life.

A tide of sadness rolls through him. The car seems to darken, as though the train has cut over from one third rail to another.

As the train sways and rocks, he gets up, threads his way along the aisle, opens the door between subway cars and enters the forward one.

At the Twenty-Eighth Street station, he stands stock-still and waits for the doors to open.

Stepping onto the platform, he stops and looks both ways.

Waiting until the platform is empty, he heads for the stairway.

It's reasonable to assume the Russians haven't followed him.

Now that he's convinced he's not being tailed, his next stop will be the apartment. But he'll take a circuitous route to make sure.

Because when it comes to the Odessa mafia, you can never be certain of anything.

9

Entering his building on East Twenty-Seventh off First Avenue, Eli is greeted by Leo, the big-bellied daytime doorman.

"Hello, Mr. Dukas," Leo says, addressing Eli by the name he uses in the building. Few tenants even know of his existence. Those who've noticed him must think he's just another anonymous soul in a city of strangers.

Eli shoots Leo a quick smile. "How're you today, Leo?"

"Just fine. On such a cold day, it's good to be indoors."

"Yes, it is."

Eli has good relations with the doormen. But he's always careful when speaking to them—or, for that matter, when talking with anyone. Even though he speaks all-American English—has what some would call a news broadcaster's neutral speech pattern—he's aware that a tinge of an accent can occasionally infiltrate his speech.

Usually, his English is flawless, lacks any regional inflection. Maybe it's because he grew up in a trilingual home—English, Arabic, and Hebrew, along with a smattering of Yiddish—and is comfortable with each language. His mother, an American-born teacher originally from New York City, said, "I want you to be as much American as Israeli." He was happy to accommodate to her wish.

Eli grew up watching American sitcoms and movies. He loved listening to American pop music and adored Van Halen, Guns N' Roses, along with Springsteen and the E Street Band and became familiar with the most well-known jazz musicians of various eras.

He read American comic books—the superheroes: Superman, Spawn, Sandman, old Batman issues, and the entire Marvel series.

A voracious reader, he read all the Tarzan books and, as a young adult, read novels in English. When it came to linguistics, he took after his mom and is capable of mastering new languages with astonishing speed. His rare mispronunciation occurs only with certain words—like when he's tired and the fricative *ch* comes from the back of his throat while pronouncing a *c*.

Gotta stay vigilant. Language is important—not only its content but its form. You'll give yourself away if you're not careful.

In the apartment—a soulless one-bedroom on the sixth floor—he realizes he didn't do his usual morning exercises. He was too focused on the prospect of meeting Gorlov to attend to his morning routine.

At thirty-nine, he's aware it now takes more effort than ever to stay fit. So he watches what he eats, avoids simple carbs, exercises regularly, and walks for hours at a time—stops only for traffic lights at street corners—and varies his route to avoid falling into a predictable routine.

In the living room, he does a set of stretches, then cracks the vertebrae in his neck and lets out a series of hollow pops.

Dropping to the floor, he does his daily push-ups—three sets of fifty—then a hundred sit-ups, followed by fifty knee-to-chest crunches while lying on his back.

Standing before a mirror, he breathes deeply, closes his eyes, and relaxes, then explodes in a series of Krav Maga moves—kicks, punches, knee and elbow strikes, the movements fluid, fast, precise. And potentially lethal. Then come more stretches—hamstrings, back, arms, and neck—to keep the muscles flexible, supple. He stands for a full minute on his right foot, then the left—an exercise designed to maintain finely tuned balance.

Eli has the same waistline he did when he was twenty. But he knows he no longer has the speed, strength, or flexibility of even a few years ago. It's an inexorable waning of the body's capacities. Advancing age is never kind.

Thoughts of Gorlov and his offer intrude. Eli's earned plenty of money over the last ten years. His offshore accounts are swollen with enough cash to sustain him for the rest of his life. Maybe he should have turned down the job.

Because there'll come a day when his reflexes will slow even more, when he'll have less stamina and will become more vulnerable to those who would harm him. Yes, the day will come when he'll no longer be a hard target and could fall prey to the same people who pay him to kill others.

And before that day comes, he'll have to get out of this life.

10

The next morning, while brewing coffee, Eli recalls the conversation with Gorlov—nearly word for word.

His memory is one of his most valuable assets. Mom used to say, "Eli, you have a memory like a steel trap. You can put it to use in many different ways. And you're smart enough to be anything you want to be. Anything."

So, with all that potential, why did he join the commandos, then the Mossad, and from there, decide to no longer be a blip on anyone's radar and move to the States?

And to become a contract killer?

He hates thinking about the reasons his life has taken this direction. Instead, he focuses on Gorlov's job. Of all the mob-related hits he's ever accepted, to assassinate a Bratva boss is unprecedented. And Ivan Agapov's death will have major consequences throughout the underworld, especially with Russian organized crime.

Focus, focus on what must be done.

There are two major impediments to this being a successful hit:

First, he's gotta meet with the mobster in person—at his restaurant—unfamiliar terrain. That'll make things far riskier since there'll be multiple layers of protection and he can't scope out the place in advance.

And second, it has to look like a natural death. Under the circumstances, how can he end Agapov's life without it looking like an assassination?

No bullets or bombs.

It's a strange and sad thing: bombs and bullets have been part of his life, all his life.

When Eli was six years old, Arab terrorists infiltrated the kibbutz in the middle of the night. They sprayed AK-47 bullets into each house. Eli's father grabbed his pistol and ran from the house along with other men in the collective.

Mom dragged Eli and his two-year-old brother, Ezra, into a closet. Gunfire and shouting were everywhere. Paralyzed with terror, Eli trembled in the dark. Mom wrapped her arms around both boys.

Only moments before the gunfire died down, a stray bullet shattered Ezra's skull. Eli can still visualize his brother's ruined corpse.

It was difficult for Mom and Pop to find meaning in anything after that. Eli's certain they never recovered from Ezra's murder.

That night was the beginning of everything that changed for Eli.

Bullets and bombs.

They've been his way of life since he was twenty-one years old.

At a Starbucks on First Avenue, he grabs a small table for two. There are still a few empty seats, so there's little chance anyone will ask to share the table. He can work at his laptop, undisturbed. After ordering an espresso macchiato, he hooks into the coffee shop's Wi-Fi system.

While the barista calls out orders for lattes, cappuccinos, and espressos, Eli checks his secure offshore account at Butterfield International Bank in the Caymans.

Three hundred thousand has been electronically transferred.

Twenty minutes later, he checks the website dedicated to the Odessa mafia.

Sure enough, Gorlov's IT man has posted a dossier on Ivan Agapov.

Ivan Agapov
Age: 50
Lives at Oceana Apartments, a condo in Brighton Beach, Brooklyn, a doorman building with a health club and indoor and outdoor pools. Swims nearly every day, indoors during the winter. A security detail is always present at the pool or in the gym.

Married 22 years; wife, Sonya, 47.

No children. Has a brother who lives in Brighton Beach, not a member of the Bratva.

Owns a Georgian shepherd, takes the dog to the office at his restaurant. The dog is protective (photo enclosed) and trained to attack.

Staring at the photo, Eli sees a tawny, thickly built dog with a broad muzzle and yellow-looking eyes. It's gotta weigh at least 70 kilos or 150 pounds. The tongue, hanging from the side of its mouth, looks like a huge slab of ham. *Jesus, it's a vicious-looking beast. There's no way an unarmed man stands a chance if the animal attacks.*

Medical: High blood pressure, controlled with medicine. Physician: Dr. Vladimir Voronin, Russian-born internist; office at 150 Brighton Beach Avenue.

Owns Valentina's, a restaurant at Brighton 6th Street and the boardwalk. Has dinner there 3 or 4 times a week. Has a table reserved. Bodyguards nearby. Has an office in a back room of the restaurant.

Favorite foods: Ukrainian borscht and veal pelmeni.

Smokes 2 to 3 Cuban cigars sent by Davidoff of Geneva on Madison Avenue, Manhattan. After dinner, usually has a snifter of Rémy Martin cognac and smokes a cigar.

Is chauffeured in a Lincoln Navigator, but while under house arrest must stay at home or at the restaurant. Wears an ankle bracelet with a GPS function. Has enough connections that allow him to visit his girlfriend (see below). Chauffeur is a

Bratva man, Mikhail Potchak. Bodyguards wait outside while he visits girlfriend.

Speaks fluent English, Ukrainian, Russian. Some Yiddish. Prefers English.

Girlfriend/mistress: Sofia Dudyk, lives at 125 Corbin Place, Brighton Beach, Brooklyn. Sees her once a week.

Additional information is in the enclosed article from June 2019 in *New York* magazine. Click on the link.

Though he'd been expecting the dossier, it's surprising to see it here on the laptop screen—a précis encapsulating the man's fifty years on earth. All transmitted in binary number coding so Eli might terminate the life these two pages summarize.

Agapov's not a soft target. Knowing he has serious enemies, he's always heavily guarded.

And there's the added complication of the dog. How does he get past the beast?

Eli peruses the *New York* magazine piece. The article reveals nothing actionable about the man.

Eli long ago hacked into the NCIC computerized database and its files, including the National Instant Criminal Background Check System and the Interstate Identification Index. It's an electronic clearinghouse of crime data available to every law enforcement agency throughout the nation. There's nothing operational that can be used to terminate Agapov's time on earth. It's just a dreary recounting of his criminal activities and long record.

Eli moves the cursor to Google Search and types Agapov's name into the search engine. There's a Wikipedia entry along with various web links. They detail that Agapov has gone to trial twice before but has never been convicted. This guy's the Russian version of the Teflon Don, John Gotti.

After reading more about the man, it's clear Agapov has enough people in his pocket to take care of most potential legal problems, but apparently the feds have come down on him with a RICO charge for which he's about to stand trial.

And the various articles make something else obvious: Agapov is rumored to have 400 loyal soldiers—first rank and secondary mobsters or affiliates—guys who'll do his bidding. And he can tap more button men from the Eastern European countries that were once part of the Soviet bloc. The guy's a serious contender for the title Mobster of the Decade.

Past wars between Bratva brothers have left blood-soaked streets, not just in Brooklyn but in Queens, the Bronx, and Westchester too. The Russians don't stick to the mob conventions depicted in the movies. Unlike the so-called *infamita* of the Italian mafia, Bratva members find nothing sacrosanct and nothing shameful. In a pinch, they'll go after your wife, your daughter, your girlfriend, even your dog if that's what it takes to put fear in your heart. Or to exact revenge.

The Agapov job would change the balance of power in the city's underworld. No wonder Gorlov's willing to pay such big bucks for the security of knowing his rival will be gone. And for the ability to leave the country and retire without worrying about the feds coming for him.

But what about the second part? What's that about? Gorlov's apparently willing to pay even more than the six hundred thousand he'll pony up for the Agapov hit.

Who's a great enough threat to Gorlov that he's willing to pay even more than what he's committed to the Agapov job?

The whole mob thing is strange.

Survival is tenuous.

Kill or be killed.

It's more than just a mob mantra.

It's emblematic of what Eli's life has become.

He again wonders if he's made a mistake agreeing to take this job. Did meeting Gorlov in person leave Eli vulnerable to revealing his identity? He's now recognizable to Gorlov, to Viktor Sorokin, and two of their foot soldiers. He's sacrificed his anonymity. He's no longer a digital ghost floating through cyberspace.

Will a sit-down with Agapov jeopardize Eli's anonymity even more than the Gorlov meeting did? How much physical exposure can he risk without endangering his life?

A dead man's switch would be a good idea. Is there anyone else who can be trusted with information that would nail the people who've hired him for assassinations over the last ten years?

There's no one else.

Not a soul on the planet.

11

Still sitting in the Starbucks, Eli wonders if there's a way to put Ivan Agapov in the ground without it looking like murder.

Death by natural causes.

While Mossad had done it before—many times—it was never an easy mission. It called for stealth, ingenuity, and above all, favorable circumstances. If conditions weren't right, the mission would be aborted.

That kind of killing means getting up close and personal. It'll be tough to do with the man under house arrest and protected by bodyguards.

Sucking down his third espresso and getting a bit of a caffeine jolt, he hits the computer icon for Google Maps and types in the address for Oceana Apartments in Brighton Beach, Brooklyn. Street View shows an eighteen-story luxury building not far from the Atlantic Ocean. It's likely that no one is admitted into the building without being vetted by the doorman and concierge.

And there's the dog. Agapov has the beast with him at home and in the office. Assume the worst: any move toward the man will set off an attack.

As for his paramour, Sofia Dudyk, Eli types "125 Corbin Place in Brooklyn" in the Google Maps address bar. Clicking "Street View," he gets a close look at her house. It's a two-story, attached brick residence with a garage that's reached by driving down a steep ramp. A flight of brick stairs leads from the sidewalk up to the front door of the house.

No doubt, when Agapov visits her, he's driven by the chauffeur, who waits in the car while the bodyguards are in a nearby vehicle.

It's doubtful there'll be an opportunity to force the man to take a neck-breaking header down that stairway.

And he can't take the guy out with a rifle or a remotely detonated device.

The kill will require subtlety and an up-close encounter.

That means the best—and only—chance to take him out will be when he meets with the pakhan—in his office, surrounded by bodyguards. And with that beast at his side.

What does the dossier reveal that could make for the possibility of an assassination looking like a natural death?

Maybe just as important is the fact that there *is* this dossier.

It's clear Agapov is being betrayed by a close associate who knows his routines, even his personal and sexual habits. The informant might be able to supply a hint about Agapov that's not obvious from the dossier. But it's unlikely the mole will take a chance on meeting with anyone connected to Gorlov. It's far too risky.

No bullets.

No bombs.

Bombs. Bombs. Bombs.

The thought of explosives causes Eli's thoughts to swerve back to when he was twenty-one years old.

Having been childhood sweethearts, he and Hannah married young, which was the norm on the collective. By age twenty-one, he'd completed his compulsory service in the IDF. His paratrooper days were over, and he'd become a reservist in the Thirty-Fifth Paratrooper Brigade.

Soon afterward, Hannah was pregnant. A sonogram revealed they'd have a boy. They decided to name him David. For the first time in years, a spark of life returned to Mom and Pop. Though they would never have acknowledged it, Eli was certain they thought of the unborn baby as being sent to them by their beloved Ezra.

On a warm spring day during the Second Intifada, having been discharged from the army only a few days earlier, Eli was in Tel Aviv applying for a job in information technology at a start-up company.

Hannah, Mom, and Pop, along with thirty-five other people, were on a Jerusalem bus when a young man entered through the rear door. When he pressed the detonator button on his suicide vest, the explosion was so powerful, it lifted the bus off the ground. Nothing was left but charred skeletal remains of the vehicle, millions of shards of bloodied glass, and the smell of burned plastic and chemicals and scorched corpses.

Including those of Mom, Pop, Hannah, and their unborn son, David.

When Eli got to the scene, the stench of death crawled up his nose and reached the back of his throat. Shock blasted by disbelief, Eli realized in that terrible moment he was truly alone in the world.

Even now, sitting in a Starbucks amid the aromas of coffee and croissants, he can smell the burnt blood and flesh and incinerated bone. It seems the odors lurk in his sinuses just waiting to be recalled, but really, they're embedded in his brain.

And they'll stay there for as long as he lives.

For weeks after the bombing, he was numb, incapable of thought or feeling, and it seemed he was living in a colorless dream state.

When feeling returned, it felt like his still-beating heart had been ripped from his chest, thrown to the ground, stomped on, and squashed.

His despair obliterated everything else. He could barely understand how the world kept spinning, continued grinding on in all its indifference. How did people talk or laugh or go to restaurants or movies or concerts and plays, and how did they empathize and love and care and fuck or function in the dreary swamp of this world?

Slowly, the pain subsided, but left in its wake is an ache that will stay with him for the rest of his life. It was more than simply pain or longing or the loss of innocence. It was a bludgeoning of the soul, an awareness of the world's ugliness, its cruelty. He felt emptied of his humanity.

The loss of Hannah, Mom, Pop, and unborn David was unendurable, and even now, it seems, grief oozes through him, robs him of the capacity to feel love or warmth or joy.

Yet it's more than grief.

It's rage, the only feeling left to him.

It's poisoned him.

And he's come to believe that in every life there lurks catastrophe.

Through the hissing of the espresso machine and the coffee shop's babble, Eli does his best to suffocate the darkness. He thought that by now he'd formed a thick outer crust protecting him from so much pain.

He's seen so much death—men, women, and children torn apart by bullets or bombs—he believed he'd been stripped of feeling, and the only purpose left to him in this life is to kill evil people.

But can he go on living this way? Is that layer of numbness now crumbling?

Get ahold of yourself. Stop pondering this shit. Do what you have to do. It's time to come up with a plan.

Closing his eyes, he struggles to think about what must be done now, to focus on Agapov, the Bratva, and Brighton Beach.

How does he make good on his commitment to Gorlov?

A moment later he realizes exactly what must be done.

12

Anton Gorlov sits behind the battered oak desk in his Brighton Beach Avenue office.

Viktor Sorokin sits in a chair across from him. Viktor is his *rodnoy brat*, the loyal brother Gorlov always wished for but never had. And brothers they will be until the end of their days.

The Q train thunders past the second-story window on the Brighton Beach Avenue el. They wait for it to pass so their words aren't drowned out.

"So, Viktor, the money's been transferred?"

"Yes, this morning. But I don't trust this Aiden."

"Listen to me," Gorlov says. "If Ivan Agapov gets a deal, he'll tell the feds everything he knows. We have to protect ourselves."

"But we don't know if this man can do it. And even if he does, there's no guarantee it won't be traced back to us."

"Tell me, what's guaranteed in this life?"

"And if we go to one of those South American countries, we can be extradited."

"So? Do you want to live in some extradition-free backwater like Libya or Chad? Or maybe a good Muslim country like Bangladesh?"

Viktor scoffs, gets up, and begins pacing about the room.

"Let's face it," Gorlov says. "The feds are on Agapov like flies on shit. I have no doubt that if he lives, he'll give us up. He'll get a deal. After a short prison sentence, he'll go into Witness Protection while we're lounging on some beach in the Caribbean. Then the feds show up, and we're extradited. And the next stop is prison." He gets up from his chair and begins pacing.

"But if it comes out that we put a hit on Agapov, all the brigades will come after us."

"Not if he dies of natural causes."

Viktor shrugs, then shakes his head. "Who knows?"

"And I've been thinking," Gorlov says. "We also have to take care of a few other people. You know who I am talking about?"

"Of course," Viktor says. "One of our financial people. But hear me out, Anton. Do you really want to live somewhere in South America?"

"Where else? Israel?"

"I don't think so." Viktor chortles.

"Remember Meyer Lansky?"

"Yes, of course."

"He went there under the Law of Return but was extradited and stood trial on tax charges. The Israelis exclude any Jew fleeing from alleged crimes."

"But why don't—"

"We can't afford to worry that Ivan Agapov will try to save his skin by giving us up. And you *know* he won't just go to prison and keep his mouth shut. He'll squawk in a heartbeat if it reduces his sentence. Unfortunately, we have to depend on this man, Aiden. Otherwise, we'll never know when the hammer will drop." Gorlov pauses as his chest tightens. "Besides, ever since Nadia died . . ."

"May she rest in peace."

An ache sinks into Anton Gorlov's chest; it's so powerful, it feels like an aura. "Imagine that—dead at fifty." He thinks about how breast cancer, the same disease that claimed Mama, shrank his wife to a withered corpse.

"Ever since she passed," Gorlov murmurs, "I've asked myself, 'What am I living for? More money? Prestige? Do I want to be a public figure like Ivan Agapov? I'm sixty years old now, and let's face it: it's all meaningless.'" He plops back down into his chair.

Sighing, Viktor shakes his head. "Anton, I know how you feel, but—"

"I want to get away from these cold winters," Gorlov says. "They remind me of Odessa and how life was back there. The winter always makes me feel sad. I want a new life away from this place."

"What about your daughter?"

"Diana? She thinks my career worried her mother to death, that I caused Nadia's cancer. She won't even talk to me." Gorlov sighs. "It's a stone in my heart."

"I understand, Anton.

"It's a shame. Our children in America, they can't understand what life was like back there. I once tried to tell Diana what we went through, but it bored her."

"These American kids understand nothing," Viktor says. "All they care about is what's on their cell phones and going to their personal trainers. They even have *life* coaches. Can you imagine that?"

"A life coach?" Anton says with a snort. "The streets of Odessa were our coaches, and they taught us well." Getting up from his seat, he begins pacing again. "Of *course* these kids understand nothing, Viktor; they've grown up in a different world. They can't understand what we went through. It's beyond them. And the more I think about it, the more I know there's nothing left for me here."

"I'm just not sure about this Aiden," Viktor says. "There was *something* about him . . ."

"Viktor, you know I've always valued your advice, but it's different now. Things are changing, and the old ways won't work anymore. We need to take care of some people, or should I say . . . some loose ends? And after things are in order, we need to get out of here. And this Aiden will take care of what needs taking care of. I know he will."

13

At eight o'clock that evening, Eli takes an elevator to the fourth floor of NYU's Langone Medical Center.

He'd gone through security on the first floor, having to show a fake driver's license as ID. A small machine made a photocopy of it and produced a visitor's pass with a head shot of Eli. The pass is now affixed to the lapel of Eli's jacket.

He gets off the elevator on the fourth floor and climbs to the tenth floor. Aside from being a precautionary diversion, using stairways is another way to get exercise.

The reason he's in this building brings back thoughts of the past.

The blast radius of that bus bomb drove Eli to reenlist in the active-duty IDF. The Sayeret Matkal was an elite counterterrorism unit. The training took seventy-five weeks.

He remembers his first commando action: he chased a member of Al-Qassam Brigades down a Jerusalem alleyway. The guy had detonated a car bomb that killed ten people. Eli yelled in Arabic, "Stop or I'll shoot." The terrorist turned, raised a pistol, and Eli triple-tapped him—put two slugs in his chest and one in his head.

Later, Noah, his team leader, asked how he felt having killed a man face-to-face.

"I feel good," he replied, though his hands were shaking.

"Once you've crossed that line, it's tough to come back," Noah warned.

At that moment Eli knew that Noah had spoken an enduring truth.

Along with Noah, Eli was recruited by the Mossad. He blitzed the entry tests and scored off the charts on intelligence. He handed in a stellar performance on aptitude tests, especially for verbal skills. "You have linguistic neuroplasticity," the recruitment officer said. "The language areas of your brain are more highly developed than anyone's we've ever seen. You can learn languages quickly and speak them so fluently, you'll never be outed as an Israeli."

The training for Mossad—involving many skills—was even more extensive than it had been for Sayeret Matkal. When it was over, he became a *katsa*, a field agent in the Mossad.

Throughout his career with "the Institute," he'd never been through the sanitized version of death—the trappings of a funeral home with the mortician's artifice, the restored face of a loved one resting on a pillow in a silk-lined coffin, and the coterie of mourners with their eulogies.

For Eli, after losing his family, death has involved the stench of blood and guts and shit and bodies riddled with bullets or shrapnel while covered with buzzing flies.

But the death of Ivan Agapov must be achieved by taking a different approach.

On the tenth floor of Langone, he makes his way along a corridor that has a vaguely medicinal smell.

Dr. Otto Bauer is a physician, professor, and research toxicologist who was once short-listed as a recipient of a Nobel Prize in Medicine for work on the osmotic transfer of particles across semipermeable membranes.

After knocking on Otto's office door, Eli hears the doctor call, "Come in."

The office is filled with an array of books, binders, and medical journals. A host of diplomas, certificates, and honoraria blanket the other walls.

Otto Bauer, a barrel-chested man in his sixties, wears a starched white lab coat, black trousers, and a dark blue cloth tie. His rimless glasses reflect the room's overhead light and sometimes make him appear virtually eyeless. His white hair forms a massive corona around his head.

Eli has always thought Otto looks like the old-time caricature of a mad scientist.

Otto rounds the desk and greets Eli with a smile on his cherubic face. They exchange man-hugs and backslaps. "Ah, Ezra, my *boychick*, it's a pleasure to see you again. You look strong and healthy as always."

With his hands on Eli's shoulders, he leans back and nods. "You've been taking good care of yourself, yes?"

"Yes, I have, Otto. And it's been a long time."

"Much too long, Ezra. I've missed our talks."

Ezra is the name Otto knows him by—he hasn't provided a last name—and Eli hasn't lost sight of the fact that Ezra is the name of his dead baby brother. Eli loves when the doctor calls him *boychick*; it reinforces the notion that the professor has been something of a father figure, offering Eli advice about staying healthy. And about life.

Otto is by far his favorite *sayan*, a word in Hebrew literally meaning "helper" or "assistant."

While he was in the Mossad, Eli had contact with many sayanim, people who aren't Israelis but are willing to help the state of Israel fight terrorism. This means having volunteers all over the world, people who help in various ways without receiving benefits of any kind.

Otto Bauer is his medical and scientific sayan.

Another sayan manages a car rental concern and provides Eli with vehicles without the need for the usual documentation.

A real estate agent arranges apartment rentals without Eli having to provide background information.

A gunsmith in Mount Kisco delivers pistols without filing the required paperwork.

A forger in Flushing, Queens, provides documents needed for his many bogus identities.

He's had sayanim in Paris, Damascus, Cyprus, and Rome. In other places too, even in equatorial Africa.

None of them know he's no longer a Mossad agent.

And they still help in different ways.

Each of them knows him by a different name, which is where his memory plays an essential role in this clandestine life. He's different people for different *sayanim.*

Though he wishes he could be more personal with some of them—especially with Otto—Eli always adheres to the credo of anonymity.

"You know, Ezra, I was just thinking of you," Otto says.

"I'm flattered. How come?"

"I got a call yesterday from a man named Moshe. I suspect he's Mossad."

"There are many *Moshes* in the Mossad," Eli says, knowing it's a common nom de guerre used by field agents. It's virtually generic for *You can't know my real identity.*

"This fellow's interested in a new medical device," Otto says. "Any idea what he might mean?"

"You know I can't discuss Mossad business."

Otto laughs while nodding as he moves back behind his desk. "Of course not. It's all secret."

Eli is certain "Moshe" is from the secretive Unit 81, a branch of Mossad that develops advanced espionage tools. Inserting cameras or listening devices into medical equipment is a Mossad kind of thing. They've also inserted bombs into components for centrifuges used in Iran's nuclear development program, devices that explode at predetermined times to take down hundreds of centrifuges in a matter of moments.

After some conversation, Otto settles into his leather chair, claps his hands together on his desk, and says, "So, Eli, you have another Nazi or terrorist to dispatch?"

Otto Bauer is especially sympathetic to the cause of Nazi hunters. Having grown up as the only child of Austrian Holocaust survivors, he has an abiding hatred of Nazis and terrorists of any stripe. Yes, Otto's morality is compartmentalized; he'd never think of harming a patient or someone who's innocent of crimes against humanity. But when it comes to Nazis and terrorists—those who kill innocents—Eli knows Otto's more than comfortable going along for the ride.

"Yes, there's another one," Eli says. "But you know I can't give you any details."

Eli regrets lying to Otto, but if the good doctor knew the true purpose of his visit, he'd never consider helping send Ivan Agapov to an early grave.

"Of course, I understand," Otto says. "Just tell me what you need, and we'll see what we can do."

"This one's gotta look like he died of natural causes."

"A *natural* death? One that looks like it has medical causes?" Otto says, raising and bending his index and middle fingers to signify quotation marks.

"Yes. Otherwise there could be repercussions."

"Reminds me of the death of Ahmed Hussein Saleh in Beirut."

Otto's referring to the operation that targeted an upper echelon Hezbollah terrorist. A Mossad agent infiltrated his inner circle and switched his toothpaste for an identical tube laced with an undetectable toxin. Every time Saleh brushed his teeth, a miniscule quantity of the stuff penetrated his gums and made its way into his bloodstream.

Over the next ten days, he began to bleed from his gums, then from his nose and rectum. He died in agony bleeding from every bodily orifice. The doctors were baffled and attributed his death to "natural" causes.

"It's somewhat similar," says Eli, "but this one can't take ten days."

Otto taps his chin, appears to be thinking. "First question," he says. "Does this individual have a medical condition?"

Eli gives Otto a rundown of the dossier's contents.

After listening carefully, Otto says, "So, other than hypertension, there's no vulnerability like diabetes or chronic heart failure."

"None."

"There are interesting technologies that can deliver toxins into the body without being obvious, and some of the latest won't even leave any biological markers. There's a liquid jet injector that can shoot a toxin into a victim's skin so fast he—"

"Let me stop you there, Otto. Bodyguards will be with him at all times. There's no way I'll get to touch him. Also, he has an attack dog he takes with him wherever he goes. If I make the slightest move toward the man, the animal will probably react aggressively."

"So, there'll have to be another way," Otto says, leaning back in his chair, clasping his hands behind his head, then closing his eyes.

"Yes, of course."

Otto tilts the chair forward. "Then there's the question of which toxin to use."

"That's your department," Eli says.

"I'm guessing you need something with a delayed onset so you won't be suspected of having given it to him."

"Yes, and here's the thing, Otto. I've done a little research. This guy's very fond of fine Cuban cigars. Is there a way to deliver something in a cigar, something that has a delayed onset . . . let's say for at least three or four hours?"

"Fine Cuban cigars?" Otto asks with widened eyes. "You *do* know that cigar aficionados can be very picky about what they smoke. Which brand does he prefer?"

"A real cigar lover will salivate over *any* brand so long as it's fine Cuban tobacco."

"I'm guessing you know cigars," Otto says with a broad smile. "Which one would you use to entice him?"

"A Cohiba Robusto."

"Aha. You *do* know your cigars. You know that Fidel Castro smoked Cohiba Robustos?"

"I do," Eli replies with a nod and a smile.

"And the CIA tried to kill him with an exploding cigar. Isn't that ludicrous?" Otto says, slapping a hand on his desk as they laugh.

"That's not how the Israelis would've approached the problem," Eli says.

"A Cohiba Robusto," Otto says, nodding. "A cigar lover will drool for one. And a cigar can be an excellent mode of delivery if the right toxin is used."

"I have a narrow window of time. The symptoms can't start for a few hours, and it has to cause death within a day or two. Can you prepare something to fit that bill?"

"I could spike a cigar with dimethyl sulfate. It's a colorless fluid with barely any odor. Any smell or taste of it would be hidden by the tobacco resins in the cigar smoke. Absorption is through the mucous membranes of the cheeks, tongue, and soft palate when smoke is drawn into the mouth. Symptoms won't start for at least eight or nine hours."

"Sounds good."

"Better yet, if he inhales," Otto continues, "it'll also be absorbed through the lungs. On contact with mucosal surfaces, DMS hydrolyzes into a variety of toxic substances."

"Assuming he'll inhale, how long before symptoms appear?"

"If he inhales, the effects will start maybe three hours after he's taken the first few puffs," Otto says. "He'll begin feeling sick when the cigar's a crushed stub lying in an ashtray."

"Sounds perfect."

"After another six or seven hours pass, toxic shock will set in and he'll die from respiratory and heart failure."

"Sounds excellent, Otto. I've brought these," Eli says, reaching into his pocket and producing three cigars.

He hands them to Otto, who holds them beneath his nose and sniffs.

"These are things of beauty," Otto says. "And they cost a pretty penny, *boychick*. A cigar lover will certainly go for this one. After all, we all want the satisfaction of mother's milk." He laughs softly.

"Prepare only *one* with the toxin," Eli says. "How long will it take?"

"Can you come back tomorrow?"

"Of course."

"Come by in the afternoon. I'll mark the spiked one with a small black dot on the rounded end of the wrapper. It'll be rewrapped perfectly. No one will ever know it was tampered with. Then, *boychick*, you'll do what you have to do."

Descending the staircase to the lobby of Langone Medical Center, Eli's reminded of how much he owes to his Mossad training.

He mastered an array of unconventional killing and survival tactics: how to make bombs from ordinary ingredients, to be a marksman with a silenced .22 Beretta, attaining black belt status in Krav Maga, becoming proficient in surveillance and countersurveillance techniques, and memorizing multiple false biographies in the event he'd ever be interrogated.

He learned the culture of any country where he'd be planted and easily mastered different Arabic accents—whether Syrian, Palestinian, Egyptian, or Saudi—so he'd never be exposed as a foreigner.

He studied the menus of top-flight restaurants in France and Italy, became familiar with top-shelf liquors, and learned an array of fine wines—anything from a Bordeaux like Château Margaux to a Sauterne like Château d'Yquem.

He studied casino games so he could mix with sophisticated players inhabiting the gambling palaces of Monaco, Spain, London, Paris, or Zagreb.

Included in his training was a thorough familiarity with the finest cigars men in those stratospheric circles tend to favor.

As he spins through the revolving door onto First Avenue, it strikes Eli that this assassin's life has given him a perverse view of the pleasures most men take for granted.

For him, a fine cigar, a vintage wine, or a single-malt whiskey holds little value other than being a potential weapon of death.

14

Three days later, Eli approaches the steps leading down to the Lexington line's Twenty-Eighth Street subway station, headed to Brooklyn.

From the top of the stairway, he hears the 6 local pulling into the station before continuing on its way downtown.

Going against the flow of people climbing the steps, he scrambles downstairs and passes the ticket booth. At the turnstile, he swipes his MetroCard through the metal slot and sprints onto the platform, but he's too late. The train pulls away, its rumble lessening as it disappears into the blackness of the downtown tunnel.

A few stragglers move toward the exit gate.

Except for one guy. He's tall, rangy, wears a black leather jacket, and has a *New York Daily News* folded and tucked beneath one arm. He must have gotten off the train that just left the station, but he hasn't moved toward the exit. Why?

The primitive part of Eli's brain does an instant threat assessment. The guy's lingering presence doesn't make sense. He could be waiting to meet someone, but time will tell. One thing is certain: when a situation defies logic, something's usually wrong.

Eli remains alert, ready to react.

A few more people trudge down the stairway and wait on the platform. There's a twentysomething woman with purple hair. She's chewing gum and her thumbs are working like mad, texting on her cell phone. An older man bundled in a heavy coat sits on a wooden bench at the far end of the platform. And there's a young man with a knapsack large enough to carry a small army.

Initial impression: he looks like a college student, not a suicide bomber.

Moments later, Eli's take on the kid is confirmed: the young man sits on the bench near the old guy, slips a textbook out of his backpack, opens it, and uses a yellow marker pen to highlight passages.

A few other people meander into view, but no one forms a blip on Eli's radar screen.

Just the loiterer remains a source of concern.

The LED display indicates the next train is due in four minutes.

Soon a distant rumbling comes from the southbound tunnel. The next 6 train is approaching. A dense vibration courses through the platform, rises into Eli's feet.

With a rush of dank tunnel air and a high-pitched squeal of steel on steel, the train roars into the station and brakes to a stop. The air smells of ozone.

The doors slide open with a hiss.

The loiterer boards the third car.

Entering the fourth car, Eli remains standing and grasps the center pole. The air smells stale, with a hint of camphor from winter coats that had been stored in closets.

Peering through the front-door window of the fourth car, Eli sees the loiterer take a seat in the forward car; he opens the newspaper and begins reading. He's not a threat.

The train begins its downtown trek.

Eli occupies himself by looking at the ads displayed above the windows but regards each person who enters the car. No one looks suspicious.

At the Broadway–Lafayette station, Eli gets off the train and walks through a series of passageways heading toward the D line, which will take him to Brighton Beach.

And to Ivan Agapov.

Eli glances back and sees no one who looks like he's tailing him.

A few minutes later, the D train thunders into the station. Boarding it, he takes a seat at the rear end of the fifth car.

Moments later the train emerges from the tunnel and clatters over the Manhattan Bridge toward Brooklyn.

After crossing over the East River, it barrels underground to its next stop, DeKalb Avenue. A few passengers disembark.

At the Prospect Park station, the train emerges from its subterranean route and continues its seesawing trip at ground level until it climbs onto the elevated tracks near the Kings Highway station, where a few more passengers get up and leave the train.

At the Sheepshead Bay station, Eli knows the next stop will be the end of the line: Brighton Beach, home of the Odessa mafia and Agapov's brigade.

Slipping his hand beneath his overcoat, Eli feels the three cigars tucked into the breast pocket of his sports coat. They're tickets to Ivan Agapov's grave. If things go as planned.

Eli thinks back to Otto's departing words when he handed the stogies to Eli. "If he lights up while you're there, make sure you don't breathe in any smoke. Though it'll be diluted, there'll still be a small amount of toxin in the exhaled smoke. If any comes your way, without being obvious, try to hold your breath. And don't stay for long in an enclosed room with him if he lights up. Just leave as quickly as you can."

The train slows as it rolls toward the Brighton Beach station.

The few remaining passengers look Russian, or maybe the correct description would be *Slavic.*

Of course they do. They're entering the neighborhood of the Bratva. It's brimming with Russians and Ukrainians.

Eli thinks back to how this meeting came about.

One of Agapov's men called him on his satellite phone.

He recalls the conversation verbatim.

"How'd you get my number?" Eli demanded.

"Our people have it."

"But how'd you get it?"

"I don't know."

Eli wonders if the sat phone's been compromised; maybe it's time to get a new one.

And once again he's breaking a long-standing rule. He's not only meeting Agapov face-to-face, but the sit-down is on the Russian's home turf, where Eli knows nothing about the setup. If Agapov's people somehow got wind of this plot, Eli's headed for the bottom of Sheepshead Bay, wearing Quikrete cement shoes.

Maybe he should have called off this deal with Gorlov, returned the money, and made arrangements to leave the country.

There's still time to do it. He could turn around, wait for the next Manhattan-bound train at the Brighton Beach station, and head back to Manhattan. After returning the money, he could say he's rethought the situation and the job's not for him. He again wonders why Gorlov refused to discuss the second half of the assignment, the *delicate* matter that would require even more *finesse* than the first part. No doubt it's another hit. But there's something about the assignment that's mysterious, maybe an undercurrent of extreme danger, as though the first part isn't treacherous enough. And when he began pressing the pakhan about the second part of the job, Eli thought he detected a change in the timbre of Gorlov's voice.

But backing out now could be dangerous: you don't break your word to a man like Anton Gorlov, not if you want to keep breathing.

And he did commit to this first part, so it has to get done.

As the train rolls to a stop on the elevated trestle in Brighton Beach, Eli knows he'll make good on the commitment to Gorlov.

The lights at the Brighton Beach station cast a dim glow on the elevated platform.

A biting wind blows in from the Atlantic Ocean, just a stone's throw away. Eli stands in place until all the other passengers disembark from the train and go downstairs to Brighton Beach Avenue.

With the train heading toward the Coney Island terminal yards, he has a good view of the platform on the opposite side of the tracks.

Beneath the dim lighting of the corrugated roof, he sees a few people—an old man, three women, and a young couple waiting for the soon-to-arrive Manhattan-bound train, the one he considered getting on if he'd aborted this assignment. A few more people climb up the stairway on the other side of the tracks and meander onto the platform.

No one looks suspicious or out of place.

He long ago learned a basic rule about assassination: *Act as though you're the one being hunted. In fact, think about how you would hunt for yourself if you were the target. You can stop feeling like prey only when the target is in your sights and you pull the trigger or detonate the bomb.*

That's when you become the assassin.

Making his way down the stairway, he sees nothing to raise his antennae.

On the avenue, he's quickly swallowed up by the tumult of a busy street.

There's no way he can know if a hit man is lurking nearby, or if someone might burst out of a crowd and put out his lights. These are the risks of the life Eli has chosen.

15

Brighton Beach Avenue, the neighborhood's major commercial thoroughfare, is clogged with pedestrians and vehicles, all moving beneath the elevated train trestle.

Bundled up against the cold, people stream past an array of storefronts, most displaying signs in English as well as in Russian.

It's dark at six o'clock in the evening, but the street is well-lit and swarms with shoppers. Eli purposely arrived an hour early and has time to kill.

Looking through the plate-glass window of Tashkent, an ethnic supermarket, Eli sees the prepared foods department. A long line of customers, most young and stylishly dressed, await their turns as they stand next to a handful of head-scarf-wearing grandmother-types.

A clot of older men huddle together on the street near the curb. They seem oblivious to the cold as they talk and argue back and forth in a slew of languages—mostly Russian, Ukrainian, and Yiddish, with English reserved for the occasional f-bomb.

The trains, which run overhead in both directions, pass simultaneously, their din momentarily drowning out the men's shouting on the sidewalk below.

An ambulance with its siren bleating and burping races down the avenue on its way to Coney Island Hospital.

Walking along the avenue, Eli comes upon Taste of Russia, a gourmet emporium offering high-end products like the tins of caviar on display in a refrigerated window display case. He debates whether or not to wander in and look around but decides it would be foolish to confine himself in a crowded and unfamiliar space.

There are few chain stores in this neighborhood, mostly mom-and-pop shops. Storekeepers thrive in Brighton Beach partly because there are no protection rackets. The Russian mob doesn't suck the blood of its own. In fact, there's virtually no street crime in the neighborhood—no muggings, carjackings, break-ins, or robberies. The Bratva won't tolerate that kind of low-life criminality.

It's strange how so many Russians and Ukrainians who left the Soviet Union as soon as they were free to do so streamed to this neighborhood at the southern tip of Brooklyn—known as Little Odessa by the Sea—a place reminiscent of the home they loathed and left.

Eli glances at his watch. It'll soon be time for the meeting with Agapov.

He walks along the avenue and turns onto Brighton Sixth, a narrow residential street lined by six-story brick apartment buildings that ends at the boardwalk fronting the beach.

Dark and deserted, the street has an eerie vibe. Unlike Manhattan streets, no security cameras are visible, either on streetlamps or attached to the exteriors of buildings. There are no doormen working in these six-story residential buildings. Not a single pedestrian is in sight. It's graveyard quiet—a perfect spot for an ambush from any secluded niche.

As he walks toward the ocean, Eli scans the interior of each parked car to make certain there's no gunman sitting in one or crouched between two vehicles, waiting for him to pass. He's unarmed and vulnerable to an attack, so he's primed, on high alert. He's aware of every sight and sound, is cognizant of everything, especially the smell of the briny ocean air wafting by his face. A faint scent of seaweed mixed with iodine hangs on the breeze.

It's nearly seven o'clock when he approaches Valentina's at the intersection of Brighton Sixth Street and the boardwalk.

The restaurant's main entrance is near the boardwalk. The ocean lies maybe fifty meters behind the building, just beyond the darkness of the deserted beach. The sound of waves crashing onto the sand on a cold winter night seems strange. In Israel, the weather was warm all year round. The sea's rhythmic tide rolling in and hitting the shoreline on this frigid evening adds a feeling of eeriness to everything, especially the unprecedented situation he's about to encounter.

In the restaurant's anteroom, Eli hears the melodic strains of a balalaika and a violin.

Standing at the entrance to the dining room, he sees two musicians wandering between tables, serenading the diners. It's very old-world, romantic, and actually a bit melancholic. Or maybe it's his own penchant for sadness. Yes, leaving the old country was a blessing for these people; it was an escape from bigotry and limited opportunities, but it's also a cause for nostalgia, even sadness, for the life left behind. But for Eli, there's no nostalgia for what he left behind, only a wish to forget the past. But that'll never happen.

A mixture of English, Russian, and what must be Ukrainian along with smatterings of Yiddish resounds through the dining room. The aromas of braised beef and roasted potatoes fill the air. No doubt the food is heavy and the patrons dine on it with sentimental pleasure.

The maître d,' a tall, dark-haired man wearing a tuxedo, approaches.

"I'm here to see Mr. Agapov," Eli says, unbuttoning his overcoat.

Without asking his name, the man nods. It's obvious: he's been told to expect this visitor.

"Certainly, sir," the man says. "Please wait here for just one moment."

He picks up a telephone from a credenza, turns his back toward Eli, and speaks softly. In Russian.

Eli gazes about the dining room, sees the perimeter is lined with velvet-covered banquettes. Well-spaced tables with thick-looking white linens occupy the rest of the room. Heavy draperies hang over the windows. A huge samovar surrounded by elaborately decorated teapots stands on a damask-covered table in the middle of the room.

Most of the diners appear to be in their fifties; some are older. They look Slavic—Belarusians, Russians, Ukrainians, maybe a few Czechs and Poles—all dining on what looks like rich Eastern European food.

Most of these elderly people probably cling to the customs of the old country. Eli recalls that when immigrants from the Soviet Union arrived in Israel, a host of Russian, Bulgarian, and Ukrainian restaurants sprang up in cities and towns populated by the Slavic newcomers.

Suddenly, out of nowhere, a giant of a man—Shaquille O'Neal tall, the guy looks like he weighs in at a solid three bills—lumbers toward Eli. He has a prognathic jaw and heavy facial stubble. He wears a shirt open at the collar over which hangs a sports jacket, and it's clear from the drape of the cloth that he's packing some serious hardware.

A blue-black tattoo of Russian Cyrillic script snakes across one side of his neck. No doubt there's ink on his back and torso, highlighting the guy's journey through the Russian prison system.

Eli sports no tattoos anywhere on his body. They weren't permitted in the Mossad. They were absolutely taboo. A simple thing such as a tattoo could give away your nationality or hint at your identity. Anonymity mandates nothing that could be even a remote indicator of your name or origins, not even something so simple or innocuous as a tattoo.

"Follow me," the Russian barks in heavily accented English as he turns abruptly and heads toward the rear of the dining room.

Eli knows he's about to enter a room filled with Bratva muscle. His heartbeat ramps up as his chest tightens. No doubt he'll be frisked. He knew better than to bring the Beretta. Before there would be even a *hint* of a confrontation, the piece would be confiscated. No matter what precautions he could have taken, he'll be unarmed in a room filled with Agapov's thugs, all armed to the teeth.

And besides, even if there were a shootout, he'd be outnumbered and would end up eating dirt.

As they walk down a short hallway, the danger of this mission soaks its way into Eli's awareness. He definitely regrets having accepted this assignment.

There were Gorlov's words: *The money will change how you live the rest of your life.*

Money, that's what matters most to these people. Those words assume he'll have a life after tonight.

But that's an open question, or at least, one open to interpretation.

Because if things go south, the only way he gets out of here is in a bag that'll be dumped in a Canarsie landfill.

16

The giant opens a door leading to a narrow hallway; he then opens another door.

Eli is escorted to a sparsely furnished room. It's overheated and the air is stale with the odor of coffee and cigarette smoke. A table and four chairs are located in a corner of the room. Cups and saucers, along with a cigarette butt–filled ashtray, are on the table.

Two men stand with their hands clasped in front of them. One wears a dark blue sports jacket, looks like something straight out of *The Sopranos*, except he's Russian, not Italian. The other is a simian-looking thug dressed in jeans and a red spandex T-shirt that shows off his bloated biceps. He sports plenty of gold on his wrists and around his neck. The handle of a pistol is visibly protruding above his waistband. A third man stands off to the side; he wears dark pants and a black T-shirt over which is draped a dark sports jacket. No doubt a holstered piece rests beneath it.

These guys have been waiting for him.

There's no sign of the pakhan. Or his dog.

The dossier was accurate: there's no lack of security for Ivan Agapov.

Eli feels quivering begin deep within his body. It's accompanied by a surge of blood in his arteries. His nerves begin thrumming like hot wires. He can't let adrenaline take over; he's gotta stay focused so he'll have an edge should things get violent.

"Here he is, Sergei," says the giant, who turns and leaves the room.

Eli sizes up the situation. He's unarmed, in a room with a closed door and three mob soldiers, each carrying hardware. And that behemoth is probably right outside the door.

Survival means staying cooperative, even passive, no matter what they say or do.

The one named Sergei—obviously the one in charge—narrows his hooded eyes, looks like he's sizing Eli up. It's not a friendly look. It's the testosterone imperative. It never fails to kick in with this kind of guy. Eli's body remains tense.

He's certain he'll have to deal with what will no doubt be Sergei's tough-guy routine. The man looks like he's straight out of a graphic novel with his skintight black T-shirt and tapered, form-fitting sports jacket, his Doc Marten lace-up boots, a gleaming stud in his left earlobe, his heavy stubble and slicked-back hair ending in a thick ponytail.

The beefy guy wearing the T-shirt stands at the closed door, blocking any exit.

The third guy, wearing a blue tracksuit, stands to Eli's right; his hands stay clasped in front of himself as he stares at Eli with stone-faced indifference.

Eli feels a tensile readiness, an inclination to move—fast and with extreme effect—but that would be getting sidetracked. And he can't afford violence because it would end badly. For him. He's here on a mission. There's no backing out now. And there are more goons where these three came from.

Just stay focused and don't ruffle feathers. Passivity is your ticket to the inner sanctum and the pakhan.

The room's lighting seems to brighten; Eli knows his pupils are dilated.

CCTV cameras are positioned on two walls. They're being monitored. Probably recorded. He should have anticipated that. Accepting this job was a mistake; a recording will make him identifiable to anyone who sees it. His long-nurtured anonymity is shredding at this moment.

"So, you're Aiden," Sergei says. A sneer teases the corners of his lips as he eye-fucks Eli. "I hear you're a *tough* guy." Hearing the smirk in the man's voice, Eli knows trouble is brewing.

Eli says nothing, knows he'll have to walk a fine line between acquiescence and resistance.

Holding Sergei's stare, he does his best to appear unintimidated, but avoids looking belligerent. A low-level buzzing begins in his skull. It's a familiar neural sensation—the harbinger of action—as though an electrical wire hisses in his brain.

"You don't look so tough to me," Sergei says as he shakes his head. He looks like he's doing a poor job of trying not to smirk.

Eli remains silent. Any response to Sergei's goading could provoke violence.

Sergei moves closer, virtually invades Eli's space. The guy bathes in cologne—marinates in what smells like Paco Rabanne. And his breath reeks of coffee and cigarettes.

"Take off your coat," Sergei orders.

Eli shrugs out of his overcoat and tosses it onto a nearby chair.

Picking up the coat, one guy goes through its pockets, inside and out. "Nothing here," he says, then drops the coat back onto the chair. It was wise not to bring the Spytec bug detector. For sure it would be confiscated. And it would set the wrong tone for the sit-down.

"Raise your arms," Sergei says.

Eli's arms go up; he keeps his hands open, palms facing Sergei. Maintaining a neutral expression, he stays composed, does his best to avoid staring into Sergei's eyes.

They begin patting him down, head to toe. Sergei works from the front while Spandex Guy searches from behind. They feel around and through his sports jacket, inside and out. Their hands cover every possible area of his body, his chest, lower back, even his crotch. And they pat his shirt over his chest, belly, armpits, and lower-back areas. They're looking for more than a weapon; they're searching for a wire or recording device, not only on his body but possibly sewn into his sports jacket or outerwear.

"He's clean," says Spandex Guy.

Holding Eli's cell phone, Sergei says, "You'll get this back after the meeting."

Eli's hands drop to his sides. Slowly. He maintains a calm facade, yet he's brimming with energy.

"These look like fine cigars," Sergei says, holding the three Cohiba Robustos he's removed from Eli's sports jacket. Setting them beneath his nose, he sniffs deeply. "Ah, I can smell the tobacco through the wrapper. I'll enjoy them," he says, slipping them into his breast pocket. That smirk finally materializes on his lips.

"They're not yours," Eli says in an even voice, though it feels like acid drips through his veins.

"They're mine now," Sergei says, shooting him a snarky smile.

"Please give them back."

Sergei's lips twist into a sneer. "Now, why the fuck would I do that?"

"Because they're mine."

"Not anymore."

"You have no right . . ."

Sergei's eyes ice over. His right hand darts beneath his jacket's left lapel.

A pistol sweeps out from a shoulder holster; it's a Glock, now hovering in front of Eli's face.

Heat flares in Eli's cheeks. A metallic taste forms on his tongue.

Standing at arm's length, Sergei holds the pistol an inch from Eli's forehead.

The gun is so close, Eli can't see the black *O* at the end of the barrel. He smells gun oil.

The man's index finger has partially squeezed back on the trigger, there's virtually no slack. "Now I have a right," Sergei snarls, then presses the muzzle to Eli's forehead. It feels like a cold circle against his skin.

Spandex Guy moves off to the side, out of the line of fire.

Eli's hands rise again, slowly, to the level of his shoulders, nonthreatening, a surefire sign of submission. He stares straight ahead, lets his eyes look unfocused.

Acquiescence. Assent. No threat. But a quivering sensation spreads through his arms. It feels like something's activated in his brain, a neural impulse. His head thrums with the rush of blood.

"Now you got somethin' to say about my rights?" Sergei snarls.

Eli shakes his head. Slightly. Slowly. Keeps his eyes unfocused, stares ahead—at nothing.

Sergei moves the pistol back a few centimeters but still holds it pointing at Eli's forehead.

"Good. Now that that's settled, let's go meet Mr. Agapov." Sergei waves the muzzle in the direction of a door off to his left.

With panther-like speed, Eli's hands converge on the gun's barrel as his head swerves down and to the left. Using both hands, he violently twists the weapon toward Sergei's belly, twisting Sergei's wrist and nearly breaking the man's index finger—a Krav Maga move—as his right knee slams into Sergei's groin.

The thug jackknifes as Eli yanks the piece away and whirls in place.

With a two-handed grip, he assumes a shooting stance and points the pistol at the two other men. His finger rests on the trigger.

Both men's hands shoot up in the air.

Tracksuit's eyes bulge. He shakes his head frantically, begging not to be shot. Eli can see the guy's pulse beating in his neck.

Spandex Guy's lips quiver. He's about to shit his pants.

Eli tilts his head, motioning for him to move closer to Tracksuit Guy.

When they're standing next to each other, Eli backs away, then turns to Sergei, who's bent over, groaning in agony. With his breath coming in short gasps, he peers up at Eli. His face borders on turning a sickly green.

Moving closer to Sergei, Eli points the pistol at his head. "My cigars, please."

Grimacing, Sergei reaches into his breast pocket.

"Slowly," Eli says.

Sergei extracts the cigars and, still bent at the waist, holds them out.

Eli snatches them and slips them into his breast pocket.

The other two men keep their hands raised, don't make a move.

Without a word, Eli's left hand moves to the pistol's slide and he racks the gun repeatedly. Round after round flies into the air and thuds onto the carpeted floor.

The bullets roll around, then come to a stop.

He presses the release and the pistol's empty magazine drops into his left hand.

He flips the gun around, holds it by the muzzle, and offers it to Sergei, handle first.

Sergei reaches out, grasps the pistol, and slips it back into his shoulder holster. He turns away and sucks air, trying to recover from the knee to his balls.

Eli tosses the empty magazine to Tracksuit, who snags it in midair.

The cartridges remain on the floor.

"Now let's go see Mr. Agapov," Eli says.

He picks up his overcoat. No way will he leave it in this front room where a portable tracking device could be inserted in the lining.

With his face still contorted, Sergei nods and turns toward the door at the rear of the room.

"This way," he says in a voice laced with pain.

17

There's no need to be buzzed into Agapov's office.

Spandex Guy simply opens the door—its hinges are located on the inside, and it swings inward from the anteroom.

Eli notices small factoids like this one. Such awareness can be the difference between life and death. He always makes note of his surroundings, ascertains how a door opens, how a place is configured, and preplans every way out—any exit possible—front door, rear door, restrooms, a hallway leading to a storage room.

A glance tells him the only exit from this office is the door to the outer room where he was patted down. If this sit-down goes off the tracks, he's trapped. And he dies.

These kinds of observations pertain to people too. The most seemingly inconsequential detail can be a lifesaver: whether a man is right- or left-handed, how he eats, dresses, how he holds his head, how he walks or talks, whether he makes direct eye contact, or how he shakes hands. These tidbits speak volumes about any individual and hint at what can be expected in virtually any encounter.

And right now, Eli's observations set his nervous system into overdrive. His legs are rubbery and his hands feel weak. The weakness is a depletion from the adrenaline dump brought on by the encounter with Sergei. But it also derives from the precariousness of this situation. He's in the inner sanctum of one of the most feared mob bosses on the planet, and he's in the company of three men who only moments ago he held at gunpoint.

The room is thick with the fecaloid odor of cigar tobacco, though Agapov isn't smoking at the moment. But a crushed stogie stub lies in an ashtray sitting on a table Agapov sits behind.

The pakhan's eyes are lasered on Eli. The man is making an assessment, sizing him up.

Agapov looks his age, fifty, is well built, and unlike Gorlov, hasn't let the passing years turn him to fat. He takes care of his body with the workouts and swimming described in the dossier. His dark, wavy hair is perfectly barbered. He has deep-set green eyes, and a weathered face, which despite its hardness could be considered handsome.

Though Eli's aware most Russian mobsters buy cheap threads, he notes that Agapov is an obvious exception. He wears a tailored gray flannel sports jacket—definitely not something off-the-rack from Kohl's—black slacks, and a fine-weave white cotton shirt open at the collar. Even a casual glance tells Eli the man spends tons of money on clothing—Armani and Hugo Boss—and buys Hermès shoes along with expensive accessories. It's the high-end look of a wealthy mob boss.

Even a brief look at the pakhan tells Eli something else: brutality lies at the core of the man's being.

Eli's eyes do a casual sweep of the room. It's windowless with overhead fluorescent lights emitting a steady hum. The walls are painted an off-white color; the ceiling has acoustical tiles.

Agapov sits behind a narrow Formica-topped table; another chair on the opposite side faces the pakhan, and a couch upholstered in blue fabric stands at the far end of the room. A stack of folded bridge chairs lie on the floor beside the couch. The place is sparse, has no frills.

To Eli, the room looks bleached white, sharply etched, as though he's standing on a movie set beneath brilliant klieg lights. That's because he's still primed—simmering with readiness after the confrontation with Sergei.

There's one bit of good news: Agapov's dog's not in the room.

Eli catches a barely detectable whiff of the diluted lime juice he'd dabbed on his wrists earlier in the evening. To a human being it smells vaguely like cologne. Knowing most dogs are repelled by the scent of citrus, Eli squeezed the juice of a fresh lime into a glass and gently applied a small amount to the inside of his wrists, hoping the beast would hesitate if ordered to attack. But it's not a worry: the dog's nowhere in sight.

Agapov doesn't get up to greet Eli. There's no offer of a handshake. There's not even a nod acknowledging him. The man's demeanor is a universe removed from Gorlov's. The only response to Eli is Agapov's sea-green eyes boring into him.

And they convey lethality.

The primitive part of Eli's brain registers a simple fact: he's being scrutinized by a predator. He learned long ago to depend on these primal indicators. Gut feelings are never to be ignored. It's a matter of survival.

He wills himself to stay calm; it means invoking a kind of Zen mindfulness learned in the Mossad training program. His heart rate begins slowing. His pulse no longer bounds through his wrists. The blanched look of the room dims. His pupils are no longer dilated.

Focusing on Agapov, he makes certain to avoid looking intimidated, yet he doesn't want to appear confrontational.

"Very impressive," Agapov says as he nods and points to a flat-screen monitor mounted above the room's door. "You disarmed Sergei—a very capable man—and you did it in half a second. How'd you do that?"

"Krav Maga."

"Looks effective. Is it an Olympic sport?"

"No. It's for self-defense. And for killing when necessary."

"I'm sure Sergei's glad it wasn't necessary," Agapov says with a snort. "Aren't you, Sergei?" He tosses a steely grin at Sergei, who nods and manages a weak grunt.

No doubt, Sergei resents Agapov's put-down in the presence of the other men. But Agapov doesn't give a shit about social niceties. He's brutally direct and keeps a thick thumb on his men, keeps them in their places, won't let them feel overly important.

"Allow me to apologize for Sergei's rudeness," Agapov says. "He should know better than to take a man's cigars—isn't that right, Sergei?"

Sergei, still looking puke-worthy green, says nothing.

"*Isn't* it, Sergei?"

"Yes," Sergei replies in a hoarse voice.

Agapov nods his approval. "Well, gentlemen," he says, "now that we've established that this man isn't armed or wired, you can leave us alone. Aiden and I have an important matter to discuss. So, go. Get *out*."

On Agapov's command, Sergei mumbles something indecipherable.

The others murmur their acknowledgment and turn toward the door.

All three men leave the room.

The last one out closes the door.

There's the sound of the lock cylinder turning.

Nothing about this situation is good.

He's alone and unarmed, locked in a room with a man whose tentacles spread throughout the criminal world, a man reputed to be the most brutal mob boss in the city, one who's known to have killed or ordered the killings of countless other men.

And three armed thugs wait on the other side of the locked door.

One of them, Sergei, has a score to settle.

A single wrong move or word, the slightest slipup, and Eli's a dead man.

18

Eli waits for Agapov to speak. It's not only prudent, but it's a sign of respect for a man who demands deference.

"Sit, Aiden, sit," Agapov says, gesturing with an open palm toward the chair across the table.

Eli folds his coat over the back of the chair and sits facing the pakhan. With his back to the door, he's violating his rule of watching any room's entrance, but there's no way of getting around the challenges of this situation.

"Don't worry about those three," Agapov says, pointing to the monitor on the wall. "They're just out there to make sure we have complete privacy."

Is this room wired for sound? Probably not because Agapov's gonna talk about an assassination. He doesn't want a word of it overheard. If I'm guessing correctly, he doesn't even want his bodyguards to hear what'll be said.

"I've heard good things about you," Agapov says, narrowing his eyes.

Eli knows he must tread carefully—it's crucial to be respectful and accommodating—but some parameters must be established up front. Otherwise, Agapov will try to assert dominance, likely press for concessions.

I don't want to get into a tug-of-war with this guy.

"How'd you get my name?" Eli says in a firm voice, yet one bordering on being deferential.

"We have our sources. Is that important?"

"I always like to know the source of any referral."

"Unfortunately, that stays my secret. Understood?"

"Yes."

Don't push this guy.

"Good . . . good." Agapov nods, and a self-satisfied semismile appears on his lips.

There's a brief pause as he eyeballs Eli, then nods almost imperceptibly. "Actually, after hearing about your . . . shall we say . . . exploits, I've become intrigued," the Russian says. "I understand you're able to track down people anywhere. Is that true?"

"I don't think so."

"Oh, c'mon, now. No false modesty here. How do you find people?"

"I also work as a skip tracer."

"Isn't that a modern-day bounty hunter?"

"You could put it that way."

Eli's Mossad training was so thorough that the only places a fugitive might evade him are those with no electronic capacity—Antarctica, the Himalayas, maybe the far reaches of the Amazon or the most remote jungles of equatorial Africa. Even then certain creative options are available.

The opposite is also true: Eli can use his skip tracing skills to help someone disappear—including himself—from virtually any set of coordinates on the face of the earth.

"So, you find people," Agapov says. "At whose request?"

"Anyone who decides to use my services."

Eli was first assigned to Mossad's Keshet service, where he learned electronic intelligence. There's barely a database he can't penetrate—whether it's governmental, corporate, or financial—a skill he'd used to find and track terrorists and to decipher the communications of enemy countries when he was with Mossad. He'd become an expert at using and detecting spyware—hacking and infiltrating—a computer, phone, or virtually any other device.

IT dexterity—a precursor to becoming a skip tracer.

And a valuable asset for an assassin.

"I think we can use your *services*—in more ways than one," Agapov says. "How does that sound?"

Instead of answering a vaguely phrased question, Eli says, "I took a considerable risk coming here, Mr. Agapov."

Nodding, Agapov says, "I appreciate that. I, too, minimize risks. That's why I only meet with people in this office." The pakhan leans back in his chair. "I appreciate that meeting me here isn't something you would ordinarily do. But I'm restricted by my legal situation.

"I'm sure you know that I'm about to go on trial. I'm out on bail, but the feds have severely limited where I can go. They've taken my passport. They're letting me run my restaurant, eat, drink, shit, and sleep—that's it. And I'm wearing an ankle monitor, so my movements are monitored by Uncle Sam."

Eli nods, says nothing. He long ago learned to listen carefully, not only with mobsters, but throughout his life. He knows listening can be one of the most effective weapons in his arsenal. And listening to Ivan Agapov is revealing: the man has an inflated regard for himself. He relishes being on Page Six of the *Post* or on the six o'clock news; he assumes Eli's read about him or has seen him on television and is aware Agapov's trial is forthcoming. He's a media whore who needs recognition, adulation. Knowing that much about Agapov, there's a chance the man's need for self-aggrandizement might make him careless.

"And, please, call me Ivan. There's no need to be formal."

"Sure enough, Ivan."

The mobster's assessing whether or not Eli can be trusted. He senses Agapov's a man with exquisitely fine antennae, a guy who can read deceit in a heartbeat. If he detects even a scintilla of treachery in this sit-down, Eli's never walking out of here.

"Would you like some Rémy Martin?" Agapov asks.

Knowing he can't risk dulling his senses, Eli says, "Thank you, but no."

"Ah, that's a shame. This particular one, the Louis XIII, Collector's Edition, costs a fortune. If you knew the pleasure of such a fine cognac, you'd be a drinking man."

Eli manages a tight smile.

Louis XIII Collector's runs minimum $3,500 a bottle. No way did Ivan Agapov drop that much cash on a bottle of cognac. His stuff fell off a truck.

Agapov gets up from his chair, goes to a credenza, and pours a finger of cognac into a snifter. Swirling the liquid beneath his nose, he inhales, then downs the Rémy in a gulp. He returns to his chair and sits.

Agapov's a braggadocio; he'll crow about his possessions, even to a stranger.

But time is being wasted. Enough chitchat.

"So, Ivan, why are we here?"

"We're here, as I'm sure you already know, because I'd like to retain your services." Agapov's eyes narrow as he again peers at Eli.

"What would that be for?"

"Tell me, have you ever heard of a man named Anton Gorlov?"

"Yes."

"How did you hear of him?"

"He's the pakhan of the Odessa mafia. I've done jobs for him."

Agapov smiles, obviously approving of Eli's answer. He closes his eyes and nods. "I think I may be able to trust you, Aiden. If you'd said you've never heard of him, I'd have known you were lying."

"How would you have known?"

"I have my sources."

It's probably someone in Gorlov's camp. Inside men are everywhere. Gorlov, Agapov . . . There are traitors in every crime organization. After all, Bratva guys aren't vetted like they're entering the Mossad.

Agapov sets his arms on the table and leans forward.

Eli notices the same tattoo he saw on Gorlov's finger: a small crown tattooed on the outer surface of his right thumb.

"Anton Gorlov is the reason we're meeting," Agapov says. "We have reason to believe Brother Gorlov is planning to leave the country for someplace where he can live the rest of his life in peace."

"Is that a problem?" Eli asks.

"Yes, it is. Because he wants to retire with no worries. He doesn't want the FBI coming after him wherever he may be."

"And?"

"Some years ago, he and I worked together on certain . . . let's call them . . . *projects*," Agapov says with a snort. "So, he wants to ensure that I won't cop a plea for a shorter sentence, that I won't implicate him in certain things we did a number of years ago. If that were to happen, he could face criminal charges. To put it bluntly, he's worried I'll give him up as part of a plea deal."

Eli nods.

"Brother Gorlov wants to make sure I go the way of all flesh. And he wants it to happen before any plea deal can be worked out."

Getting up from the chair, Agapov begins pacing back and forth. He stops and fixes Eli with a bone-chilling stare. "Given these circumstances, certain conclusions are obvious, don't you think?"

Eli says nothing. It's always better to let the other party broach the subject.

"Brother Gorlov wants my demise to happen soon. So, it's in *my* interest that he takes a long nap. And that it happens very soon, before he can put his plans into motion."

Agapov shoots a smirk at Eli. Something dark flickers behind the mobster's eyes. Pure menace bleeds through that nonsmile.

Eli knows Agapov is still taking his temperature. And he's wondering if Eli's willing to take out a man who's paid him handsomely for past services.

"So, Aiden, that's why my people contacted you," Agapov says, turning his head slightly to the side as his eyes narrow, a sure sign he's still appraising Eli.

Eli nods, remains silent.

"Now, be truthful with me. Do you have any qualms about sending Anton Gorlov to his grave, a man who's no doubt paid you well over the years?"

Eli shakes his head. "I have no qualms about it."

"Just to make sure, I'm prepared to pay you five hundred thousand for this job."

"That's a great deal of money, Ivan."

"It's a down payment on my future."

"I understand."

"It'll be half up front, the other half when the job's done. How does that sound?"

"It's very generous of you."

"I believe in paying my contractors well. So, you'll take the job?"

Eli nods. Reaching into his shirt pocket, he extracts a card. "Please have the first half wired to this account as soon as possible."

Agapov sits and glances at the card. "Ah, an offshore account. Very smart. I've heard you're a man of considerable intellect." He grabs the card and waves it in the air. "The money will be transferred as soon as you leave. Two hundred and fifty thousand." Agapov snorts, apparently appreciating some internal bit of humor. "Tell me," he says, "are you worried I'll stiff you after the job is done, that I won't pony up the second half?"

"It's not a concern."

"Why not?"

"People pay because they worry that nonpayment will make them my next target."

Agapov appears to be absorbing this statement like a chemical molecule crossing through one of Otto Bauer's membranes. After a pause, he says, "I understand. You have a reputation to protect. As do I. Rest assured the second payment will be made."

"If, for some reason, I don't get the job done, the money will be returned."

"Why would you not get the job done?"

"It's just my way of saying that I can be counted on to fulfill the contract."

Agapov tosses Eli a knowing nod.

"How soon do you want it to happen?" Eli asks.

"Gorlov wants me out of the picture quickly. So, you must *act* quickly."

"Any preferred method?"

"However it gets done, I want it done soon. Just don't get caught."

"That goes without saying."

"But if you *are* caught, can I count on you not giving me up?"

"I won't be caught. But in the unlikely event that should happen, I'll never talk."

"How can I know that?"

"You have to trust me."

"Why would I trust a paid assassin?"

"Because I'd go to prison. And there isn't a prison in existence where I'd be safe. If an inmate doesn't get to me, some corrections officer on your payroll will get it done."

"I see you know the system."

"It turns out we have ways of keeping each other honest."

"True," Agapov says with an icy smile.

Eli notices that Agapov hardly ever blinks, just stares. There's something robotic about him.

"Tell me something, Aiden . . ."

Eli knows Agapov's about to test him. Because trust is hard to come by in the killing business, especially when you're sandwiched between two men intent on taking each other out.

"What if Gorlov had gotten to you first and asked you to kill me? Would you do that?"

"Do you know the story about Willie Sutton?" Eli asks.

"I don't think so."

"When he was asked why he robbed banks, he said, 'That's where the money is.'"

Agapov's laugh is a guttural rasp. His face reddens as he chortles to himself, obviously approving of the answer. "So, you go where the money takes you."

"Don't we all?"

"What if, after Gorlov already paid you half up front to get me, I offered you even more money . . . let's say six hundred thousand . . . half up front? What would you do?"

"A bird in the hand," Eli says.

Agapov's lips curl into a smile. "I like you, Aiden. You think the way I do." He slaps his hand on the tabletop. "Then it's settled," he says, leaning back in his chair. "It's a done deal."

"Yes, it's settled."

"My lawyers can't ask for another continuance. Make it happen soon."

"It'll get done."

Agapov nods his approval.

"But," Eli says, "to make certain you're not linked to this arrangement, our discussion must never leave this room."

"Of course," Agapov says.

"Do the men out there know why we're meeting?" Eli tilts his head toward the door.

"They know nothing."

"Does anyone else know why we're meeting?"

"Not a soul."

"Then it's our secret . . . between you and me."

"Yes, of course," Agapov says. "Now, can I convince you to have a snifter of the Rémy? It's a fine way to cap things off."

"No, thank you. But I will join you in a good cigar."

Agapov's eyebrows rise.

Eli reaches into his breast pocket and produces the three cigars, holds them out toward Agapov.

The pakhan leans forward, inspects them, and his eyes widen. "Cohiba Robusto? Ha! They're among the best in the world. How could I refuse? Are you a cigar lover?"

"I appreciate a fine Cuban cigar."

A nearly invisible black ink dot at the bottom end of the wrapper tells Eli which one to pull out and extend toward Agapov.

The pakhan grabs it, regards the label, smiles, tears off the wrapper, and sets the cigar beneath his nose.

After a deep inhalation, he says, "There's nothing better than the smell of Cuban tobacco. You'll join me, yes?"

"Of course," Eli says, and rips open the wrapper of a second cigar. He tosses the third one—still wrapped—onto the table. "Here's one for later. I'm sure it'll give you pleasure."

There's something between us now—maybe a slight connection.

"I appreciate the gesture," Agapov says, setting the third cigar into his breast pocket. He fishes into another pocket, produces a cigar cutter, then slices off the rounded end of the cigar he intends to smoke.

Eli bites off a piece from the blunt end of his cigar, transfers it from the tip of his tongue onto his fingertip, and sets the piece into the ashtray sitting on the table.

Agapov pulls out a gold-plated lighter, flips open the top, rolls the thumbwheel, lights up, and rotates the cigar between his thumb and index finger to get it going evenly.

Closing his eyes, he inhales, then lets out a smoky stream through his nostrils.

Eli leans back in his chair, keeps his distance and holds his breath.

A moment later the Russian pulls the cigar from his mouth and peers at it. His nostrils flare as he closes his eyes and sniffs the air. A deep furrow forms between his eyebrows.

A chill pervades Eli. Despite feeling cold to his core, sweat prickles at the back of his neck.

Shit, he detects something off about the stogie.

Eli's pulse thuds in his ears.

Stay calm. Don't even blink. Act like nothing's wrong.

"May I?" Eli asks, pointing to the lighter.

A slight diversion might do the trick.

Momentarily distracted, Agapov hands the lighter to Eli. He again regards the cigar, then closes his eyes and sniffs once again.

Trying to stay calm, Eli lights up, gets the cigar going, and sets the lighter back on the table.

Sucking on the cigar, Eli sends a billowing gray cloud toward Agapov. Hopefully, the smoke stream will blend with the pakhan's smoke and disguise anything that may be slightly off or detectable. It'll also keep Agapov's smoke on his side of the table.

The mobster opens his eyes and reinserts the cigar between his lips. He sucks in more smoke, then exhales a languid cloud that snakes slowly from his mouth upward into his nostrils. He wrinkles his nose.

The taste must be off a bit. Otto put too much toxin in the cigar.

Agapov's eyes shift from the cigar and focus on Eli.

Fucking guy knows something's wrong.

"Tell me," Agapov says, "other than sex, is there anything this divine? The purpose of life is pleasure, don't you agree?"

"I do."

Between the cognac and the cigar, his taste buds are dulled. He can't detect a thing.

Agapov gets up and returns to the credenza. "You're sure you won't join me in a drink?"

Eli glances at his watch. "Thank you for the offer, but I have to go. I have things to take care of."

"What things?" Agapov slips the cigar between his teeth and pours another finger of cognac into the snifter, then sips. The cigar goes back between his lips, and he sucks in more smoke.

"I have to make arrangements for what we've agreed on."

Eli gets up from his chair, sets the cigar between his teeth, grabs his coat, and shrugs into it.

Agapov approaches, holding the cigar in one hand, a snifter of cognac in the other.

Eli sucks in air and holds his breath; no way will he breathe in the man's secondhand smoke.

"The money will be wired to that account tonight," Agapov says. "The second half will arrive after it's done."

"It'll get done."

"Then we'll talk about some other jobs," Agapov says.

Eli sucks in a mouthful of smoke, then expels it toward Agapov.

He nods at the pakhan. Without shaking hands, he turns and walks toward the door. His heart kicks like a stallion. Blood surges through his brain with a clangor that feels like a hammer beating on copper.

He turns back to Agapov.

They hold each other's eyes for a moment, but there's nothing more to say.

"I look forward to hearing from you," Agapov says. "And I'm sure I'll hear about Mr. Gorlov's unfortunate demise in a few days."

Eli nods again, then pulls on the door handle.

It's locked.

"Knock three times," Agapov says.

Eli raps his knuckles against the wood, then stands back.

A moment later the lock turns and the door opens inward.

Spandex Guy stands there. He hands Eli his cell phone. Sergei and Tracksuit stand at the table in the corner of the room.

Eli takes the phone, nods, slips it into his pocket, enters the anteroom, and glances to his right. Sergei is standing next to the table and stabbing a cigarette out in an ashtray. The man glares at him.

Eli turns away. While crossing the room, he wonders if these three will go back to where Agapov sits and breathe in his cigar smoke. If they do, they could be goners too. Or they might fall slightly ill from the diluted smoke. If that happens, the cigar will have been the common denominator, and they'll know Eli was the source of the problem.

Why think about that? Just get outta here.

Approaching the outer door, Eli feels Sergei's eyes boring into his back. No doubt the guy's giving him the death stare.

He walks down the hallway leading to the restaurant.

Making his way through the dining room, he arrives at the entrance, nods at the maître d', and leaves.

Thankfully, he'll never return to this place.

On the street, he tosses the lit cigar between two parked cars and walks into the night.

19

What am I doing? Eli asks himself as he rides the subway heading back toward Manhattan.

He's done a complete 180. Before this he'd never met with a client.

He'd never allowed himself to be seen, hadn't spoken directly with any of them unless he used a sat phone, and even then direct communication was a rare thing. Interface has been through secure websites on the dark net. He'd been a mystery to those who'd hired him, had remained a shadow at the periphery of their awareness.

But in the last few days, he's had back-to-back face-to-face meetings with two Russian honchos. He was seen by Gorlov, Sorokin, Agapov, and both men's bodyguards.

At Agapov's restaurant, he was also viewed on a video monitor. And there's little doubt he was recorded. A photo from the video can be extracted and emailed or texted anywhere in the world. His anonymity is now a thing of the past because he's physically identifiable to virtually anyone in the Russian Brotherhood.

What the hell is wrong with me? I'm risking everything. For what? For money I don't even need.

Is it because he's grown tired of living an assassin's life?

It's now obvious: he's increasing his chances of being dumped into an early grave.

If I want to live, there's only one solution: get out of the life.

20

The train slows as it approaches Fourteenth Street.

Still thinking about how it went down in Valentina's, Eli is reminded that Agapov isn't the first man he killed in a way that appeared to be either a natural death or an accident.

Years earlier, there was Khaled Khan, a Saudi playboy who donated support money to the families of suicide bombers who'd detonated their bombs in a crowded Israeli marketplace or outside a concert hall. Because the money he gave was considered by those in the upper echelons of the Mossad to be an added incentive for young men to sacrifice their lives, Khan was considered a "ticking time bomb" and marked for elimination.

At a meeting of Eli's team, a high-ranking officer explained that Khan's death had been approved by the prime minister. Since the man was connected to Saudi royalty, an outright assassination could have political repercussions. So, to ensure the government's plausible deniability, the man's demise had to look like a natural or accidental death.

No bombs or bullets. Just the way it is with Agapov.

Infiltrating Khan's bank accounts, Eli saw clearly that the man had given support money to the family of Mohammed Taher, the teenaged suicide bomber who'd killed Mom, Pop, Hannah, and David that day in Jerusalem.

For Eli, killing Khaled Khan would be more than just another hit.

It would be personal.

The team tracked Khan from Monaco to Paris and London.

That spring he decided to vacation in the Greek islands. Between trysts with prostitutes, Khan enjoyed cruising back and forth between Corfu and the island of Kefalonia on the Ionian Sea, a distance of one hundred kilometers.

Arriving at Corfu with Jordanian passports, Eli's four-man Mossad team feigned being tourists and rented a motorized yacht to go deep-sea fishing.

The next morning Khan's yacht set out from the Corfu harbor, heading south toward Kefalonia. Keeping out of sight, the team used night-vision binoculars and shadowed the 242-foot Benetti craft. That night Khan's crew anchored the boat a few miles offshore.

Having bugged the vessel while it was in port—Ari, a Mossad team member, posed as a ship chandler—they could hear drunken conversation between Khan and his three-man crew.

At one o'clock in the morning, under a moonless sky on a calm sea, wearing black wet suits, Eli, Noah, and the two other operatives paddled a black rubber dinghy toward the vessel. Other than the boat's navigational lights, only dim illumination came from Khan's stateroom.

Pulling alongside the yacht, they tied a rope to a docking cleat. They climbed aboard, where Ari and Emek waited on the yacht's port side with suppressed Rugers. Eli and Noah made their way to Khan's sleeping quarters.

Khan woke with a start as Noah slipped a thick forearm across his throat and held him down. Reaching into a pouch, Eli removed a needle and a 100 cc syringe. With Khan pinned, Eli pulled back the syringe's plunger and slipped the needle into a vein on the Saudi's forearm.

"This is for my family," Eli whispered, pushing down on the plunger.

Moments later Khan spasmed, then died from an air embolism that traveled through his bloodstream and compressed his heart.

Eli and Noah carried the body to the deck, where the team slipped it silently into the sea, then paddled the dinghy back to their boat and returned to Corfu harbor.

When the body washed up on the shore, it would appear as though Khan had fallen overboard while drunk that night. The puncture mark in his forearm would escape detection because seawater would have eroded the outer layers of skin. And fish would have nibbled at the body, obscuring the small needle hole.

Paddling back to their boat, Eli whispered the words of the prophet Ezekiel, which he'd committed to memory.

And I will strike down upon thee with great vengeance and furious anger those who attempt to destroy my brothers. And you will know my name is the Lord when I lay my vengeance upon thee.

But killing Ivan Agapov was different: it wasn't an act of vengeance. It was done for money and to ensure that another criminal, Anton Gorlov, could make a safe exit from mob life.

Tonight's assassination wasn't a righteous kill. Nor were the deaths of so many other mobsters over the years. Killing is how he makes a living. And he feels not a shred of remorse.

Because after losing those he loved, something inside Eli died.

And he's not certain he cares.

21

At 11:50 that night, Anton Gorlov's burner cell phone trills. The readout tells him who's calling. "Yes, Viktor."

"Ivan Agapov's been taken to Coney Island Hospital. He's having chest pains and trouble breathing."

"It sounds like he might be very sick," Gorlov says, doing his best to sound surprised and concerned.

This is probably Aiden's doing.

Despite using a secure phone, Gorlov speaks in coded language in the unlikely event the call is being monitored. "I never knew he had heart problems."

"He seemed like a healthy man," Viktor replies.

"It just goes to show, you never know what can happen."

"Yes, life is unpredictable, and we have to make the most of every day."

"Very true."

There's a pause in the conversation.

"Have you heard back from the travel agent?" Gorlov asks.

"Yes. There are some beautiful beachfront properties, furnished and unfurnished. We can either rent or buy."

"You're sure Oksana is ready for a move?" Gorlov asks, though he already knows the answer.

"Yes," Viktor says. "She's tired of these winters. How about Katerina?"

"She says she'll go if I promise to marry her."

"So? Marry her. She's a good woman."

"I know that, but no one can replace Nadia."

"Anton, you wouldn't be replacing anyone."

"We'll talk more about it at another time," Gorlov says.

"Of course."

"Have you begun making arrangements for the next part?"

"I'm working on it."

"Do it quickly. And then contact Aiden. There isn't much time."

22

At 11:50, Eli finds himself in the East Village.

Except for the incident with Sergei, the Agapov kill went as smoothly as could be expected. Yes, it was hairy when Agapov looked at the cigar, but it turned out he suspected nothing. If Otto was right, it's only a matter of time before he goes down. Does he feel anything about the man's demise? Probably not, yet he's beset by a strange sense of melancholy.

After getting off the subway at Fourteenth Street, Eli took a taxi uptown to Twentieth and Lexington, then switched cabs and told the next driver to take him to a location six blocks away from where he's now standing. He's reasonably certain he hasn't been followed.

After the second taxi dropped him off, he began walking in what he sometimes thinks of as a dream state. Unable to recall the route he'd walked, he now realizes he's only one block from East Fourth Street in the East Village.

As he strides through the nightscape, the streets appear strange. It's an eerie look, almost dreamlike, as though this is his first time in the East Village. But he's been here many times before, which makes the feeling of unfamiliarity even more bizarre. Passing a deli, a tattoo parlor, a laundromat, and a series of stores and clubs, he realizes he hadn't consciously thought about where he was going. But he now knows the destination.

He's about to pass an Indian restaurant when the door opens and the aromas of cumin and coriander pervade the air.

Then it happens.

In a heart-stopping moment he sees her.

Leaving the restaurant, she walks down the street with another woman. For a half second he thinks it's Mom, and he's blindsided by the shock of recognition followed by a swell of sadness.

It can happen at any time. Mom, Pop, or Hannah can appear anywhere. There's no warning, no specific situation or context: it just happens, a momentary sighting lasting a mere second or less—a sudden flash, nothing more. Or if he sees a ten- or eleven-year old boy, he thinks of David, who would be that age by now.

It happens less often these days, but when it does, he's overwhelmed by a gust of memory. It can happen under different circumstances: a woman steps out of a taxi or leaves a store or turns a corner and suddenly there she is. It's Mom. Or Hannah. And his heart feels like it's dropping in his chest. There's an intense pang of longing followed by a tide of melancholy.

Then comes a craving both bitter and sweet. The pain and regret are unbearable.

It feels like he's being punished for living.

As the woman walks away, he waits for the sorrow to fade.

At the corner of Second Avenue and East Fourth, he enters the club.

It's happened before: he hadn't thought of coming here, but after wandering in some strangely altered state of awareness, he ends up here.

Casey's is an East Village hangout frequented by jazz lovers. For some reason it's a favorite watering hole for Israelis visiting New York. Eli used to drop in frequently, but it was starting to become a predictable pattern, so he stopped coming. But the thought of returning to his apartment—of being alone amid the dreariness of the place—is intolerable. So here he is.

It's crowded for a weekday night, especially since there's no live music scheduled. The front room's lighting is kept dimmed; no matter the time of day, it's always nighttime in Casey's.

The bar is packed three deep with people speaking a polyglot of languages.

Peals of laughter coming from the drinkers make Eli feel especially alone.

The back room, with its stage and small round tables, is dark.

It's disappointing that there won't be any musicians tonight, not even from a local ensemble trying to get a foothold in the business, let alone from an appearance by the likes of Norah Jones or Diana Krall.

Threading through the bar crowd, Eli spies an empty stool. Making his way toward it, he notices two hard-looking men sitting at the far end of the bar—wiry-looking guys with shaved heads, stubble-covered faces—likely IDF commandos. His assumption is confirmed when he hears their distinctive phonological Hebraic speech.

Settling onto the bar stool, Eli catches a glimpse of himself in the mirror behind the bar.

He doesn't like what's staring back at him.

What the fuck am I doing with my life? It's nothing more than kill or be killed.

He turns away from his reflection, peers down at the bar top as his thoughts turn to Agapov.

If Otto was right, the guy'll soon be lying on a steel table in the morgue. And an autopsy won't reveal how he died. Another job cleanly done. No evidence of violence. No residue of a toxin in his system.

Seeing the Israelis at the end of the bar reminds Eli of the assassinations he and Noah carried out as Mossad operatives. Unlike tonight's job, most were accomplished with extreme violence.

There was the gunning down of Abdullah al-Masri. He'd planned attacks on the American embassies in Kenya and Tanzania, along with other atrocities against Israeli civilians and those of other nationalities. Given refuge in Iran, he lived anonymously in Tehran. The CIA and Mossad had been tracking him for years. With full approval of the prime minister, Noah and Eli stalked him for weeks.

One summer night, al-Masri was driving his sedan in Tehran's fashionable Pasdaran district. Eli and Noah followed him on a souped-up Kawasaki motorcycle. Drawing abreast of the car, Eli, sitting in the rear seat, fired five shots from a silenced Beretta, blowing the man's brains out. Noah gunned the bike, and they sped away.

Or when a chemical engineer at the Natanz uranium enrichment facility was driving in Tehran. Noah drove a Honda NC750X motorcycle abreast of the car. Eli, sitting on the back seat, attached a magnetic bomb to the engineer's vehicle and they sped away. The bomb detonated when they were far ahead of him. He was killed instantly.

But, tonight's killing was different: it was stealthy, silent, undetectable.

No bullets or bombs.

A natural death.

And now the second part of the assignment is waiting. Whatever that may be.

Gorlov's words return. *Ah, that's a delicate matter, one that will require even more finesse than this one.*

Delicate?

Finesse?

Eli can't buy into some absurd notion that his work is like that of some skilled artisan. Delicate. Artful. No way. Killing another man is the crudest, most primal thing you can do to someone, especially if it's done close-up with a gun or knife.

Or by poison.

Or an air embolus injected into a vein.

Is he now soulless, dead in spirit?

Yeah, he's still breathing, but for what purpose?

To kill again, and again, and again?

He could turn down the second part of the job. He hasn't been paid for it and can easily forgo the money.

But I can tell you this: the money involved will change your life.

Not true. The money would change nothing.

Just pick up and leave. Find a peaceful place. No bombs, no bullets, no assassinations either violent or more subtle. Begin a new life away from all this.

Catching the bartender's eye, he orders a Maccabee beer, then drops two fives onto the bar.

The conviviality of the crowd deepens his funk. He feels disconnected from the everyday pleasures the people at this bar take for granted.

There's no laughter in his world. No drunken silliness. No camaraderie.

The bartender sets the beer in front of him.

"Keep the change," Eli says as the young man scoops up the bills.

Gazing at the bottle, he anticipates the deliciously slow seep of alcohol to his brain.

For some reason, tonight's hit is taking an unexpected toll on him.

Regret? Remorse? Shame?

What did Agapov ever do to him, or to someone Eli loved?

Nada.

And soon there'll be a newly minted widow crying her eyes out in Brooklyn. If not now, in a few hours her husband will be gone. Does she deserve the suffering Eli's dumped upon her? There's gotta be something more to life than being an instrument of death. Is there a cause more worthy than dispensing vengeance or so-called justice? Not out of some principle, but for money?

Of course there is, but here he is, sitting at a bar, having just killed another man for money. It feels like a sledgehammer blow to the chest: there's nothing he does that's noble or serves a cause higher than himself. He's just a paid killer.

He thinks back to what he and his fellow *katsas* did after successful assassinations of terrorists. They'd hit a Tel Aviv bar. Polish off Gold Star and Maccabee beers. Gorge on falafel, pita, and hummus. They'd talk about anything else—soccer, the basketball leagues, the top players and teams, not about Mossad and certainly not the kill.

Discussing the hit was forbidden.

Besides, it was routine, just another day at the office. It was simply what they did: kill and disappear.

But those were righteous kills.

There was nothing honorable about tonight's kill.

Or what he's been doing since leaving Mossad.

23

When the guy sitting at the bar to his right gets up and leaves, a young woman plants herself on the empty stool.

She has short black hair, a metal piercing above her left eyebrow, and a rhinestone stud penetrates the flange of her left nostril. Three small ringlets pierce her left ear shell. Her lips shine with crimson-colored gloss.

He catches a whiff of her perfume: it reminds him of the kind Hannah used. So simple a thing as a fragrance can bring on that ache. Closing his eyes, he tries to suffocate the memories.

The barkeep approaches; the woman orders a gin and tonic on the rocks.

When her drink arrives, she swirls the swizzle stick in the glass, takes a sip, leaving a red impression of her lips on the glass, then shoots Eli a smile.

He's about to say something when a solid thud lands on his shoulder.

He whirls around, ready to launch into a series of Krav Maga moves.

There stands Noah, his commando partner and fellow *katsa*—his blood brother and Team leader—a guy he hasn't seen in years.

Eli jumps off the bar stool.

Embracing, they hug and backslap each other. "Jesus, I was just thinking about you," Eli says. "Where've you been all this time?"

"In Israel. Been here for a week."

Noah's dark hair is slicked back with gel. It's a different look from when they went on missions, when his hair was shaved to the scalp.

Even in dim lighting, Eli can see the scars on Noah's cheeks. His face was lacerated during commando training when he jumped bare-chested from a moving Jeep into a patch of thornbushes. In the macho culture of Special Forces, he had to prove he feared nothing.

Noah, a natural-born killer. Perfect for the Sayeret Matkal or Mossad.

When Eli left Mossad, he could no longer tolerate living in Israel. Everything he saw, smelled or heard reminded him of Hannah and the loss of his family. Noah gave him the name of his cousin, Boaz, living in Brooklyn. Boaz was a member of the Israeli underworld and knew people in the Russian Brotherhood. Thinking his most marketable skill was killing, Eli contacted the Bratva and became a contract assassin. Killing evil men had become a way of life.

"What're you doing in the city?" Eli asks.

"Visiting relatives."

"How long will you be here?"

"For five more days. Then it's back home to the wife and kids."

"I never figured you for a family man."

"Neither did I, but Devorah changed everything."

"So you got out."

"Hell yeah. When I turned forty, I realized I couldn't take another day. What about you?"

"I live here."

"You married an American?"

"No. I'm not married. I just had to get away."

"Too many memories, right?"

Eli nods.

"I know, I know." He pats Eli's shoulder. "You sleeping better?"

Eli shakes his head.

"Still having those dreams?"

Eli nods again.

From their days together, Noah knows what haunts Eli. "Yeah man, that shit can stay with you forever," Noah says.

"What're you doing now?" Eli asks, just to change the subject.

"IT work with a start-up company in Tel Aviv. The 'Institute' training came in handy."

"Any regrets about what we did?" Eli asks.

"Nope. Lots of people are alive because we punched those bastards' tickets. Any time I have doubts, I think about Mombasa. Remember that?"

"How could I forget?"

Eli recalls how the team arrived at different times from six points in Europe and Africa, then tracked a band of Al-Qaeda terrorists through Kenya and the Congo.

"After what they did to Ari," Noah says, "those bastards got what they deserved."

The terrorists had captured Ari, the team's surveillance specialist, dragged him to a river, and fed him to the crocs. They filmed him being eaten alive and sent the tape to the Mossad station chief in the Congo.

Noah sets his beer bottle on the bar top. "I still think about how we wired their safe house," he says. "It was good watching those shitheads get blown sky-high."

Eli grabs his beer. "To Ari," he says.

They slap their bottles together.

When the bartender approaches, they order another round.

"So, what're you doing now?" Noah asks.

"I do some skip tracing."

"Who do you go after?"

"Deadbeats, people who've jumped bail and skipped town."

Here he is with Noah, a man he trusted with his life, a man who knows him as Eli, not as Aiden or Ezra or Richard or any of the fake monikers he uses in this poor excuse for a life—a man who saved Eli's life years ago, and he's lying to the guy.

Jesus, my life is so fucked up.

"We should stay in touch," Noah says, reaching for his cell phone.

Because of their shared past, Eli realizes Noah's not making an empty suggestion.

"Yes, let's swap numbers," Eli says.

"Sure. We can plan our next operation," Noah says with a laugh.

When they've exchanged numbers, they begin recounting their years of service and their camaraderie.

And they throw back more beers.

Noah talks about his wife, the kids, the in-laws, his job, and his plans for the future.

For Eli, Noah's description of his home and family brings on a withering realization.

Now more than ever Eli's aware of how empty his life has become.

24

At noon the next day, Anton Gorlov's cell phone lets out its ringtone.

The readout says it's Viktor.

"I hear Ivan Agapov died," Viktor says.

"Really?" Gorlov replies, feigning surprise just in case they're being monitored. "How did you learn that?"

"Through the grapevine," Viktor says, playing along with the charade. "The doctors don't know what went wrong, but he passed away peacefully."

"An autopsy will tell them what happened, yes?" Gorlov asks as a spasm of worry seizes him.

"According to what I heard, the doctors don't feel there's a reason to do an autopsy."

"Perhaps his blood pressure finally got him."

"Poor guy. He was too young to die," Viktor says.

Viktor's a good actor, knows how to play at being empathic. Yes, all the world's a stage.

"Find out where and when the funeral will be. We'll send our condolences."

"I'll take care of it."

Changing the subject, Gorlov says, "You know, I was just thinking, we still have some business obligations to take care of."

"Don't worry," Viktor says. "It will all get done."

Gorlov knows Viktor will wire the rest of the money to Aiden's account. The pathway to retirement is being cleared, but they'll have to move quickly because you can never know who may betray you and where it may lead.

In fact, there was the accountant, Grigory Sakharov. That weasel knew too much and was trying to protect himself by creating a flash drive with all that financial information on it. There's no doubt he'd have handed it over to the feds. But his disappearance was handled quite efficiently. There's no paper or digital trail for the feds to follow.

"Oh, Viktor, speaking of business, what about our IT man? I think he deserves a bonus," Gorlov says, speaking in code.

Our IT man, little Vasily Kamkin. That little worm.

For the love of God, Anton thinks, why must we always speak in code? The world's become so complicated with triangulating cell phones and computer hacking and viruses and worms and these damned secure sites. You have to assume every word is being monitored, if not by the feds then by your rivals. And now there's Bitcoin, this cryptocurrency thing, something Anton can't get his head around. And there are NFTs, nonfungible tokens, whatever on God's earth they may be. It's all beyond comprehension.

How does anyone keep up with this technology? It's so intricate, so convoluted, they now have an IT specialist working for them—Vasily Kamkin—on a full-time basis. The little guy sits in front of a monitor all day, clicking away, and he says they should start doing their banking online. As if cash isn't good enough; God, nothing's real anymore. It's all digital with virtual reality, teleconferencing, quantum computing, even imaginary money. What's the world coming to? Before you know it, you'll need an IT maven to wipe your ass.

An uncluttered existence would be so much better—a simple life where you don't have to worry about cybersecurity or some geek you've hired sending out an encrypted dossier. Where you don't have to wonder who's going to betray you for a few lousy dollars.

I'm too old for this. I can't wait to get out of here and relax on a lovely beach somewhere, anywhere, just so long as it's not Brighton Beach and the Bratva or the Italian mafia or the Albanians or Dominicans or whoever it is that makes the next power grab.

"You mean a bonus for Vasily?"

Viktor's words break Anton's train of thought; he's back in the moment. "Yes. Vasily's done such a fine job, I think he deserves a bonus," Gorlov replies.

"Yes, are you giving me the okay?"

"Let's wait a while," Gorlov says with a sigh. "We can't be sure of anything—at least not yet. Meanwhile, we need him to go ahead and help arrange for the next part of the project."

"You're sure about the next step?"

"Yes. Absolutely. We must think of the future, Viktor. So finish setting it up."

"I'll have Vasily contact Aiden."

25

Sitting in his apartment the next afternoon, Eli thinks about having run into Noah last night.

The guy's gotten beyond the ugliness of what they did for Mossad.

Yes, Noah's moved on.

But Eli can't.

He knows his life, or whatever passes for one, is static. It's like an old phonograph's broken record. The needle's stuck, and all he hears are the same pitiful notes over and over again: kill or be killed.

But this isn't the Middle East, and he's not killing for the right reasons, like that time he and Noah were in Syria on a Mossad operation.

The team had been tracking Abu Awad, a Hamas engineer who designed explosives for suicide bombers. Containing nuts, bolts, and scraps of metal, they were designed to kill, injure, and maim as many Israelis as possible.

For months they reconnoitered Awad's villa on the outskirts of Damascus and managed to bug every room in the house. On the night of the planned assassination, Eli, Noah, along with Ari and Emek, heard Awad go upstairs. He said good night to his son and daughter, talked to his wife, then returned downstairs to his study.

Armed with suppressed Berettas, Eli and Noah crawled toward the house. After Noah picked the lock, Eli entered the vestibule while Noah kept watch outside.

Awad's study door was closed. About to open it, Eli glanced to his left.

Standing there was Awad's son, a pajama-clad four-year-old.

"Are you the Prophet?" the boy asked with wide-eyed wonder. "Or are you Santa?"

Eli put his finger to his lips. "Shh."

"Nasim, I hear you out there," Awad called from the study. "Go back to bed—*now*."

"But, Papa . . ."

"Nasim, upstairs *now*."

The child cast a befuddled look at Eli, then headed for the staircase and disappeared upstairs.

I'm about to murder this boy's father. He's the age David would now be.

Eli's hands began shaking, but he breathed deeply and steadied himself.

A moment later he burst into the room. As Abu Awad rose from his chair, Eli put two bullets into his chest.

Another into his head.

Another triple tap.

He unplugged the computer and carried it out of the house.

On the road, he and Noah were picked up by Ari and Emek in a van.

Heading back to the border, Eli consoled himself knowing it was another righteous kill.

To this day he still hears that little boy: *Are you the Prophet? Or are you Santa?*

Now his targets aren't terrorists committing crimes against humanity.

Yet he's still mired in the tar pits of his past.

An hour later, sitting at a corner table in a Starbucks, Eli boots up his laptop.

He goes to the VPN website dedicated to Gorlov's brigade.

As expected, there's a message:

See the transfer. Please confirm receipt.

He wipes the message clean, then clicks on the link to Atlantic International Bank, Ltd. Located in Belize. Another $300,000 electronic deposit was made. The time stamp says it occurred an hour earlier. In the last few days he's been paid $600,000 by Gorlov and $250,000 by Agapov. A total of $850,000 wired to his accounts, all sent in binary code, undetected, tax-free blood money he doesn't even need to live for the rest of his life—away from the tracking, the internet, the killing.

Such is the life.

He sends an email to Gorlov's IT man confirming receipt of the money.

Now there's the second part of the job.

Does he really want to do it?

Why not put up his entire life for revision?

Why not get away from the killing?

Why not begin a new life?

If there is such a thing.

26

Anton knows Aiden must be contacted for the next part of this assignment.

And it must happen soon.

He knows this because people in this business will betray you in a heartbeat. Actually, people in any walk of life will turn on you if given the chance. Self-interest and greed always win out. It's the way of the world. There are enemies everywhere.

He remembers what Mama said about life in Ukraine.

"No one will ever care for you but your own family. Trust no one else."

Mama knew this all too well. In 1944, she was a fourteen-year-old girl living with her family in Kiev. "We were poor, but we were happy," she said. "Until the Germans came."

The Nazis ordered all Jews to pack their belongings and assemble in the city square. The Ukrainian government, every bit as hate-filled as the Germans, complied with the request.

"I tore up my identity card," Mama said. "I claimed I wasn't Jewish, that I was just seeing a friend off. But the Germans didn't want me to witness what they were doing and forced me to join the crowd.

"We were ordered to gather in the city's main square. Then we were paraded through the streets at gunpoint. Our neighbors, people we'd known for years, lined the streets and cursed us. *Dirty Jews. You're going to hell.* Then they ransacked our houses, took whatever they could. Remember, Anton, even your closest friends will betray you the first chance they get.

"We were marched en masse to a ravine at the edge of the city, a place called Babi Yar. We were forced to undress, and our clothing was left in separate piles: shoes, underwear, outerwear. At the edge of the pit, I looked down and saw hundreds of naked bodies below.

"German soldiers and the Ukrainian police were behind us," she continued. "They sat on stools, drinking coffee and smoking cigarettes, just waiting for us to be lined up at the edge of the pit.

"They began mowing us down. I jumped just before they opened fire and landed on top of the bodies. I played dead while they walked on top of the bodies and shot anyone they thought was still alive.

"Then they covered the pit with a layer of soil. They were going to shoot more people in the morning, so they didn't fill it up with more dirt. When it was dark, I crawled out of that pit soaked in blood. I got dressed, and hid in the woods."

Mama made her way south to Odessa, where family friends, Orthodox Christians, took her in. "They treated me like a daughter."

Ten years later Mama married a man who'd also survived the killings at that ravine.

"And a year later, Anton, my love, I gave birth to you."

When he was a year old, his brother Oleg was born, but he died a few days later of pneumonia.

And then there was Papa.

"Anton," Mama said, "your father never recovered from the loss of his family. Like me, he was filled with indescribable sadness, and he drank himself to death."

The Holocaust left Papa with a broken spirit from which he never recovered.

He died when Anton was four years old.

Anton Gorlov knows life is steeped in betrayal, death, and despair.

And survival depends on being ruthless.

27

At six the next morning, Eli's head throbs.

It's a pulsing headache for which Advil will do nothing. It'll take a tincture of time to wear off and maybe three or four cups of strong coffee. Trying to shake off the haze, he trudges into the kitchen and pours water into a kettle.

He drank too much beer at a neighborhood tavern last night. Meeting Noah two nights ago dredged up far too many memories, and he tried drowning them in alcohol.

Right now he feels so strange, even detached, as though he's watching himself pour a cup of freshly brewed coffee. Two cups later, the headache has subsided. After another cup of the brew, he steps into the shower. As water sloshes over his head, he closes his eyes, soaps up, rinses, then turns the hot water handle all the way to its limit. It's nearly unbearable, but he suffers through the deluge.

He suddenly recalls the dream. It returned last night.

Walking along a Jerusalem street, he sees a bus heading toward the Old City. As can happen in dreams, he has foresight, knows Hannah, Mom, and Pop are on the bus. It stops to pick up passengers. And there's that kid boarding through the open rear door. Knowing he's a suicide bomber, Eli sprints toward the bus, desperate to stop what he knows will happen.

But an immense fireball erupts, and the percussive shock wave knocks him to the ground. Screaming, he lies on the pavement, knowing once again, he couldn't stop what happened.

As always happens at the end of the dream, he shuddered awake, quaking amid sweat-soaked sheets.

Jesus, this time he even smelled the smoke, felt the heat, and when he woke up, his throat was raw from having screamed. And his back ached as though he'd actually been thrown to the pavement.

Will the dream ever stop?

It's as though his mind keeps reliving that day.

Until Noah asked about it, he hadn't had the goddamned dream in months.

Stepping out of the shower, he grabs a towel and wipes mist from the medicine cabinet mirror. In the bathroom's light his skin looks milky white. Dark circles are slung beneath his eyes, which seem to have sunk into hollows in his skull. Deep creases are etched into his forehead.

He sees something else in the mirror: rage.

Smoldering like embers, it eviscerates his soul.

While shaving, he inadvertently cuts himself. Blood trickles down his chin. Crimson red droplets splatter onto the sink, forming serrated-edged starbursts.

Turning on the water, he watches a reddish swirl disappear down the drain.

Grabbing a tissue, he presses it to the cut.

His thoughts reel as he recalls the men he's killed.

It's a parade of death.

And little Nasim's voice screams in his head.

Are you the Prophet? Or are you Santa?

There's another voice—his own, or is it Mom's?—and it asks, *What have you done with your life?*

Seeing Noah has set off this assault of remembrance. And regret so deep, it sears him.

Eli's stomach does a slow roll as a wave of sadness rolls over him.

Dropping to his knees, he crawls toward the toilet and hangs his head over the edge.

There's a wrenching sensation as vomit races up his gullet and spews into the bowl.

A few hours later, he's sitting in a Starbucks on Third Avenue at Thirty-Third Street, one of the many coffee shops he uses to hook into a Wi-Fi system.

He boots up the laptop. There's a message on the VPN website reserved for Gorlov's brigade.

It's from Gorlov's IT guy.

> We need to discuss the next part of the project. We can meet at the same place. You pick the date and time. Please respond ASAP.

Why do the next part? Just get out. Do it. Now.

He has enough money saved to live comfortably for the rest of his life.

The rest of my life? How long will that be?

He can ignore the message, make arrangements to get out of the city, leave the country, and be gone.

But when they met, there was something about Gorlov that hit him, some strange sense of connection.

Eli knows the pakhan wants to get out of this life too.

What the hell. I'll hear him out. I can always say no.

Typing quickly, Eli responds to the post.

> Have Gorlov call me.

The satellite phone is secure, and Gorlov's IT guy won't be able to triangulate cell tower signals to learn his location.

He hasn't made a commitment, and he's been paid for the first half of the assignment. So there's nothing lost by hearing what the man has to say.

Or is he just fooling himself about walking away from this life?

28

Shortly before twelve thirty in the afternoon, Anton Gorlov and Viktor Sorokin round the corner of Brighton Fifth Street and trudge against a strong wind sweeping along Brighton Beach Avenue. The wind is so harsh, Gorlov's cheeks and ears burn.

Suddenly Gorlov notices a disheveled man sitting on the sidewalk between Russakoff's Bakery and Eugenia's clothing store. He'd seen plenty of beggars on the streets of Odessa, but it's a rare sighting in Brighton Beach. Poor fellow looks to be about thirty years old. He wears a tattered coat—no doubt retrieved from a dumpster—along with torn jeans and hole-ridden sneakers with no laces.

Homeless and on the street in this cold weather? Such a pity.

The guy hasn't bathed in months; the reek of him nearly reaches the curb. Staring ahead vacantly, the man holds a piece of cardboard on his lap. On it, crayon-scrawled in English, are the words HOMELESS. PLEASE HELP.

Gorlov stops and stares at the man's ceramic bowl. It contains a few coins.

Mama's ordeal with the Nazis was real suffering, Anton thinks, not the plight of some guy who had all the advantages of growing up in America but wasted his life sucking down alcohol.

But how can you ever know what another person has been through?

Walk a mile in my shoes.

Gorlov says a few Russian words to the man.

The fellow peers at him, seems not to understand a word of what was said.

Gorlov switches to English.

Same lifeless response.

Gorlov pulls out his wallet, holds his breath, and drops a ten-dollar bill into the bowl. He says, "Here, get something to eat."

He and Viktor climb the stairs leading to the office located above Novinka Foods. They're greeted by Gennady, a bodyguard stationed at the office door.

A moment later Vasily Kamkin, their IT technician, emerges from his work cubicle.

Peering at Vasily, Gorlov wonders why he doesn't trust the man. He's always thought of him as a *laska*, a weasel. He doesn't talk, he whines, whether in Russian, Ukrainian, or English. But the poor bastard has his own troubles, a sick wife who isn't long for this world, which hits Anton in the gut. Nowadays, whenever he sees Vasily, he's reminded of Nadia's death.

"Anton, I received a message," Vasily says in his puling voice. "It's from that fellow we sent the dossier to a little while ago. He wants you to call him."

"He said nothing else?"

"The message was, 'Have Gorlov call me.'"

Anton assumed Aiden would never meet twice at the same place. They were lucky to have met with him even once. That fluke wouldn't be repeated. The assassin has always been unpredictable. But now he may not even want to hear about the second part of the job. This could mess up their plans. They have to clean up this matter before leaving the country.

Back at the apartment, Eli kills time by playing game after game of solitaire, but the computer keeps dealing him shitty hands. He's lost five games in a row.

Or is he not concentrating? Is he too preoccupied waiting for Gorlov's call?

There's little doubt that the second part of this job will be another hit.

Will it be another pakhan?
An Albanian *kyre*?
An Italian don?
Or a Dominican drug lord?
All snakes who should be eating dirt.
And he's become part of this filthy scenario.
Yes, it's time to get out of this life.

Gorlov sits behind his desk.

Viktor sits across from him.

"It seems Aiden doesn't trust us," Gorlov says.

"Why should he?" Viktor replies. "He lives a life of treachery."

Using his encrypted cell phone, Gorlov dials the number.

"Yes," says a flat voice.

"We speak again," Gorlov says. "I assume Aiden is still your name."

"It's whatever you feel comfortable calling me," the assassin replies.

I could never feel comfortable with this man. Something about him makes my skin crawl.

"As you requested, I'm calling," Gorlov says, aware he sounds placating. "Just so you know, Viktor is sitting here with me, and I have you on speakerphone."

"I'm sure whatever you have to say has already been heard by Viktor."

"Congratulations on a job well done," Gorlov says, trying to inject a bit of camaraderie into the conversation. "It's quite impressive."

The silence is so dense, Gorlov momentarily thinks the line's gone dead.

Shaking his head, Gorlov glances at Viktor, whose eyes narrow. The book is obviously closed on the Agapov matter. Aiden won't utter a word about it.

"I understand," Gorlov says. "A magician never reveals how he does his tricks."

More silence.

A knot of frustration forms in Gorlov's chest.

He must think we're wired so he'll say nothing to implicate himself. In fact, he might be wired, so I'd better be circumspect.

"What about our next meeting?" Gorlov asks.

"You had your onetime face-to-face. Now tell me about the second part, and I'll let you know if I'm interested."

"I thought we were in agreement that you would take it."

"We agreed to nothing."

"Did I assume too much?"

No response.

"We would like to discuss a sensitive matter," Gorlov says, aware he's approaching this conversation gingerly. Like when he was a young boy facing the Odessa gangs, when he was too small to confront them, when he resorted to flattery and placated them with words.

"I'm listening."

"This is an unusual situation, so let me give you some background."

The assassin says nothing.

Gorlov finds the man's silence to be daunting.

"A short time ago, we lost someone in our organization."

"You lost someone?" the assassin asks.

"Yes. An unfortunate fellow who committed suicide," Gorlov says, keeping his voice modulated, aware he's lying and he's certain Aiden knows it. "He was very depressed."

Viktor is nodding again.

"It seems," Gorlov continues, "that in a moment of despair, he jumped from the window of his apartment building."

Gorlov anticipates Aiden will ask for details or express some curiosity. But he says nothing. The silence feels like it's sucking the air out of the room.

This man is like a sphinx.

"So, this situation leads to the second part of the job," Gorlov says, knowing it would be wise to proceed cautiously. "Actually, this part of the assignment will require even more cunning than before."

"Go on."

"And I think you're just the man to accomplish what must be done."

Again the assassin remains silent.

29

The delicacy of Gorlov's phrasing strikes Eli as a euphemism. Or, more likely, a surefire sign that the guy's bullshitting him. There's also a hint of sarcasm in his voice. It borders on scornfulness, hints at treachery.

Whatever this job is, it requires more cunning than the Agapov hit?

He can tell Gorlov's waiting for a response. But there's no need to fill the silence. It's better to let it draw itself out because it makes Gorlov uncomfortable. This man is accustomed to people giving in to his every demand, and Gorlov's mounting unease will push him to fill the void.

Another few seconds pass.

"I assume you would like to know about the next part of the job?" Gorlov asks in a voice rising in pitch.

"This *unfortunate* fellow who committed suicide," Eli says, purposely using Gorlov's words, "Why did he kill himself?"

"Because he was our accountant, and the feds were looking into our finances. We believe he was afraid he'd be indicted for what the feds would allege were certain financial irregularities. He was worried because whatever went on, he had a hand in it. And, of course, he had to hand over certain records and books. We think that was what drove him to kill himself."

So the guy knew too much, Eli concludes. In accounting terms, he became a debit and they made sure he was no longer on the books. "And if I may be so bold as to ask," Eli finally says, purposely injecting a tone of impatience into his voice, "what does *any* of this have to do with me?"

Gorlov clears his throat. "After this poor fellow died, we

became aware that he probably had gotten his hands on some sensitive information."

"What information?"

"I am sorry, but I am not at liberty to discuss that."

"You became aware of his having this information *after* he died?"

"Yes. And we believe it still exists—on a flash drive."

Eli says nothing, thinking he'll be asked to find that device. And that will mean killing someone.

"This fellow violated company policy by creating that flash drive."

"I assume you're certain this device is still around."

"We think so. Unfortunately, we don't have it, which is why you and I are talking."

"And that's because . . . ?"

"Because our plans could be compromised if what's on that device becomes public."

"And you want *me* to find it?"

"Yes, if you can."

"I can't help you."

"Why not?"

"I find *people*, not flash drives."

"This involves more than just finding it."

"In what way?"

Whatever he says next is why he's been beating around the bush.

"This accountant's name was Grigory Sakharov. He has . . . or I should say, he *had* a sister, a woman named Irina Sakharov. Not that *she's* dead. She recently came to New York from Moscow, and now lives in Manhattan with her cousin. We think Sakharov may have given his sister the flash drive before he killed himself. Or he may have given her a copy of it."

"Why would he have done that?"

"Our guess is he felt it would be insurance in case we learned he'd stolen this information. Not that we would want to harm him."

Eli hears a sardonic edge, even a smile, in Gorlov's voice.

"We think there's a good chance he gave it to her for safekeeping."

"But you're not certain she has it."

"No, we can't be completely certain, but we suspect that she does. Or that she could get her hands on it."

"Does she know what's on it?"

"We don't know. She may not even realize it exists."

"It could be in a safe-deposit box somewhere," Eli says, "in which case you'd never get your hands on it."

"We're certain it's not. He didn't trust banks, and he'd only leave it with someone he trusts—in this case, his sister."

"An *accountant* who doesn't trust banks?"

"Yes, he knows how corrupt they are," Gorlov says with a snort. "We're quite certain he left it with his sister. And we worry she might eventually read its contents, though as far as we know, she doesn't have a computer. No matter what she knows or doesn't know, it's *crucial* that we locate the flash drive before it falls into the wrong hands."

"And?"

"We would like you to retrieve it. You can start by meeting the sister."

"Why pay me for what one of your men could do?"

"The feds have been snooping around and could be keeping an eye on this woman, this Irina Sakharov. We don't want to approach her directly. On the other hand, if she meets someone socially, *that's* a different situation. We'd like you to get involved with this woman."

"Involved?"

"Yes, get to know her. For a good-looking man like you, that should be easy."

"I'm not interested. It's not the kind of work I do."

"All we ask is that you find out if she has the flash drive—or if she's even aware of it. Either way, we would like you to do your best to learn its whereabouts and, if possible, to get it back to us."

"What plans do you have for this woman . . . this Irina Sakharov?"

"If she's innocent, we mean her no harm."

"You must think I was born yesterday. There's no way she stays alive. You'll have her put in the ground, and *that's* what you're really asking me to do."

"I can assure you—"

"Find someone else. I'm hanging up."

Eli begins pulling the phone from his ear, is about to cut off the call.

"*Hold* on. Just hear me out," Gorlov says in a voice that borders on sounding frantic.

"I'm listening. But you'd better make it quick." Eli's foot begins tapping on the floor.

This is absurd. I know how these guys operate.

"I'm glad you brought up the unlikely prospect of harm coming to this woman. That tells me you are not recording this conversation."

"Of course not. I said make it quick. I'm waiting."

"Here's the situation," Gorlov says. "She's a twenty-nine-year-old woman who's now living with her cousin, Sasha Bortsov. We know Sasha quite well. She has a good heart. She offered to let this Irina stay with her until she's more settled in New York."

"So?"

"Since her brother's death, Irina Sakharov has been feeling sad, which, of course, is understandable. She has no family left. We're quite sure she would be vulnerable to, shall we say . . . the charms of a handsome man such as yourself."

Charms of a handsome man? Fucking guy's gotta be losing his mind.

"Through her cousin, we can arrange for you to meet her. She might let you know if she's aware of this flash drive. And if so, where she has it."

"So you think that aside from being naive, I'm a Casanova?"

Gorlov's chortle reeks of cynicism. If they were meeting face-to-face, Eli would get up and walk away. It's an absurd scheme, something he wants no part of. Eli sighs heavily, making sure Gorlov hears it.

"Listen to me, Aiden, this involves nothing more than meeting and being sympathetic to a young woman who, by the way, I understand is quite lovely. There's nothing else to it."

"And if she *does* know about the flash drive?"

"We can relieve her of it."

"How would you do that?"

"Oh, there are many ways. Once we know she has it and where it's kept, a simple robbery would be easiest. We could gain access to Sasha's apartment, toss the place, and make it look like it was a break-in."

"I see. And since there's a chance she might know what's on the device, you'll eliminate her."

"We won't touch her. You have my word on that."

"Why this elaborate scheme?"

"It's the best way for us to get what we want without attracting attention from the feds. Of course, it involves our future. Viktor's and mine."

"And this woman . . . this Irina Sakharov? What's *her* future?"

"If the flash drive is lost or destroyed, we forget about it. She goes on with her life. And so do we. Doesn't that make sense?"

There's a brief pause.

"I swear to you," Gorlov says, "no harm will come to her."

"I don't do this kind of work."

"What kind of work?"

"Conning or killing innocent people."

"She won't be hurt. You have my word on that."

"Words are cheap."

"Let me assure you, Aiden, this will be the most pleasant job you've ever had. And we're prepared to pay five hundred thousand for your efforts—all of it up front."

Eli isn't certain he's heard Gorlov correctly. "Five hundred thousand?"

"Yes. I want you to know how important this is to us."

A brief pause follows.

"Let me remind you," Gorlov says, "along with the payment for the first part, the total we'll be paying is one million, one hundred thousand. I want you to appreciate how much this means to us . . . to our futures."

"The money means nothing to me."

"Understood. But this is vitally important to us."

"And the woman?"

"I swear to you no harm will come to her."

"How long do I have to try getting this information?"

"We would like to find out within the next two weeks, sooner if possible."

"That's not much time."

"I understand. But there *is* pressure."

Eli says nothing.

"Well?" Gorlov says. "Will you do it?"

Eli is certain Gorlov will do whatever he can to recover the flash drive—if it exists.

Of course, these guys never leave any loose ends, not when this device could mean Gorlov and Viktor end up in prison for money laundering and tax evasion. You could probably add wire and securities fraud into the mix, all serious crimes punishable by long prison sentences. That's precisely why Grigory Sakharov took a flier out that window. Because Gorlov's business model includes making sure all evidence evaporates into thin air. No matter what she does or doesn't know, Irina Sakharov will most likely end up at the bottom of Gravesend Bay.

These guys are the vermin he's been exterminating for the last ten years.

Maybe there's something worthwhile in what he does. Yes, there could be something virtuous in short-circuiting their plans.

And it's a good payday.

He can meet this Irina and tip her off about what's coming. Whether she believes him or not is another issue. But he can do his best.

Gorlov wants to get this thing done. His first impression of Anton Gorlov at Cipriani Dolci was on target: *He's an impatient man, finds it hard to delay gratification. He wants this done now, without delay.*

Eli says, “You guarantee that no harm will come to this woman?”

“I do.”

“Who do you love most in the world?”

Silence.

“Who’s the most meaningful person in the world to you?” Eli asks as a flash of Hannah goes through his mind. His throat constricts.

Nearly choking, Gorlov says, “My wife . . . Nadia.”

“Swear to me on Nadia’s life that no harm will come to this woman, Irina Sakharov.”

“I swear on Nadia’s life,” Gorlov says in a quivering voice.

Eli hears Gorlov’s breathing quicken. The man is emotional; Eli’s hit a raw nerve. He can actually feel Gorlov’s pain. He’s a man capable of deep love. Losing his wife would be an unbearable burden for him.

“Providing Irina Sakharov stays safe, I’ll do it. If I get the slightest hint she’s in danger, I’m gone.”

“Understood.”

“That being the case, I’ll need a dossier on her.”

“We’ll post it to the secure site. Where shall we wire the money?” Gorlov’s voice has resumed its usual pitch and tone.

“To the same account.”

“It will be done this afternoon. Another five hundred thousand.” A short pause. “And let me say, Aiden, this is a great favor, one I won’t forget.”

30

Eli knows that if the feds get their hands on that flash drive, Gorlov could be charged with a shitload of crimes, mainly financial, but there could be details on the device implicating him in other felonies as well. Crimes that go beyond white-collar stuff: extortion, kidnapping, human trafficking, or murder.

No matter what Gorlov says, Irina Sakharov will be nothing more than collateral damage for Gorlov and Viktor.

This woman is innocent, has nothing to do with Russian organized crime.

Yet she's going down. As for her brother, when Gorlov suspected he'd been disloyal, he ended up leaving this world.

This is how the Bratva operates.

That's why Eli deals with digital data, encrypted satellite phones, and an array of burners.

As far as his clients are concerned, he exists in cyberspace only, not in the flesh.

It's kept him safe from the same people who've paid for his services.

But now he's changed his protocol by meeting with Gorlov, Viktor, and Agapov. He was not only seen but most likely was recorded. In the digital age he's vulnerable: there's facial recognition software such as FaceVault, Fotobounce, and dozens of others. He can be recognized and picked up in a heartbeat if the right software is used.

And there's that question he's been considering for a while: why not get out of the life?

He has enough technological savvy to recalibrate everything, to leave the country, become a different person, and begin a new life, one far removed from this one.

He can live in a witness protection program of his own making.

There's enough money stashed away to live well—not lavishly, which has never been his style—wherever he wants to spend the rest of his life. There are spots in the Caribbean—Saint Lucia or Antigua in the West Indies—where he can live without worrying about threats from the mobs that have hired him over the years. And there are safe havens like Singapore, Kuala Lumpur, Java, or Bali, where plenty of expats live. Where he could get lost among those who've exiled themselves from their birthplaces and the burdens of their pasts.

The skip tracer could skip town and never be traced.

Why keep living a life that's nothing but a tangle of lies and deception?

And murder.

As though he's still a Mossad operative.

31

The next morning Eli visits a different Starbucks, this one farther downtown from the apartment.

Sitting at a corner table, he boots up the laptop, then goes online.

He checks the bank account for Gorlov's deposit. The money's been electronically transferred, $500,000, which now totals $1,100,000 from the Odessa mafia, not to mention the money transferred from Agapov's brigade before his death. Plenty of money, none of it really needed to live a good life far from New York or Tel Aviv or any of the European capitals.

It's time to go to work. Using the search engine Tor, he scours the dark web for something about Grigory Sakharov.

There's nothing.

Google Search will no doubt be useless, but he tries it. There's one mention of Grigory Sakharov from Brooklyn, and he finds a brief article in the *New York Post* from two months earlier.

> Grigory Sakharov, a New York City bank executive with Allemegne Bank, in an apparent suicide, jumped from his apartment window in the Brighton Beach section of Brooklyn. Sakharov was being investigated for involvement in financial matters related to Russian organized crime.

The guy had no social media presence—no Facebook, Twitter, LinkedIn, or Instagram.

Link after link on the internet reveals nothing more about his death or life. Except for the brief article in the *Post*, it's as though he disappeared from the face of the earth.

Going to Wikipedia and Yahoo, Eli finds a plethora of entries about Allemegne Bank.

Scouring a few more websites sheds a bit more light on why Grigory Sakharov died.

One site explains that in 2018, government prosecutors alleged that Allemegne Bank had been involved in money-laundering activities along with the Danish bank Danika. Bank executives were accused of having helped wash $10 billion for Russian money launderers.

A web search of Danika Bank turns up links detailing a US Department of Justice criminal investigation of money laundering. The inquiry concluded that Danika, along with Allemegne Bank, had allowed billions to flow through one of its branches. The scheme is noted to have involved certain unnamed US citizens thought to have ties to Russian organized crime both in the Russian Federation and in New York City.

While there's no specific mention of Gorlov or the Odessa mafia, it's clear that money was being washed through a complicated chain of security purchases—mostly NASDAQ stocks—and by an elaborate series of shady transfers of bank funds.

Yes, that's how sophisticated laundering schemes work—by the buying and selling of stocks through networks of shell companies. The money stays offshore, where the US government can't access it.

The bottom line seems clear: Grigory Sakharov, a mob-connected bank executive, probably gathered incriminating financial information about Anton Gorlov and his second-in-command, Viktor Sorokin. Fearing he might be discovered and for his own protection, he transferred the data to a flash drive. But somehow Gorlov learned what Sakharov had done.

And now, Grigory Sakharov is history.

But Irina Sakharov is still around.

That flash drive, if it's available, could become part of a federal probe into Anton Gorlov and his associates.

So, Irina Sakharov is the next target. Next he does a web search for Irina Sakharov. While a number of people with the surname Sakharov live in the New York area, only two are women.

Neither is named Irina, and there's no description of anyone who recently moved to the United States. There are other entries, but they're in Russian, a language he doesn't speak.

A few clicks later, Eli sees the dossier on Irina Sakharov posted to the secure site.

A color photo—a long shot obviously taken with a high-powered lens—shows an attractive, fair-skinned woman with Slavic features. She has prominent cheekbones, a heart-shaped face. The photo was taken in a public place—the background has the look of a cafeteria—and was apparently shot without her awareness.

He peruses the dossier. It gives a skeletal picture of the woman.

> Irina Sakharov is 29 years old, lived in Moscow and was sole caretaker of her widowed 64-year-old mother who died recently of heart failure. Came to New York 3 months ago.
>
> Lives with a cousin, Sasha Bortsov, in a 2-bedroom apartment at 161 East 18th Street, Manhattan. Works as a receptionist at Sasha's fitness club, Healthworks, located at Third Avenue and 21st Street. Brother died 2 months ago (committed suicide) soon after she arrived in New York.
>
> Speaks fluent Russian, Ukrainian, and Polish. Command of English is somewhat limited but communicates well. Has no other relatives in Russia or the United States. Single, never been married.

Closing down the laptop, Eli considers the situation.

If that flash drive ever surfaces, Irina Sakharov—knowingly or otherwise—could endanger Gorlov and Sorokin for their financial crimes.

No matter what she does or doesn't know, whether the flash drive is intact or not, Anton Gorlov will make sure Irina Sakharov never becomes a threat to his plans.

She might as well be dead.

32

As he prefers it, Anton Gorlov has the steam room at Vanya's to himself.

As a favor, Boris, the spa's custodian, usually directs other men to the smaller and less commodious steam room so Anton doesn't have to share the space with anyone. But Boris isn't working today, so it's likely Anton will soon be joined by other men.

Anton loves being alone with his thoughts. It's such a pleasure to be enveloped by steam and sweating while looking forward to a hot shower. He relishes the chance to strip naked and sit on a wooden bench in this old-time Brighton Beach bathhouse. It's one of the few bathhouses left in the neighborhood and reminds him of the old country. When the old Russians and Ukrainians die off, the community will no doubt gentrify. It's already started; new fancy restaurants are opening. They'll stop serving borscht and pelmeni, and there'll be plenty of New American food, whatever the hell that is.

Now his thoughts turn to Aiden. Can this man be trusted? Anton has paid plenty of good money over the years to this assassin and still knows nothing about him. But time is short, and there are few other options available. They have to disappear before a war erupts between the brigades. There's always a lull and then it starts. Again. After what happened to Ivan Agapov, it will only be a matter of time before the streets run with blood.

Will Aiden do what he's been asked to do? He knows Anton and Viktor are under the pressure of time—so he's holding all the cards. It was surprising that he didn't want more than the $500,000, but he seems like a man for whom money doesn't mean all that much.

While Aiden's always taken care of business, there's always the possibility he could just walk away with the money. And they'll never find him. God knows, they've tried locating him, but he's much too savvy and untraceable. If he takes off, they'll have to devise another plan—a more direct approach, which will be tough to do. But it's too early to take that route. Discretion and indirection are more suitable—for the time being.

It's hard to imagine Aiden making a romantic approach toward this woman, this Irina. He may be too much of a loner to get the job done. Time will tell. And there's not much time left.

The plan they've engineered is a callous one, and for it to succeed, Aiden must do his part.

Anton knows next to nothing about this Irina. And there are many moving parts, too many unknowns about both Aiden and this woman, so it's difficult to feel confident that things will work out. It's unsettling because Anton loathes the unknown. It leaves him with feelings that harken back to the past—those of weakness, futility, and a soul-shredding sense of vulnerability, the way he felt as a young boy in Odessa.

He much prefers simple, quick solutions to any problem, generally dislikes subtlety and indirection. But here there's little choice.

Recently he's felt doubtful about so many things. Maybe it's because he's gotten older and now realizes the fragility of life, how finite it all is. How death lurks around a nearby corner.

Anton's thoughts turn to the uncertainty and brutality he's seen in his lifetime. And it saddens him.

As a young boy, Anton was picked on relentlessly by bullies.

One day, when he was ten, he was cornered in an alley by a group of five older boys. "Jew," growled Nikola, the leader of the gang. "What're you doing in this neighborhood?"

"I'm going home," Anton said, sensing the hatred seeping from Nikola's pores.

"Going home?" the older boy snarled. "Not now," and he punched Anton in the face.

All five boys converged upon him. He was big for his age and fought back but was pummeled and kicked to the ground.

The blows were relentless and landed with shouts of, "Die, Jew. Die."

When he awoke, he was lying beneath a heap of garbage they'd dumped onto him. But that day changed him, became part of what made him the man he now is. Or maybe it was a series of things beginning even before he was born, like what happened to Mama's family back in Kiev at Babi Yar. And the slaughter of Papa's entire family too.

There was little but horror and brutality.

By fourteen Anton was a veteran street brawler. At fifteen, to survive, he joined a gang of ethnic Ukrainians, Russians, and Jews roaming the streets of Odessa, robbing and mercilessly beating anyone who resisted. He mastered the brutality of the streets.

By seventeen he was the group's leader.

He had many encounters with the police but was able to buy his way out of going to prison.

When he was nineteen Mama was diagnosed with advanced breast cancer.

On her deathbed, he took her hand and leaned close to her. "Mama, please don't leave me."

"Anton, my love," she whispered. "I must leave you, but you must survive . . . for me . . . for your father . . . for your little brother, Oleg. Promise me you will find happiness in this world."

"I promise, Mama."

Happiness?

I barely have a memory of Papa.

Mama died so long ago.

My beloved Nadia's dead.

My daughter won't talk to me.

There's very little happiness for me.

There was no joy in the Soviet Union and none when he made his way to Mama's relatives in Hamburg, Germany. So he crewed aboard a freighter out of Hamburg, headed for the United States. Once it docked in New York, he disappeared into the underworld of Brighton Beach, here in Brooklyn, Little Odessa by the Sea.

It didn't take long to prove his worth and rise through the ranks of the syndicate.

And now he occupies the exalted position of pakhan.

But to what end?

Does it really matter?

At sixty, except for what now seems the oh-so-brief interlude with Nadia, he still hasn't found the happiness Mama wanted for him. Nadia was the light in his life, and her death left him so bereft, it seems little in this world matters.

With the sound of the room's door opening and closing, Anton Gorlov's stream of thought vanishes. Three men can be seen through the steam room fog; naked but for towels across their laps, they sit on a ledge across from him. When he peers at them, each man averts his eyes. Not one of them dares meet his gaze. Because he's the pakhan of a brigade known for its ruthlessness in the madness of this world.

How did it come to pass that he's a man to be avoided, a man so feared that other men won't even look his way?

Lately he's been thinking more about how he became the man he now is.

Maybe we don't get to choose the people we become. Not when you think about life and the way of the world. It could be that what he's become was stamped into his genes, that it's merely a matter of biology, that he was born to be pakhan, that nature made him who he now is.

Or, he may be the man he's become as a result of life's tragedies. Maybe it was the series of misfortunes that preceded his having been born: there were the horrors of the Nazis and Kiev and Babi Yar and the catastrophes that befell his family—the deaths of Oleg and Papa, lost not just in the flesh but to memory as well—and then there were the days of his youth: the threats, the beatings, the corrupt police, the street gangs, and of course there was Mama's early death, and then coming here to Little Odessa by the Sea, where in order to survive, he joined the ranks of the Russian underworld.

Even more than biology, it seems these calamities created a path that led inexorably to what he's become: an apex predator.

33

A day later, Eli is sitting at a table in another coffee shop on First Avenue, where he's hooked into the Wi-Fi system.

A soft ding comes from the laptop. It's a message on the secure website from Gorlov's IT man.

> A gathering this Friday evening at 8:00 at Sasha Bortsov's apartment, 161 East 18th Street, Manhattan, Apartment 12-N. You will have a chance to meet Irina Sakharov.

So he prepares himself for what will be the last task in his career as an assassin.

On Friday evening at seven—following his usual precaution of arriving early for an appointment—Eli walks past 161 East Eighteenth Street.

It's a white brick structure that appears to be about twenty stories high. Boxwood hedges form a neatly trimmed border in front of the building. A glance skyward reveals the upper stories are recessed in a wedding cake architectural style. From a distance of nearly ten meters, Eli stops briefly and looks through the lobby's glass facade.

As people stream in and out of the building, the doorman picks up the intercom to announce visitors. There's no CCTV camera visible in the lobby, though he'll know for certain when he enters the place. It looks like a typical Manhattan residential security setup. A doorman, nothing else. Nothing about the place raises his antennae.

Though it's an unusually frigid evening, Eli decides to go through his usual anti-surveillance maneuvers since the Odessa mafia knows precisely where he'll be tonight. With his hands thrust in his overcoat pockets, he meanders along a few side streets in the upper teens, taking a circuitous route to make sure he's not being tailed.

He's left the Beretta at the apartment; there's no sense in going to a social gathering while carrying. Especially if he's on a mission like the one tonight. But sitting in his right hip pocket is a Tac Force spring-assisted knife. With a three-and-a-quarter-inch blade length, it's easily hidden and can make a difference in close-quarters combat. Of course, it's no match for a pistol, but at close range, it can be effective. It's far better than being completely unarmed.

After circling the block once more, he crosses East Nineteenth Street, backtracks, and is reasonably certain he's not being tracked. With nearly a half hour to kill, he enters O'Malley's Pub on the northeast corner of East Eighteenth Street and Irving Place, one block from Sasha Bortsov's building.

The tavern is filled with a boisterous barroom crowd. The camaraderie of these places always makes Eli feel disconnected and alone. He'd ordinarily avoid this kind of saloon with its noisy crowd of drinkers packed two or three deep along the length of the bar; there's the risk of an assassin slipping through the press of people, getting close and using a box cutter or a knife to slash your femoral artery. If that happens, your life's blood pours out in less than a minute. But that seems to be a small risk in this place. And it's too early to show up at the party. Besides, the frigid air has forced him indoors.

Glancing about, he notices the pub's dark wood walls and old mahogany bar. Looking up, he sees a coffered tin ceiling, which likely dates back to the late nineteenth century. Framed black-and-white photos of old-time Irish boxers—Jack Dempsey, Gene Tunney, Mickey Walker, and others—hang on one wall. The flag of Ireland is draped on another. The stacked bottles behind the bar are backlit with kelly-green lighting. The place definitely has an Irish vibe.

From the bar area, Eli can see into a rear room, with its brick-lined walls and tables napped in green-and-white-checkered cloth. At the far end of the dining room, comfortable-looking booths with faux-leather seats are arranged along one wall. It looks like a welcoming space for chowing down on traditional pub fare.

Catching the bartender's eye, he orders a bottle of Bud and tosses a ten-dollar bill onto the bar top. The beer gets slapped down in front of him. The barkeep grabs the ten-spot and gives him a questioning look.

"Keep the change," Eli says with a wink.

The guy nods, shoots him a quick smile, and makes his way to the cash register.

Eli uses the mirror behind the bar to scope out the area behind himself. Scanning left and right, he eyeballs the drinkers. No one looks suspicious. He wonders how many times in his life he's used barroom mirrors and glass storefronts to check his surroundings. By now it's virtually reflexive.

The guy to his left speaks loudly in a voice thick with alcohol. He's drinking scotch on the rocks. The stuff smells like low-octane gasoline. Eli puts the beer bottle to his lips, takes a small slug, and glances at his watch. He'll kill another ten minutes and leave.

After downing two more sips of beer, he sets the bottle onto the bar top. The tavern is getting even more crowded, and the noise level is now approaching an ear-bleeding level. He waits another three or four minutes, glances at his watch, then weaves his way toward the front door.

It's ten minutes past eight o'clock.

Party time.

34

He enters the lobby.

The doorman stands next to a sign that reads ALL VISITORS MUST BE ANNOUNCED.

There's no evidence of CCTV cameras anywhere in the lobby. After calling upstairs, the doorman directs him to apartment 12-N.

Eli opens his overcoat and approaches the elevator.

A man and woman—two thirtysomethings—are waiting for the elevator. They speak to each other in French. Though he doesn't speak the language, from their vocal tones and facial expressions, Eli's certain they're having a low-level argument.

An arguing couple can be an effective distraction as a prelude to an assassination. Eli's seen Mossad use that ploy in Beirut. Though it's unlikely to occur with these two, he can't assume anything and won't take a chance.

When the elevator arrives, Eli gestures for them to enter the compartment. The man nods, gives him a semismile, and they both enter the elevator. Eli follows them with his right hand in his pants pocket, ready to pull the knife and slash their carotid arteries if there's a sudden movement.

The couple is now whispering to each other. The guy sighs, looks frustrated, then presses the button for the eighteenth floor. Watching them from the corner of his eye, Eli pushes the button for the sixth floor and leans against the elevator wall, facing the couple. They all stand in silence as the elevator rises. At the sixth floor, the elevator stops, the door slides open, and Eli slips quickly out of the elevator. He walks along the hallway, enters a stairwell, and climbs to the twelfth floor.

A coat rack on wheels stands near the door to apartment 12-N. Based on the number of coats, he estimates there are at least thirty people at the gathering.

He hangs up his overcoat, wondering if any Odessa mafia operatives are at the party. It would be surprising if none are present. After all, it's unlikely they trust him enough to let him approach Irina Sakharov without some kind of scrutiny. Or is he being overly cautious?

Entering the apartment, he recognizes the resinous odor of marijuana. He passes through a small foyer into a crowded living room. People are sipping champagne, chatting, and nibbling finger food. Soft jazz is coming through a sound system; the piano sounds like Bill Evans playing his version of "Autumn Leaves," a song that for Eli has always had a melancholic feel.

A bartender wearing black slacks, a white shirt, and a red bow tie stands behind a portable bar at one end of the living room. He serves flutes of champagne while a young woman, dressed in similar attire, carries a tray of hors d'oeuvres around the room.

Weaving her way through the throng, a woman with dark hair and liquid brown eyes approaches. She appears to be almost slinking toward him. It's clear she's been waiting for him to arrive. "Hello there," she says as a smile creases her face. "I'm Sasha Bortsov. And you must be Aiden." Extending her hand, she moves closer, so near, he gets a whiff of her perfume.

The handshake goes on too long for Eli's taste. Her palm is moist and hot. *She knows me by sight; she must have seen my photo. Where and when was my picture taken? It must have been at Grand Central. I've been careless. Another good reason to get out of this life.*

"Yes, I'm Aiden," he replies, keeping his voice even. "Glad to meet you."

Her grip is firm, and she holds on to his hand for another few moments, far longer than necessary. It's clearly a message: *I know who you are and why you're here.*

Sasha Bortsov is a good-looking woman of about forty, maybe a bit older, but it's tough to tell. In the room's subtle lighting, he's not sure if crow's-feet radiate from the corners of her eyes. He thinks he sees a lattice of fine lines on her face. She has pale skin made more noticeable by the generous application of ruby-red lipstick. Gold earrings dangle from her ears. Her fingernails are covered with mint-colored polish but for the fourth finger of each hand, which is painted with a high-gloss black. She wears a black sheath dress that shows a generous amount of cleavage.

"How did you recognize me?" he asks, annoyed at his own carelessness with Gorlov, with Agapov, and now, meeting someone who's connected to the Odessa mafia.

"Oh, a friend described you," Sasha says with a half smile forming on her lips. "And I'm always on the lookout for a good-looking man."

Yet another hint that she knows not only who I am but why I'm here. She's the one who'll be watching me approach Irina Sakharov.

"Who's this friend?" he asks, ignoring her comment about his looks.

There's a playful glimmer in her eyes as her lips curl into a smile. She's toying with him, seems to find him amusing. "Oh, a friend of mine who lives in Brooklyn told me about you," she says.

There's a laconic casualness to her response, and despite the dim lighting, he thinks he sees her eyes roll upward.

Of course she's alluding to Anton Gorlov.

"Are you originally from Brooklyn?" he asks.

"Yes, but I left a long time ago."

"And you live here now?"

"Yes."

Her eyes brighten as she shoots him another smile. She's giving him nonverbal signals about his role this evening. And it's likely she's aware of the work he's done for the Odessa mafia.

There's little doubt she's connected to the syndicate.

Is it possible Gorlov has a stake in her health club? Sure, why not? Mobsters infiltrate legitimate businesses to launder money. Allemegne and Danika Banks aren't the only vehicles Gorlov uses to wash funds. Just as the Odessa mafia has different revenue streams, it has different ways to scrub away evidence of its activities.

As she makes small talk, Eli finds himself recoiling inwardly, knowing Sasha Bortsov is involved in a scheme to set up her own cousin.

And very likely have her killed.

Or kidnapped, spirited away to a foreign country, and forced into the sex trafficking trade.

That's one of the ugly things about these mobs—family or not—when you boil it down to basics, betrayal is always part of the picture. There's no room for attachment or loyalty or a shred of sentiment. There's this mantra about blood connections between and among mafia members of any ethnic persuasion—all this crap about family, brothers, honor, loyalty—but it's all bullshit.

In the end it's all about money.

And self-preservation.

"Can I offer you a flute of champagne?" she asks in unadulterated Brooklynese, glancing toward the bartender.

Strangely, she doesn't have a hint of a Russian or Eastern European accent. Was she born in Brooklyn?

"No thanks," he replies. "Not right now."

She nods. "Why don't I introduce you to a few people?" she says, grasping his arm and guiding him toward the center of the room.

He again notices her casual affability. She greets and exchanges ladies-who-lunch air kisses with a few guests she apparently hadn't talked with earlier. She's adroit at social banter, but her geniality feels counterfeit. And there's something else: she radiates a distinct feral quality, a not-so-subtle hint of predation, yet somehow remains attractive, even appealing.

"How'd you get here?" she asks as they move through the crowd.

"By subway," he replies.

"Was the train crowded?"

She says "train" not "subway." Spoken like a true New Yorker.

"For a Friday evening, it wasn't bad," he says, doing his best to give her a casual response.

Eli scopes out the other guests; his eyes dart left and right, looking for anyone who has what might be considered to have a "Russian" appearance. Though there's no single copyrighted look, there's a certain Slavic-type face mixed with subtle Mongol features—something often viewed as a semitypical Russian appearance.

But there are no hulking men with shaved heads; not a single guy in the room is wearing an ill-fitting suit and looking like he could snap your backbone in a second. But appearances can be deceiving, so situational awareness is definitely called for.

Then there are the women. Other than Sasha Bortsov, there's no woman in the room with that pouty Russo-Balkanized look he associates with Melania Trump or Anna Kournikova.

And there are no heavy Eastern European accents to be heard—from either men or women—though the blended babble of the guests makes it difficult to isolate any single speech pattern.

There, too, lack of an accent doesn't necessarily mean a thing. After all, Eli speaks several languages with flawless accents. And he's always kept current, learned to use local idioms and contemporary turns of speech so he'd never be outed as a foreigner.

Everything about this gathering feels false. Especially Sasha Bortsov. Deceit and misdirection are the reasons he's here—to meet Irina Sakharov and gain her confidence.

So she can be relieved of that flash drive.

And then either kidnapped or murdered.

Still hooked on to his arm, Sasha introduces him to a few guests—some teachers, an attorney, a doctor, and two neighbors who live in the building. There are casual introductions along with small talk, a social skill Eli long ago mastered through Mossad training. With repeated exposure, he learned to banter with strangers in four languages, though mostly in English—at embassies, in consulates, on yachts, at glitzy casinos, and at staid conventions.

Sasha introduces him to a British couple. The wife has huge brown eyes that remind Eli of a lemur. The husband's Adam's apple bobs up and down as he gulps champagne and looks unsteady on his feet.

After some inane chitchat, Sasha turns to him and says, "I'll leave you to yourself, Aiden, so you can circulate and meet a few other people." That enigmatic smile plays on her lips—this one has a conspiratorial tinge so obvious, Eli decides he dislikes Sasha Bortsov. Intensely.

Her eyes swerve to the far corner of the room, then back to Eli's before she turns abruptly and fades into the throng.

He waits for a few beats and then, without appearing obvious, peers across the room to where Sasha's gaze had settled momentarily.

Amid the buzz of conversation, he spots a woman who just may be Irina Sakharov.

35

She stands alone, gazing out a window with her back to the crowd.

Though he can't be certain, she looks like she could be the woman in the photo, Irina Sakharov. Nearly six feet tall in heels, with her blond hair pulled back into a French braid, she's the only woman in the room whose body type and stature appear to match that of the picture in the dossier.

Threading through a clot of people, he drifts toward the window where she stands stock-still, staring out at the cityscape.

He stops a slight distance behind her. Peering over her shoulder, he too looks out at the cityscape. The lights seem to flicker in the wintery night air.

Still gazing out the window, she has no idea he's standing behind her.

He moves a bit closer.

As though she suddenly senses his presence, she turns, looks momentarily startled as her mouth opens, and her eyebrows rise inquisitively.

Yes, it's Irina Sakharov.

And the photo didn't do her justice: she's gorgeous. It may be her height or the lustrous blond hair or something indefinable, but in a moment of stunning clarity, Eli realizes he could be looking at a mature version of Hannah.

The flash memory of his long-dead wife brings on an aura so powerful, his heart jumps and the room seems momentarily to sway. Collecting himself, he realizes that Irina Sakharov's sapphire-blue eyes are the feature most evocative of Hannah. But it's an emotionally driven illusion. This woman is beautiful in her own unique way.

With her hair pulled back, her heart-shaped face is striking. She has a high forehead accentuated by her hairstyle. And that hair: it's a natural golden-blond highlighted by the room's subtle illumination. Her skin appears pale, smooth, and dewy. Her chin has a soft, rounded underbelly set below full, sensuous lips. Her prominent cheekbones emphasize an exotic Slavic look, one that seizes him in a stunning moment. The overall effect is one of gentle beauty.

And there's a burgeoning sense of sadness.

A long moment passes as his thoughts spiral. He tries gathering them, but it's difficult. He's never felt so tongue-tied as he does at this moment.

But then the words come to him. "Were you looking at something interesting out there?" he asks, so near her now, he thinks he smells a distinct floral fragrance, perhaps lilac or honeysuckle.

"Yes, it is interesting, but is a mystery. I was looking at sky," she says in a voice that has a breathy alto quality. It's not a sensual affectation; it's her natural sound.

Her accent and speech pattern are lyrical.

"What kind of mystery?"

"Here, in city, I see no stars at night."

The dossier: her command of English is somewhat limited, but she communicates well.

"Yes, the city lights hide them at night," he says. "You have to be in the country to see the stars."

She smiles, seems to blush, and casts her gaze downward.

It's obvious she's shy, has trouble making direct eye contact. And it's likely she's not very skilled with people, doesn't fall into conversation easily, especially with a stranger who approaches out of nowhere and begins speaking to her.

The sound system is putting out the languorous melody of "Time on My Hands." The trumpet solo reminds him of Chet Baker's horn. The tone is so smooth, Eli senses he's floating on a soft ribbon of sound. He feels momentarily woozy, yet hasn't had a drop of champagne. The image of Hannah is gone as he stares at Irina Sakharov.

"I'm Aiden." His heartbeat feels like it's storming through his chest.

He moves a half step closer.

Her eyes drift upward to meet his gaze. "I am Irina." Her eyes then flit down and away.

Though the lighting is dim, he's certain her face is flushed.

This is uncomfortable for her. She has very little confidence.

"I don't know anyone here," he says, knowing it's true, and more important, he senses a small opening that might allow a conversation to begin. He's always been able to get people talking, though at this moment he has little trust in his social skills and realizes he's searching for something to say, anything to prolong the conversation.

"I know only cousin," she says, again making fleeting eye contact.

"Who's your cousin?" he asks, feigning ignorance.

"Sasha. She owns apartment. I am guest here."

"Yes, I just met her," he says, continuing the charade. "We talked for a while. She's lovely."

"She is very kind person," Irina says, blinking rapidly.

There's something engaging about this woman. He senses she's not only self-conscious—even timid—but is exquisitely vulnerable. Yes, she's guileless, an innocent, untutored in the ways of the world. Or is he jumping to an unwarranted conclusion?

He knows from Gorlov and the dossier that her father died years ago and she recently lost her mother. And her brother committed suicide, as Gorlov would have the world believe. Except for her cousin Sasha, she's adrift in a strange city far from everything she's ever known. She's alone in the world. And has no idea she's ultimately going to be in the crosshairs of the Odessa mafia.

My God, what am I doing here? Why have I allowed myself to become part of this obscene scheme?

"I stay here with Sasha," she says. "For some months I am here, but soon I will get place of my own. Sasha has friend who owns place and is soon leaving for Europe. It is where I will be staying."

"So, you recently came to New York?"

"Yes. I been here only a few months."

"Where did you come from?"

"Russia. From Moscow."

"It must be a big change to come to New York."

She looks directly at him, finally holds his gaze. "Yes, but Sasha makes it easy for me. She is very good to me even though we never seen each other before now. She is cousin on mother's side. She let me stay here and gives me good job."

"Doing what?"

"I work at gymnasium, Sasha's Healthworks on Third Avenue—a few streets from where we are here. I answer telephones and make appointments for customers. And she pay good money, enough so I save for place of my own."

"What did you do in Russia?"

She hesitates, seems reluctant to answer.

He genuinely wants to know more about her, more than the dossier revealed. He could never have guessed he'd be so curious about this woman.

"I study to become actress. I make some television commercials. Nothing more. It was not working out for me. There is little work for me there, and after Mama dies, I leave. And here I am now."

She mixes up her tenses in a delightful way.

"Russia. I've never been there. What's it like?"

"Life is hard. Putin is rich. The people, not so rich," she adds, shaking her head. "It is very hard place. It is not for me."

He nods, knowing there must be an enormous contrast between Moscow and the sophisticated Gramercy Park section of Manhattan.

"What do *you* do?" she asks, now holding his gaze.

"I work with computers."

"Oh, technologic, yes?"

"Yes."

There's another pause. Eli searches for something to fill what might become a conversational vacuum. He's always been verbally adroit, but at this moment he's not sure what to say. He doesn't want to lose her for lack of something to discuss. "Do you have other relatives in New York?" he asks.

She shakes her head. For a moment she says nothing and her face remains neutral.

Eli senses she's gauging whether or not to reveal more, and if so, how much to divulge.

Suddenly her eyes grow moist. Her face turns red, then twists into the beginnings of a grimace. Vertical furrows form between her eyebrows, and her lower lip begins quivering. She looks as though she'll burst into tears.

"Did I say something that upset you?"

"No, no . . . it's just . . ."

Of all things, he feels a pang of sadness and is overcome by the strangest wish to console her.

"Just what?"

"My brother."

"Your brother? What about him?"

Iridescent tears form at the corners of her eyes, collect at the lower lids, then begin a slow trek down her cheeks.

Feeling a rush of pity for her—it's something tender and empathic—he stifles the temptation to gently brush her tears away. And then too, a shiver of excitement overtakes him. It feels electric.

"I am sorry," she whispers, then takes a shaky breath, blinks a few times, rapidly, and swipes at her tears with the tip of her index finger.

"Oh, don't be sorry. Don't . . ." But he doesn't know what else to say.

It was wrong to ask about other relatives. He already knew the answer and should have realized the question would upset her. God, he can barely tolerate this ruse. It's a quiet kind of cruelty to have asked about her brother. There's no doubt the poor bastard was helped out a window by Gorlov's thugs.

Eli feels more than deceptive; he feels dirty.

And he feels an attraction. It's more than merely physical.

Something about her touches him. Deeply.

And it suddenly strikes him even more powerfully than before: the Bratva will eliminate her for no other reason than the possibility that she may someday come to possess that flash drive, which could expose Gorlov's financial crimes.

She's a loose thread in his plan to begin living a new life.

Irina Sakharov's fate has already been decided.

And now Irina Sakharov is much more than a name and a brief description on a dossier. She's a sad and beautiful young woman who has no idea of the danger lurking at the edges of her life.

"I didn't mean to upset you," he whispers. "I don't want to . . ." He can't find more words.

He's at a conversational dead end.

"Is not your fault," she says as her chest heaves. She takes a few shaky breaths. "It's just that . . . my brother, he died."

She now gazes directly at him with those wet eyes. They glimmer in the lighting, and the tears make them look like they're changing color, from sapphire to a grayish blue.

Hannah's eyes did the same thing.

"I'm so sorry," he says, knowing he truly means it. He understands her loneliness, her sadness, her feeling of being bereft in the world. She's truly alone, burdened by a sense of loss, of desolation, feelings he knows all too well.

She lives with a distant cousin who is part of a cabal trying to extract that flash drive from her. And then kill her. Or traffic her to some remote corner of the world as a sex slave.

It's because of her looks that Gorlov won't have her killed when the problem of the flash drive is behind him. She has no family—other than Sasha Bortsov, who doesn't give a shit about her—so they won't have to threaten her family to keep her from trying to escape. No one will know or care that she's disappeared. The mob will have her locked away in an underground brothel somewhere in Europe or the Middle East, use her for the customers' satisfaction until she's older, maybe in her late forties, when she's no longer sexually marketable. Then, to maximize her value, she'll be killed and her organs will be harvested to be sold in the illegal transplant market.

That's the emotional valence of these mobsters. They see everything as a business opportunity. They're vile. Scum.

All these gangsters deserve to die. They're every bit as cruel and loathsome as the terrorists he's killed. At least those guerrillas were fighting for a cause. For the mob, it's just about money.

Throughout the room people are nibbling on food, sipping champagne, chatting, laughing, enjoying themselves, while now the sound of a saxophone solo seeps through the sound system. And in the midst of all this normality, he's part of an ugly scheme to end this woman's life as she now knows it.

Something tugs at him, threatens to suffocate him.

It's grief, a cold shadow coming over him.

And now it feels like a claw burrowing into his chest, squeezing his heart.

Yes, it's the anguish of loss—his own and hers.

It's also regret.

For what he's doing. For the life he's led.

He reflexively reaches for her. "I'm *so* sorry," he whispers, his throat constricting.

He suddenly realizes that without thinking he's set his hand on her shoulder.

He's tempted to embrace her; it would be both empathic and sexual, but he can't succumb to the urge.

How did it come down to this? This whole thing is insane. What am I doing here?

He tries to smother the sorrow he feels for her.

And the attraction.

Yet his hand remains on her shoulder.

With her head bowed, she raises her arm and sets her hand on top of his.

Her touch makes his skin tingle.

A rush of thoughts streaks through his mind: how lost and alone he is, how hollow his life—his soul—has become after all these years of tracking and killing and seeking revenge. He thinks of Hannah and David, the son he never had, the son who now would be nearly eighteen, but his was a life unlived. Ezra and Mom and Pop and Hannah are now only distant recollections.

Everything that was meaningful is now no more than a memory.

And this woman's sorrow makes him realize the misery-laden life he's been living since they died.

This will end badly for her, and he knows even now—less than five minutes after meeting her—he feels more than attraction for her. They share sadness, soul-crushing grief.

But he's just a cog in the machinery of her inevitable demise.

For the first time since he approached her, she holds his gaze.

He moves toward her; so close the scent of her skin and the fragrance of her hair are intoxicating.

His hand envelops hers and he whispers, "Have you had dinner?"

She shakes her head, still gazing at him with those sad eyes.

"There's a pub just down the street," he says. "We can get something to eat."

He can barely believe how anxious he is for her to say yes.

She nods as a single tear trickles down her left cheek.

He wipes it away with his index finger.

She smiles and tilts her head at him, as though she's waiting for a kiss.

Through the babble of conversation and background music, with his heart kicking crazily, Eli takes her arm gently and says, "Let's get out of here."

36

Anton Gorlov moves his knight to a new position on the chessboard.

"Ah, Anton, that was a fatal mistake," Viktor says, dipping his head to peer over his reading glasses. He moves his bishop to a position where checkmate is now inevitable.

"One thing is certain," Gorlov says, "I'm no Garry Kasparov."

Anton acknowledges to himself that Viktor has won this game, as he so often does. A smart man, he sees four steps ahead of where they are at any given moment. It's a good quality to have, especially for a pakhan. A quality that's served Anton very well. Yes, Viktor would have been a good pakhan if he'd had the ambition to slash his way to the top as Anton did.

"It makes me feel terrible to beat you," Viktor says, shaking his head. "I have no right to defeat my pakhan."

"Ah, Viktor, you should never feel that way. When the game is over, the king and the pawn go into the same box."

Viktor smiles and nods. "So true. When the game is over, death waits for us all."

"Lately I've been thinking about that—maybe too much, but I suppose it's inevitable once you reach a certain age." With a heavy sigh, Gorlov shoves the chess pieces aside and looks at his watch.

"You haven't played well lately." Viktor's lips spread into a thin line.

"It's because all I can think about is this fellow Aiden and what's going to happen with this woman, Irina Sakharov." He glances at his watch. "It's nine thirty. He's probably met her by now."

"Yes, he was asked to get there by eight. Let's hope a small spark ignites between them."

"We can hope, but who knows," Anton says. "Let's face it. We don't know a thing about this woman. And we know even less about Aiden. So who knows where this may go."

"I agree. As you know, Anton, from the beginning I've had my doubts about this arrangement. There are too many unknowns, and it makes me uneasy. I'm surprised we're doing it this way. I've never known you to feel comfortable when you don't know the outcome of a situation before it comes to pass. It isn't like you."

"Very true, but we have no choice here. And hopefully we're coming close to the finish line in this business. I've grown tired of the deception, the things we must do to keep things going. I think that after all these years, it's worn me down, the constant vigilance, the fights for territory, the wars. What's the meaning of it? What good comes from it? I'm glad it will soon come to an end."

At that moment Anton's stomach squeals and groans, sounds like a boiler factory. A spurt of acid shoots up his gullet and sears the back of his throat. This heartburn happens when he's under stress. Or when he eats too much and too fast. Dr. Voloshin, his cardiologist, didn't like the way his heart looked on an echocardiogram. He said, "Anton, your heart is enlarged because you're not controlling your blood pressure. You must lose weight and eat less fat." And he harps on him constantly, says the way he eats—rich food he tears into like a starving wolf—worsens the acid reflux, which he calls GERD. On top of that, the good doctor says Anton's weight—275 pounds—is putting a strain on his heart, and he insists that it would be wise to lose forty or fifty pounds because if Anton keeps gaining weight, his heart will fail.

So, if that happens, his life will be over. To die a natural death would be different from what he's expected all these years. It would be better to die in bed than to suffer a violent death at the hands of a criminal organization. So much for watching his weight. He'll take his chances.

Just eat what you want, enjoy the comfort of good food, and live as good a life as possible. And don't worry. Whether because of overeating or violence, one way or another, death will come for you, as it does for everyone.

He reaches for the bottle of extra-strength Rolaids, extracts two tablets, pops them in his mouth, and begins chewing. Relief will come soon. And maybe he'll begin dieting just to please Katerina and get her off his back. Perhaps he'll do it after they've left the country and can live in peace without all this Bratva business.

"Getting back to this situation with Aiden and Irina Sakharov," Viktor says. "I don't want to harp on this, but I can't help but be pessimistic about the chances of it working the way we want it to. Let's face it: matters of the heart are never easy to understand. And as you yourself implied, we have no control over what happens between Aiden and this woman . . . this Irina."

"Ah, Viktor, I can't disagree with you, but don't you believe in love at first sight?" Gorlov says with a smile forming on his lips, knowing he's asking a loaded question.

Viktor laughs. "Love at first sight? That's fiction. Sexual attraction? Lust? Yes. But love? No."

Gorlov picks up his glass of warm milk and sips without taking his eyes off Viktor. He sighs. "Before I met Nadia, I never believed in it. But there *is* such a thing. I know because the moment I saw Nadia, I fell in love."

My God, it seems like only yesterday. Where have all the years gone? And now they fly by faster and faster. I fear it's all heading toward the end.

"I'll never forget that moment," Anton murmurs through a wash of sadness. "It was like something struck me in the chest and burrowed into my heart. I was sitting with Boris at that restaurant Varenichnaya, on Brighton Second Street. This beautiful woman walked in with this no-goodnik. I was so taken by her that I was tempted to go over to their table and pull her away from him."

"Knowing you, I'm surprised you didn't do just that," Viktor says. "So, what happened?"

"I called the maître d' over. He told me her name was Nadia Belyanko and said she lived on Brighton Eighth. So when I got home, I looked up her number and called her that very same evening, only a few hours later, and said I saw her at the restaurant and that it was impossible for me to forget her."

"You actually *said* that?"

"Yes. I was desperate to see her. At first she resisted; she thought I was some kind of lecher or maybe I was insane. But I persisted and told her a little about myself, and luckily, I knew a few people she knew, so there was a connection. And she gave in."

Recalling her voice on the telephone that night, Anton feels heat in his cheeks. But at least the burn at the back of his throat is gone. Thank God for Rolaids.

"So, what happened?" Viktor asks.

"We went out two evenings later, to a French restaurant in Manhattan, a place in the West Thirties," Anton says, recalling the bistro's Parisian atmosphere. At this moment he can virtually taste the French onion soup and the coq au vin. "We couldn't read the menu with all those French dishes, but it didn't matter. We had such a good time, I realized I'd never felt that way in my life. Four months later, we were married."

He pictures Nadia all those years ago: tall, dark haired, and elegant, with the most soulful eyes. "I tell you, Viktor, she had a musical voice. That voice of hers *sang* to me."

Viktor nods. "Yes, I remember her voice. It was lovely."

"And then at forty-two, the breast cancer took her—the same thing that took my mother."

"But now you have Katerina," Viktor says, pouring a splash of vodka into a glass, then downing it in a gulp. "Once we leave, it will be a new life."

"Ah, Katerina is a fine woman, but she is not my Nadia." He nearly chokes on his sadness.

Gorlov hates displaying sentiment to a subordinate. But there's no need to keep up a pakhan's facade with Viktor. He's truly a brother. And the man is one lucky son of a bitch: at sixty he's been married to Oksana for thirty-five years. They have two grown daughters who love Viktor the way a Russian loves borscht.

"But back to this Irina," Gorlov says as he sips more milk, then drains the glass. "If she and Aiden become a couple, maybe everything will be taken care of."

Viktor nods. "I still think it's a long shot, but we can hope. You mentioned everything being taken care of. Speaking of *everything*, I'm reminded there are some other people we have to take a look at."

"Yes, I was thinking that, too," Anton says, setting the empty milk glass on the table.

"Anyone specifically?"

"Another financial person," Gorlov replies.

"At the bank?"

"Yes," Gorlov says. "We can leave no unfinished business here. There can be no loose ends."

37

O'Malley's Pub is more crowded than before.

The bar is so jam-packed that despite the cold weather, patrons are standing in the entranceway. With bottles of beer or drinks in hand, they don't seem to mind the rush of icy air blasting over them each time the door opens.

Eli and Irina wend their way through the bar crowd and head toward the rear room.

Standing at the entrance to the dining area, the maître d' nods at their approach. "Good evening. Table for two?"

"Yes, please, for dinner," Eli says. He points to a booth in the far corner of the dining room. "How about that booth?"

"I'm sorry, sir, that's reserved for four."

Eli slips him a crisp twenty already folded in his palm.

The maître d' slides the bill into his pocket, smiles obligingly, grabs two menus from his lectern, then leads them to the corner booth.

Two guys at a nearby table laser in on Irina as she and Eli are escorted across the room.

They stare so lustfully, Eli's tempted to toss them a *fuck-off* look. But that's ridiculous, even more than immature. Knowing he could demolish them with a few Krav Maga moves, he stares straight ahead as he and Irina are led to the booth.

Ordinarily, he'd sit with his back to the wall, but not tonight: he'll let Irina have a view of the room. So he sits facing the brick wall behind her.

"I am glad we leave party," Irina says as they settle into the booth.

"I am too. We can talk here."

A wall sconce bathes Irina in buttery light. Even more than at Sasha Bortsov's apartment, Eli's mesmerized by her beauty.

An aproned waiter—a crew-cut thirtyish guy—introduces himself as Eric. "I'll be your server tonight." Eric strikes Eli as cloyingly officious as he jabbers smarmily about the place having "the best pub food in the city."

Eli wonders if Irina has mastered enough English to negotiate a menu, even the relatively simple fare of an American pub.

"Would you care to start with a drink?" Eric asks.

"Maybe a glass of white wine?" Irina says, peering at Eli.

"We'll have two glasses of the house white," he tells the waiter.

"It's an oaky Napa Valley chardonnay—an excellent choice," Eric says.

After a few more unctuous statements, he disappears.

"What looks good to you?" Eli asks.

"Maybe the *soup de jour*," she says with a French accent and a quick smile.

"Do you speak French?"

"*Un petit peu.*"

"We'll find out what kind of soup it is."

When Eric returns with their glasses of wine, Eli asks about the soup.

"It's butternut squash. Delicious and very popular."

Irina nods, obviously approving.

"We'll each have a cup of that," Eli says. He turns to Irina. "What else would you like?"

He's aware he's speaking slowly, using simple words, and hopes he doesn't sound patronizing.

"*Le hamburger.*"

"How would you like it cooked?" Eric asks, bending close to her.

"With red inside, but not much red."

"We'll have two burgers, medium rare," Eli says.

"Another good choice, sir," Eric says. "They're grilled on an open fire and come with the best french fries in the city."

When Eric disappears, they clink their glasses together and sip the wine.

"It is very nice," she says with a smile and sets her glass back on the table. "Like oak," she adds with a laugh, gently mocking Eric. Laughing, they touch glasses again and sip more wine.

Eli's aware he's abandoned caution. Right now a button man could be loitering outside the tavern, waiting for them to walk out to the street. Or he could walk casually into this back room and blow him away. With his back to the entrance, Eli would never see it coming.

If a hit man comes for him, Irina would be collateral damage. Eli's once again reminded that he forfeited his anonymity by meeting with both pakhans. And Gorlov's people know precisely where he is tonight. So right now he's a soft target.

But Gorlov has an investment in Eli's getting this job done, so for the moment he's safe.

But if Agapov's men ever learn what he did with that cigar, they'll come for him.

"I think you are very kind man," Irina says, gazing at him.

Her words interrupt his preoccupation.

"Really?" he replies, feeling remorse for his duplicity. If this poor woman knew why they're here now, she wouldn't think he's so kind.

"When you asked about brother," she says, "I could see the sadness in your eyes."

"And I could see the sadness in yours. I could *feel* it in you."

"Did you ever lose someone you love?" she asks.

"Yes, it was a long time ago." Even as he says it, he visualizes the medics in orange and red vests, the charred and twisted remnants of that bus, the blood-soaked asphalt, rows of covered bodies, and the sickening smells of burned plastic, charred flesh, and blackened bone crawl into his sinuses. Stifling the perceptions, he focuses on her.

"Tell me," she says.

"Maybe some other time. It's too sad to talk about right now."

She nods. "I will listen another time."

She's willing to see me again.

"But your brother," he whispers, feeling corrupt for pursuing it. "I mean, if you want to talk about it . . ."

She draws a shaky breath, then fixes him with those crystal-clear blue eyes. "It is sad that he would do such a thing, to kill himself," she says.

"He killed himself?" Eli whispers, feigning surprise even as he feels a pang of self-loathing.

"Yes."

"Do you know why?"

She shakes her head. "He never was sad man. Maybe years ago when girlfriend leave him back in Russia, he was upset, but that was long time before. I think he was happy coming here to US."

"So, what happened?"

She draws another deep breath. "He called me that day," she says in a near whisper. "He says to me he is feeling so sad, and nervous too. Very nervous."

"Did he say why?"

"He was working for bank. There was money they don't find. I don't know what he was talking about. He was afraid for going to jail. He said he has big troubles. But . . ." She hesitates and draws another deep breath.

"But what?" he asks.

"His voice," she says, "it sounds strange to me. Like he been putting on brave act for me, maybe hiding something. He sounds scared, like people maybe want to get him. But I dunno." Her eyes gleam in the room's lighting.

"Why would they want to get him?"

She shrugs. "It was just a feeling I have. I drop everything at work and tell Sasha I must go see brother, that Grigory sounds sick. I rush to his house on Seventy-Nine Street.

"When I get there, I see crowd outside building. And I see police with lights and sirens and ambulance too." Her voice is strangled. "And . . . and I see . . . lying on the ground is body covered with blanket. They tell me that Grigory . . . he jumps from window, that he lands on sidewalk and dies."

A soft, choking sound comes from deep in her throat. A lone tear spills from her eye, runs down her cheek.

There are no words to convey the rush of feelings overwhelming him. He'd sound insincere offering condolences. And his voice will surely quaver and break. Swallowing hard, he says nothing as his hands slide across the table and slip gently over hers.

Looking up, she gives him a wan smile.

Her hands move out from under his and latch on to them. She squeezes his hands, and he feels a moment of intense connection with her.

In a voice thick with feeling, she says, "I dunno if he kill himself or maybe something else . . ."

"Something else? Like what?"

Jesus, this fakery is repulsive.

A deep ache overtakes him. The pain is as much for himself as for her.

She peers at him. "And you, Aiden? Who in your life do you lose?"

She's still holding his hands in hers.

He wants to share things with her but knows it's so difficult in the midst of this ruse. "My brother. When I was six and he was a baby."

"What happened?"

More lies. More deception.

This is torture.

"He died from an infection in his heart."

"And your family?"

"They're gone. A long time ago."

"*All* gone?" Her mouth opens.

"Yes. All of them."

"Oh, how sad." She squeezes his hands again. "What happened?"

"An accident. They were on a bus that crashed and caught fire. Everyone died."

My life's a complete lie, even about death.

She shakes her head and squeezes his hand.

He won't say a word about the nightmares or the memories that flood him. He banishes the image of the burial grounds on the Mount of Olives and the parades of mourners weeping in the grief of living beyond those they loved.

"And now," she murmurs, "you want to be happy?"

His throat tightens as he shakes his head. "I don't trust happy."

Her face conveys empathy, along with sadness and regret.

For both of them.

"We are both orphans," she says in a voice barely above a whisper.

He nods, aware they share terrible loss along with abiding sadness.

He knows he'll try to find out about that flash drive and then warn her about Gorlov. He'll buy time, as much as possible. Eli can tell Gorlov she isn't opening up so easily, that he needs more time—enough time for her to feel comfortable with him so when he tells her what's going on, she won't think he's conjuring some sick tale. It might allow him to learn what, if anything, she knows about that flash drive, and then he can get himself out of the country and end the insanity of his life.

It'll take time because, despite this moment, he's a stranger to her. It'll be a while before there's enough closeness for her to divulge things.

And when that happens, he'll do what he can to help her escape the horror of what awaits her: death or enslavement.

38

Eric appears with the soup.

They agree that the waiter was right; it's delicious, and its warmth is soothing on this cold night.

Then come the burgers—half pounders, perfectly chargrilled to a juicy medium rare—arriving on oversize oval-shaped plates. A heap of sizzling hot and crispy french fries rests alongside each burger, accompanied by the requisite sliced tomato and spear of kosher dill pickle.

Eli notices that despite her sadness, Irina eats robustly. Unlike so many women he's known over the last few years, Irina enjoys food with the same gusto his wife did. She's definitely not a "dressing on the side" kind of woman.

Seeing Irina enjoying her food lightens his mood. Even thinking about Hannah's similar passion doesn't darken his spirits. In fact, watching Irina devour that burger makes him feel more alive than he has in a long time.

After dinner she describes her life in Russia. "It was hard taking care of mother and to make living. I wanted to come to US to be with Grigory, but I must be with her and be a nurse. She has very bad health. When she die, I come here."

"Do you have pictures of your family?"

"Just a few."

"Of your brother too?"

"That's all I have now. Pictures of him and mother and father."

"Did he leave you anything?"

"Just clothing and a little money."

He can't ask about a safe-deposit box. It would seem completely out of line at this point in their—in their—what? What do they have at this moment? What *are* they to each other? Is this the beginning of a *relationship*?

It's impossible to even *imagine* feeling comfortable asking about a flash drive. Not when they met only a few hours ago by what appears—to her—to have been sheer happenstance.

"Tell me about you, Aiden," she says. "I want to know your life."

As a Mossad agent, he learned to construct many a personal life story, each going beyond a false name and occupation. Over the years Eli's mastered the art of recalling all the identities he's assumed.

He was told by the Mossad evaluation team that he has an eidetic—or photographic—memory. He sees something once, he sees it forever. It's served him well, and he's yet to have slipped up. To some people he's a reporter; to others a screenwriter; a few know him as a skip tracer (when he's tracking down some mobster living in Arizona as part of the WITSEC program).

The Mossad trained him to become a master of deceit and an expert liar.

But it would feel liberating to give up the lies, the chameleon-like fronts, the deceptions, to be able to talk freely.

Yet he holds back. He can tell her more another time, in the future.

But will there be a future for her?

Will she survive?

Tell me about you, Aiden. I want to know your life.

She already knows he does "technological" work. So, he describes a fictional life in New York, helping people with their computer setups and technical problems. He even relates some humorous anecdotes about his clients.

Then he changes the subject. "You said you studied acting before you came here?"

"I study, but there is no work for me."

"No work? The way you look. You're so . . ."

She blushes and looks down at the table, then gazes at him with a weak smile.

"Don't tell me you've never been told you're beautiful."

It's clear she's embarrassed. It's the curse of those who feel they don't measure up to some standard imposed on them as children, then internalized to haunt them for the rest of their lives.

"When I was little girl, I was not looking good. I had bad skin and flat chest. Other girls make fun of me."

She needs to deflect the compliment.

"But, of course, that changed," he says, knowing the compliment might embarrass her.

"When I was eighteen, the skin got good. And I became developed."

"And then?"

"Then I study acting."

"And why was there no work for you?"

"Because I won't do things . . . things people want me to do."

He knows precisely what she means. "And here?"

"My English is not good enough to be actor."

"And it would be the same here," he says, thinking of the Harvey Weinstein types. And he again realizes that her beauty would work to her detriment, as it will with the Russians, whether or not they get their hands on that flash drive.

"I gonna study English in spring and see what I can do."

"I could help you with that," he says, knowing it's unlikely they'll have enough time together for him to make good on the offer.

"Really? You will do that?"

"Of course. With me, you'll learn English very quickly."

"That will be nice." She smiles and reaches across the table. Clasping hands, she says, "And now I have money to get apartment. I will leave Sasha's place in a few days. And maybe get different job, something better."

"Good for you. Where's the new place?"

"Only few streets from here. Sasha helps me find it. A friend of hers owns it; it is how do you say? A condo is what it is. And she is going to Europe for a year. Sasha helps me with lease. She even take lease to lawyer who makes sure it is all legal. She is good cousin and helps with everything."

He lifts his empty glass. "To your new digs."

"Digs?" Her eyebrows rise.

"Slang for your new place."

She laughs and nods. "Yes, I stay with you and learn more English." She raises her empty glass in a toast, then sets it back on the table.

"And you, Aiden. What is your name? Your family's name?"

"West," he says, giving her the surname he uses when calling himself Aiden.

Yes, his web of misdirection grows more tortuous each day of his life. It means immersing himself in yet another pseudo-life. The stream of lies is more than a burden on the memory; it's a strain on the soul.

"Aiden West," she says. "I like that name."

My whole life's a sham.

"And I like your name—Irina. It's a beautiful name. What does it mean?"

"Irina? In Russian it means peace."

"Peace," he says. "I like that."

"We both find peace, yes?" she asks with her eyes widening.

"Yes, we'll find peace."

"I am toasting peace," she whispers, raising her empty glass.

39

They emerge from the restaurant to near-freezing temperatures.

The wind has strengthened, the cold air bites at his face. The bare sycamore trees form a swaying tracery overhead as they walk back toward Sasha's building. He's exquisitely aware of Irina at his side, feels close to her in a way he could never have anticipated only a few hours earlier.

They've already shared things about themselves—mostly their grief—and because of that there's a small chance something good will come out of this.

Maybe he can extract some information from her. And then take whatever steps may be necessary to keep her safe. To ensure she'll survive. But there must be more going on than that because the thought of seeing her again fills him with something he hasn't felt for a long time: a sense of anticipation. It's the strangest thing because for the first time in years he's thinking of being with a woman for more than a night or two.

The wind slicing in from the East River lashes at their faces. The street is virtually deserted, the whoosh of Third Avenue traffic sounds muffled in the distance.

He slips his arm around her waist, and she leans closer to him as they walk. He can feel warmth radiating from her.

As they approach the building, he asks, "What's it like living with Sasha?"

"Sasha is good to me. She like big sister. But she worry too much for me."

"Why does she worry?"

"She think I don't know New York. That I should not be alone here. I tell her I come from big city, Moscow. It is busy and noisy, like here. Things not too different there."

Now they're standing beneath the hunter-green awning of Sasha's building. Eli glances about. The streets are deserted; no one's been following them. The doorman is seated behind a counter in the entranceway, looks like he's reading a book. No one is entering or leaving the premises. It's eerily quiet for a Friday night, most likely because of the cold air blowing in off the East River.

As they stand facing each other, clouds of breath vapor billow from their mouths, only to be whipped away by the wind.

She smiles and says, "I think maybe Sasha worry about me now."

"Why?"

"Because I am not at party. She think something happens to me, and she will be looking to find me."

"You're safe with me."

She laughs softly. "She don't know I'm with you."

Yes, she does. Your cousin knows very well you're with me. And she's hoping something happens between us. Sasha only wants what Anton Gorlov wants. And what do I want?

Looking into Irina's eyes, he feels a shudder of desire.

And it's mixed with fear.

For her.

For what will happen to her.

Unless he can do something to prevent what's inevitable.

He moves closer, brushes the backs of his fingers against her cheek.

She closes her eyes, seems to luxuriate in his touch.

Then she opens them, looking into his.

It feels like she can see into his soul.

His fingers remain on her cheek.

She's so near, he smells her skin, or could it be her hair, or the fragrance of some lotion or body wash, something botanical? Whatever it is, it's intoxicating.

Her mouth opens slightly, and he sees the white curve of her upper teeth, feels the moist heat of her breath, and breathes in her scent. There's something delicious about it, the warmth of it, the aroma of wine and of her.

He draws nearer as her face tilts upward, comes closer still.

Her hand rises to his; her fingers rest on his as they remain on her cheek.

He moves his thumb back and forth gently, savoring the softness of her skin.

"Oh, Aiden," she whispers.

His knees feel weak, as though they can no longer support him.

They're so close her face is a blur, and he hears her breath quicken.

It's happening, something he'd thought could never be possible—it's a strange sense of warmth, a wish to be close to someone, to have her in his life.

And he loves it.

If somehow time could stop, suspend itself and never resume, he could luxuriate in this moment. If only things were different.

Even as he thinks this, her hand slips behind his neck, rises to the back of his head, pulls him toward her, and he feels her body against his.

It happens naturally; they're kissing lightly.

He's overwhelmed by the feel of her lips, by their plush softness and moistness, by the taste of her, and he feels the tip of her tongue against his. A current of excitement runs through him—a tremor begins in his legs—and he's aroused in a way that's been absent for so many years.

She pulls back and whispers, "If we could only . . ."

The kiss leaves him breathless.

His heart feels like it's jumping in his chest.

He hasn't felt this way since the first kiss he shared with Hannah, when he realized he wanted to be with her. Always.

"Another time, Aiden . . . Yes?"

"Yes, another time."

"When I have my place, not at Sasha's."

"I understand," he whispers. "Give me your number."

Reaching into her purse, she removes a cell phone and they exchange numbers.

"I call you after work," she says. "Two days from here, after I move to new place."

"I'll be waiting," he whispers.

"Soon," she murmurs, then plants a light kiss on his cheek, turns, walks toward the door.

Still feeling her lips touching his cheek, he watches her walk—her gait so lithe, so sexy.

His chest heaves and his legs feel weak, wobbly.

He can barely believe the desire he feels.

He delights in wanting to see her again, to be with her, to protect her.

There's no way he can let Gorlov's plan succeed.

Not now, not a week from now.

Not ever.

But is it wise to get mixed up in the mob's business?

It's foolish to think he can stop what will happen.

But there's Irina—the sight, the scent, the sound, and the sexiness of her will drive him to do what must be done.

He just needs to figure out what that will be.

40

Walking away from Sasha's building on East Eighteenth Street, Eli passes O'Malley's Pub.

He's tempted to reenter the place and order another drink, maybe head toward that back room and glance at the table where they'd been sitting.

Don't get sentimental. Just think practically about how to get yourself and her out of this situation. I've been in tight spots before this one and have always come out of them on top.

He's not an infatuated kid overwhelmed by feelings the way he was that day when he first saw Hannah. Jesus, he was only twelve years old that day and knew nothing about life. He was filled with wonder, with hope. Back then the world seemed tinged with magic.

And despite the pain of it all, he returns to those days again and again, yearns for them in a way that's both sad yet has its own forlorn kind of beauty. There are times when it seems he's swallowed by memories of Hannah and what they had, when he sees her in momentary flashes, as though she's still with him. And it feels like she owns him every day of his life. As though he's lost in a realm of remembrance.

Call it what you will: heartbreak or sorrow or despair.

But now there's Irina.

After all that's happened to her—losing her entire family—misfortune will strike her again.

Very soon.

And it'll be deadly.

Unless he can divert it.

There must be a way.

But it'll take time to figure out and execute whatever plan he might devise.

Walking toward Lexington Avenue, he reconstructs the evening. He reimagines first seeing Irina as she stood at that window. That moment will stay with him for a long time. And when she turned to face him; how lonely and broken she appeared. He recalls every word of their conversation—first at the party, then at O'Malley's, and then during their walk back to Sasha's building.

There was that kiss. He can still taste and feel her warmth even as he walks along the street. And it's so strange: he feels the same elation he felt with Hannah that day in the apple orchard so long ago. It was a sense of anticipation for what will come. Or is he remembering it as lovelier than it was because there's no way to reclaim the past or Hannah or the time he might have had with her? There are nothing more than memories.

And now there's more than a distant memory; there's the possibility of a future.

As he approaches Gramercy Park, the wind kicks up. There's no way to catch a taxi in this weather, especially on a weekend night. The apartment is only nine short blocks away. There's very little pedestrian traffic on a night this cold. A quick glance around confirms there are no unoccupied taxis.

He gets to the south side of Gramercy Park and begins walking around its fenced perimeter.

At the north side of the park, he turns onto Lexington and heads uptown.

He again relives the evening, realizes Irina rekindled embers that have been buried for so long. It's strange how the capacity for feelings never truly disappears.

Suddenly the iciness of the wind chills the back of his neck even though his collar is raised.

It's a familiar sensation: the harbinger of danger.

Glancing back, he sees two men barely a city block behind him.

A bit farther along Lexington, he gets another glimpse. They're now closer and moving quickly, with purpose.

A pool of dread forms in his chest.

His instincts scream: it's a tail.

Another glance.

They're gaining.

Oh shit. Why didn't I take the Beretta?

Now they're running toward him, closing in. Fast.

Another guy crosses Lexington from the west side of the street, joins the other two.

Three on one.

Something flares in his head, then through his entire body—a bolt of kinetic energy—and suddenly his legs churn as he sprints north on Lexington.

There's a subway station at Twenty-Third Street.

He can get there, but then what happens?

Don't overthink it, just run.

He races by stores, passes buildings, parked cars, and plastic garbage bags. Blood pumps furiously through his body—into his lungs, his arms, thighs, and calves—and he keeps going.

A glance back. They're a half block behind and coming fast.

He lengthens his stride, pushes harder, wills his legs to move faster.

There's a desperate intake of breath and a burning sensation in his lungs, and now there's a stitch in his side and it feels like he's been running forever. It's a marathon, and there's a leaden ache in his legs—it's lactic acid buildup, a sign of fatigue—and he knows he'll never outlast them because no matter how well conditioned he is, he's not a young commando, and soon he'll be running on fumes.

The weariness is building, and it's only a matter of time before they get close enough to take him down with a volley of shots.

Nearing Twenty-Third Street, he realizes he's made a mistake: the subway station's on Park Avenue South, not Lexington; it's one block west.

Gotta move. Or I'm done.

At the corner of Twenty-Third Street and Lexington, he stops and glances at the stream of cars heading downtown on Lexington.

There's an opening.

Leaping onto the roadway, he bursts into the flow of traffic.

A horn blast comes from his right. A taxi nearly swipes him.

There's the screech of brakes, but he keeps going as another horn blares and rubber squeals on asphalt.

A third car's tires shriek as the vehicle swerves and barely misses him.

He stutter-steps, whirls, moves ahead, gets to the far side of Lexington.

A shout comes from behind. Then words. Russian. They're coming fast, crossing Lexington, right on his tail.

Brakes howl, horns trumpet.

He sprints west on the south side of Twenty-Third Street, passes Cohen's Optical, an AT&T store, then a Starbucks, and now he's at the corner of Park Avenue South. The subway entrance is on the far side of Park.

Gotta move. Gotta get to the station.

He lunges onto the northbound lane of Park.

A horn blares from his left, then comes the squeal of tires as a car veers around him, misses him by a hair.

He keeps going; more horns; a guy curses from an open car window.

There's the solid crunch of steel on steel. A car has rear-ended another.

There's more shouting.

At the median divide, he waits for an opening, sees oncoming headlights coming from uptown, but he leaps onto the southbound lane, jumps out of a taxi's path.

Another vehicle screeches to a halt.

An opening appears.

He sprints across the roadway, gets to the curb, now he's on the sidewalk, he's at the station entrance, glances back.

He's extended the lead. But they're coming.

Scrambling down the subway stairs, he stumbles, nearly falls but regains balance and descends quickly.

He leapfrogs the turnstile, staggers, nearly flops onto his face, regains his footing, keeps going. He's on the subway platform.

Where to go? People are waiting for the train. One woman sees him, seems to realize there's trouble. She extracts a cell phone, begins pressing buttons.

He stops, looks left, then right.

Is there a way out?

Can he head to the other end, barrel up the far stairway, get back to the street?

Then what? Go where?

Not a choice. He can't keep going. They'll run him down.

Can he fight off three guys?

Not out in the open.

Mouth dry, heart thumping, thoughts swirling, legs quaking, what to do, where to go?

Desperate glances, left, right, then a one-eighty.

There it is.

A door.

A sign:

MEN
RESTROOM
CLOSED
12 MIDNIGHT–5 A.M.

He grabs the handle, pushes down, and the door swings inward.

He's inside.

He slams the door shut.

He sucks in air. His chest heaves like a bellows.

In seconds they'll burst in and be on him.

41

The room is maybe four meters long by three wide.

White tile walls, fluorescent lighting, a near-blinding glare.

One toilet stall.

A filthy sink, two urinals.

A metal bin overflowing with used paper towels.

The lingering odor of bleach mixed with the smell of piss.

The closed door will open inward and away.

He stands with his back to the wall, knows the door will open away from where he's positioned.

Mossad training: Find a choke point. Exploit it. Shoot each one as he barges into the room.

He reaches for the Beretta.

Shit, it's not there.

Stupid. Just plain stupid.

Get the switchblade out. Move. Do it. Now.

His hand shakes, and he fumbles; he can't find the pocket.

Gotta use his hands, Krav Maga, quick short thrusts. Go for the soft spots—eyes, nose, throat, groin.

There's a loud thump.

The door blasts open, slams against the opposite tile wall with a deafening clap.

The first guy barrels in, momentum carrying him straight ahead.

Eli's fist slams into his Adam's apple. There's a cracking sound. Snapped cartilage. A strangled grunt comes from his ruined throat. His windpipe is crushed, collapses in on itself. The thug flops facedown to the floor. His pistol slides across the floor, comes to rest against the wall inside the toilet stall.

Grab it. Go for it. Get the gun.

Not enough time.

The next one barges in and nearly trips over the prone body of the first one.

Eli's knee slams into the guy's groin. An explosion of breath comes from his mouth. He doubles over, sags, is about to fall as the heel of Eli's palm smashes upward into his nose. There's a sharp snapping sound. Flattened nasal bones. Blood sprays in the air. He groans as he drops down, immobilized with blinding pain. His knife clatters onto the tiles, then skitters across the floor.

Eli's about to turn to the third one but his throat closes off.

He's being choked, can barely breathe. The third guy has him locked in a choke hold from behind. The grip is viselike. Eli gags.

The pressure on his neck lessens as the guy's right hand rises and a knife rises, then begins a downward thrust, aiming for the heart.

Eli clutches the man's wrist with both hands, pins the knife sideways against himself, bends at the knees, thrusts an elbow into the guy's gut, tucks, spins sideways, lifts the guy's feet off the floor, and slams him against the wall. The man bounces off the tiles and drops to the floor, onto his belly. The door swings shut.

The knife slides across the floor.

Eli pounces onto his back, sits on him, straddles him with one foot on either side of his torso, slips his left forearm around the man's neck, locks it against his right biceps, and yanks upward.

The guy's neck is stretched; he gurgles.

A glance at his face. It's Sergei, Agapov's pony-tailed thug.

"Why're you here?"

Sergei grunts; he can't breathe. His face is crimson, his eyes are closed, and drool drips from his lips.

"Talk to me, or it's over."

Eli loosens his grip.

Sergei grunts and honks; he can hardly draw a breath but manages to mutter, "You killed Ivan Agapov."

"Who told you?"

Sergei tries to push himself up, but Eli's weight on his back is too much for him. Sergei's pressed to the floor beside his two companions; the pressure of Eli sitting on his back and compressing his chest makes it difficult for him to breathe. If he stays this way for a few minutes, the man will suffocate and die. Or Eli could give Sergei's neck a sharp crank and snap his spine.

"Tell me or you die." He lets up on the pressure. Just enough to let Sergei speak.

Gurgling, Sergei whispers, "We have an inside man at Gorlov's. We got an email after Ivan died."

"Who is it?"

Eli increases the pressure. A few more seconds will cut off Sergei's carotids. It'll starve his brain of oxygen. He'll lose consciousness.

Eli loosens the hold. "Who?"

"I don't know," Sergei rasps.

A quick glance at the other two.

One guy lies on his belly and moans. He's crawled forward, toward the commode stall. A runnel of blood streams from his crushed nose, shimmers on the tile floor. He'll recover, but he'll need the skills of a plastic surgeon to keep from looking like a gargoyle for the rest of his life.

The other one lies crumpled on the floor near the door, beside Sergei. His trachea is crushed; he can't breathe. He'll be brain dead soon. Just then he lets out a fluttering rasp, and the stench of feces fills the room. He's a corpse.

Gotta get outta here.

Out of New York.

Out of the country.

Still holding Sergei's neck in a death grip, he whispers, "If anyone else comes for me, I'll kill them. You hear me?"

Sergei grunts. "Yes."

"And I'll kill *you*, motherfucker."

He leaps to his feet, flings the door open and dashes out to the platform.

Reaching the exit, he pushes through the gate and bolts up the stairway.

42

On Park Avenue South, he bends down, sets his hands on his knees, gasps for breath.

He feels faint, and his heart is pumping like crazy. He can barely breathe, and breath vapor pours from his mouth in gray clouds and is then whipped away by the wind.

He's being hunted like prey. The Russians will never stop until they get him. And he wasn't thinking back there. He should have rummaged through their pockets, grabbed their cell phones, emptied their wallets, left them with nothing, not one miserable dollar.

And he should have taken the first guy's pistol.

Stupid, so fucking stupid. But not as stupid as the three assholes lying on the floor in that restroom.

Jesus, he's killed again.

Will it ever end?

Forget it. Just get outta here.

He can't go back to the apartment, not now. He'll have to get to the safe house.

But he might be followed.

Where to go?

He'll touch base with Noah.

Maybe he's at Casey's.

He glances at the traffic pouring downtown on Park Avenue.

A lucky break. There's a taxi on the downtown side barreling toward him. Its roof light is on.

He jumps onto the roadway, waves it down.

The driver pulls over.

He rips the right rear door open, jumps in.

"Where to?" the cabbie asks.

"The East Village."

"Anyplace in particular?"

"Just the East Village."

The driver hits the meter's button. He has the radio tuned to WFAN; two guys are arguing about basketball, comparing Michael Jordan and LeBron James. Who's the better player? Like it fucking matters?

The rear seat has a concave depression from a thousand asses. It's vinyl, cracked, patched with duct tape.

The driver hits the gas, and the taxi joins the flow of traffic, a phalanx of vehicles heading downtown. The taxi's shocks are gone; the suspension is lousy. They hit bump after pothole, then more bumps; the taxi bounces and rattles as it speeds downtown with the traffic light wave. It's a sick blur as the nighttime sounds and sights of the street blow past them.

A quick glance back.

No one's following. No, they're back there, still in the station, gathering their wits, licking their wounds. And one of them is dead.

They tracked him after Agapov's people got ahold of Gorlov's communication about the hit. The pakhan's internet connection isn't secure. And there's a mole in his operation. The infiltrator obviously read the message about Sasha's party.

The new leader of Agapov's brigade—whoever that is—sent them.

And now Eli's in their crosshairs.

If he doesn't get out of the country, he's a dead man.

He'll be as dead as Agapov. Or as dead as that goon with a crushed windpipe at the Twenty-Third Street station.

It's only a matter of time.

43

Sitting in the taxi, his arms are rubbery and his hands feel weak, like they can't hold anything.

And it feels like he might shit his pants. It's the depletion after being so jacked on adrenaline his body was in overdrive—like a car that's been driven at high speed in low gear.

Now electrical twitches begin in his chest; shock waves course through his skin.

He's so sweat-slicked, it feels like stress is seeping out of every pore of his body.

A tingling sensation surrounds his lips. His fingertips go numb, then comes a pins-and-needles sensation. He's hyperventilating.

This never happened when he was with Mossad. Back then he thought he was missing the fear gene; he had no awareness of the possibility of his own death. And even if he had, no matter what the danger, he'd felt an inner calm, always found that serene place inside himself, especially as he was preparing for a mission.

But he's older now; no longer invincible.

He gulps lungfuls of air, but his trachea feels like it's closing.

Deep breath in, deep breath out. Like it was before storming a house crawling with terrorists.

A flash: he's crouched, waiting for the order to move in.

He's point man for the squad.

When there's a tap on his shoulder—it'll be Noah telling him they're ready to burst in and waste the bastards inside. There's a glaring white sky, a hot wind, and sand on the Gaza streets; there are Uzis, a Galil assault rifle, stun grenades.

Is this a fever dream?

The taxi hits a pothole; the jolt is so hard it rattles his teeth.

He's back in the moment.

For sure his photo's been circulated.

They know what he did to Agapov.

And they can track him.

They'll spare no effort to get to him.

An eye for an eye—it's a mob mantra.

Heading back to the apartment, he'd been thinking of Irina, had no awareness of his surroundings. A fatal mistake.

He pulls out his cell phone. His hands are shaking. His fingers cramp, won't do his bidding.

The streets rush by in a kaleidoscope of blinking lights and traffic with the clopping of the taxi's tires on the roadway.

Finally, Noah's number comes up.

One ring.

"Yes?"

"Noah, it's Eli."

"Shalom, my friend. Good to hear from you."

There's background noise, the blather of voices, bursts of laughter, clinking glasses, a sax crooning in the rear room.

"You at Casey's?"

"Yeah, bro. What's up?"

A sudden storm of static.

Then silence. Is the line dead?

"Noah, can you hear me?"

Staccato bursts of sound, no words, then comes a hissing sound followed by a buzz.

"Noah, you're breaking up. You there?"

He's about to press End Call but hears, "Eli, you okay?"

"Noah, stay where you are. I'll be there in a few."

"See you soon."

Two blocks from Casey's, he tells the driver to pull over.

Leaning through the Plexiglass opening, he drops a ten-dollar bill onto the front seat and jumps out of the cab.

44

Standing at the curb, he's not sure he can make it the short two blocks to Casey's. His legs feel heavy.

Trudging ahead, he thinks he must look like something out of *The Walking Dead*. The streets look dark, eerie, forbidding, and the buildings seem to crouch over the streets. Though he's been here before, everything looks strange, unfamiliar, unreal, like stage scenery.

A half block from the club, he moves with a slow shambling gait, like an old man.

He's at Casey's front door.

He opens it to a wall of noise.

The place is seething with life. In the dimness, drinkers are bellied up to the bar, three and four deep, even at the front door. There's barely enough room to squeeze beyond the entrance. It's surreal, looks overwhelming, alien.

It's Friday night: live jazz and the crowd it brings.

In the back room—a quartet is going at it—piano, alto sax, bass, and drums. The sound threads through the roar of the bar crowd. People are pressed together, talking, shouting, and laughing. It's a teeming mass of humanity, seems to be heaving back and forth. The din is earsplittingly loud; his head throbs.

He peers left and right, tries to spot Noah but can't see him. Not in this press of flesh.

Men, women, drinks in hand, dim lighting, ghostly looking faces, a maelstrom of noise and movement. Complete overload. Unreal.

There he is—Noah, at the far end of the bar, talking with two hard-looking guys. Shaved heads, three days' stubble. Former IDF commandos for sure.

Threading through the crush, he gets to the group.

Noah greets him. Introductions are made.

Eli can barely stand in place. He hears nothing being said. The throb of the mob drowns out their words, yet the sound of the drum from Brubeck's "Take Five" spools out from the back room, creates a thumping bass sound reverberating through the floor.

The end of the drum riff ignites a furious round of applause from the back-room crowd.

Amid the bar clamor and the kaleidoscopic sense of light and fury, Noah's eyes meet Eli's in a flash of understanding.

Eli tilts his head toward the restroom.

Noah nods. "Excuse me, guys," he says to the other two, "Eli and I have to discuss something." He turns and begins jostling his way through the crowd.

Eli follows in his wake.

Eli closes and locks the men's room door, takes a deep breath.

He sheds his coat, holds it in his hand.

Another restroom.

Brightly lit.

White tile walls.

Two porcelain urinals.

Two stalls.

A floral scent mixed with the stringent smell of deodorant cakes.

The crowd's thunder pulses through the door.

Noah's eyes question Eli. "Hey, man, you look like shit. What's up?"

Eli trusts Noah more than anyone on the planet. The guy saved his life when his Tavor rifle malfunctioned and he was cornered by two Hezbollah fighters in Lebanon. Noah stitched them with lead from his micro Uzi. Theirs is a bond men who've been in combat together can have.

"Lemme catch my breath," Eli says as he bends down, sets his hands on his knees, and sucks in more air.

Noah places his hand on Eli's shoulder. "Deep breath in, then out," he says.

Jesus, just like in Lebanon.

Finally, Eli straightens up and faces him.

Breathing shakily, Eli describes the way he's spent the last ten years, then goes over the last two weeks: meeting with Gorlov and Viktor, the hit job on Agapov, the second part of Gorlov's assignment—the arrangement with Sasha, meeting Irina, the party, walking her back to Sasha's place, the chase to the Twenty-Third Street station and what happened there.

"So, the skip tracing's just a cover. You're in the killing business."

"I couldn't get out."

"Hey, man, you made a choice."

He nods, swallows hard, and says, "Okay. That's the way it happened."

"Life isn't what *happens* to you. It's the choices you make."

Eli nods. "I've made bad ones."

"Let's face it, brother. The Mossad did it to you. You're fucked in the head."

Noah's right. Eli's been stuck in some shitty gravitational pull, and he's never pulled out of it. He's been stuck in time, living out some shit-ridden version of the past, nurturing rage and a hunger for vengeance.

And here he is now, being stalked by the Russians.

"So, what're you gonna *do* about it?" Noah asks.

A stab of emptiness threatens; it's that dark space that makes Eli's life feel like he's drifting through space, empty, devoid of meaning, lifeless with no chance of a future.

"You can't pussyfoot around, bro," Noah says.

"I know, I know."

"I have one question for you."

Eli closes his eyes and waits.

"How much money do you have?"

"Plenty."

"How much?"

"I have *fuck you* money."

"Then get out. Make peace with everything and go home. I can hook you up with someone who'll get you a good job and—"

"I can't."

"Why not?"

"Too many memories."

"Give it another chance."

Shaking his head, Eli mutters, "I can't do it."

"It was a long time ago. Things are changing."

"No, man. It's the same shit: terrorists, bombs, shootings. It's an endless fucking war."

"They're talking about a two-state solution."

"It'll never happen."

"What? You have the gift of prophecy?"

"I can't go back."

Noah's hand slips onto Eli's shoulder again. "Listen to me," he says. "It's time to make another choice, one that'll be the difference between living and dying. You were the best soldier I ever had under my command, and I always admired you. But you gotta think straight now and make a decision, one that'll take you through the rest of your life."

Just like Noah, never minces his words, says what's on his mind.

"Think about it and think *clearly*," Noah says. "The choice is simple: you're either gonna live a normal life back home, back where you'll work a regular job with regular hours and be with regular people, or you'll be a goddamned fugitive, always looking over your shoulder. Because the Russians are everywhere, and I mean *everywhere*, and you're on their to-do list."

"I can't go back. Ever, it's not where I can live. Even seeing the streets there makes me sick. I just can't do it."

Noah shakes his head. "Okay, so your life there is over. But you gotta get away from *here*. You gotta find a new life. There's the Caribbean, South America, Southeast Asia. Places with lots of expats . . . Americans, Israelis, Brits. Just get away, and make a fresh start. You have the money and—"

"There's this woman. If I can get her away, then—"

"The *Russian*? Oh, c'mon, man. Forget her. She's as good as dead. And if you hang around waiting for her, you'll be dead, too."

"But—"

"But *nothing*. If you don't get out now, you'll be just another corpse rotting away in some God-forbidden place."

There's a loud pounding on the door.

"What's goin' on in there, you goddamned queers? I gotta take a dump," calls a voice.

"One second," Noah shouts.

"Listen, Eli, I'm staying at an Airbnb on Houston Street. Bunk with me tonight, and then get to a safe house. You have one?"

"Yeah."

"After that you know what to do. You have two choices: get out now, or stick around and die."

Eli's mouth goes dry.

"Do yourself a favor—take Door Number One. Because whether you want to admit it or not, you're radioactive."

45

At eight o'clock in the morning, much earlier than he usually gets to the office, Anton Gorlov sits at his desk thinking about this Irina Sakharov and the hit man, Aiden, or whatever his name may be.

Is this scheme going to work? If not, we'll have to take a more direct approach. That may require a different kind of creative thinking. There's not much time, and we need to clean up these loose ends before we leave.

A knock on the door interrupts his thoughts.

"Come in."

It's Viktor. His face looks ashen.

"What's wrong. Viktor?"

"I didn't want to call you so late last night, but I heard from Aiden."

"Yes?"

"He was attacked by three men after the party at Sasha's place. They were from Agapov's brigade. The new pakhan, Leonid Koskoff, must have sent them."

"How does he know they were Agapov's men?"

"He overpowered them and got one to talk."

Every nerve in Anton Gorlov's body jangles.

"They know we were behind Agapov's death," Viktor says.

"Did he find out how they know?"

"There's an informant in our brigade."

Gorlov's mouth opens as he sucks in air. "This is unbelievable. Who is it?"

"He couldn't find out," Viktor says, "but it has to be someone who knows our plans."

"This has been our secret," Anton says, feeling his heart accelerate.

"There's only one man who could possibly know about it," Viktor says. "Vasily."

"Vasily?"

"Yes. He posted the dossier on that website," Viktor says. "And he sent Aiden the notice about Sasha's party. It *has* to be him."

Anton shoots to his feet. "Vasily? That worm. After all I did for him? We should have taken care of him weeks ago. It's my fault."

"No, Anton, it's my fault. I should have pushed harder to give him that *bonus*."

"This is bad, Viktor. We'll have to move the time line up."

"Understood."

Through a maelstrom of thoughts, Gorlov says, "Have Vasily brought to the basement."

Viktor hates the basement. It's dimly lit and damp. And it smells of mold.

The walls are lined with gray cinder blocks. The room is lit by the ceiling's fluorescent lights. They hum and flicker constantly and remind Viktor of being interrogated by the Odessa police back in the old days.

Vasily Kamkin, their IT technician, is a slight man with pale skin and dark hair. He wears thick glasses, which now lie on a workbench table. He sits in a chair alongside the table.

Two huge men, Vadim and Dima, stand beside Vasily. Viktor chose them because neither one speaks a word of English. He can't take a chance on yet another leak.

Plastic tie strips secure Vasily's hands behind his back. His head rests snugly between the jaws of a large bench vise clamped to the edge of the table.

"*Pozhaluysta,*Viktor, *ne delay etogo*," Vasily squeals.

"English, Vasily. English."

"Please, Viktor, don't do this."

"We must speak in English, Vasily. This is just between you and me. Do you understand?"

"Yes . . . yes . . . I understand." The man shudders visibly. Droplets of sweat drip from Vasily's brow to the floor. Huge sweat stains now permeate the shirt beneath his underarms.

"I didn't do anything. Please, you have to believe me."

It's a shame, Viktor thinks. Greed is such an enduring part of human nature. Over his sixty years, he's watched so many men die for the love of money.

There are many ways to extract the truth. Forcing a man to undress reduces him to the level of an animal, degrades and humiliates him. Being naked bespeaks vulnerability, helplessness. Above all else, it strips him of dignity. The man breaks down and tells the truth. But he senses that they don't need to strip Vasily of his clothing.

Of course, they could torture Vasily in any of a number of ways, and he'd give it up. But Viktor prefers the vise. There's something otherworldly about having your head clamped between the steel jaws of the device and knowing your skull can be crushed with a few turns of the handle.

Viktor nods at Dima.

Dima begins turning the vise handle clockwise. The movable jaw squeaks and rachets as it slides closer to the fixed one, squeezing Vasily's skull.

He lets out a yelp. "Please, Viktor. Please, I don't deserve this." Droplets of sweat drip from the tip of his nose. Snot dribbles from his nostrils.

"Just tell us the truth, and there will be no further consequences."

"Please . . . I have a family."

"We all have families. But we never betray our brothers."

"*Ya ne sdelal nichego plokhogo*," the man screams.

"English, Vasily. English only."

"I did nothing."

"If you tell the truth, you'll have a life. Sadly, it won't be with us. But it will be a life."

Viktor nods once again.

Dima rotates the handle a bit more. The moving jaw creaks as it slides closer to the fixed one.

Vasily cries out, "Please . . . *please*."

Rivulets of sweat drip from his forehead. He sucks in snot and tears through his nose.

Intense fear can turn a man into an animal, Viktor thinks. And as happens with all animals, Vasily's instincts scream for him to stay alive, so he'll break down and give it up.

Viktor nods once more.

The sliding jaw ratchets a few millimeters closer to the fixed one.

"Okay, okay," Vasily screams.

"Yes?"

"My wife has cancer."

"I'm sorry to hear that. And?"

"I went to Anton and told him about it."

"And?"

"We don't have insurance, and she couldn't get into a clinical trial. I told Anton I needed money for her treatments."

"Yes?"

"He was sympathetic and said, 'I know all about cancer. It's a death sentence.'"

"Yes?"

"He gave me twenty thousand dollars."

"And?"

"It only covered two treatments. But she'll need infusions for the rest of her life . . . every two months. I saw no way out."

Vasily's words sound choked as he sobs.

"Why not go to him again?"

"I did, and he gave me another ten thousand but said there would be no more."

"Why not?"

"Because of what happened to his wife, he thinks chemo does no good. He said I'd have to accept the inevitable."

"And what then?"

"I reached out to Agapov's people."

"How much did they give you?"

"A hundred thousand."

"And?"

"I sent them the post, the one you had me put up on that assassin's website."

"And then?"

"I sent them the notice of Sasha Bortsov's party."

"And you agreed to send more communications in the future, didn't you?"

"Please, Victor. I was on the hook." Vasily's lips begin moving in silent prayer.

"Have you ever communicated with anyone else about our business?"

"No. Please believe me." More sobs, high-pitched, frantic.

"I believe you."

"Please, let me go. I swear I'll never—"

"It's such a shame, Vasily. If you'd come to *me*, not Anton, I'd have seen to it that your wife's bills were covered. But instead, you chose to betray your brothers."

"Please, Anton. I didn't mean—"

"I understand, Vasily. I do."

Viktor nods to Dima.

Dima pulls on the vise handle. The jaws tighten. Dima struggles with the tension. He slips the handle shaft completely through the spindle to gain more leverage. Putting all his weight on one end of the bar, he leans down and presses.

The sharp sound reminds Viktor of an eggshell cracking open.

Vasily's skull caves in.

Something drops to the floor with a wet plop.

Years ago, Vasily's skull being crushed would have sickened Viktor. But the Bratva life hardens the soul. Regrettably, it comes to this, he thinks. Because betraying one's brothers is unforgivable.

He looks at the men standing beside the table with Vasily's head-crushed corpse now dangling from the vise. Vadim turns away from the table; his face has a greenish hue; he looks like he's about to puke.

Speaking Russian, Viktor says, "What's the matter, Vadim?"

Nearly choking, Vadim mutters, "It's disgusting."

"I don't pay you to be *disgusted*. I pay you to do what's necessary. Understood?"

"Yes."

Viktor turns to Dima. In Russian, he says, "You know what to do, yes?"

Dima regards him with what Viktor recognizes as wary devotion. "We clean up this mess, take the body to the tub, cut it up."

"And then?"

"Put it all in a bag, drive to that swamp near Gerritsen Beach, and dump it there."

"And the bag?"

"We burn it."

"Very good. And don't forget those glasses. Get rid of them, too."

"We'll take care of everything."

"Good," says Viktor, thinking Dima's a good man; he's not squeamish like Vadim.

"Use a heavy-duty trash bag," he tells Dima. "The kind they use in construction. I don't want anything spilling in the trunk of the car. And drive carefully so you don't get stopped by the cops."

Sighing, Viktor thinks, *So much violence. It's a shame.*

He gets up and leaves the basement.

46

Eli wakes up to the aroma of coffee brewing.

It's nine thirty in the morning.

After having breakfast, Eli thinks back to having called Viktor Sorokin late last night and telling him what went down after the party at Sasha's place.

Viktor's heavy breathing and shaky voice told Eli the man was shocked to hear about the attack. There's no way he and Anton Gorlov had anything to do with it. In fact, they must be worried that a Bratva war is about to break out.

As Noah's getting ready to leave the apartment, he says, "I'll be at my aunt's place. You going to the safe house?"

"Yeah, but first I have to change my look."

Noah opens the closet door. "Here, wear this," he says, handing Eli a quilted black ski jacket. "And this too." He tosses a blue wool watch cap to him. "Leave that coat here. And put this scarf over your nose and mouth," he says, handing Eli a wool scarf. "It's cold enough to use without looking like you're hiding your face. There's a drugstore downstairs. I'll head there and buy you a pair of sunglasses. "

"I can't get these back to you."

"No problem. I'm leaving tomorrow and won't need them back home."

Noah goes downstairs.

When he returns, he gives Eli the sunglasses.

"How much do I owe you?"

"Forget about it. Just stay safe and get out of the country." Noah falls silent, then says, "You're sure you don't want to go back home?"

"I'm sure."

"Eli, why not give it a chance? You can have a life back there."

"I can't do it. If I see a bus on a street, I get sick to my stomach. If I hear Palestinian Arabic, I get queasy. I can't stand looking at men in keffiyehs. I can't live a life there, either as a civilian or in the military. I tried getting past it, but I couldn't. That's why I came here. I just can't go back."

"I understand." Noah sets his hand on Eli's shoulder. "Listen up, you have my cell number, so you know how to get in touch with me. You can always call, and I'll do whatever I can to help you."

"Understood. Thank you. You've always been more than a commander to me."

"Just don't be a stranger, Eli. Once you settle down, wherever it is, stay in touch."

"Will do. Hey, man, I'm gonna miss you."

Noah nods. "And I'll miss you . . . have for years. We went through a lot together."

Eli's eyes grow wet as they exchange man-hugs and backslaps.

When Noah is gone, Eli knows his last connection to what once had been his life is gone.

And it's never coming back.

A short while later, he's back on the street.

It's ten in the morning.

Using his encrypted cell, he calls Irina.

A robotic voice says the number is not in service.

To make sure he'd dialed correctly, he tries again.

Same message.

There are three possibilities:

One: he punched in the wrong number last night.

Two: because of the language barrier, she mixed it all up when she gave him the number.

Three: she purposely gave him the wrong number to blow him off. But that seems unlikely.

Whatever the reason, he's gotta get ahold of her. After what happened with Agapov's men, there's a good chance she's in danger. No doubt those guys were watching them as they stood in front of Sasha's building.

He's gotta make sure she's all right.

He opens the Chrome search engine on the cell phone and plugs in "Sasha's Healthworks, Third Avenue, NYC."

The address comes up along with a description of the place.

He can get there easily. Wearing a watch cap with his face covered by the scarf and sunglasses and dressed in a different jacket, he doesn't look like he did last night.

He'll take a chance and go to the health club.

47

Sasha's place is on Third Avenue, next door to a SoulCycle outlet and just a few blocks from her apartment on East Eighteenth Street.

The place is so upscale, Eli is certain Russian mob money is behind it.

He enters the club feeling confident his changed look and circuitous route have minimized any chance of being followed. Beyond the reception area, a carpeted expanse is dotted with treadmills, exercise bicycles, Nautilus equipment, and racks of chrome-plated dumbbells. A sleek-looking juice bar stands off to the side.

A group of thirtysomething women wearing sports bras and yoga pants pedals stationary bicycles to the beat of piped-in techno music. At the far end of the room, a muscle-bound behemoth flexes his biceps and adopts a bodybuilding pose in front of a mirrored wall. The guy looks like he gobbles anabolic steroids; his balls have no doubt shrunk to the size of shelled peanuts.

Eli removes the scarf and takes off the watch cap and sunglasses. A moment later, Sasha emerges from an office near the reception area.

When she notices him, Eli thinks he sees surprise showing on her face. She recovers quickly. "My, my, aren't *we* bundled up for the cold." A smile forms on her lips.

There's something private about that smile, something unknowable, as though she's carrying a secret. Wearing black yoga pants and a sweatshirt, she looks like she's ready for a workout.

"Aiden, I never expected to see you here," she says, approaching him with her hand extended.

As they shake hands, her eyes appear questioning. Eli knows anything he says will find its way back to Gorlov and his sidekick, Viktor. "I just wanted to drop by and say hello," he says, trying to sound casual even as his pulse bounds through his body.

"And you wanted to see Irina too?" she says with a half-smile.

"Yes, of course." His lips spread into a grin, hopefully not a sheepish-looking one. "I tried calling her, but the line isn't in service."

"Oh really?" Sasha tilts her head. "I think I recall her saying something about the telephone company—some kind of mix-up with her account. She pays her bills by postal order, and I've told her again and again the mail is unreliable. She needs to get a checking account or pay her bills online."

Eli nods.

"Come into my office and we'll talk." She tilts her head toward a nearby door.

There's something custodial—even maternal—about her demeanor, as though she's protecting Irina.

Sasha's office is furnished with a glass-topped desk the size of a helipad, two plush-looking chairs, and an oxblood leather tuxedo couch. Crimson-colored carpeting covers the floor. Eli sits in one of the chairs.

"Irina's not in today," Sasha says, lowering herself onto the sofa. "The poor girl suffers from migraines. I think she's hassled because she's moving into her own place. It's very stressful for her, and I'm guessing that brought on the headache. But I'm sure she'll be glad to hear you dropped by."

Getting up from the couch, she says, "While I fix us some herbal tea, tell me a little about yourself, Aiden. Where're you from?"

"Originally, from California," he says, keeping his voice even. "But now I live here . . . in Manhattan."

Isn't she going to talk about Gorlov? Here they are, two people involved in the same cabal, each pretending they don't know the other's role in this charade.

"Tell me more," she says, fiddling with the machine and then handing him a mug of tea. "I understand you do IT work."

Anything I tell Irina could be discussed with Sasha and find its way back to Gorlov. Noah's right. It's time to get out.

"Yes, I have a private clientele."

"Is business good?"

"I get by," he says, knowing her questions are all diversionary. She knows he's a hit man.

This is a bizarre cat-and-mouse game.

He sips the tea. It's too hot, so he sets the mug on a small end table.

After more small talk, Sasha says, "Irina told me that you and she hit it off quite well."

"Yes, she's lovely."

Sasha nods. "I must confess, Aiden, even though she's a distant cousin . . . how shall I put it? She's become like a little sister to me."

Is Sasha even trying to con me? Why this charade about protecting Irina?

And yet it continues.

"After all that's gone on in her life, I think she can easily be hurt," Sasha says in a voice so honeyed Eli feels like cringing.

She suddenly glances at her watch, and her mouth opens. "Oh my God, I almost forgot. I have an important call I must make. They're expecting me on the phone in the next minute. I'm so sorry." Sasha's face darkens, which tells him more than words ever could.

She wants him gone. The less he sees of Sasha, the better. She's dangerous, and she's trying to play him for a fool.

"Please tell Irina I came by," he says, heading for the office door, "and I hope she feels better soon."

"Will do," Sasha says, virtually leaping up from the couch to open the office door for him.

Walking out into the cold, he feels like he's exited the stage at the end of the third act in a play.

It's theater of the absurd.

And it's lethal.

48

At two that afternoon, Anton Gorlov sweeps his hand across the chessboard and knocks the pieces to the floor.

"I can't concentrate," he says. "My mind is too filled with this trouble to play chess."

"Mine too," says Viktor, pushing his chair away from the table.

"Let's speak Russian, Viktor. There's something comforting about our mother tongue." He sighs. "I'm worried about this Agapov business. With Leonid Koskoff taking over, there *will* be war. I'm certain of that."

"We could call for a sit-down. That might calm things enough before it all goes to the dogs."

"No, it won't," Gorlov says. "I know Koskoff. He's gathering his soldiers as we speak. The man will do anything to get revenge."

"Anton, we have three hundred loyal men. We can flood the streets."

"All-out war?" Gorlov shakes his head. "When we're making arrangements to leave? It's the last thing we need." A sense of bleakness floods him. "I'm still thinking about that worm Vasily. The betrayal, the deceit . . . It's part of the despicable world we live in, where no one can be trusted."

"I must confess, I'm tired of this life too. I'm glad we're getting out."

"We have to push up the timeline," Anton says. "We must get out within the week. Call Volkov and make sure the passports and the other documents are ready."

"It'll get done."

"And you're familiar with this Bitcoin thing?"

"Yes, I know it. We're financially secure."

"Everything is changing. I swear, Viktor, the world has gone insane. I don't know how we live in it." A wrenching sadness threatens to seize Gorlov. There's been so much death in his life, he must fight for a new one, far from Odessa and Ukraine and Russia and Belarus and Brighton Beach and the Bratva.

But enough of these morbid ruminations. There's too much going on in the here-and-now.

"I have to confess, Viktor, I'm worried about this business with Aiden and this Irina woman."

"Sasha seems confident that they'll become lovers. In fact, she called today to tell me that Aiden came to the health club to see her—not Sasha, but Irina. But she thinks it might take a while before something happens."

"We have very little time," Gorlov says. "Things must move quickly."

Viktor gets up from his chair, goes to the cabinet, and pours himself a half finger of Stoli. He guzzles it down and then turns to his pakhan. "Anton, do you ever regret the things we've done?"

"Ah, the agony of regret," Gorlov says. "We did what we had to do to survive. The streets of Odessa were dangerous, especially for us. At least here we're with our own kind. And we've done well. There was no other choice."

"Understood. But the things we've done . . ."

"The things we've done? I can live with them."

"Even murder?"

"We've only murdered evil people . . . people like ourselves." Gorlov chortles.

Viktor laughs and raises his empty glass. "Here's to a peaceful life far from here."

Gorlov nods. "A fine sentiment, Viktor, but we have to take care of business with this Irina. She's an unknown, and who knows what will happen with those two."

"Agreed."

"Contact Aiden," Gorlov says. "We have to push him. Let's get it over and done with."

49

At three that afternoon, Eli considers everything that's happened.

The secure site's been compromised. He can't trust any communication with Gorlov's people because there's a chance it'll be seen or heard by a third party. The only way to have contact with Gorlov is by satellite phone, but even that could be risky. There are always burner phones, but who knows how much technology has now made them useless. The Israeli NSO Group has developed spyware called Pegasus that can remotely surveil smart phones, even burners. Who knows what the Russians have purchased lately?

Email is no longer safe.

Both Gorlov's brigade and Agapov's people knew he was going to be at Sasha's party.

Jesus, he's lucky to be alive.

But if he stays in New York, it's only a matter of time before he goes down.

These days technology is advancing exponentially. There's no such thing as an impenetrable firewall. Hackers and malware can penetrate any database. Even nuclear facilities can be infiltrated, like when Stuxnet fouled up the operational capacity at the Iranian Natanz facility in 2010. It was a CIA and Mossad mission.

He'll have to get ahold of a new sat phone.

By now the Russians may know where he lives. And they know about his involvement with Irina.

Yes, he has to get out of the life. Why live this way, where there's no truth, no loyalty, no family or friends, where there's no sense of belonging anywhere? It's a life where anyone can be used as a tool, a life in which no one even knows his goddamned name. The way it is with Otto and the other sayanim.

It's a counterfeit life, a life of fiction.

Noah's right.

It's time to get out.

But first things first.

He'll leave this apartment and never return.

He'll erase any trail—paper or electronic. There'll be no forwarding address, no uncollected mail, no credit card or telephone bills, no travel records. He'll take a few bathroom articles and the clothes on his back. That's it. Everything else is nothing more than a meaningless possession—the clutter of life.

This place is no different from any other apartment he's occupied for the last ten years.

Temporary.

Transient.

His real estate sayan makes certain any rental includes utilities, so there's no account with the electric company or any utility. The landlords always accept electronic payments.

Nothing can be traced to a credit card or mailing address.

The only snail mail he receives are advertisements addressed to "Occupant."

He's left no digital footprint in New York or anywhere in the world.

He'll take only the letters Mom wrote to him when he was in the army, along with a few photos of Hannah, Mom, and Pop. These mementos are the only reminders that he once had a life anchored to people he loved, that he had relationships, that he'd lived a life with meaning.

It's time to get to the safe house, a furnished sublet on Bleeker rented under yet another assumed name. It's stocked with enough supplies to last for a month—not that he'll be staying that long. It's the way his safe houses were throughout Europe and the Middle East.

It's tough to live anonymously in the twenty-first century, but he does it.

It's time to contact the forgery sayan in Queens. The guy can create a passport that'll pass muster at any customs terminal in the world. He does birth certificates and driver's licenses too.

He'll stay at the safe house until he leaves, which will be a few short days from now.

But before then he'll warn Irina she's a target. That's the best he can do before he tries to find a new life.

His next birthday's in two months.

He'll be forty, not yet an old man.

There's still gas left in the tank.

After all these years, there has to be a better reason to wake up in the morning, open his eyes, and put his feet on the floor.

Maybe he can salvage something from this blighted life.

Is there such a thing as a new life?

Maybe it's possible.

But where?

50

For a change, Anton Gorlov isn't thinking about the prospect of all-out war or the scheme with Irina Sakharov.

He glances at Katerina, whose brow is furrowed. She sighs and shakes her head. She's upset, and he knows it's with him. "What's troubling you, darling?"

"You know what's wrong, Anton. We've been together for five years and nothing's happened. It's all been the same, and things are different now."

"Different? How?"

"How? How can you ask 'How'? You're asking me to leave Brighton Beach . . . to leave the *country* and leave everything behind—my sister, my friends, my hair salon, my whole *life*. But it's the same old story; you won't make a commitment."

"Oh, Katerina, you know I love you."

She shakes her head again and her lips turn down. "Anton, let me ask you something."

"Yes?"

"Does marrying me mean somehow you would be betraying Nadia?"

God, this is excruciating.

He's at a loss for words.

"Be honest with me, Anton."

He recalls how he convinced Nadia to undergo chemotherapy, even though the cancer had spread to her lungs, her bones, even her brain.

No, I don't want them to drip any more of those poisons into my veins.

And yet he'd insisted that she go to the hospital for that one last infusion.

Anton, the hospital is where people go to die, she said, moaning in pain.

At the hospital, as the IV dripped steadily, she gazed up at him and murmured, *Anton, I want to go home.*

Nadia. Please don't give up. Just finish this one last treatment.

I hate this place. It's torture. I want to go home. I want peace.

The morphine dripping into her vein made her drowsy. She was in a twilight world and she slipped slowly and inexorably toward the other side of life. He watched helplessly as her jaw slackened and her cheeks sagged.

Then her eyes clouded over.

Yes, he saw the moment life left her.

God forgive me for making her spend her last hours in that place.

"Anton, answer me," Katerina says. "Do you feel marrying me means you've betrayed her?"

He sighs. "Katerina, I'm sixty years old. You're fifty-five. Is getting married really so important at this point in our lives?"

"You know, Anton, life's about coming to terms with things. It's about moving on no matter what's happened before."

She's right. I can't live in the past.

"Okay, okay. We can get married whenever you want."

"Why not tomorrow? I went to the City Clerk's website. We can go to the office on Joralemon Street. We just fill out a form. We'll have a civil ceremony. Just you and me. And our future."

Will there ever be another woman like Katerina? She's treated me with tenderness, with such kindness, and yes, with so much love. Despite everything that's happened, I'm a lucky man.

"Okay, we'll do it."

"What about Diana?" she asks.

"My daughter has no use for an old crook like me."

"Are you sure?"

"I'm sure, darling. You and me, Viktor, and Oksana . . . we'll leave together and begin new lives."

51

It's nearly four in the afternoon, time to get out of the Twenty-Seventh Street apartment.

Sergei and those other thugs were a wake-up call. He came as close to death as when he was trapped by those Hezbollah fighters in Lebanon.

But now there's no Noah to save him.

He gathers his New York State driver's license, his bogus birth certificate, passport, social security card, and anything else that could identify him as Mr. Dukas, then grabs a pair of scissors and turns it all into confetti.

In the hallway, he opens the door to the compactor room and dumps the scraps down the chute.

Instead of wearing sunglasses, he slips on a pair of clear, plastic-framed nonprescription glasses. His nerd lenses is what he calls them. Though not a real disguise, they change his look enough to make him a bit less recognizable. And he dons Noah's wool watch cap.

A canvas case is strapped over his shoulder. It contains his laptop and a few bathroom articles. Any other items he'll need—clothing, another winter jacket, soap, shampoo, toothbrush, and various odds and ends—are at the safe house.

He double locks the apartment door, makes certain it's secure.

Not that it matters because he won't be back. There's no need to worry about fingerprints anywhere because his prints—even his DNA profile—aren't on a database anywhere in the world. Not even the IDF databank. Once he became a Mossad agent, his entire personal file was expunged from government archives. Eli

Dagan evaporated into thin air. Just as there's no digital footprint, there are no biological markers to identify him anywhere in the world. It's all fluid, changeable.

As Mom said—jokingly, of course—he's a chameleon.

Ordinarily, he'd take the stairway down to the basement and leave the building through the garage. But today he'll stop off at the lobby.

There's only one person on his goodbye list: Luis, the daytime doorman. Over the last six months, he and Luis have established what could be called a friendly rapport. Getting even marginally close to anyone is a departure from his usual protocol, but Eli made an exception for Luis, a really good guy. He gets off at four o'clock; Eli's glad he'll get to see him before leaving.

Things are pretty fucked up when the most meaningful relationship in your life is with your doorman.

As Luis says, "Good afternoon, Mr. Dukas," a smile breaks out on his face.

"And a good one to you, Luis. How's the family?"

"Good. Good. I've been meaning to tell you—Angela's been accepted at Bronx Science."

"Congratulations. It's gotta be great to have a really smart kid. You must be very proud."

Beaming, Luis says, "Oh man, I can't begin to tell you how good it is."

After they exchange a few more words, Eli clops him on the back, then leaves.

So much for Luis.

Not even a goodbye. Nor an excuse such as "I'm leaving on a business trip and will be back in two weeks."

Nothing. The less said, the better.

It's time to simply disappear.

Knowing he'll miss Luis—and Otto, too—Eli suffocates a

swell of nostalgia. Whether it's Luis or Otto or any of his sayanim, it doesn't matter. They're all dispensable relationships.

In the life Eli's chosen, everyone's disposable.

It's all temporary.

Transitory.

Fungible.

And it's so sad.

52

At 4:05 on a weekday afternoon, rush hour has begun.

The city's madness is in high gear.

It's the worst time to try catching a taxi in Manhattan.

A parade of yellow cabs, vans, eighteen-wheelers, and passenger cars streams uptown on First Avenue. It's a honking symphony of chaos. Street construction slows the vehicles to a crawl amid a pall of fumes. A jackhammering Con Edison crew is at work in a trench at the corner of Twenty-Eighth Street. The traffic clog isn't helped by double-parked delivery trucks narrowing the roadway. The sky is darkening, and car headlights slice through the air. It won't be long before dusk falls. Traffic signals blink along with the usual WALK–DON'T WALK signs in a display of optical turbulence. A medley of sirens wails in the distance, merging with the blare of car horns.

Standing on the corner at the intersection of Second Avenue and Twenty-Seventh Street, Eli can't spot a single cab with its roof light on. There's neither a Boro taxi nor a gypsy cab in sight. And there's no way he can call an Uber or a Lyft because they require an account registered to a credit card—which could be a potential hint at his identity, even with bogus plastic.

Catching an unoccupied taxi is out of the question, which means taking the subway. So he'll walk a few blocks to the nearest station. To make certain he's not being shadowed, he'll use a few diversionary moves. Can't be too careful after what happened last night.

Walking toward Lexington, he scans the street for the possibility of an ambush. He's antsier now than he's ever been in all the years he's been in New York. After the smackdown with Sergei and his goons, Eli's radar is primed to the edge of paranoia.

Smokers loiter in front of commercial buildings. Having been exiled from their offices, they take their last desperate puffs before heading back to finish a day's tedium. Walking along the street, Eli scans every one of them as well as passersby. No one looks suspicious.

Two guys unloading a refrigeration truck glance at him. There's something surreptitious in one guy's look; he turns away the moment Eli's eyes fasten on him. The guys begin talking to each other in Spanish.

Though he doesn't speak the language, he tries to discern their tone.

They could belong to the Dominican mob.

Maybe the Bratva outsourced the hit to them.

Having just passed their truck, Eli stops in front of a store window and eyes them in the reflection. They keep working. After a full minute of observation, it's clear: they're just two guys offloading food to a Thai restaurant.

It feels as though every millimeter of the city is trip-wired for an ambush.

At the corner of Third and Twenty-Seventh, he notices orange traffic cones set on the asphalt around a stalled city bus. Its front end is being hoisted by a heavy-duty tow truck. Men wearing reflective red and yellow emergency vests swarm like ants around the disabled vehicle.

There's a flash of the Jerusalem street and the skeletal bus wreckage with its charred steel, the stench of burned flesh and bone, the scorched blacktop and acrid smoke in the air. Having played out in his mind a thousand times, it's ready to intrude in a millisecond.

For a sickening moment, Eli feels rage and despair, knowing he'll be haunted by that image for the rest of his life.

Jesus, don't think about it now. Just keep going.

He keeps walking west on Twenty-Seventh Street.

At Park Avenue South and Twenty-Eighth, he scrambles down the subway entrance stairway. Though the Bleeker Street place is downtown, he'll head uptown as a diversion.

The station, with its dank air and stale smell, reminds him of the fight with Sergei's crew. He walks along the crowded platform and positions himself to board the train in a middle car—usually the fourth one—typically the most crowded and, therefore, the least dangerous.

There'll be safety in numbers.

More people descend the stairs. No one looks remotely suspicious, though you can never know anyone's intention.

He moves back from the platform's edge, stands against the station's white tiled wall. Why take a chance on being pushed onto the tracks as a train approaches?

Though it must be only a few minutes, the wait seems endless.

Preceded by a rushing wall of damp air, the 6 local roars into the station. Brakes screech as it comes to a stop.

Eli waits for most of the crowd to board the train, then joins the horde pressing itself into the fourth car. It's packed so tightly, a few coats and backpacks get caught in the doors, preventing them from fully closing. Every time they reopen in an attempt to shut, more stragglers squeeze into the cars, and again the doors jam when the conductor tries to close them.

On the fourth try, the rubber bumpers thump together and the train begins its trek to the next stop: Thirty-Third Street and Park Avenue South.

Though it feels like being crammed in a cattle car, the odds of an ambush occurring are less likely amid the packed-in crowd of straphangers.

He'll be getting off at Grand Central, the stop after Thirty-Third Street. In the press of the car, no one's able to move, so anyone near enough to pose a threat will be visible.

Shifting his gaze to a small opening between passengers, he sees nothing suspicious.

For the moment, he's safe.

At the Forty-Second Street–Grand Central Terminal station, he joins the exodus leaving the train.

The crowd moves glacially along the platform, bobs its way slowly up the stairs toward the terminal's concourse. Looking back, he sees an undulating sea of souls trekking behind him.

There's no way to know if a threat lurks somewhere in the rear.

He climbs the final stairway, and amid the slow-moving mob, strides along the Lexington passage.

At the main concourse, the oceanic noise resounds off the cavernous vault that passes for a ceiling with its painted zodiac constellations. People eddy and crisscross in every direction. The roar of the crowd and its incessant flow seem dreamlike, bring on a dizzying sensation.

Circling the expanse, he sticks to the perimeter, passes gates to trains that will head north through Manhattan toward Westchester and Connecticut.

A glance up at the west balcony reminds him of meeting Gorlov at Cipriani Dolci. Just a little more than a week ago—probably ten days have passed since then—he and Gorlov sat there and discussed the hit on Agapov. Or has it been longer? The days now seem like a dread-filled continuum.

At the west end of the concourse, he scrambles down a stairway to the food court and the lower-level train gates. He moves past jam-packed food concessions with their incessant babble and where people are buying late-afternoon snacks. The air smells of pizza, onions, and garlic.

At Shake Shack, a line of people stands behind theater ropes waiting to order hot dogs, burgers, and custards before boarding trains to the suburbs.

He joins a stream of men and women funneling into the corridor leading to the restrooms. Veering left, he heads into the men's room. He doesn't really have to take a leak, but he'll empty his bladder just to be on the safe side. Needing to piss or empty your bowels can get in the way of an effective countermove if violence breaks out.

The U-shaped men's room is crowded; its marble walls are lined by nearly two dozen urinals. Standing at one, he relieves himself, shakes, tucks, and zips, then washes his hands and dries them under a hand blower.

After leaving the men's room, he climbs the stairway at the east end of the food court.

Back at the Lexington passage, he passes a series of high-end retail shops, then hustles down a stairway to the platform for the Lexington line's 4, 5, and 6 trains stop.

The 4 express and 6 local roar into the station together on either side of the platform.

When the doors of the 6 train open, passengers disgorge from the cars, while those waiting on the platform push their way on board. Swept up in the movement, Eli's forced into the third car. It's the same press of flesh as there'd been on the uptown train.

It's a similar routine with the doors, but finally they remain closed and the train pulls away, heading toward lower Manhattan.

With each successive station on the way downtown, more passengers leave the train than enter it.

The next stop, Bleeker Street, is where he'll get off.

As soon as the train reaches the platform, he's at the door, ready to sprint upstairs to the street.

53

The safe house is a fully furnished fourth-floor studio apartment in an eight-story building located at the intersection of Bleeker and Lafayette.

Eli's rent is paid by monthly electronic transfer of funds to a management company. Eli never writes a check and has nothing to do with any apartment's owner or a management company. His current safe house is in a building that was converted from a commercial structure to a condo a few years earlier. Its thick walls ensure privacy for each apartment. Many of the owners are absentee landlords who lease their apartments as an additional source of income. The realty sayan addresses any problem that may arise during Eli's tenancy.

Rather than enter through the front door, he approaches the service entrance on Bleeker. The door is always locked. A CCTV camera is perched above the door. The doorman can view whoever is making a delivery and can release the lock mechanism by pressing a button at the front desk. As a tenant, Eli knows the entry code.

Eli presses the code numbers on the keypad beside the door; the lock clicks, and he enters a dimly lit hallway.

The heavy, spring-loaded door slams shut behind him.

Avoiding the elevator—they can be death traps, and these days many have CCTV cameras—he climbs the stairway to the fourth floor.

The hallway is deserted.

The apartment is located at the end of the corridor. He unlocks the door and enters the place.

It smells musty. Not a surprise. The apartment has been locked tight for months. The carpet looks gray and dingy. Baseball-size dust bunnies have collected in the corners. A radiator knocks, sounds like a death rattle.

Jesus, this place is depressing.

Despite the tightly closed double-pane windows, a patina of dust is visible in the late-afternoon light filtering into the studio. But it doesn't matter because he won't be staying long—at most another few days.

He opens the pantry closet. He'd stored cans of soup, beans, corned beef hash, and dried pasta, along with tins of tuna and salmon. The place has to be move-in ready at all times. And just like any other apartment in which he's lived, it can be abandoned in a heartbeat.

It's equipped with towels, sheets, blankets, soap, laundry detergent, all supplied by the owner. It has everything needed for a clandestine existence.

He checks the freezer: plenty of frozen vegetables and steaks, enough to last for weeks, not that he'll be staying anywhere near that long.

When he opens a closet door, the dust mites float through the air and create a tickle in his throat.

A canvas satchel sits on the floor beneath a pile of clothing. He unzips the bag and removes a pistol wrapped in a hand towel. It's a .380 Glock, an ultracompact pocket-size lightweight piece. Fully loaded, it weighs just over a pound. It has enough firepower to do plenty of damage.

He unwraps the towel, removes the magazine, makes sure it's empty, checks there's no round sitting in the chamber, then assumes a shooting stance and practices dry firing the pistol.

It's clean and well oiled. Good to go.

Opening a box of cartridges, he loads the magazine with a full complement of rounds, slaps the mag back into the grip, racks the pistol so a cartridge is sitting in the chamber, and sets the gun on the coffee table. The weapon has no safety lever, but a double pressure trigger acts like a safety and makes it unlikely to fire by accident.

He prefers the Beretta and only uses the Glock as backup.

Sitting on the sofa, he opens the laptop, boots up, and hopes he won't have to hit another coffee shop to hook into a Wi-Fi network.

Sure enough, the next-door neighbor still has an unsecured Wi-Fi connection. The guy's router is only one wall away. The signal is strong—five full bars—and gives excellent internet access. Months ago, Eli connected his laptop to the man's network and clicked on the Connect Automatically checkbox, ensuring an instant hookup into the neighbor's Wi-Fi so long as it's not password protected.

Most people are lackadaisical about security. The guy in the adjacent apartment—whom he's never even seen—is no exception. If he changes over to a secure network, Eli will have to find another public place to access Wi-Fi setup—a coffee shop or café—but he won't be in the city long enough for it to be an issue.

A moment later he's online and checks the secure website.

There's no message from Gorlov's IT guy.

He's reminded he has to call the forgery sayan about getting new documents.

It's time to change the monikers for the shell company and both bank accounts. It's just a matter of contacting the banks and providing his so-called identifying information—mother's maiden name, favorite sports star, city where he was born, all bogus factoids—then filling out the forms sent by both banks over secure messaging sites.

Now it's time to settle on a new identity.

It suddenly hits him: it'll be a name—a pseudopersona—he'll use for the rest of his life, however long that may be. It means getting a new birth certificate, passport, and driver's license.

And it has to be done now.

Even with a superb memory, it's getting tough to remember all the pseudonyms and life stories he's adopted since leaving the Mossad. Sometimes they begin to blend, one fictitious character—and his fabricated life story—begins seeping into another. There could come a time when he'll slip up and give himself away. But not if this new identity becomes permanent, not if he lets it seep into his being and, in essence, becomes this person.

He logs on to the bank websites, answers a few identity questions—all listed on a drop-down menu—then changes the user names and passwords for the accounts.

It's another task for his memory because he never writes down anything. It's getting harder to remember all this mundane information; it's almost like memorizing nonsense words. On top of that, each site requires a completely different password each time it's changed.

He now has to enter his new name in the accounts.

He pauses.

Never before has he given much thought to choosing an alias. But this one will be for the rest of his life. Hopefully. If his luck holds out, he'll never have to scrounge around for another identity.

Glancing around the room, he searches for some source to spark his thinking. He's always chosen names based on a nearby object or person so the newly assumed moniker isn't simply an easily forgettable abstraction. Rather, it's attached to some tangible object, situation, or place, making it easier to recall.

And there it is—on a tag attached to the bottom of a fringed ottoman: Ainsley Furniture.

Yes, from now on he'll be Eliot Ainsley. It's a good enough moniker. The name "Eliot" isn't too far from "Eli," so there'll be a similarity to his given name, which will make for easy name recall and recognition. Besides, the surname is the most important identifier when changing your identity. And your birthdate; a descriptor he never changes.

As usual, when taking on a fresh identity, he must create an elaborate biography far beyond assuming a fake moniker. He sifts through a series of newly created life facts—his birthplace, education, job history, even a false history of family life: where he was born and raised, his parents and their professions or occupations, and everything that will be needed to become a different person—all devised to fit his newly minted self.

He repeats the information to himself—twice—and a freshly acquired life history is now embedded in his brain. Yes, he's more than a chameleon. He's a shape-shifter, almost like the cyborg coming after Schwarzenegger in *Terminator 2*.

He'll need to conjure up two more aliases and life stories to be kept in reserve in the unlikely event other identities will become necessary. It'll be another memory task, but it's gotta be done. The sayan will take care of those documents as well.

He changes the names and access information on both accounts and does the same for the shell company.

Now he'll call Eichelberger—the guy's probably the most skilled forger on the planet—to give him the information for three new sets of documents.

After that he'll wait to hear from Irina.

It's likely she'll get in touch late today or tomorrow.

After speaking with Eichelberger, to whom he's wired money for the fee, he sits quietly.

He hasn't done his crunches, sit-ups, and push-ups for the last few days. Nor has he practiced his Krav Maga combinations. And he hasn't taken those long walks to maintain stamina. He's been too preoccupied with Gorlov's job, with Irina, and with the near disaster with Agapov's crew. And by the danger now facing Irina. Once he gets out of the country, there'll be plenty of time for staying in shape.

Sitting on the sofa, he closes his eyes.

Suddenly there's a sound coming from the hallway. It's not a voice. It can't be the next-door neighbor because no matter what the hour, that guy's always talking on his cell phone, even while walking along the hallway.

Something's being dragged along the carpet.

He strains to hear it again.

Footsteps, coming closer, nearing the door.

And there's that dragging sound.

With his pulse pounding, he picks up the Glock.

Pulling himself up from the sofa, he moves toward the door.

He peers through the peephole but sees nothing out there.

Then he hears it: the key turns in the lock cylinder next door. There's squealing as the door of the adjacent apartment opens. It's followed by a clunk of what must be the wheels of a roller suitcase bumping over the saddle threshold, then coursing along the wooden floor of the neighbor's place.

Eli's muscles relax.

He returns to the sofa and sits. Leaning back, he feels bone weary. He closes his eyes and begins drifting into a twilight sleep. His thoughts spool through so many things: there's the Bratva and Gorlov and Agapov and Sasha and Irina, and there's a strange melding of past and present because now Hannah's standing in that orchard holding a basket of apples and he's back to that magical day when he first saw her and his heart soared and of all things she's here in this moment and that lovely smile spreads across her lips as he gazes into her eyes—so luminous and soulful—and now she's sitting next to him as shafts of sunlight stream through the apple trees, and he's about to tell her he loves her, yet for some reason the words won't come as he struggles to say what he wants to, and suddenly his chin drops onto his chest and his eyes pop open and he realizes none of this is real.

How long did that reverie go on?

Maybe a minute.

Or was it only seconds?

God, how I wish you could come back to me, Hannah, he thinks.

Or did he say it aloud in a voice drained by despair?

Jesus, now I'm talking to myself.

Fully awake, he no longer hears the muted sounds of traffic or the clamor of the street or the ticking of his wristwatch or any sound from the neighbor's place.

He hears only the hush of the apartment.

54

An hour later, he again opens the laptop.

There's a message on the secure site, which isn't all that secure anymore:

> Call me as soon as you can.
> Viktor

Using the sat phone, he dials Viktor's number.

"It's Aiden."

"Good, good," Viktor says. "Have you made progress with Irina Sakharov?"

Hearing her name sends a low-voltage charge through Eli's chest.

"Yes, but I've only met her once."

"Will you be seeing her again?"

"She said she'd call me."

"Why don't you call *her*?"

"In my experience, the best way to make a woman lose interest is to seem too eager," Eli says, aware the pressure from Gorlov is mounting. It'll be tough to temporize. There must be a way to draw this out, though how much time can there be with the thugs from Agapov's brigade tracking him?

"You have so much experience with women?" Viktor asks, a hint of sarcasm infiltrating his voice.

A long silence follows.

Waiting, Eli hears the man's breathing.

"Anton is getting impatient," Viktor finally says. "He needs this thing taken care of very soon."

"I can't force anything with her. If I do, she'll get suspicious."

I can't be unreasonable, but I gotta play for more time.

"We need you to make a move now," Victor responds in a truculent-laced tone that makes Eli realize he's pushing the envelope too far.

"It'll take more than another meeting to gain enough of her trust for me to bring up anything about the flash drive."

Viktor sighs. "Tell me, Aiden, do you read the papers? Or watch television?"

"Sometimes. Why?"

"Because last night we lost two men. They were gunned down on the street in Coney Island. We know it was Koskoff's doing. We're at war."

"Koskoff?"

"The new pakhan, who took over after Agapov died. And Koskoff is not a man to be fooled with. We need something to happen . . . *soon*."

"I'll do the best I can," Eli replies, aware his voice is softening. He has to make it appear that he's moving quickly, yet it could take some time to gain Irina's trust enough to tell her what's going on.

"Make something happen *fast*," Viktor says. "Find out what you can and contact me as soon as you do."

"Okay. I'll do it as fast as possible."

Victor ends the call.

Eli sits in stunned silence. He doesn't give a shit about those Russians. War between the brigades might just knock off the entire Odessa mafia. And Koskoff's brigade too. After what happened the other night, he's tempted to tell Viktor it's too dangerous to continue with this scheme, but if he pulls out, Gorlov will take matters into his own hands. And that'll be the end of Irina.

So something's gotta happen—fast—for Irina and for himself.

Then it's time to leave the country. Permanently.

Eli long ago accepted that after his family was destroyed, he'd never have an ordinary life, one filled with the simple pleasures people take for granted. There'd be no new wife or a baby or a house with its everyday routines. Once that bus exploded, it was never gonna be in the cards. There'd be nothing in his life that could be remotely seen as normal, whatever *that* might be.

Because something within him—perhaps his soul—died that day in Jerusalem.

But now there's been a change.

And it's not just that he's met Irina, the first woman since Hannah for whom he feels something. It must have started before that night at the party. He was aware of it the night he took Agapov down, when afterward he went to Casey's and ran into Noah. When the guy talked about his wife and kids, Eli felt a pang of jealousy for the life Noah's allowed himself to have.

Yes, it was envy—a powerful craving for something he doesn't have. It's a feeling of wanting something, even desperately wishing for it. And of all things, it's a welcome feeling.

It could mean there's hope for something beyond the life he now has, that there might be a different future.

It might be more than kill or be killed.

Is there a way out of this emptiness?

Is there a possibility of a life with some meaning?

Maybe there is.

But he'll have to make something happen *fast*, if not for Irina, then for himself.

55

When his cell phone rings, he picks it up.

"Yes?"

"Hello, Aiden."

It's Irina, with that voice and its smoky timbre.

His heart starts kicking, and a tingling sensation ripples through the skin at the back of his neck. "Irina, how are you feeling?" he manages to ask without his voice quivering.

"Much better. Thank you. Headache is gone. Sasha says you come to health club to say hello."

"Yes. I wanted to see you."

"That's so nice of you."

"Are you going back to work tomorrow?"

"No. I will be at new apartment and must take care of so many things. I will have day off. Like I said, I am renting from Sasha's friend who goes away for one year. So I stay here now. It is . . . how do you say? Sublet?"

"Yes, a sublet."

"It has all the furniture. Sasha's friend gives me a break on rent. I am lucky."

Should I tell her about Gorlov now? No, not over the phone. It's better done in person.

"That's wonderful," he says. "We should go out to dinner and celebrate."

"That will be so nice."

"Are you free tonight?"

"Oh, Aiden, I have much to do. Unpack clothes, get place ready, go to bank and open account, get checks, and so many things. And Sasha will be taking time off to help me. I must leave time for that. Is it good for you tomorrow night?"

"Yes, that works. How's eight o'clock?"

"That will be good."

"You'll be at your new place?"

"Yes."

"I'll come by and pick you up."

She gives him the address; it's a building on East Twenty-Second Street, not far from Sasha's apartment and the health club.

"I tried to call you, but your phone wasn't in service."

"Yes, I have trouble with telephone people. They say I don't pay the bill but I do. It is driving me crazy. But I am on that phone now. It is all fixed up. And now I will have landline too. It is good to be on my own now."

To make sure he has the correct number, she gives it to him again. Yes, it's the one he'd stored in his contacts.

Though they speak a few more minutes, Eli senses she's anxious to get back to the rest of her chores. Her voice is filled with the excitement of beginning a new chapter in her life.

"I'll see you tomorrow night at eight," he says, reluctantly ending the call.

She's so enthusiastic about having her own place and seems so trusting of Sasha, she'll have trouble believing a word of what he'll tell her. After all, he's nothing more to her than a man she met at a party and with whom she shared a pub dinner. Yes, they also shared a kiss, but the reality is simple: he's an interloper in her life.

On the other hand, Sasha's been like her guardian angel.

But there's no choice. He'll try to get her to understand the danger she'll face, and then he'll leave.

Listen to Noah. And to your gut. It's time to get out. To a place where you can make a new life.

But as he gets up to brew a cup of coffee, he recalls part of the conversation he and Irina had at O'Malley's.

I like your name—Irina. It's a beautiful name. What does it mean?

Irina? In Russia it means peace.

Peace . . . I like that.

We both find peace, yes?

Yes, we'll find peace.

I am toasting peace.

Eli thinks, *Yes, Irina . . . here's to peace. May we both have it for as long as we live.*

And he knows something else to be true: walking away from her won't be easy.

56

After finishing his breakfast of fried eggs and kasha, Anton sips coffee while looking out onto the gray wintery waters of Little Neck Bay.

He thinks back to the days when he lived in Odessa and looked out over the Black Sea. The Atlantic Ocean is far more impressive, and once they leave the United States, he'll be gazing at the Caribbean, where he's been told the water is a crystal-clear aqua blue, and where he'll swim every day all year long beneath a tropical sun.

It's a windy day, and whitecaps churn on the rise and fall on Little Neck Bay's choppy surface. The arc of the distant Throgs Neck Bridge is visible through the heavy morning mist. The air itself looks gray and thick and ominous. It's such a dreary scene, or is it merely his mood after what's happened these last few days?

Since this trouble with Koskoff's brigade began, Victor arranged for Anton and Katerina to stay at his cousin's house on Shore Cliff Place in Great Neck. Although it's a luxurious place filled with modern art and expensive furniture, it feels like he and Katerina are living behind a walled garrison. And the military feel of the place is reinforced by the fact that Anton's posted four of their best men strategically around the property. Right now two of them are patrolling the area in the back, where there's a covered swimming pool and a small dock at the water's edge. Both men are braving the bitter cold and carry micro Uzis beneath their overcoats.

Though he hates admitting it, being holed up here makes him feel like a fugitive running for his life. Which, in fact, is true.

Viktor feels the same way. He and Oksana are staying with his relatives in their house at Shippan Point in Stamford.

Katerina's not happy with this arrangement. "This is no way to begin a new life," she complained. "Why don't we leave right now, just get out of the country?"

"Because there are a few details that must be taken care of," he'd said.

"What details?"

He shook his head, and she knew better than to pursue the issue beyond that question.

Yesterday, with heavy security, he and Katerina risked leaving this grand house and were driven to the courthouse in downtown Brooklyn.

Judge Moreno, for whom Anton had done many favors over the years, waived the twenty-four-hour waiting period and arranged for their marriage license to be readied and brought to his chambers. They were married by the judge, with his bailiff and clerk acting as witnesses. They were then whisked back to Great Neck by Anton's chauffeur.

Katerina's a good woman, far better than he deserves. She accepted that they couldn't even celebrate with lunch at what he's been told is a fine Peter Luger steakhouse on Northern Boulevard. It's far too risky, even at a restaurant that's nowhere near Brooklyn because Koskoff's assassins could be anywhere. He could have farmed out the hit to any one of a number of local gangs, so distance from Brooklyn doesn't mean Anton's out of Koskoff's reach.

After the little ceremony in the judge's chambers, they headed straight back here. He spent an hour scrounging around to see if Viktor's cousins, who are vacationing in Palm Beach, had any vodka or maybe a bottle of champagne somewhere in the house—anything he could use to toast his new bride.

And to toast their new life in the Caribbean, away from all this scheming and killing. They've decided on Antigua, a lovely island in the Antilles, where they'll be unknown and untroubled by all this Bratva business where all his underlings with the exception of Viktor are waiting to pounce on him like a bunch of scorpions. And where there's no organized crime.

Though Viktor preferred Costa Rica—they nearly had an argument about it—he finally agreed that Antigua is better since Costa Rica is now plagued by a substantial criminal element. The reach of the Mexican cartels is getting to be nearly as great as that of the Bratva.

Anton's grateful Victor is taking care of all the details and that he and Oksana will be moving to Antigua with them.

There's enough money to last them all for the rest of their lives. And they won't have to worry about competing brigades or assassinations or the government's bureaucrats and corrupt puppets coming after them. Once this business with that woman is taken care of, they'll be free of any possible entanglements that could come back to haunt them.

Their new identities are ready. He and Katerina are already practicing using their new names.

Viktor is smart: he arranged for Volkov to forge documents using their real first names, but changed the surnames. If they had new first names, there's a chance they'd mistakenly call each other by their real names and give themselves away.

And Viktor went online, contacted a real estate agency, and is in the process of renting two adjacent houses at Galleon Beach on the southern tip of the island. When the time comes, they'll find permanent homes and live the rest of their lives on a lovely Caribbean island.

With Vasily and both accountants gone, they've taken care of nearly all unfinished business. Now there's only one loose end that needs to be taken care of.

Yes, the only thing left is this business with Aiden and that Irina woman.

57

Late the following afternoon, Eli prepares to leave the safe house.

He's grown antsy waiting for today to end and eagerly anticipates this evening with Irina.

It would be wise to stay in this hideaway until he meets her tonight, but he has to come up with an idea about how to tell her what's going on. He's always done his best thinking when walking at a brisk pace, when blood flows through every part of his body and perfuses his brain. And he needs to walk because he feels restless being cooped up in this dust-filled studio. Also, a fast-paced hike to Brooklyn might begin to make up for the lack of exercise over these last few days.

After heading down the stairway, he leaves the building through the side-street service door.

At the corner of Bleeker and Lafayette, he turns and walks on Lafayette toward the southern tip of Manhattan, heading for the Brooklyn Bridge.

On this bitterly cold afternoon, he wears jeans, a heavy wool sweater over a denim shirt, a waist-length black leather jacket, and Noah's watch cap. The Beretta is tucked into his waistband. He's wearing the nonprescription eyeglasses to shield his eyes from the harsh wind whipping up Lafayette Street. He's not wearing gloves, so if necessary, he can pull the pistol and quickly slip his finger behind the trigger guard.

He walks past what had once been old factory buildings, purchased by either NYU—which turned them into dormitory, office, and classroom space—or developers, who've hollowed them out and created multimillion-dollar loft condos.

Either way, the once bohemian charm of Greenwich Village has almost completely disappeared, and it's rapidly becoming just another gentrified neighborhood.

Same goes for nearby NoHo, SoHo, and Nolita, with their converted loft apartments, high-end condos, hip art galleries, designer-label clothing shops, and trendy restaurants.

Long gone are the mom-and-pop storefronts, cozy coffee houses, and welcoming pubs.

I won't miss one bit of this pretentiousness, Eli thinks as his stomach growls, and he looks for a simple place to pop into for a quick bite to eat.

It takes another five blocks before he picks up an enticing aroma wafting from the vents of a souvlaki joint sandwiched between a hair salon and a fancy-assed bootery.

The proprietor must own the building to be able to operate this dive in such a pricey neighborhood, Eli thinks, as he enters the hole-in-the-wall storefront.

The interior is warm, humid, and redolent of Middle Eastern spices.

At three o'clock in the afternoon, he's the only customer.

Wearing a white T-shirt and trousers, the counterman has a potbelly that looks like a sandbag drooping over his belt.

Eli orders a gyro.

Another guy behind the counter is busy slicing down a large chunk of lamb set on a vertical rotisserie.

Though posters of Greek tourist attractions hang on the wall—the Parthenon, the Acropolis, some of the Greek islands: Mykonos, Santorini, and Rhodes—neither guy is Greek.

Not by a long shot.

They're speaking to each other in Arabic with a distinct Syrian dialect. A portable radio behind the counter plays softly. Eli recognizes the sound of the Tunisian rock band Myrath. The music and voices make him jumpy, remind him of Damascus and of operations he and Noah carried out around the city.

And of that pajama-clad little boy, Nasim, standing outside Awad's office.

Are you the Prophet? Or are you Santa?

For a moment he's tempted to get up and leave, but hunger wins out. Trying to divert his thoughts, he focuses on the counterman, watches him slit open a pita bread, then stuff it with the lamb, diced tomato, a slice of onion, and tzatziki sauce.

And he thinks about tonight with Irina. Anticipation is almost always part of what's worthwhile.

Eli pays with cash, then sits at a Formica-topped table facing the door and polishes off the gyro. After sucking meat juice from his fingers, he wipes them with a paper napkin and realizes the aromas of lamb and spices remind him of street vendors in Tel Aviv and Be'er Sheva. Then come images of Damascus, where he once lived in a safe house while tracking the movements of a high-ranking Hamas operative who's now history.

As another image of little Nasim begins to intrude, he reminds himself he's not in the Middle East. He's in New York City on a cold winter day, about to head off to Brooklyn and the neighborhood where his mother lived during her high school and college days. And he realizes that he regrets having never asked questions about his mother's and father's pasts, their upbringings, their experiences; he'd been too young, too preoccupied with his own little world.

Sitting in this little shop, a simple thing like a familiar aroma, hearing Arabic, or the strains of Middle Eastern music can bring on a flood of memories—and feelings—so powerful, he might as well be on a Mossad mission in Damascus.

He again tries to reroute his thoughts from the Middle East or Gorlov and the plot to ensnare Irina. He can stay away from the safe house for a few hours; there's a hotel in Brooklyn Heights—the Bossert on the corner of Montague and Hicks Street—where he could hang out in the lobby to minimize time spent in Manhattan. Yes, he'll buy a newspaper, sit in the hotel's lobby, and catch up on the news. There's no way he can be tracked to Brooklyn, especially if he goes on foot.

Afterward, he'll take the subway back to Bleeker Street and get ready for the evening with Irina.

Back on the street, he hits a steady walking rhythm and heads downtown.

He's lost in thought about what he'll say to Irina. She'll probably recoil in horror when she hears about Gorlov's scheme. And when she learns of Sasha's involvement, she may not believe a word of what he tells her. How could a cousin with whom she's lived and who's given her a job betray her? It seems to Eli an impossible task, but there's no way he can let this scenario play out to its conclusion.

58

The Brooklyn Bridge walkway is nearly deserted.

On this cold and windy day, few people brave the weather and trek across the bridge, a distance of nearly two kilometers. An occasional bicycle rider passes by in the bike lane. The temperature is so low it makes summer seem unimaginable. It always seems that way in the middle of winter, and yet the seasons change and warm weather returns.

Midway over the river, a frigid gust of wind hits him with such force he has to lean into it to keep going. His ears burn, and despite wearing glasses, his eyes water. Wiping the tears away, he lowers the watch cap over his ears.

Nearing the Brooklyn side of the river, he casts a look back to make sure he's not being tailed.

Once in Brooklyn, he heads over to Cranberry Street and walks past nineteenth-century row houses and brownstone mansions.

He gets to the promenade, a wide pedestrian walkway cantilevered over the Brooklyn–Queens Expressway. The view of the New York harbor is spectacular—picture-postcard perfect. The crenellated lower-Manhattan skyline always reminds him of medieval battlements—and of the walls of Jerusalem's Old City.

The view extends from the Statue of Liberty at the south to the tidal basin of the East River passing beneath the Manhattan and Williamsburg Bridges. He could never tire of looking at the Gothic towers of the Brooklyn Bridge.

The sun is setting behind lower Manhattan to his west. In the gathering darkness, an orange glow backlights the serried skyscrapers of the financial district. Thousands of window lights form a latticework of luminescence against the gloaming sky, which looks like a fiery red-orange mandorla behind the buildings.

As the world fades into night, the reflection of the window-lit skyline glimmers on the inky waters of the harbor. There's a rippling iridescence to the surface of the estuary. In the distance to his left, the Statue of Liberty looks pistachio green bathed in the floodlights of Liberty Island.

Traffic traversing the span of the Brooklyn Bridge creates a flickering trail of headlights in the direction of Brooklyn, while a necklace of winking red taillights flows toward Manhattan. The cars crisscrossing the bridge create a distant thrumming in the night air.

From this vantage point, the cityscape—a glittering giant in the distance—has a voluptuous vitality that always energizes him.

The promenade lamps cast discrete pools of pinkish light on the walkway.

The cold temperature ensures the pathway will be virtually deserted except for an occasional pedestrian hurrying to get out of the cold.

Eli again wonders how best to warn Irina about the danger she faces. No matter what he says or how he puts it, she'll ask how he's come by this information. He'll have to reveal his role in it all.

She'll never want to see him again.

Can he describe it in a way that won't frighten her to death?

Concentrate. Talk it out to yourself. You can do this.

Suddenly, he picks up movement in the periphery.

Two men approach from his right.

They're about fifty meters away, closing in.

His internal alarm begins clanging. It's a signal from the archaic part of his brain, one that sends a chill shimmering through his chest.

The message is primal and clear: predators are coming.

59

They wear heavy coats.

One guy has a parka hood raised over his head. The other wears a watch cap pulled down over his ears. Their hands are jammed in their pockets, where no doubt they have guns.

The deliberateness of their gait is a giveaway: unlike the other pedestrians, they're not rushing to get out of the cold.

Because they're on a mission.

Yes, they're Koskoff's men.

Or hit men to whom he's outsourced the job. Albanians, maybe Chechens or Dominicans. It's impossible to tell from this distance.

Shit. Even walking all the way to Brooklyn wasn't safe. They must know the location of the safe house and managed to tail him from there. It was only a matter of time before they would get to him.

And the time is now.

A prickly feeling scours his skin. He feels a throbbing sensation in his neck.

The isolated expanse of the promenade is a perfect kill point. After shooting, they can run down a quiet Brooklyn street and get to the subway station at either the Clark Street or Montague Street station.

That sense of menace heightens. It's the biology of instinct.

Mossad training taught him about a small, almond-shaped part of the limbic system—the amygdala, the brain's primitive alarm system. In a moment of threat, it pours a flood of impulses that activate the body and ready it for a survival response.

Fight or flight. The mantra for staying alive.

But there's no flight here, no fleeing, no panic, just an eerie calm as his hand moves slowly beneath his jacket to the inside of his waistband, and even as his palm wraps around the Beretta's grip, he's calculating angles, speed, trajectory, and now the pistol is nestled in his hand and the ball of his thumb is on the safety lever, moving it so the locking mechanism is turned off and the gun is ready to fire, and since a round is already chambered, there's no need to rack the slide, and when he raises the gun and pulls the trigger, a .22 long rifle slug will sink into the first guy's chest; he's the larger of the two men, the one walking on the near side closest to where Eli's sitting, and before the second guy even registers what's happening, a forty-grain bullet will smash through his skull and his lights will go out. And he'll pour more lead into them and then walk away. He'll worry about where to go after these guys are dead.

They're less than fifteen meters away and coming.

They're talking to each other, as though they're just having a casual conversation as they walk along the promenade, impervious to the weather because they're on a mission and he's the target.

The Beretta is now resting against his thigh, where it can't be seen by them. His finger sits on the trigger, partially pressing it, taking up slack, which will give him an advantage for speed firing when even a tenth of a second can be crucial in getting off the first shots. And staying alive.

The world seems to slow as he continues with a series of mercurial calculations—of time, distance, motion, and speed. The slug from the Beretta has a muzzle velocity of more than 300 meters per second—faster than the speed of sound—and he can empty the magazine in two and a half seconds. The bullets will shear flesh, shatter small bones, and lodge deep in a man's organs. Rapid firing at a moving target is embedded in his muscle memory, and once he makes a move, it'll be over.

They're closer now, maybe five meters away, and carrying on the wind, their words reach his ears.

They're not Russians or Ukrainians or Dominicans or Chechens or Albanians.

They're speaking English.

Americans.

Talking politics.

They pass by, looking straight ahead, walking steadily, still jawboning.

Yet Eli waits. His eyes follow them, and he's ready to raise the Beretta and shoot because they might turn suddenly, whip out hardware, and start firing.

But they don't.

They just keep walking, as though Eli isn't even there, sitting on a bench only ten meters behind them.

Though they were harmless and ultimately meaningless, they were potent reminders that the mere twitch of a finger can put an end to life.

A single movement of an index finger can mean Eli's a dead man.

60

When his heart rate slows, he begins shivering in the cold. It's that postadrenaline depletion that leaves him feeling like jelly.

Forget about hanging around the Bossert Hotel. It's time to head back to the safe house and get ready for the evening. He'll take a circuitous route to lessen the chance of being successfully tracked.

He gets up from the bench and makes his way along Montague Street toward the subway station at Borough Hall.

Those guys on the promenade were a false alarm, one of many he's had in this life.

Thoughts of Irina flood his mind. When he tells her about Gorlov and Sasha, it'll be like a thunderclap to her.

He tries imagining the conversation.

Irina, you're in terrible danger.

What do you mean?

Your brother created a flash drive. It has information about criminal activity. If the police get their hands on it, certain people in the Russian mafia will go to prison. They think you have it.

Mafia? What are you talking about? How do you know this?

Does he tell her he was hired to get close to her and learn the whereabouts of that device? That he was hired to facilitate Gorlov's plans? That they'll make sure she never tells anyone about that flash drive? That she faces death or enslavement in a foreign country once Gorlov's people either have the flash drive or realize it's nowhere to be found?

Will she tell Sasha whatever he reveals? If she does, Sasha will tell Gorlov, and that'll seal Irina's fate.

Noah's advice resounds in his head: *The Russian? Oh, c'mon, man. Forget her. She's as good as dead. And if you hang around waiting for her, you'll be dead too.*

As the temperature plummets and the wind kicks up, Eli wonders why he thought it would be a good idea to head out to Brooklyn.

Did I really think being near where Mom grew up would make me think more clearly? As though Mom would magically advise me about what to do? I should never have left the safe house. I'll return Gorlov's money and get out of here.

Those goons are in the middle of a war, and maybe this flash drive problem isn't at the top of their to-do list.

I could forget about the date, just not show, stand her up.

Do the smart thing, just get out.

61

Standing in the shower, Eli realizes there's no way he could just pick up and leave without warning Irina of what's coming.

And he's been anticipating this evening more than he'd like to acknowledge. He'll decide when it's best to tell her about Gorlov's scheme and its ramifications. And he'll let her know about Sasha. Nothing will happen in the next day or two. Letting her know what she faces is all he can do.

Then he'll get out of the country.

Dressed and ready to leave, he momentarily thinks about leaving the Beretta behind.

Not a good idea. No way can he make the mistake he did when going to Sasha's party. So he tucks the pistol in the back of his waistband, dons a sports jacket, and then slips into an overcoat.

After a short subway ride uptown, he walks from the Twenty-Third Street station toward Irina's apartment building.

The air is as frigid as it was on the night they met. He's glad to be bundled up against the cold by covering his mouth with Noah's scarf. And there's a small bonus: the scarf also gives him a slightly changed appearance should Russian thugs be anywhere in the vicinity. Though being tracked is a possibility, it seems unlikely.

Irina's place at 233 East Twenty-Second Street is in a newly constructed building on the north side of the street located midway between Third and Second Avenues.

To Eli's surprise, Irina is braving the cold and waiting for him beneath the building's awning.

Seeing her standing beneath the pinkish glow of a nearby streetlight, he feels an eagerness he hadn't anticipated until this moment.

"Aiden, I been waiting for you," she says as he nears her. Her lips spread into a welcoming smile.

They plant light kisses on each other's cheeks.

"Why're you outside on such a cold night?" he asks as they clasp hands.

"Because I want to show you apartment, but not now, later—yes? We have nice dinner and come back here—okay?" A mischievous smile spreads across her lips.

That frisson of desire quivers through him, reminds him of the kiss they shared in front of Sasha's building.

Yet an undercurrent of dread slithers through him.

It's not about the possibility that they're being followed. It concerns how she'll react when he tells her about Gorlov's scheme. Will she get up from the table and run from the restaurant? Will she ever want to see him again? He's always faced dilemmas with confidence, but tonight he's uncertain what to do. There's still time to figure out how and what to tell her.

Irina chatters on about her apartment, about how much she loves the building, and mentions having set up a checking account. "And now I have a savings account too," she says. "Only three apartments are sold and everything is new in the building. Not so much noise like place in Moscow."

"The building looks lovely."

"After we have dinner, we come back here, yes?" she adds, with that smile again spreading across her lips.

"I hope you're hungry," he says as they walk toward Second Avenue. "I've made reservations at an Italian restaurant."

"I dunno Italian food. You will show me how to order, yes?"

"Of course."

"Where is it?"

"Greenwich Village."

"I never been there. I hear it is fun place to be going," she says, squeezing his arm.

"We'll take a short tour before we go to the restaurant," he says, despite wanting to minimize their time on the street. *Walking a few blocks on a crowded street won't put us in too much danger. Not in a place like the Village, with its crowds and tumult.*

They're in luck: at the corner of Twenty-Second Street and Second Avenue, he sees an unoccupied taxi and waves it over to the curb.

The warmth of the taxi's interior is welcoming.

"It is so cold tonight—feels like Moscow," Irina whispers, pressing close to him.

They head downtown amid a swarm of taxis and a medley of honking horns.

He's delightfully aware of her nearness; it portends intimacy. He drapes his arm around her. She responds by nuzzling close to him, and he takes in the fragrance of her hair.

The nagging worry about revealing Gorlov's scheme competes with the excitement of having her so near.

The taxi drops them off at Bleeker and LaGuardia Place.

Ironically, they're only a few blocks from the safe house. Walking amid a tide of pedestrians—couples, NYU students, tourists, bands of teens—they're in the commercial heart of the Village. Despite the chilled February air, the street pulses with the crowds.

He suddenly realizes he hasn't scanned his surroundings. He's been careless. Doing a quick perimeter check, he realizes how perverse his life has been. No matter where he may be, he's always aware of what's around him, the people, the situation, anything that seems even remotely unusual. He can never afford to be careless. But that'll change once he gets away from the city.

As they pass a jazz club, the House of Blues, the door swings open and a couple emerges. The muted notes of the Miles Davis version of "Stella by Starlight" drift out to the street.

Eli thinks of the times he's enjoyed listening to music—rock or jazz or pop—when he and Hannah felt the music down to their souls. They'd often go to nighttime concerts at the ancient Roman amphitheater in Caesarea and afterward at a club in Tel Aviv to dance.

"Maybe someday you take me to jazz place," Irina says. "We have good jazz in Moscow."

He imagines taking her to a club and sharing a bottle of wine while enjoying the music. As enticing as the fantasy may be, it won't happen anywhere in New York. Is there a possibility they could be together somewhere else?

Am I thinking of going away with her? Jesus, that's just a kid's fantasy. Grow the fuck up.

As they walk toward the restaurant, Irina seems to be taking everything in with a joyfulness that makes him feel truly alive, just as it was with Hannah so long ago. It's as though the past has returned.

But it hasn't. They're immersed in the present, in the danger of what's happening now. In the risk that exists for each of them.

And he'd better figure out when to tell Irina what awaits her.

Maybe it'll be easier after a few drinks, or it might be best to tell her when they get back to her place.

It has to happen soon.

Because time is running out.

62

Umberto's is a low-key place on Thompson Street, between Bleeker and West Houston.

Eli's been here many times but with intervals of a few months between visits, so he's never fallen into a predictable pattern.

Umberto, the chef-owner, faithfully maintains the culinary traditions of his native Naples. No fancy-ass risottos with shaved white truffles are served here. Neither is pumpkin risotto with hot gorgonzola sauce on the menu. This isn't one of those pretentious uptown eateries. Down-home southern Italian dishes are the mainstays here. Savory, tomato-based sauces served over generous portions of handmade pasta dominate the menu.

The restaurant's ambience—straight out of a long-lost era—appeals to Eli much more than what you find in the sleek (and overly priced) trattorias on the Upper East Side. There's no jet-engine noise level at Umberto's. Nor are any millennials using cell phones to snap pictures of their food for posting on Twitter or Instagram.

Brass sconces on stucco walls cast a welcoming peach-toned glow onto well-spaced tables napped with starched white linen cloths. Candles flicker romantically on each table.

The dining room's sound system plays Neapolitan love songs, but never at a volume that interferes with intimate conversation.

Yes, intimate. That's the most fitting description of Umberto's, and Eli's certain it's the right place to have *the conversation* if he can figure out just when and how to broach the subject.

They descend three steps, entering a small anteroom that has the bar. With just three stools, it's no more than a service bar, but it doubles as a convenient perch where patrons can enjoy a drink while waiting to be seated when the place is busy.

But at this hour of the evening, the dining room is only half full.

Mario, the effusive maître d', finishes seating another couple, then rushes to the front room's podium to greet them. "Ah, Mr. West, we haven't had the pleasure of seeing you for a long time," Mario says breathlessly in his thick Italian accent. "Just as you requested, we've reserved table number four for you and your companion."

Aiden West is the name he uses, not only with the Odessa mafia, but when he dines at Umberto's, as well.

As Eli and Mario shake hands, a folded twenty-dollar bill passes discreetly from Eli's palm into the captain's hand. Ever grateful for the gratuity, Mario says, *Grazie, signor*, bows lightly, takes their coats and hands them to the woman standing behind the Dutch door of the coatroom.

Irina is wearing dark slacks, a black sweater, and high heels that accentuate her height. A delicate choke chain surrounds her neck. Small pearl earrings adorn her earlobes.

Mario leads them to the dining area at the rear of the restaurant. As they walk toward their table, the room falls silent. Heads turn and eyes focus on Irina. Eli guesses it happens each time she enters a room. She's definitely a traffic-stopper.

As Eli had known when he reserved the corner table, Irina would be seated facing the other diners, while he'd have a good view of the entrance and bar area off to his left.

With a flourish, Mario pulls out the chair where Irina will be sitting. As she sits, he again bows slightly.

"Have you ever tried a Negroni?" Eli asks when they're seated. He's always enjoyed starting an evening with that aperitif at Umberto's.

"No, never," she says, "but I try it, if you say it is good. You take me to such beautiful place." Her eyes gleam as she takes in the room. Eli notices people at nearby tables staring at her, but she seems not to notice.

"Two Negronis, Mario," Eli says.

"I'm so pleased you like our *ristorante*," Mario says, beaming before he heads to the bar area.

A minute later Eli sees a burly man wearing a black leather car coat enter and sit at the service bar.

There's something off-kilter about the guy. He obviously has no reservation. He's alone, doesn't take off his coat, and says nothing to Mario. In his late thirties, rough-featured with dark hair and a fleshy face, he looks like he's part of the bridge-and-tunnel crowd; probably drove into Manhattan from Brooklyn or Queens. He peers about as though trying to get a bead on the restaurant's layout.

Eli's antennae shoot skyward. The guy could be a hit man.

Irina's glancing about the room and commenting on the ambience and how she was so looking forward to this evening.

But Eli is lasered in on the guy at the bar.

The bartender pours the man a glass of red wine.

He picks up the glass, takes a sip, sets it down on the bar, then narrows his eyes and looks around again. Yes, he's scoping out the place.

Shit, this guy's as obvious as a dog's balls.

Eli realizes he could have been tailed from the safe house to Irina's place, then shadowed on the way to the restaurant.

The guy picks up his wineglass, puts it to his lips, and drains the rest of his wine, then sets the glass down on the bar.

Eli waits to see his next move.

But suddenly a party of eight enters the restaurant and congregates in the front room. The crowd blocks Eli's view of the bar. The guy could slip through the throng and saunter into the dining room with a pistol dangling next to his thigh.

And then open fire.

Can't take a chance; gotta check him out.

"Umberto is the name of the owner?" Irina asks.

"Yes. And I want to tell him something. Will you excuse me?" he asks, doing his best to sound casual, though his heart is battering his chest wall.

"Of course."

"I'll be right back," he says, getting up from the table.

With his pulse thundering through his skull, he heads toward the front area.

He feels coiled, ready for anything.

What do I do?

Grab a stool and sit next to the guy?

Tell him he's being watched and if he makes a move, he'll be taken out?

Eli weaves through the people in the front room.

He focuses on the bar.

All three bar stools are unoccupied.

An empty wineglass sits on the bar top.

The bartender is mixing a gin and tonic.

"The man who was sitting here," Eli says, pointing to the empty stool.

"Yes, sir?"

"Did he leave?"

"Yes, just a moment ago."

"Did he say anything?"

"No, sir. He drank his wine, paid up, and left."

He might be lurking outside waiting for us to leave the restaurant.

Back at the table, Eli realizes he's living moment-to-moment immersed in a sense of danger.

Something's gotta change. Soon. It's impossible to go on living this way.

While they're sipping their aperitifs, he wonders if this is the time to tell Irina about Gorlov's scheme.

He'd composed a speech earlier in the evening.

Irina, I have to confess that our meeting the other night wasn't accidental.

But his heart's only now beginning to decelerate from the jackrabbit pace of moments ago. Maybe it would be better to tell her when they're alone; when there are no distractions. When they're back at her place.

Besides, he's still not sure how to put it to her. It had seemed fine when he'd run through it back at the safe house, but now it feels canned, rehearsed—which it definitely is.

Later in the evening will be a better time.

Franco, a waiter at the restaurant since the Bronze Age, appears at the table.

A short, stocky, gray-haired man in his fifties, he wears black pants, a white shirt with a black bow tie, and a gold-colored Eton jacket with black lapels.

Franco regards being a waiter as a profession, not an interlude between auditions like the twentysomething guys working the East Side bistros. He's waited on Eli many times over the years and appreciates a patron who tips generously—in cash.

"Good evening, Mr. West," he says with a broad smile on his face. "Welcome back. It's a pleasure to see you."

"It's nice to see you again, Franco."

Warm feelings and a sense of bonhomie wash over Eli. He appreciates Franco's familiarity more than ever before.

"And welcome to Umberto's," Franco says to Irina as he extends her a slight bow.

She smiles. Her gaze then flits to Eli, as though she's not quite certain how to respond to the waiter.

"Will you be having wine with dinner?" Franco asks.

Eli gazes at Irina. "Let's order a bottle," he says, knowing he's about to abandon another well-established routine: he'll need some wine to warm up for what he must tell her, even if it's later at her apartment.

Smiling, she nods. "Red is nice for me."

"We'd like a Barolo," Eli says.

"Which do you prefer?"

"The finest in the house," he tells Franco. "You choose."

"As you wish, Mr. West. My pleasure."

A minute later, Franco returns with a bottle of 2010 Ceretto Barolo Brunate.

Jesus, it's good to have money. This top-shelf Barolo is gonna run a few hundred.

Franco pops the cork, moves it toward Eli for him to sniff—but he demurs by shaking his head.

Franco pours a splash of wine into Eli's glass.

After tasting it, he nods his approval. While Mossad schooled him in sophisticated drinks, the whole wine routine always seemed like pretentious bullshit: the ceremonial reverence of presenting the bottle, the splash of wine into the glass, the swirling and sniffing for its bouquet, the whole enchilada.

Franco deftly pours wine into both their glasses. "*Salute*," he says, and gently sets the bottle on the table.

They raise their glasses, toast each other silently, then sip the wine. It has a delightful bouquet of cherries and raspberries. Swallowing a mouthful, Eli loves how one or two glasses will bring on a hazy sense of well-being. And now Pavarotti's voice on the sound system is angelic as he holds a high operatic note for what seems like forever.

"This is delicious," Irina whispers. "I never have wine so good."

Eli agrees. The wine smooths out the dread lingering in his awareness.

Franco delivers the menus.

Irina peruses hers, looks up at Eli, and says, "What do I order?"

"Do you like pasta?"

"Oh, yes, I love pelmeni filled with meat. That is pasta, yes?"

Eli's heard of pelmeni, an Eastern European dumpling. "Pork- and veal-filled ravioli would be a good choice for you," he says. Eli's aware that many ethnic cuisines throughout the world have similar dishes, whether they're called ravioli, pierogi, shish barak, or kreplach.

He luxuriates in shepherding Irina through the menu, just loves being—what is it—a caretaker? Yes, that's it. He's something of a guardian, a protector.

"And I'll have the same thing," he says to Franco. "We'll start by sharing a small plate of antipasto."

Eli loves how Irina chews each mouthful; her movements are delicate, yet she obviously takes great pleasure in food.

Though still ruminating about how he'll begin the conversation, he distracts himself by asking her about Russian food.

"The food is very heavy. You gain much weight. I must always watch myself. But not tonight."

"Yes, if you watch what you eat, then you'll be looking good," he says with a smile.

She laughs. "Do you make fun of my English?"

"No, I love your English."

In the buttery light cast by the sconce and candlelight, he thinks he sees her blush. And he notices a barely perceptible tremor ripple through the skin of her neck.

This woman's love of life, mixed with her shyness, is irresistible.

Eli feels more than an attraction; he realizes he could spend a lifetime being with her.

But Anton Gorlov and Viktor Sorokin have other plans.

63

While they're sipping the last of their espressos, Umberto, dressed in his chef's whites, set off by a red-and-white checkered neckerchief, approaches their table.

It's obvious Umberto can't take his sixty-year-old eyes off Irina. "I hope you and your beautiful companion have enjoyed your dinner," he says, as his eyes keep swerving back to her.

Knowing the chef is being flirtatious, Irina blushes and lowers her head.

"As usual, Umberto, it was delicious," Eli says. "And let me introduce you to Irina. She's recently moved to the city from Moscow."

"Well, that calls for a celebration." A smile erupts on Umberto's grizzled face. "I'll have Franco bring you some Vin Santo, it's the perfect way to end a meal and celebrate life. And don't be such a stranger, Mr. West. Come back soon. Make sure this lovely woman is with you. No meal can truly be enjoyed unless it's shared."

With his eyes remaining on Irina, Umberto bows slightly, then turns and disappears into the kitchen.

Soon Franco is back at the table with two digestif glasses of the liqueur. He sets them down with a flourish and wishes them good health.

Sipping Vin Santo, Irina says, "This is delicious. Such a wonderful meal. It is the best I ever have. And the company . . ." She lets out a laugh.

"Yes, the company is great," he says. "We'll have to do this again."

She nods. "Yes, we do it again."

Gazing at Irina, Eli realizes she's hypnotically beautiful. She's a study in perfection of the human form. She has the most lovely heart-shaped face he's ever seen, and her lips are full, luscious-looking, have that classical bow shape.

He loves watching her every movement, the tilt of her chin when she turns her head, the shape of her lips as she speaks, how she sips the Vin Santo, then sets the glass down and regards him with those incredible eyes. Even her hands are beautiful: graceful with long fingers and perfectly shaped fingernails.

He's so immersed in Irina's beauty, he suddenly realizes he's lost track of the conversation.

But there's *another* conversation that must be had. "Tell me a little more about Sasha," he says, thinking it may offer a segue to the Odessa syndicate, if not here, then at her apartment.

"Because of her I have a place to stay and I have job, too," Irina says. "And the job is for good money. I dunno what to do without her."

"Do you know how she started the health club?"

"I think she saves her money . . . or maybe she gets loan."

"From your brother's bank?"

"I don't think so. It was before Grigory come to US."

She blinks rapidly, and her lower lip quivers. She looks uncomfortable, as though his mentioning her brother has tapped into a well of sadness.

"Do you mind my mentioning your brother?"

She shakes her head. "I miss him. But it is in my life now. I must keep going."

A few more questions about Sasha lead to nothing revealing, so he drops the entire line of questioning.

The Barolo—and now the Vin Santo—leave him with a buoyant feeling but, at the same time, a strange mixture of delight and dread swirls through him.

"Your brother," he says, tentatively, "did he leave anything for you?"

Her eyes grow wet as she shakes her head. "Just some clothing and family pictures from Moscow. Now I have only the memories."

He nods, understanding her feelings. "Did he leave you any money, anything that might help you here in New York?"

"He had small bank account . . . a few dollars. That is all."

"Did he have a computer?"

"Yes, a small one, a laptop. Sasha says when she has time she will sell it for me."

"Did she tell you there were photos on the computer, things you might want to print and save?"

"She don't say anything about pictures."

"Did he leave any CDs? You know, maybe some jazz music?"

"Oh, no."

"How about a flash drive?"

"What is flash drive?"

"A small stick that fits into the laptop so you can store things like pictures."

"No, he leaves only computer."

It's more clear than ever that she knows nothing of her brother's involvement with the Bratva.

Her cell phone lets out a soft trill.

Apologizing, she opens her purse, removes the phone, peers at the screen, shakes her head, and sighs. Her lips tighten and curl downward as though she's smothering a frown. She's obviously displeased by the intrusion. Glancing at Eli, she smiles—looks apologetic, even embarrassed—then puts the phone to her ear. "Hello?"

After listening for a few moments, she speaks in Russian even as she's still gazing at him.

She shakes her head again, and a quivering movement begins at the edges of her mouth, as though she's growing increasingly annoyed with the caller.

"No, Sasha, Aiden will take me home," she says in English, obviously for his benefit.

She casts a wide-eyed look at Eli, presses her lips together, shakes her head again, looks exasperated, then peers into his eyes and silently mouths the words "I am sorry." She sighs heavily, loud enough to let her cousin know she's impatient. And irritated by the phone call.

Eli reads her demeanor as saying, *Can you believe this? She's calling me while I'm on a date.*

After a few more words in Russian, she says in a clipped voice, "*Dobroy nochi.*" She then translates the words, apparently for Eli's benefit. "Good night, Sasha." She presses the End Call icon and, again shaking her head, returns the phone to her purse.

"I must say sorry again," she says. "It is such silly business. Sasha wants to come for me and take me back to apartment. Like I am a child. I tell her no, that Aiden take me home. Back to *my* place. I don't need . . . how you say . . . chaperone."

Eli smothers a smile. "Really? She must think I'll take advantage of you."

"Not possible. We only do good things for each other."

Smiling, she extends her hand to him.

He takes it in his and then sets his other hand on top of hers. "You're very close to her, aren't you?"

"Yes—too close. She make me feel like little girl."

He says nothing in return. Why badmouth Sasha? It would serve no purpose other than to perhaps make Irina grow defensive of her cousin.

"But I don't say something to her because it would be like I am not thanking her for what she does. She makes my life easy in New York. But it is not good to depend so much on someone. So now I move to new place. And I will be boss of myself."

"Yes, that's a good thing."

"And good things will happen there," she says, a smile spreading across her lips.

With his heart kicking, Eli squeezes her hand.

In a moment of intimacy, her eyes invite him to share more.

It's nearly eleven when she says, "We can go now. Yes? I want now to show you apartment."

64

Traffic is light on this frigid night.

The taxi barrels its way north on University Place and gets to Park Avenue South. As the streets scroll by, Irina nestles into him. Her hair has that delightful scent he already identifies as uniquely hers, one deliciously reminiscent of lilac.

He slips his arm around her shoulders, feels her warmth even through her overcoat.

She murmurs something in that lovely, aspirated whisper of a voice; it's Russian—he catches that much, but he has no idea what the words mean. It's affectionate, and no doubt, sensual—that much is easily conveyed—but the words themselves are a mystery. The feel of her breath on his ear makes his skin tingle; the sensation travels to his groin, then to his toes.

"I wish I understood Russian," he whispers.

"I said it feels good to be close to you."

She tilts her head up, and they kiss lightly, then more deeply as their mouths open and their tongues roll over each other. The taste of her is delicious—Barolo and Vin Santo are blended with the plushness of her lips and the softness of her tongue, the feel, taste, and scent of her.

Even as he delights in all of it, there's the unsettling realization of what she'll be facing in the next week, maybe sooner now that a Bratva war has broken out. Now that there's a war going on, it's certain Gorlov's timeline has been moved up.

Is this the time or place to tell her? Maybe not, but I can edge toward it.

"Irina, I want to tell you something," he says in a near whisper.

"Yes?" she murmurs, with her head still buried against his chest.

How do I tell her without sounding like a paranoid soul?

As the taxi slows and stops at a red light, he struggles to find the words.

"What is it, Aiden?"

If I mention her brother or Sasha, it'll sound like I have an agenda. Jesus, what do I say?

"It's something about me," he says.

"About you? I will listen," she murmurs, keeping her head pressed to his chest.

What can he say to begin getting beyond the insanity of it all?

The light changes, and the taxi continues heading uptown.

"What is it?" she whispers.

"I've done some things," he says.

"Yes?"

"Things I'm not proud of."

The words won't come to him.

How do you tell someone you kill people for a living?

"Like what?"

"Well . . ."

She lifts her head from his chest. Even in the dimness of the taxi, he can see her staring at him, wide-eyed, uncomprehending.

"What things you done?"

"I . . . I've . . ." His voice sounds distant, small, tinny. It's nothing like the one he always hears, and he wonders if Irina now sees and hears a man she no longer recognizes.

"Oh, Aiden, we all do wrong things," she says, shaking her head. "What is it you done?"

What can he say that won't sound as though he lives in some fictional universe?

"Please tell me, Aiden."

My God, she doesn't even know my real name.

How does he tell her their being together was designed to dupe her, to rip her from the life she knows?

Or to end her life.

If only he could feel nothing, just go numb, be ignorant of the madness hovering over their lives.

She brings her hand to his neck and caresses it. Then her lips find his throat and she plants a light kiss on his skin. "Tell me," she whispers. "Please."

No, it'll have to wait. Until later when they're in her apartment.

If not tonight, maybe tomorrow.

But there's so little time. Gorlov wants results. Now.

He opens his eyes to the surreal look of the night with the streetlights and stores and the blur of pedestrians and the rush of traffic as the taxi speeds uptown.

It's like being trapped in a nightmare.

Like the dream about the bomber approaching the back door of the bus—the inevitability of what will happen, that very soon it will all explode.

"How would you like to get away for a few days, maybe for a week?" he asks.

"A vacation?"

"Yes. We could go somewhere for a while."

Does he propose that they pack up, grab enough clothing for one week, and take a taxi to Kennedy Airport, hop on a plane, and get away from New York? Tonight? Or in the morning?

They could get away from the cold, from the traffic and tumult of New York. He could tell her about Gorlov and Sasha while they're lying on the beach sand at Bottom Bay in Barbados; he's heard it's not developed or touristy, that it's serene, absolutely beautiful—or they could get on the next available flight to Aruba or Grenada, where there's no Russian mafia, no Mossad, no Hamas, no ISIS, no Hezbollah, where there's warmth and sand as soft as talcum powder and crystal-clear water for swimming and snorkeling, and above all, where there's safety—it could be any unspoiled Caribbean locale where they'll be far from here and where she might accept the truth of what he'll say to her.

Because if he tells her now, she'll never believe him, not when it comes from a stranger she met only a few evenings ago. But in a place far away from here, in an idyllic setting, when they've had a few days together and there's a chance for—for what?

What does he want? What will he try to do?

"A vacation?" she whispers.

Yes. Let's leave together, he could say. *Just you and me. We'll go to another country, where we can make plans to start over, begin a new life—just the two of us.*

A new life?

With her?

Out of the blue, as though we can each begin with a clean slate? As though nothing has ever happened before this night? As though we can have a new life together, like a married couple?

Absurd. I'm a stranger to her.

It's not gonna happen.

Ever.

How did this go from getting her away from Gorlov to their starting new lives together?

"Vacation, Aiden? The club is so busy. I don't think Sasha lets me take time away. And I have no other job yet."

Do I tell her I have plenty of money, that I'll take care of everything? That she'll never have to worry about expenses—about anything—for the rest of her life? That she'll be safe with me? That I can protect her from Sasha and the Bratva—always? That she'll have a new name and it won't be West or any of the other false monikers by which I've been known? That I can keep her safe from danger she doesn't even know exists? That maybe we can open a mom-and-pop shop on some island and live simple lives away from the tumult of New York? It's ridiculous. Am I crazy?

It's a stillborn fantasy.

How can he tell her the reality when he's a spectral being, a ghost floating among mob factions for the last ten years, that he's lived a life of crime, and knowing it or not, she's now involved in that life and there's not a scintilla of doubt that she's doomed and he can't possibly offer her anything real or enduring?

Not even his real name.

It's all been deception and tracking and killing, and he's nothing more than a bundle of lies.

A new life?

We have the lives we have. Nothing more.

"Aiden?" she says.

"Huh?"

"I don't understand about vacation. Maybe because my English is no good."

"No, no, no. Your English is fine."

He plants a kiss on her forehead. It's a protective gesture, and yet there's no way to shield her from what's going to happen. And for certain everything's going to come to a head very soon.

"Sasha won't let me take vacation, not now."

"I understand. Maybe we'll talk about it tomorrow."

"Yes, we talk tomorrow, but now I want to show you apartment."

Jesus, only this evening they were an ordinary couple, two people in a restaurant, enjoying the food and the wine and the atmosphere. It all seemed so natural, so normal, and yet it was light-years away from his life and from what's about to happen.

And he's lost in some farfetched fantasy of running away with this woman, beginning a new life in a different place on an island more than a thousand miles from here, as though such a childish wish could become reality.

There's no way it can happen, not now, not in the future.

Because in thirty-nine years, life has taught him that nothing changes. Ever.

65

The taxi pulls over to the curb in front of 233 East Twenty-Second Street.

The street looks deserted.

Wind gusts blow in from the East River, adding more bite to the night chill.

Traffic on nearby Second Avenue is muted, sounds like it could be miles away.

Eli pays the driver, and they get out of the cab.

Unlike earlier this evening, he'll stay vigilant. Casting subtle glances up and down the street, he sees nothing to raise his antennae. The bare sycamore branches sway in the wind and cast dancing shadows on the street. An occasional snowflake streaks through the air. When the wind abates for a few seconds, a few flakes drift slowly down to the sidewalk.

If Irina weren't with him, he'd take evasive action. Despite the cold, he'd walk around the block, find a coffee shop where he'd spend a few minutes reconnoitering, maybe even order a cup of coffee just to get caffeinated and heighten his senses, then backtrack to the building. Even then it'd be wise to stand across the street and scope out the building's entrance for a few minutes. Only then would he feel comfortable entering the lobby. But it's unlikely they've been shadowed from Umberto's to Irina's place.

Pushing through a revolving door, they enter the lobby, a brightly lit expanse. Floor-to-ceiling glass windows form a facade facing the street. The walls are covered with light beige stonework. The floor is a highly polished, creamy-hued marble. Hanging ferns and groupings of palms give the place the feel of a semitropical atrium. The space looks more like a hotel reception area than the lobby of a residential building.

The doorman, wearing a blue uniform with yellow epaulets, sits behind a semicircular granite-topped counter. A computer monitor rests on the countertop.

The guy's eyes seem to brighten as he recognizes Irina. His lips spread into a smile as he nods at her. She's been living here for one day and Eli can tell the guy's already enchanted by her. Is there a man alive who wouldn't be attracted to this lovely woman?

She returns his smile with a sheepish one of her own.

Two strategically placed CCTV cameras are perched high on the wall behind the concierge desk. They're the kind you see in banks overlooking the tellers' windows. They obviously record people entering and leaving the building or anyone stopping at the concierge desk.

If they're operational, he and Irina are being videoed as they walk through the area. No doubt the devices are digital and store images on a drive; it's likely the signals are sent to a secure server somewhere off premises. That means the videos are stored and accessible for a long time to come. There's going to be a permanent record of him entering this building.

He should have anticipated hi-tech cameras in a condo this new. Technology is transforming the city into a vast surveillance system. Cameras are now hidden at street corners, traffic lights, storefronts, subway stations, and office towers.

And now in the lobbies of newer residential buildings.

Eli again realizes he hasn't been as heads-up as he should have been this evening.

Gotta stay more alert. If not, I'll be history.

"You said only a few people have bought apartments?" he says.

"Yes, Sasha say her friend is only third person to move in. It is mostly empty now."

That seems to be true since the place is uncannily quiet. And there's the smell of fresh paint coming from a hallway to the right of the bank of elevators. Their footsteps click on the marble floor as they walk across the lobby.

The elevator doors have brushed-chrome veneers. Everything about the building screams money. Even a studio apartment—if there's one in a building like this—must go for a solid seven figures.

Ordinarily, Eli would take the stairs to any floor lower than the sixth, but not tonight, not with Irina at his side.

Her index finger nears what must be a heat-sensitive button on the wall near the elevator door.

The elevator seems to be taking a long time to get to the lobby.

Turning to him, Irina says, "What is it you wanted to say before in taxi? What is it about what you done?"

"Just . . . I wanted to say . . . I think we're good for each other."

"Yes, we can be good together. I know we have things . . . how do you say? We have things together . . . in common?"

"Yes, we have things in common."

"That is important for people to be good together."

He smiles and nods. "I agree. We're good together."

There's a soft ding. The elevator door slides open.

They enter the cubicle, a mirrored compartment with a black plastic dome affixed to the ceiling. A CCTV camera is positioned inside it for pictures of people's faces. He and Irina are being recorded—close up—in the confines of the elevator, and the video is being stored somewhere, perhaps for thirty days. The recording or a still frame can be retrieved and, if needed, can be sent anywhere. As far as the entire Russian mafia is concerned, Eli's faceless existence is over. On a strictly physical basis, he's identifiable.

But it won't matter. He's still nameless. There are no government-issued photos, no fingerprints, no files with local police or NCIC or, for that matter, with any government agency anywhere in the world. And there are no DNA samples on any database that could be identified as belonging to one Eli Dagan. There's no documentation of his existence.

His identifiable self exists neither on paper nor as a digital being. Yes, he's a ghost.

Of course, there's facial recognition technology. But even though he's been seen and recorded, his features aren't attached to a name, nationality, or an identity anywhere on the planet.

Of course, it's all academic because he'll be leaving the city.

Then getting out of the country.

He'll disappear. Forever.

Irina presses the button for the second floor.

When the door slides shut, she turns to him and their eyes meet.

She moves closer.

His knees go weak.

As they kiss, an erotic charge bolts through him.

He knows there won't be any talk of leaving New York, not this evening. There'll be no talk about a vacation or his past or what awaits Irina if she stays in the city. For the moment Anton Gorlov and Viktor Sorokin and this new pakhan, Koskoff, don't exist. Eli's radar detects no blips, not while he's staring into Irina's eyes. Maybe in the morning they can talk about what's coming. Yes, he'll bring it up when tonight's a lovely memory.

As they kiss, her hand slips behind his head and presses him closer.

Once again the taste of her is exquisite. The closeness of her body and the aroma of her skin and hair—that subtle floral scent—are arousing in a way that's been missing from his life for so long.

The elevator rises slowly, silently.

There's another soft ding.

The door slides open.

They arrive at the second floor.

His heartbeat feels like a metronome thudding through his body.

66

Irina fishes in her purse, removes her keys, unlocks the door, and they enter the apartment.

The decor is contemporary, with lots of chrome and high-end woods—mainly blond oak with a few touches of teakwood. The living room is softly lit by table lamps placed on each side of a sectional sofa, forming a conversation pit. A gas-burning fireplace is set in the wall facing the seating arrangement. A colorful Kashan rug covers much of the hardwood floor.

"Do you like it?" she asks, turning to him.

"Very stylish. The chrome reminds me of Sasha's club."

"Yes, it is like the French say—chic. Sasha says her friend is rich. Now she takes long trip to Europe so I stay here until she is back. Then I find own place where I will be for good."

They fling their coats onto a chair. She drops her purse on top of them and turns to him.

They move toward each other.

He senses her yearning, feels its power as it draws him closer.

As they embrace, he presses his lips to her forehead, tenderly, knowing there's something almost paternal in the kiss.

She whispers, "Aiden . . ."

His lips move to her cheek, then to her mouth. It's a gentle kiss, light, sweet, and she returns it. Her breathing quickens and he feels the soft flutter of her lips, so moist and pliable against his. Her mouth opens, and her tongue slides gently over his. She moans as the kiss deepens.

She slips her hands beneath his sports jacket and pulls up on his shirt, unaware of the pistol tucked in the waistband at the small of his back.

His jacket is now crumpled on the chair. Without her noticing, he slips the Beretta from behind his back and slides it beneath the jacket.

Now they're moving toward the dimly lit bedroom. It's hurried, hungry, inexorable.

They shuffle toward the bed as he kisses her face, then her neck, and she moans with pleasure. There's an urgency—it's overwhelming, and he knows she feels it, too—and he can barely believe this is happening. Only yesterday it was a fantasy, but now it's real and it's wonderful.

This is everything.

This is the world.

This is why we live.

The room swirls as he tastes Vin Santo and Barolo on her lips. With alcohol-fueled abandon, he feels the warmth and wetness of her mouth as their tongues roll over each other's, and in a rush of desire they're on the bed, where he's sinking into the delicious sensations of a world that's been gone for so long.

In a naked embrace, he's lost in the softness and heat of her as she climbs on top of him, and in a moment of exquisite tenderness, he's inside her.

She moves slowly, rhythmically, and in the midst of a hot soaking sensation, he sets his hands on her buttocks and pulls her closer so he's more deeply inside her as her arm moves away from him, and his hand slides along the length of it, reaches her wrist, and she suddenly yanks it back with such force his eyes pop open.

A pistol is in her hand, nearly pointing at him.

Even in the shock of the moment, his instinct takes over and his hand clamps on to her wrist as she tries to wrench her arm from him, but he holds on.

She twists the weapon so the muzzle almost faces him, and her finger is inside the trigger guard.

In a reflexive motion, his hand slams into her chest, and she's hurled backward. She tumbles from the bed onto the floor.

Recovering quickly, she gets to her feet; she raises the weapon.

Rocketing from the bed, he grabs the barrel and, with a powerful motion, twists the gun out of her hand.

He holds the weapon; it's small, lightweight; the safety lever is in the off position.

Nearly reeling in astonishment, he shifts his eyes to her.

She rears back with a clenched fist.

He dips his head to the right.

The punch misses by centimeters.

Shifting her weight and leaning back, she raises her left foot to thrust an oblique kick at him. If it lands, his knee will blow back, will hyperextend, and the joint will snap.

He pivots and bends at the knees, and the kick lands high—midthigh on the outer surface. No damage.

With his weight to his right foot, he whirls clockwise and slams a spinning backfist to her jaw.

Her head snaps back, and she flops to the floor.

She's unconscious.

Standing above her, he's shell-shocked, frozen in place, trembling.

His thoughts whirl. *The fucking gun was under the pillow, just waiting to blow my head off. This is how it happens. This is how the end comes when you least expect it. I almost bought it.*

She's on her back, lying inert on the carpet. Her head lolls to the side; blood trickles from her mouth.

With his heartbeat pulsing through him, he watches her chest rise and fall, listens to her breathing. His fist may have shattered her jaw, but she'll regain consciousness in a matter of minutes. He's gotta do something right now; if not, he's a dead man because she can't be in this alone. There have gotta be others. This was planned, organized down to the last detail, and there're bound to be more of them. They'll come for him, and it'll be soon. They may be on the way right now as he stands and peers down at her. It's only a matter of minutes. He's gotta get out of here.

This is unbelievable. She's an assassin.

With the pistol in his hand, he moves toward his clothes, stumbles, nearly falls, regains his balance, but weakness overcomes him. It's in his flesh, in his muscles, seeps through every part of him, even his bone marrow. He can hardly summon the strength to move.

The room tilts, then sways, and feeling faint, he manages to stumble toward the bed and drop down on it. He closes his eyes. His heart pumps with pile-driver intensity. He sucks in a chest full of air, lets it out, then in, then out. Again and again.

Stay awake, stay alert, don't pass out. If you do, you're a dead man. Get hold of yourself and just get dressed and get the hell out of this place.

There's that sickening postadrenaline weakness—it feels like he's draining away.

When he opens his eyes, pinpoint specks of white light—little stars—appear, and a swell of vertigo threatens to send him crashing to the floor.

He drops his head between his knees, lets blood flow to his brain.

When he opens his eyes, the room's washed-out appearance is gone.

Irina lies at his feet, still unconscious.

He sits upright, shakes his head, and peers at the pistol in his hand.

Did this really happen? Yes, it did. It's the shit show of my life. She was gonna put a bullet in my brain.

Now come the shakes; trembling takes over—in his fingers, his hands, his thighs, even his insides, and it's worse than it ever was in Gaza or Lebanon or Syria.

It feels like something's ruptured inside him.

I wanted to love you, hoped you could love me no matter what I've done. I wanted so much more than tracking and killing; I needed something better than the life I've been living. I wanted more, much more. I wanted peace. I wanted to be somewhere else, physically and emotionally. Maybe it would be with you. But that's never gonna happen, not for me.

In the reality of the moment, in its truth, he realizes his future is etched in stone: he'll always be a hunter and he'll forever be prey.

Even with this woman, this Irina, this sad, beautiful, vulnerable woman.

This pretend innocent, this ingenue.

This liar.

This assassin.

I know we have things . . . how do you say? We have things in common?

Yes, we have something in common, he thinks. *We kill.*

Nothing will change.

Not for him.

Ever.

He gets up from the bed—slowly—makes his way toward his clothing. It's like walking underwater, wading through its solidity.

Jesus, gotta get outta here now. Move, move, get out.

He drops the handgun onto a chair, grabs his clothes, begins dressing.

Stepping quickly into his pants, he stumbles, nearly falls, regains his balance. His hands are still shaking. He pulls his pants up, slips into his undershirt and shirt, and finally he's dressed.

He feels raw, like a nerve dipped in the ocean.

He peers at the gun. It's a Beretta Bobcat, a .22-caliber weapon. Small, lightweight. A perfect purse gun. It fit easily beneath a pillow, where it was planted before they came to this apartment. It was all a setup.

He presses the release button; the magazine drops into his hand. It's fully loaded. Six rounds are stacked inside the mag. He flips the tip-up barrel. A cartridge sits in the chamber. It was waiting for the firing pin to hit the primer and send a slug into his head.

And he'd be a corpse lying on the bed.

Who lives here? How'd this happen?

But there's no time for questions. It's time to get out.

He extracts the cartridge from the Bobcat's chamber, goes to the far side of the bed, lifts the mattress, and slips the slug and loaded magazine beneath it.

He drops the empty Bobcat into his pocket, then looks down at Irina.

An assassin hired to kill an assassin.

The ache of it is unbearable. It's like a splinter in his heart.

Gorlov wants me dead.

Death by Irina.

Or whatever her name is.

Who knows how long it'll be before she regains consciousness? He could drop down on his knees, clasp her head in both hands, and a violent neck crank would snap her spinal cord. It would be the price she'd pay for her treachery.

But it's not in his heart. He can't do it.

God, how easily he fell into the oldest trap on earth—the lure of a gorgeous woman.

Like Samson and a thousand other men.

A honey trap.

The Mossad used it. So did the PLO. Spy agencies all over the world have taken advantage of the most basic urges—the need for sex and the wish to be loved.

It's the power of yearning, the force of self-delusion. He was snared by loneliness and by overwhelming desire. His judgment was hijacked by his urges.

But there's no time for regret.

Or for thinking about what might have been.

There's time for only one thing: to ensure survival.

To get away from this place.

When Irina wakes up, it'll take time for her head to clear.

Then she'll look for the Bobcat but won't find it.

Get the hell out of here.

Just do what must be done.

67

He rips the quilt from the bed, drops it over her.

The thought crosses his mind once more: he could put an end to her. She's unconscious and would feel nothing, and in a half second it would be over.

But he's not that hardened to life. No matter what he's done as a commando and *katsa*, despite the bombings and shootings and bloodletting, even though she's a heartless assassin, he hasn't lost the ability to care. Not yet. He's still a human being, though he's certain his soul has been ruined. But how can you be certain of anything in this world of cruelty and betrayal? It's been a life of ruination, of blight, of loss.

There's only one certainty now: they're coming for him.

Fucking Gorlov. And Agapov and Koskoff. The whole Bratva and the other ethnic mobs. All snakes.

In the living room, he grabs his sports jacket and slips into it.

He picks up the Beretta and slides it into his waistband.

He shrugs into his overcoat.

There's no need to wipe down the Bobcat. His prints aren't on any database. He tucks the unloaded pistol beneath a sofa cushion.

Picking up Irina's purse, he snaps it open.

There's no weapon. He grabs her cell phone, tries to open it, but it's password protected.

He rummages through the purse: no wallet. Just lipstick, a set of keys—one for this apartment and other keys for who knows where else?—a compact, a pack of tissues, three hundred-dollar bills, four twenties. No credit card, no receipts, no scraps of paper, no address book. No driver's license. Nothing that might reveal her identity.

She's a nameless killer.

Just as he is.

Of course, when you're on an assignment, you take only what's needed to do the job, and then you disappear.

Should he take her cell phone, ask his IT guru to break into it, learn her contacts, find out how this went down? Not a good move. The phone has a GPS function. He could be tracked wherever he goes. It would put his tech sayan, Kevin Vallerie, in danger.

Just get away before they come.

For sure they'll show up to take care of what should have been his dead body.

He tosses the phone to the floor, is about to stomp on it, but hesitates.

Stomping on it will make noise. They might be coming now—any second; they could even be in the corridor at this moment—and they'll hear his foot crashing on the floor.

Just make tracks.

He shoves the phone beneath another sofa cushion.

There's only one thing left to do, and it's a no-brainer.

Get away from this building.

Leave New York.

And go where?

There's time to figure that out.

About to head for the door, he notices a card lying on a console table near the door.

He picks it up.

Crescent Moon Properties offers the unparalleled luxury and comfort discerning New Yorkers deserve. From our fully equipped health club with its own indoor pool to the landscaped rooftop deck, ideal for sunning and socializing, our property answers your every need.

Spacious apartments, equipped with only the finest top-of-the-line amenities, our indoor garage and 24-hour concierge service set Crescent Moon Properties apart from everything else.

A personalized tour of the building and prices available upon request.

We look forward to introducing you to your new home.

Please call 917-555-0123.

Jesus, it's a model apartment, a showplace for prospective buyers.

Yes, the place has that "decorated" look. It's "staged," from the sectional sofa to the Picasso reproductions on the walls. There's even a vase filled with silk flowers standing on this console. It's all faux. Fake. Bullshit. Just like Irina and he are fakers.

No one lives here.

Sasha's so-called friend doesn't exist.

Somehow, Gorlov's people got the key and arranged to have this place tonight.

For his execution.

That's why Irina met him outside. She didn't have access to the building, except to this model apartment. It would be here for them when they returned from dinner. It was all planned, down to the last detail, waiting for his execution.

That's what the call from Sasha at Umberto's was about. Speaking Russian, Sasha and Irina were coordinating the hit. Sasha called at a prearranged time. Irina told her they'd be leaving Umberto's soon.

And the real doorman or concierge, what about him? It's obvious: the Russians took care of the poor schmuck at the concierge desk—who knows where they stashed him? And replaced him with one of their own, a Bratva soldier. The smiles he and Irina exchanged weren't innocent greetings; they were acknowledging their complicity in the execution that would take place in the apartment a few minutes later. The guy was waiting for Eli and Irina to show up.

For Eli's death.

Slipping the Beretta from his waistband, he moves silently to the door.

He peers through the peephole. No one's in the hallway.

He opens the door a sliver, sees nothing suspicious.

He opens it a bit farther, looks again.

Nothing.

Now he'll do what must be done.

68

In the hallway, he assumes a shooting stance, turns left, then right.

He sees no one. It's deathly quiet.

The corridor smells like naphtha. It's a new-carpet smell he hadn't noticed when they got off the elevator. Desire had dulled his senses other than those lasered on Irina. That's what enchantment can do, narrow your focus, steal your awareness of what's really happening. The carpet odor—that naphtha smell—catches at the back of his throat, makes his sinuses feel like they're burning.

Moving toward the elevator, he hears music coming from a nearby apartment. It's Shakira singing "Hips Don't Lie."

But what if your whole life's a lie?

How do you turn away from it, begin a new one?

What if he'd never met Irina?

What if, what if?

Forget the what-ifs.

There's no time for regrets.

He bypasses the elevator. Elevators are death traps, best avoided whenever possible. In Beirut, he and Noah shot two Hezbollah honchos using Ruger .22 pistols fitted with silencers and laser pointers as the terrorists stepped out of a hotel elevator.

He'll move quickly. The longer this takes, the greater the chance the guy at the concierge desk will decide to come upstairs to check things out. Or call his Bratva brothers, who'll be there in a heartbeat.

He opens the stairwell door, peers down the staircase.

He sees no one.

It's silent but for Shakira singing behind a closed door.

He closes the stairwell door; the music fades to a base beat.

He descends the flight one step at a time.

He negotiated dozens of stairways in Gaza and the West Bank, never knowing if a jihadist was waiting just out of view. Climbing up a stairway, you lead with your head. An unseen gunman can blow you away from above. But going down is less risky.

At the first floor, he stops. Does the door open directly into the lobby?

I should've been more aware when we entered the building, but there's no sense in self-blame.

Standing at the door, he waits, hears his own blood drumming in his skull.

He strains to hear something. But there's only silence so dense, he hears his own blood rushing through his ears.

That drained feeling is gone, replaced by tensile readiness.

Opening the door, he's thankful it doesn't creak or squeal. Peering through the narrow crack, he sees the hallway leading to what must be a storage area. The lobby must be in the other direction.

Slipping into the corridor, he eases the stairwell door shut—slowly, silently—turns the handle and holds it in place so there's no clicking of the latch bolt.

Now he's inching along the wall, heading toward what surely is the lobby.

He stops.

Waits.

Listens.

A few more steps, slow, methodical. Silent.

The Beretta is racked and ready.

The lobby is preternaturally quiet; nothing but the sound of an occasional car whooshing by on the street and the whine of the wind.

Holding his breath now, and the only sound is the thunder of his heartbeat.

Peeking around the corner edge of the wall, he sees him. The same guy—the so-called doorman or concierge—sits behind the desk.

He has no idea he's being watched.

The Beretta's safety is in the Off position.

Rounding the corner, Eli steps into the lobby.

Soundlessly moving forward, slowly, trying to look casual, he's filled with readiness.

The pistol dangles midthigh; his finger is on the trigger.

Nearing the concierge desk—he's slightly less than two meters away, a bit less than six feet—a perfect distance for a kill shot.

Suddenly, the guy looks up. His eyes bulge with disbelief.

He explodes out of his chair, thrusts his hand beneath his lapel.

The Beretta lets out a metallic-sounding *pfft*, and a slug enters the man's throat. As he's thrust back, his hands rise to his neck. The slug goes through the windpipe, bursts through his esophagus, crashes through the neck vertebrae, and slams into the wall behind him. His spinal cord is severed; it's a decapitation.

Another pull of the trigger. A sharp popping sound.

A head shot. A .22 round hits the guy's forehead, sounds like a wet punch. Blood blooms above his right eye. There's no backsplash as the slug cracks through his skull and lodges in his brain.

The man drops to the floor behind the desk.

The air fills with the pungent smell of gunpowder.

Two brass casings were kicked out of the ejection port; they lie on the floor. Eli picks them up and slips them into his coat pocket.

A glance at the CCTV cameras: they're high up on the wall behind the desk—can't be reached. They can't be deactivated or blocked unless you have a ladder.

He's been recorded shooting a man. If he knew the building's layout, he could go to wherever the chip containing the CCTV footage is stored. He could remove the chip or wipe clean the hard drive before the signal is sent off premises. But that won't happen.

Don't worry about it. You're just a face with no name; you're a complete unknown to these people, and you'll never be identified or located.

He steps behind the counter, reaches inside the dead man's jacket, pulls out his pistol, slips it into his coat pocket.

Gotta get the hell outta here.

He shoves the body up against the inside of the semicircular counter. Blood leaks from his neck and head; the man's heart no longer pumps; the blood seeps out of him onto the floor, forms a slowly spreading pool on the marble. Neither the corpse nor the blood can be seen from any point in the lobby. Someone passing the counter will simply assume the doorman's left his post.

About to move toward the revolving door, he glances through the lobby's front window.

A black Cadillac Escalade is parked at the curb. Its contours gleam in the light cast by a nearby sodium vapor lamp. The engine is running; its headlights are on. Clouds of pink-tinged exhaust can be seen in the glow of the vehicle's taillights.

Shit. It's the Russians.

They must be waiting for Irina to come downstairs from the apartment.

After he'd been turned into a corpse.

Ducking back behind the concierge counter, he again peers at the vehicle.

A driver sits behind the wheel. The rear windows are darkened; it's impossible to tell if anyone's sitting in the rear of the vehicle.

If someone is there, it's a good bet he's a highly placed member of the Bratva. Or maybe there are two or three of them. It's only a matter of minutes before they decide to go upstairs to see Irina's handiwork and get rid of the body.

By now Irina must be getting dressed. She'll come downstairs, get in the Escalade, and tell them what happened. Then they'll come for him. Or she'll telephone the people in the vehicle.

He should have searched the apartment for a landline, found it and ripped the connection from the wall.

Stupid, stupid, stupid.
Now he's gotta deal with this shit.
No way can he stay behind the counter. He's a sitting duck.
It's time to take a chance.
He'll be quick and quiet.
Suddenly there's a *ding*.
It's happening.
The elevator's arrived at the lobby.

69

After pushing the doorman's chair back, Eli crouches beside the body.

Is it Irina coming down in the elevator? Who else would it be?

If what she said is true—only three apartments in the building are occupied—there's a good chance that when the elevator door opens, it'll be her. She'll go outside and get into the Escalade. The Russians are probably watching the entrance and haven't seen him leave. They'll know he's still in the building.

They'll come back for him.

They'll see that the guy who'd posed as the doorman isn't there.

There'll be no choice but to open up on them.

So what can I do?

Grab her the second the elevator door opens? Force her to stay with him behind the concierge counter? Not doable.

Pressing against the corpse, he waits. The counter's a four-foot high, semicircular barrier. Unless someone leans over to look behind it, neither Eli nor the dead man can be seen.

The elevator door slides open.

"Where's Edgar?" asks a man.

"Probably on a bathroom break," replies a woman.

"That means the door's locked."

"Use your passkey."

"I left it upstairs."

"Not smart, Charles. We'll have to wait till he gets back."

"What's that smell?" Charles asks.

"Someone's been smoking," she says.

They smell gunpowder. Shit, shit, shit. And Irina's gonna come down here any second.

A metallic taste forms on Eli's tongue.

The elevator door slides shut.

The footsteps recede. The guy's heading for the door.

Then comes the sucking sound of the revolving door's rubber seal sliding against the glass.

"Son of a bitch, he didn't lock it," Charles says. "He's supposed to lock the door when he takes a break. I'm calling management first thing in the morning."

The man's heels click on the marble floor as he walks back toward the counter.

"C'mon, Charles. The door's unlocked, so let's just go. Anne's in labor."

"I wanna write a note. Let the bastard know we're onto him. You have a pen?"

"No, I don't. Let's *go*."

"Maybe there's one behind the desk."

"You're wasting time. Let's get to the hospital."

"Ellen, this is important."

"Not as important as a baby. Bye."

"Where're you going?"

"To the hospital. We don't have time for this."

The rubber sealant makes a whooshing sound as the revolving door circles through the surrounding glass tube.

"*Ellen*," Charles calls.

Eli presses closer to the counter.

"Shit," Charles mutters.

He slams a palm onto the countertop.

His footfalls recede as he hurries across the lobby, then pushes his way out through the revolving door.

It's time to move.

Staying in a semicrouch, Eli makes his way across the lobby.

Closing in on the door, he peers out to the street.

The couple is gone.

Any moment now Irina will be in the lobby.

Gotta move now.

Both pistols are in his coat pockets.

In a squatting position, keeping as low as possible, and using both hands, he pushes against the revolving door's glass. It requires strength—maybe more than he has at this moment—as the rubber weather stripping creates powerful suction against the circular glass enclosure.

Duckwalking, he pushes in a counterclockwise direction against the lower section of the door.

At first it doesn't move.

Finally, it begins to turn.

Slowly.

It makes that sucking sound.

The revolving door picks up speed.

Gotta hope no one in that Escalade sees it turning.

A quarter turn.

Half turn.

Three-quarters.

Another push, and he's out in the open at the building's front door.

70

The air is so cold his eyes begin tearing and his vision blurs. He blinks, then wipes the tears away.

Snowflakes flutter downward and land on the sidewalk. A gust of wind drives them sideways. His breath sends vapor pluming from his mouth.

Since he's backlit by the lobby's lighting, whoever's in that vehicle might see him.

Gotta move before Irina comes out of that elevator and sees me in front of the building.

He takes the Beretta out of his pocket and in a semicrouch, inches across the sidewalk.

He looks left and right; the street is deserted.

The wind kicks up again, lashes at his face, but he keeps moving.

Closing in on the Escalade, staying low, he veers toward the vehicle. He's at the curb, near the left rear quarter panel, pressing against the cold steel, almost there.

The Beretta is in his right hand, racked, ready to fire.

Gotta move quickly. If not, there's a chance the driver will see him in the side-view mirror.

Inching along the Escalade, staying low, he's at the rear door on the driver's side.

Gotta hope the door's not locked. If it is, I'm toast.

Grabbing the handle, he leaps to his feet and yanks.

The door swings open, and he clambers onto the back seat.

71

Beneath the dim glow of the dome light, Anton Gorlov sits on the far side of the rear seat.

Eli slams the door shut behind him.

The driver swivels toward the back seat, grunts in surprise, and reaches beneath his lapel.

Eli pulls the trigger, puts a bullet into the back of his head. The man slumps against the steering wheel, then keels over across the front seat.

Seeing the brass casing on the carpeted floor, Eli makes a mental note to retrieve it later. Right now Gorlov is the main focus. He pivots toward the pakhan and points the Beretta at the Russian's head.

Staring straight ahead, Gorlov stays frozen in place.

The dome light dims slowly, then goes out.

The interior of the Escalade fades into gloom. Even in the weak lighting from a nearby streetlight, Eli can see Gorlov's face go pale. It's the body's wisdom at work, the physiology of fear: in such circumstances blood drops from the face and pools around the heart to be pumped to the muscles for that fight-or-flight response.

But Gorlov has no option: he can't fight, and he can't flee. He says nothing, shows no emotion. There's only the paleness of his features.

The SUV's heated interior fills with the coppery odor of blood and the burnt residue of gunpowder.

There's a moment of silence as Eli and Gorlov remain in place, unmoving.

Eli shoves the Beretta's muzzle into the Russian's left ear.

The man tilts his head slightly away. It's instinctive—the need to distance himself from the threat—but it can't be done. The muzzle moves with him, stays buried in his ear.

"Don't even *think* of turning toward me," Eli says. "There's no slack in this trigger, and the slightest twitch of my finger puts a bullet in your brain."

Staring ahead, Gorlov remains stock-still and says nothing. He won't try anything, not if he wants to survive.

Though they're alone right now, it's likely Gorlov has men nearby.

And Irina could come out of the building at any moment.

Eli pushes on the door lock button. The knobs sink with a solid *thunk*.

"Any of your men around?"

"No."

"If anyone comes near this car, you're a dead man."

72

"Why do you want me dead?" Eli says, pressing the pistol more deeply into Gorlov's ear.

The Russian winces but says nothing.

Eli wiggles the pistol.

Gorlov grimaces.

"Tell me."

"Because you know too much."

Gorlov's voice is soft, strained, but steady. There's no quavering, no stammering; the man has nerves of steel. Eli's seen many men who thought they were about to die, but never has he encountered a man possessing such eerie calm.

"I know too much. Meaning?"

"We've had people killed. You know the names, dates, and places. After all, you did so many jobs for us. We felt you were a liability."

"First Agapov and then me, right?"

"Yes."

"No loose ends?"

"That's right."

"Before you leave the country."

"Yes."

"What about my dead man's switch?"

"I don't believe you have one."

He has to give Gorlov credit; he knows bullshit when he hears it. His street smarts are one of the reasons he not only survived the Bratva wars but became a pakhan. And, surprisingly, Gorlov answered the question directly, didn't equivocate or go for indirection or deception. Maybe believing he's about to die brings cooperation, makes a man willing to deal.

The wind gusts, whistles past the Escalade. The vehicle rocks.

"Now I suppose you'll kill me." Gorlov's voice is steady; no shakiness, no sign of fear. The man projects a cold steeliness, a rarity in a man held at gunpoint. He knows resistance is useless. He's certain his life is over.

"That could depend on what you tell me."

"What can I say that will *possibly* make you spare me."

It's more a statement than a question. Yes, he's resigned himself to death.

"We'll see, won't we?"

Gorlov stares straight ahead, says nothing more, seems to wait for what he's convinced is coming.

Eli glances toward the sidewalk, then across the street. No one is in sight.

There's no sign of Irina. Not yet. It's only a matter of time before she leaves the building and approaches the Escalade.

"I have some questions for you."

"Really?" Gorlov says. "I can answer them, but is there anything I can say that will change your mind about killing me?"

Yes, there's acceptance in his voice. He's certain he'll die.

"We'll find out, won't we?"

"Then ask."

A brief pause and a glance to the street. No one approaches.

"Is there really a flash drive?"

"No."

"Was there ever one?"

"Yes. We took it from Grigory Sakharov."

"Before he died, right?"

"Yes."

"And you had him thrown out that window?"

"Yes. He was a traitor." Gorlov's voice sounds deadened. Still staring ahead, he seems as calm as before.

"Cleaning house, yes?"

"Yes."

"So this whole thing was concocted to get to me?"

"Yes," Gorlov murmurs, then sighs.

"Why go to such lengths?"

"Because we could never find you or learn who you are. It was the only way to get to you."

"Who is she, this Irina?"

"I don't know."

"You don't *know*?"

He digs the muzzle more deeply into Gorlov's ear.

The man winces again. "We don't know her real name. Just like we don't know yours. You assassins are all alike."

"What name do you know her by?"

"She calls herself Irina. But I'm sure that's not her real name."

"How'd you find her?"

"We made inquiries. She's new to the game."

"*Game*? Is this a game to you?"

"No, it's not a game, Aiden—or whatever your name is. It's a matter of life or death. Or it could be prison for Viktor and me. Getting to you was supposed to let us live the rest of our lives in peace."

"The rest of your life in peace?"

"Whatever is left of it," Gorlov says in a near whisper.

Yes, he's waiting for a bullet. He's accepted his fate. But with a man like this, you can never be sure. He's a survivor. His cooperation at this moment could be a ruse.

Stay vigilant. And keep the trigger pressed near the firing point. Don't get sidetracked, and don't give this fucker an inch of wiggle room.

Eli's eyes swerve left and right: a man walks on the far side of the street. Heading toward Third Avenue, he's huddled against the wind, keeps his hands in his pockets, and walks quickly. He could be a Bratva soldier.

Watching the guy from the corner of his eye, Eli keeps his finger on the trigger, exerts pressure near the point of no return.

Midway down the block, the man enters a brownstone. He's not a threat.

A glance at the building entrance. No sign of Irina. Not yet, but she'll come out soon.

"Tell me the truth—are there other men here?"

"No."

"How can I be sure?"

"You must trust that I'm telling you the truth."

"But you see, Anton, you've abused my trust. I have none left for you."

"I can do nothing about that," Gorlov says.

Wind sweeps down the street so powerfully, it rocks the Escalade.

"Your plans to leave the country . . . Where are you going?"

"It could have been Belize or Antigua . . . maybe South or Latin America. Or somewhere in the Caribbean. Viktor preferred going to Costa Rica but no matter where it would be, we'd have been leaving in a few days."

He uses the past tense, is convinced these are his last moments, believes he's about to die.

An attaché case lies at Gorlov's feet.

"What's in the case?"

"Money."

"She won't be collecting it."

"Did you kill her?"

"Why do you ask?"

"Curiosity."

"Even though you may die?"

"If you kill me, the Bratva will come for you."

"Maybe so, but they won't find me. Remember, I'm a ghost."

Gorlov stares straight ahead. "And *you* remember, Aiden, we're international. Eluding us will be like trying to run from the darkness of night." His voice is no longer one of resignation. While the words are spoken softly, it's the voice of a leader, a man with resources beyond imagination, a man of power.

"That's of no consequence to me."

"We're all over Europe and the Middle East. Even South America and Asia. We have connections you could never imagine. You above all people should know that."

"It doesn't matter to me."

"Killing me will make you a fugitive for as long as you live."

"I have to do what I must to survive. I can't worry about your people coming after me."

"It *will* be something to worry about."

"So be it."

Another glance out the window, left, right.

No one. The street's deserted.

The flakes of snow have stopped falling.

"How much were you gonna pay her?"

"Two hundred."

The pistol still rests in Gorlov's ear. "Pick up the case and put it on your lap. Before you open it, turn it toward me so I can see what's inside."

"It's cash."

"Is there a pistol inside?"

"No, just cash."

"It better be. If I so much as flinch, you're a dead man. So, pick up the case and do what I told you to do. Do *not* put your hand inside it."

Gorlov reaches for the case, picks it up, sets it on his lap, swivels it toward Eli, releases the snaps, and lifts the lid, keeping his hands on the leather top.

Bundled stacks of hundreds fill the inside.

A quick glance: there are at least twenty packets—$200,000 in Ben Franklins.

All old, crumpled. A cash payment for his death.

"Close it."

Gorlov lowers the lid, pushes the clasps down. There's a clicking sound.

"Slide it over."

Eli keeps the muzzle pressed into Gorlov's ear.

Gorlov pushes the case toward him. Slowly.

"Hands back on your lap," Eli says.

Gorlov does it.

"Clasp your fingers."

Gorlov does as he's told.

With the Beretta still in position, Eli slips the briefcase onto the floor. He pulls the doorman's pistol from his coat pocket and drops it onto the floor, then picks up the shell casing that was ejected when he shot the driver, and pockets it.

Are there other questions for Gorlov? He'll answer them because the urge to live burns like a flame in every living soul. Anton Gorlov wants a tomorrow. He hopes for a stay of execution, wants to see another day.

"So, it was all a sham," Eli says. "Irina's brother, the accountant . . . It was all bullshit, right?"

"Yes."

"The accountant wasn't her brother, right?"

"Yes, that's right."

"Tell me more about this so-called Irina."

"She's from Russia, originally, but she's been here for a while. I don't know how long, and I know nothing else about her. Like you, she's a mystery. A ghost who comes and goes. All I know is that she's a professional."

"And a good actor."

"I suppose so."

A brief pause.

"Your crimes were safe with me, Anton. There was no reason for me to expose you."

"There could be a reason."

"Such as?"

"If you're ever apprehended, you'll strike a deal and give us up."

"What makes you think that?"

"That's how the world works."

A siren shrieks somewhere in the distance, then the sound fades in the night.

What do I do with this man? Let him go? Kill him in cold blood? I've been killing people for years, and if ever murder was justified, it's now. If he lives, they'll come for me. If he dies, they'll want revenge and come for me.

"My fate is in your hands, Aiden."

"We make our own fates, Anton."

"If you kill me, you'll never survive. You'll be a hunted man."

"What makes you think it matters to me?"

"If I die, so be it. Death waits for us all. I have no fear of it."

73

Anton won't beg.

Not now, not ever.

He won't humiliate himself; he isn't a sniveling weakling, a helpless ten-year-old being pummeled by the Ukrainians in that garbage-filled alleyway back in Odessa. He's not a victim standing at the edge of a pit at Babi Yar. He's not some helpless Jew being led from a cattle car down a ramp to the gas chambers at Auschwitz or Treblinka or Birkenau and then to have his corpse thrown into an oven and burned to cinder and ash that would float in the air above Poland or Germany or Ukraine.

He has no fear of Nazis or fascists or communists or anarchists or crime bosses or their henchmen and hit men. Or of an assassin like this man who calls himself Aiden, a man who's killed scores, if not hundreds, of others. He won't get down on bended knee and plead for his life.

He suffers no illusions about the malice of men, the evil that lurks within them, their treacherous and self-serving ways. He won't crumple or tremble or cajole or wheedle or beg to be spared like some puling weakling.

No, that won't happen after the life he's led and after seeing so many men die; it won't be the way he faces death after losing Papa and Mama and baby Oleg. Not after Nadia's death and the pain it brought, the unendurable anguish that lives within him, the agony that will stay in his heart for as long as he lives.

No, he cannot beg for his life after Kiev and Ukraine and Odessa and Germany and Brighton Beach and the Bratva wars and after clawing his way to the top of a criminal enterprise, where he's reigned for years as pakhan. Not after wielding such power and meting out such violence and having survived while so many were killed.

No, he wasn't born to be who he is. It's not genetics or biology or his DNA that has determined who he's become. To blame it on biology would be a lame justification for what he's done. *Life* itself—his experiences, the indifferent cruelty of the world—has made him the Anton Gorlov of today.

Now his thoughts spiral to a remembrance of warmth and beauty: how Mama held him in her arms after the other boys beat him and made him feel so small, so weak, so hated, so vulnerable.

"*My darling,*" she'd say, "*don't worry. Someday you'll be as big as Papa was. And when that day comes, they'll have good reason to fear you.*"

How lovely her voice was, especially when she sang that Ukrainian lullaby to comfort him, to ease the humiliation. He still remembers the words: *Oy Khodyt Son Kolo Vikon*, The Dream Passes by the Windows. How beautiful her voice was when she sang, and how it soothed him, how she made him feel the world was safe and secure and good and loving and if only he could relive those days. Yes, Mama singing that lullaby is more a part of him than whatever may happen in this moment as death closes in.

It's all so sad.

As sad as when Mama lit a candle each Friday night while tears streamed from her eyes and she murmured a prayer for Papa's soul and she prayed for her family—her mother and father and her two sisters and her brother, her aunts and uncles and cousins—all perished at Babi Yar like so many cattle in a slaughterhouse, and she prayed for the soul of little Oleg, whose life had hardly begun. There was so much pain and remembrance and so much death in her life. And in his own as well.

After this assassin kills him, will anyone light a candle in his memory?

Will tears be shed for him?

By Katerina?

By Viktor?

By any of his underlings in the Bratva?

Will Diana mourn him? His own flesh and blood who refuses to see him?

No, she won't shed a tear for him, and it's such a shame because he loves her so.

Is the worth of your life measured by the number of people who mourn for you?

Perhaps it is.

Don't we all picture the mourners at our own funerals, and don't we hear the eulogies given about us? Or is it only me who thinks this way?

And now, as this assassin holds a gun to his head, a swirl of memories seizes Anton—some sweet and others bitter—and he's consumed by the sights and sounds and feelings of the evil in his life but even more by the people who've been precious to him, especially his beloved Nadia, whose nearness filled him with warmth, with happiness, even exhilaration, the beloved who made him feel life had meaning, that it was worthwhile.

Oh, Nadia, to be with you forever is my fervent wish and has been for all the years since you were taken from me.

And he now realizes that every moment of his life until this single moment is no more than a memory, is but the sum of so many yesterdays that live within him.

That entire world he's known and all those thoughts and feelings and memories—beginning with his first fragment of cognizance—are glowing embers of the soul.

But embers cool, their glow diminishes, and they're extinguished.

And that's death: the ending of the light within.

This assassin needs only apply the slightest bit of pressure, bend his finger a few millimeters, and it all comes to an end.

When this life is over, will he see Mama and Papa and Oleg and his beloved Nadia?

Will he once again be with those who'd been the bedrock of his life, those who made it all worthwhile?

Yes, he'll be with them again; it must be that way, because if it's not, then this thing we call life is nothing but a pointless existence, a journey through some vast and useless wasteland.

If he can once again be with his loved ones, if they can stay forever in some beautiful firmament, then what happens in this moment is a blessing.

Or is that just a wish before dying?

The wind buffets the vehicle once again.

Anton comes out of the reverie, and his thoughts shift to this moment.

74

Though he's holding a gun to Anton Gorlov's head, Eli's thoughts flash back to Irina and what happened in the apartment.

She still hasn't left the building.

He's certain she's still alive; that punch wasn't powerful enough to have killed her. If she approaches the car, what will he do?

Will he end her life?

Is this what it comes down to?

Again?

To kill or be killed?

Can he do it?

Can he wait until she leaves the building, approaches the car, reaches for the door handle, and he'll pop open the locks so when the door opens he'll pull the trigger and put an end to her?

Everything in his life—the sad wrongfulness of it all—has funneled down to this moment, where he sits beside a man whose treachery and scheming nearly had him killed by a woman for whom he felt such sadness, such empathy, a woman who made him believe she's suffered in her own way as much as he has. A woman with whom he began to envision a future, or was he simply trying to revivify the past, recapture the precious times with Hannah, the cherished feelings he lost so long ago, and it now seems he was attempting to reconstruct a life that began before the fateful blast that took his family away? God, how he yearns for those lost days and the people who had such meaning, who made life worthwhile.

And now, sitting here with this man, he must make a decision—to kill or not.

Is this the way it must be?

Can he keep going this way, living this life of rage and violence and revenge for what happened during the days of his childhood and youth?

Was the death of his loved ones the defining moment of his life? Has it driven him to live a life of never-ending grief, an empty life reflecting the terror of what he endured beginning as a child and culminating in that explosion on the bus, the detonation that caused him to grow to be the man he's become?

This brutal life must come to an end, either by changing his way in the world or by his own death.

Is there a way to renounce the rage, the violence, the need for vengeance?

If only he could forgo the deaths and regrets, maybe things could be different. Perhaps he can live a life of tranquility and serenity, far from here or Europe or the Middle East. But that's self-deception so profound it borders on delusion.

Because it seems there's no coming back from what he's become and there's no way to renounce a life brimming with bitterness, with grief, and with rage so monstrous it consumes his every waking moment.

This fury has gnawed at him, has ravaged his soul, has made him a murderer, a loner, a man floating through this life devoid of remorse for the things he's done. And there's no forgetting the tragedies that befell his family and their forebears, and none of that can be undone. The murdering, the obscene hatred of others—the Russians, the Poles, the Ukrainians, the Arabs, the Germans, and all the nations—the loathing they have for his people will stay with them for all time to come and its repercussions will be with him for as long as he lives. So will the misgivings about what he's done because his life has been filled with evil deeds.

And who am I to judge who shall live and who shall die? he thinks even as he knows there are times when a man must do bad things for good reasons.

Is killing evil people no more than an anemic attempt to try forgiving himself for the life he's led because he can never be absolved from his crimes, his sins that are too many to count?

And now he must decide the outcome for Anton Gorlov, a man who has been a ruthless killer, a predator responsible for the deaths and enslavements of others, a man who had him marked for death.

Anton Gorlov is an evil man, a callous man who's been the architect of so much despair in the lives of so many people and their families.

And for what reasons?

It's all been for money, to satisfy his need to stay in power so he could do more evil and make more money.

Eli struggles to recall Anton Gorlov's last few words.

What had he said?

Now Eli remembers.

If I die, so be it. Death waits for us all, and I have no fear of it.

75

Coming out of his reverie, Eli says, "It's good that you don't fear death, Anton, because you're right: it *does* wait for us all."

"I'm certain you have no fear of death, either," Gorlov says. "And I suspect something else about you."

"Oh? What's that?"

"That you've suffered terrible loss in this life. Perhaps as great as mine, maybe even deeper loss than I have, though each man's loss is his own burden to bear."

Strangely, Eli wants to hear more. "Meaning exactly what?"

Anton Gorlov stares straight ahead and says, "It's the same tragedy that happened to me. I believe death and tragedy have been the arc of your life. You've become who you are because of the suffering you endured in this life. There can be no other reason for living the way you do."

"You may be right, Anton, but at this moment, my losses and suffering are irrelevant. The only thing that should matter to you is whether you will live or die."

"Death is inevitable. No one gets out of this life alive."

"Well put and very true, Anton."

"Is there a way I can convince you to spare me?"

"Are you trying to negotiate with me?"

"No. I'm asking if you can find it in your heart to let me live."

"After what's happened, why should I do that?"

"Because I want to get away from America and begin a new life."

"There are no new lives, Anton. We live the lives we've made for ourselves."

"I've sometimes thought I was born to be the way I am," Gorlov says. "But I now know that's not true. The terrible things that happened in my life—the losses, the evil, the deaths, the horrors—are what made me who I've become."

"But you may be right, Anton. Perhaps it could have been different because, despite the tragedies, I too had choices. And I made them. I alone have made my life what it is. We've each made our lives what they are. And there's no going back. There's no innocence left for us to retrieve."

"Very true, Aiden. And you're right: death waits for us all. It may be my fate to die tonight. So be it. In the end, death always wins, but that doesn't mean I must grovel before it. I have no fear of it."

Eli pulls the trigger, and a bullet slams into Anton Gorlov's brain.

Four Days Later

76

At nine in the morning, a man casually makes his way to the United Airlines check-in counter at JFK International Airport.

He's nearly forty years old, but his lithe movements give him the appearance of a considerably younger man. In fact, though he's on the far side of his prime, he looks very much like an athlete. He wears a gray sports jacket, dark blue denim pants, and a white shirt open at the collar. His overcoat is gray and stays unbuttoned. His hair is dark blond and shaved down to a crew cut. He wears clear plastic-rimmed eyeglasses.

Walking with a confident stride, he looks like a seasoned international traveler. Without a large suitcase, he won't have to wait at his destination's baggage claim area, and it appears he'll be away for a short time, a few days at most, perhaps no more than a week. A nylon laptop case hangs from a strap slung over his shoulder.

He carries no weapons, having dumped the Beretta into the East River two nights earlier. He left the $200,000 with his financial sayan who is depositing it into Eli's Belize account.

The man's name is Eliot Ainsley. He's an American who has been living in New York City and is traveling alone. His new passport bears no stamps indicating prior trips out of the country.

He took a taxi to the airport after having spent his last night in New York at the Hampton Inn on 135th Avenue in Queens. He registered there and paid for his room with a credit card that's not in the name of Eliot Ainsley. He used a different credit card with a different name. The motel is only a few minutes from JFK and the United Airlines terminal.

In addition to the documents identifying him as Eliot Ainsley, he carries two sets of identity papers provided by the Queens sayan. One of them was the name on the credit card he used at the motel.

Each set of documents describes a different individual; each persona has a passport, a credit card, and a driver's license. At the airport and for this trip, he's using only those documents belonging to Eliot Ainsley, which hopefully will be his identity for the rest of his life. The other two sets—being held in reserve—are tucked behind a barely noticeable flap in the laptop case sealed with a strip of Velcro. If the Ainsley identity is compromised, he can resort to either of the other two. It's just a matter of slipping into yet another character.

As always with an alias, Eli Dagan has adopted the emotional bearing of this new persona. He does more than simply change his outer self as would a chameleon. He *lives* a different identity. It's a complete makeover, down to the bogus memories of a faked former life. In a sense, he becomes the new person, as though he's always been who he now claims to be.

At the check-in counter, he uses Eliot Ainsley's newly minted credit card to purchase a round-trip ticket to San José International Airport in Costa Rica.

Ever since 9-11, buying a one-way ticket to a distant destination is certain to arouse suspicion, as would paying for the airfare with cash. Either attempt would ensure his being escorted to an interrogation room by Homeland Security agents at any US airport. Of course, he has no intention of ever using the return ticket.

The ticket agent is an attractive red-haired woman who takes care of the purchase. The transaction goes smoothly, with no unanticipated questions asked. He gets his seat assignment, a window seat in the middle of the craft.

Batting her eyelashes at the conclusion of the transaction, the agent smiles and wishes Eliot Ainsley a good holiday in Costa Rica.

Airport security is predictable. His carry-on baggage consists of only the laptop in its canvas case. Aside from the laptop, which he removes and shows to the security agent, the case contains two sets of fresh underwear, a toothbrush, and a tube of toothpaste. The agent rummages through the case and finds nothing unusual. The traveler's wallet contains identification as Eliot Ainsley and three hundred dollars in twenty-dollar bills. There's nothing on his person that will set off the metal detector: no keys, no watch, no loose change, nothing other than a leather belt with a metal buckle, which he drops into the plastic tray. After taking off his shoes—which are put on a conveyor belt and scanned by a metal detector and scanner—he walks through the X-ray scanning machine. He's past security in less than thirty seconds. Traveling lightly has its advantages.

With his shoes on, he walks to the departure waiting area, where multiple rows of seats are arranged back to back. A few passengers are already seated, waiting to board the plane.

He takes a seat facing a series of floor-to-ceiling windows, which provide an unobstructed view of the tarmac and the accordioned aerobridge leading to the plane now parked at the terminal. The empty seats behind him face in the opposite direction. Anyone who sits in them will be facing away from him and looking back toward the security area.

There's no need to worry about who may enter the departure lounge area since high-tech security cameras and an array of security devices scan each person heading toward the area. And Homeland Security personnel are everywhere, so there's little chance of anyone entering with a weapon.

For the first time in many weeks—perhaps months or even years—Eli Dagan aka Eliot Ainsley feels relaxed, as though life can be filled with promise, as though there may be a future. It could even be a feeling of serenity because his life might be on the cusp of changing.

As Eliot Ainsley, Eli hopes he's on his way to beginning a new life, or at least, the semblance of one. For the moment it's only a matter of waiting for the steward or stewardess to pick up the microphone of the PA system to announce the boarding procedure. Then, once on the plane, it's a matter of waiting for takeoff.

To Costa Rica and a new beginning. At this moment, his anonymity—the feeling of aloneness, of being unknown by any living soul—seems precious, lifesaving.

He waits patiently—unobtrusively—as he did for years as a Mossad field agent when he spent countless hours in airports and bus terminals waiting for a target to appear. Or when he'd lingered at a train station, anticipating the arrival of fellow *katsas* who'd traveled by different routes to their prearranged meeting place, all using counterfeit passports from an array of countries.

It was an operational imperative to meld into a crowd, to be unnoticeable. As part of the spearhead of the Israeli targeted-killing program, they would then set out on their assigned mission.

Eli knows how to blend in and never arouse suspicion. He's adept at finding a sense of calm within himself, can ease himself into stillness of mind, that usually elusive sense of tranquility he now finds so precious.

Because he's not on a mission of death or retribution.

He's on a different mission, one that will hopefully allow him some peace.

Or is that merely wishful thinking?

He'll begin making arrangements when he arrives in San José. The real estate sayan contacted an agent at the RE/MAX office in the city, a Mr. Michael Simons, an American living and working in Costa Rica. Eli's already used his sat phone to call the agent and set up an appointment for tomorrow morning.

He'll rent an apartment in San José, where he'll stay for a month while he scopes things out; then, if no threat from the Bratva materializes, he'll look into buying a house. It'll be a small place on the Pacific coast, with its pristine beaches, where the weather isn't too different from the conditions of Tel Aviv or

Caesarea, where he and Hannah used to swim and get sun-drunk on those lovely Mediterranean beaches.

He'll find a permanent place that will be close to a medium-size city so there'll be an opportunity for some semblance of a social life. These days, with online house tours, you can see more than twenty or thirty houses on any given day.

The departure area is filling with fellow travelers, ordinary citizens—mostly middle-aged men and women in search of a week or two away from the winter cold of New York City. They all take seats in the waiting area.

After about fifteen minutes, he begins drifting into a twilight sleep—that surreal alteration in awareness, where reality and the dreamworld seem to fuse in some strange nether land.

Suddenly, the hazy feeling evaporates. His senses sharpen.

Because he hears a man's voice immediately behind himself.

The guy is sitting in the chair facing in the opposite direction, so they're back to back with only inches separating the backs of their heads.

Though the man speaks softly, Eli recognizes the sound and cadence of the Russian language.

A bolt of alarm shoots through him.

They're here, right behind me. They've found me. Gorlov was right; there's no escaping them. Do I get up and walk away? No. Stay where you are. Don't move or do a thing. Wait it out and see what happens.

It feels like an iron claw grips his heart. His scalp dampens, and sweat oozes to the surface of his skin, begins soaking his shirt and chills him.

A woman responds to the man in a near whisper. Yes, they're speaking in Russian. There's no doubt about it. And there's a conspiratorial tone in their voices, as though they're speaking in a prearranged code.

This is it.

It's a hit team sitting behind him.

He's about to go down.

How could they have known he'd be here?

Have they been tracking him for the last four days?

From the safe house to the hotel on the Bowery, then to the Hampton Inn in Queens?

How could that have happened?

He'd taken every precaution possible, seen and heard nothing that even began to arouse a scintilla of suspicion. And yet they're right behind him, only inches away and facing in the opposite direction, waiting to board the same plane he'll be taking to Costa Rica.

Gorlov's words come to him: *We're all over Europe and the Middle East. Even South America and Asia. We have connections you could never imagine. You above all people should know that.*

Somehow they learned his escape plan.

They even know which flight he's taking; they may even know which *seat* he's been assigned.

And there's a good chance they'll be sitting behind him on the plane. Less than an arm's length away.

How on earth did they arrange all this?

It's uncanny.

Gorlov was right. Running from the mob is like trying to escape the darkness of night.

Is the woman behind him Irina?

He can't make out the pitch or timbre of the Russians' voices because they're whispering back and forth to each other.

So she's now working with a partner.

Is this the end of the line?

Yes, they'll take him out.

They won't do it here, not in the departure area. It would be too obvious. Any move here will be seen by scores of people. They'd be apprehended by security only seconds after putting a slug into his head.

On second thought, even if they managed to get a gun past the metal detectors, they won't use it here. Nor will they shoot him on the plane. No, they'll do it once he leaves the airport in San José.

But that's all too crude, too pedestrian, too risky.

They won't shoot him at all. That's not how the Russians

assassinate people these days.

It'll happen in a better way, one that will go unseen, unnoticed, undetected.

This is how they'll do it: they'll use a sonically powered liquid jet injector, the kind Otto mentioned when Eli was at Langone.

Or better yet, they'll use a small spray canister.

Whatever they use, it'll contain an untraceable toxin, maybe dimethyl sulfate, the poison Eli used in Ivan Agapov's cigar.

Or they'll use a nerve agent—VX—like the Koreans used on Kim Jong-un's half brother at the Kuala Lumpur airport.

Or they'll use Novichok, the poison Putin's assassins used on Alexei Navalny. It's slow acting and lethal. And undetectable by ordinary laboratory methods.

Once it's delivered—the toxin's either absorbed through the skin or inhaled—it reaches the brain, heart, and lungs, and Eli's history.

Actually, they won't care if the toxin is detectable or not. After all, he'll just be a dead guy, an unknown corpse lying on a steel table in a morgue, and they'll be long gone back to wherever they came from.

He must do something.

Anything to avoid certain death.

Slowly getting to his feet, appearing nonchalant, he stands up, keeps his back to the Russians.

Never let the enemy know you're onto them. Stay cool. Without being obvious, turn your head—slowly, slightly—just enough to get a view of them out of the corner of your eye.

Only the backs of their heads are visible. Because the weather in New York is so cold, they're bundled up in winter clothing as though they're in Moscow—heavy coats and fur-lined hats, typical Russian outerwear—so their features are obscured. The woman's hair is being worn up, stuffed beneath the hat so he can't tell if she's Irina.

Neither is identifiable from behind.

He can't even make out their ages.

They look quite ordinary, like a tourist couple about to go on a vacation.

Of course, it's an act.

Do they realize I've made them?

Suddenly the man turns his head and leans toward the woman and whispers into her ear.

She turns to him and murmurs a few words in return.

Eli is stunned, shocked into near immobility.

Viktor Sorokin sits next to a middle-aged woman—she must be his wife.

Of all places on the planet, they too are going to Costa Rica.

Anton Gorlov is dead, and Viktor Sorokin is leaving for Costa Rica.

With his heart beating rampantly, Eli moves away.

Walking slowly, carrying the laptop case, he ambles around the periphery of the departure area as though he's simply stretching his legs.

Leaving the lounge, he makes sure to keep looking away from the couple.

In the men's room, he enters a stall, closes the door, locks it, opens a flap inside the laptop case, and removes a different passport, another credit card, and a second driver's license. He slips Eliot Ainsley's documents inside the hidden pocket, closes the flap, and presses down on the Velcro edge.

After leaving the men's room, he passes security and heads to the United Airlines ticket counter. He'll have to go through a security checkpoint again, but it's not a big deal.

No way does he want to deal with the young woman from whom he purchased the first set of tickets. If he can't use another ticket agent, he'll go to a different airline terminal and begin the whole process again.

But he's in luck. An older man stands behind the counter.

It's a good thing the sayan provided him with three sets of credit cards in different names, issued by different banks. And three sets of identification documents. A true trifecta. You have to be ready to change identities at a moment's notice. When he gets to his final destination, he'll decide whether to stick with Eliot Ainsley's character or resort to another identity.

The information display board says the next flight leaving for a South American destination will be headed to Bogotá, Colombia, and it leaves in two hours.

Using different documents, Eli purchases a round-trip ticket to Bogotá. The flight to San José, Costa Rica, will take off in less than a half hour. It'll be gone without him on board. The flight manifest will show his name, but his person won't ever have been on that plane. The airline will assume any of a number of reasons for his absence—maybe he changed his mind or he might have become sick or for some unknown reason missed the plane. It sometimes happens.

Now he'll kill some time. He won't pass through security again until the flight to Costa Rica has boarded with Viktor and his wife on board.

The waiting area for the flight to Bogotá is on the far side of the terminal, but he won't go to its departure area yet. Why take a chance on being seen by anyone there?

He heads to the food court in the presecurity area.

Sitting at a corner table in Starbucks, he waits for his heart to slow. How utterly strange that he and Viktor were about to leave for Costa Rica on the same plane.

He now recalls Gorlov talking about moving to Antigua or some other South American destination. And yes, he mentioned that Viktor preferred Costa Rica.

And that's where he's going.

So, Colombia will be the next but not the last stop on what Eliot Ainsley hopes is a road to a new life.

He'll spend one night at an airport hotel in Bogotá, then catch a flight to another country. Some online research will help with the decision about which one might become a permanent home. He may have to puddle hop to a few countries before making a choice. It won't be Bolivia, where Butch and Sundance went down in a barrage of bullets.

Whichever country makes the cut, it'll be one with relatively little crime and, hopefully, without too much political turmoil. But it'll be a convoluted route to wherever that final destination may be.

Changing one's life must involve more than simply moving to a different location. There must be something else, something fundamental, something internal and enduring.

Can it be done?

For years, terrorists, criminals, bombs, guns, tracking, and killing have been at the center of his life. He'd deluded himself into believing there was something noble in ridding the world of evil people.

But that's over.

And what about the time spent with Irina?

If only things had been different, but that's no more than wishing neither of them was who they actually are.

She acted a part and, in doing that, held out a promise for him.

But she was a mirage.

It's now clear that, without realizing it, he hungered for what she seemed to offer.

She was no wide-eyed ingenue.

Nor was she merely a chameleon.

She was something more—maybe *she* was a shape-shifter.

She looked deeply into his soul and understood the emptiness of his life.

She knew what he wanted and, in so doing, became in his longings what he desperately craved, though it was beyond his awareness.

Without her intending to do it, she gave him a gift.

The gift? A wish for a future.

But wishes are nothing more than dreams that haven't yet

come to life.

Irina's brief presence in his life fostered a sudden realization that may tide him over in the coming years, one he never dreamed would materialize: despite the wounds to his soul, he's not a hollow shell of a man. He's more than a cold-blooded assassin. He now realizes there's still room in his heart for love to fill it once again.

Irina's gift to him is simply his awareness that there's hope to rediscover love.

Maybe there's a future filled with beauty and mercy and even a modicum of grace.

Maybe he can rid himself of the shackles of the past and hope for a new life.

And for the moment, the world seems less tragic, less mired in catastrophe. There's the promise of wholeness, even of rebirth in some strange way, the wish for a new way of being.

Is a new life conceivable when only a few nights ago he told Anton Gorlov, *There are no new lives*?

Can there be a new life for Eli Dagan?

Or will Eliot Ainsley fall into the same hideous trap that held Eli Dagan prisoner for so long?

One thing is certain: life as Eli Dagan is over.

Eliot Ainsley's has just begun.

But as Eliot Ainsley, must he always be looking over his shoulder?

Can Eliot Ainsley truly live a new life so long as Eli Dagan draws a breath?

Time will tell.

A Note to the Reader

In *Assassin's Lullaby*, I did my best to tell a story that would, above all, be entertaining.

As always when writing fiction, I've taken liberties with politics, time, places, and other details. Occasionally, I've used real institutions, events, and places in the service of fictional verisimilitude. (Yes, it's an oxymoron.)

Other particulars have been revised beyond recognition or have been wholly fabricated. Any alterations in the names of institutions, in locales, even of history are, in my view, of little consequence to the main objective, which was simply to tell a story, one that derives from imagination.

After all, I'm just a storyteller.

I hope there's some truth in the story you've just read, whether it's about the power the past holds over us, the struggle between good and evil, the question of nature versus nurture, or matters such as identity, vengeance, acceptance, the capacity to evolve, to love, and the struggles that bedevil us as human beings.

I've always believed what Albert Camus famously said: "Fiction is the lie through which we tell the truth."

Acknowledgments

It's often said that writing is a solitary endeavor.

But really, I never write alone.

I take with me whatever I've learned living my life.

And when it comes to writing fiction, I take with me the collective wisdom and experience of certain writers whom I've been fortunate to have as friends and people who've been extraordinarily generous: foremost among them are Don Winslow and his wife, Jean; David Morrell; Jon Land; Simon Toyne; and Lisa Gardner.

There are many other authors with whom I've enjoyed lunches, dinners, email communications, and telephone conversations. And of course, there are the occasional Zoom conferences.

I've learned so much about writing fiction from each of them, and I treasure these relationships. These writers have been great company, and in a sense, each of them is my coauthor.

I would not have whatever insight I possess about the human condition were it not for the influence of three extraordinary teachers I was fortunate to have as a psychiatric resident so many years ago: I owe an enormous debt to the late Dr. Bill Console and to Drs. Dick Simons and Warren Tanenbaum. Over the years, Dick and Warren have become treasured friends who make my world a far better place than it would otherwise be.

Two people who have been essential in my writing life are Kristen Weber, a great editor who introduced me to the way of the novel, and Sharon Goldinger, an expert on all things books. I'm eternally grateful for what they've done on my behalf.

Many others have been important in my writing life, including Fauzia Burke; Victoria Colotta, a talented conceptual artist;

Joel Friedlander; Penina Lopez, a great copy editor; and Skye Wentworth. They've helped me navigate the wondrously arcane world of books.

Friends, relatives, and other authors have been great sources of encouragement. Some have been enormously helpful first readers, having made suggestions that vastly improved the novels I've written. All are appreciated. Deeply.

Among them are Ace Atkins, Joseph Badal, John Burke, Ann Chernow, Reed Farrel Coleman, Michael Connelly, Claire Copen, Dr. David Copen, Rob Copen, Tal Copen, Alice Davenport, Amy Davenport, Melissa Danaczko, Kent Doss, Lenora Doss, Bob Elton, Randall Enos, Sharon Esposito, Linda Fairstein, Dr. Helen Farrell, Joseph Finder, Nancy Gazo, Bruce Glaser, Elissa Durwood Grodin, Andrew Gross, Mysia Haight, Dianne Harman, Dorothy Hayes, Martin Isler, Elizabeth Joseph, Connie Kaufman, Helen Kaufman, Phil Kaufman, Dr. Faye Kellerman, Dr. Jonathan Kellerman, Dr. Jeff Ketchman, Niki Ketchman, Cindy Bloom Lahey, Elaine Tai-Lauria, Phil Lauria, Dr. Peter Le Jacq, Lou LeJacq, Courtney Lilly, Phil Margolin, Holly Maxson, Hilda McVey, Harvey Morgan, Valentina Belyanko-Morgan, Dr. Barry Nathanson, Susan Nathanson, Arnold Newman, Elaine Newman, Linda Nyselius, Abernathy Paterson, Dr. Kimberly Simons Patterson, Christopher David Peterson, Dr. Daniel Pildes, Dr. Andrea Polins, Dylan Pratt, Scott Pratt, Laura Rahtz, Dr. Roger Rahtz, Linda Robbins, James Rollins, Jeannette Ross, Dan Santos, Tina Schwartz, Harriet Senie, Bert Serwitz, Joyce Serwitz, E. J. Simon, Alan Steinberg, Mindi Stark Steinberg, Dr. Donna Sutter, Karen Vaughan, Dr. Howard Welsh, Cathy Werner, Martin West, Ann White, Steve White, Judith Marks-White, and June Zeitz. They've all helped in more ways than they could possibly know.

I owe a great deal to the librarians who have been so kind and gracious having arranged for author talks and luncheons. Foremost among them is Elaine Tai-Lauria.

A multitude of thanks to the bookstores and libraries that have invited me to present author talks, especially Yale University Library, Wilton Library, Stamford Library, New Canaan Library, Norwalk